PRAISE FOR WRAY DELANEY

'Shades of Sarah Waters … irresistible'
Guardian

'Compelling'
Sarra Manning, *Red*

'A bawdy, romping affair'
The Times

'This is one hell of a read'
Sun

'A fun, explicit romp with real stakes that will have you
trying to finish this book in one sitting'
Stylist

'An irresistible world to drop into'
Emerald Street

'An amazing book… like a box of treasures'
Meg Rosoff

Wray Delaney is the pen name of Sally Gardner, the award-winning children's novelist, who has sold over 2 million books worldwide and been translated into 22 languages. She lives in East Sussex, and this is her second adult novel.

The Beauty of the Wolf

Wray Delaney

ONE PLACE. MANY STORIES

HQ
An imprint of HarperCollins*Publishers* Ltd
1 London Bridge Street
London SE1 9GF

This edition 2019

1

First published in Great Britain by
HQ, an imprint of HarperCollins*Publishers* Ltd 2019

Hardback ISBN: 978-0-00-821735-8
Trade Paperback ISBN: 978-0-00-821737-2

MIX
Paper from
responsible sources
FSC™ C007454

This book is produced from independently certified FSC™ paper
to ensure responsible forest management.

For more information visit: www.harpercollins.co.uk/green

Printed and bound in Great Britain by
CPI Group (UK) Ltd, Croydon, CR0 4YY

To Julia, the wisest woman I know, whose love
and patience have been my greatest anchor.

THE SORCERESS

When I go musing all alone
Thinking of divers things fore-known.
When I build castles in the air . . .

THE ANATOMY OF MELANCHOLY

ROBERT BURTON

I

I woke when the mighty oak screamed.

No mortal heard the sound those roots made when their weighty grip upon the soil was lost to them. No mortal saw the desperate clawing at the earth, the very life snapping from the trunk as the ground crumbled, shivered with the cacophony of destruction. How could I sleep, tell me, for it had awakened the very rage in me.

My oak trees outlive men by hundreds of years, yet it is these mortals with but a few seasons to their names that claim the wisdom of God in their insect hours upon this earth.

I have no time for sweet, enchanting tales that fool the reader with lies and false promises. Too long I have lived and seen, and seen yet never said, been counselled strong to leave off the telling of my tale. What care have I for such timid sentiments? Let the Devil make his judgment.

Do you not know me? I was born from the womb of the earth, nursed with the milk of the moon. Flame gave me three bodies, one soul. In between lies my invisibility. I am the maiden, the mother, the crone, in all I am one. You think that I am unlike you. Look again. I am the dark side of the glass, proud to own my power for good or for ill.

My sorcery, unlike your malcontent prayers, cannot be undone. I relish my powers to shift my shape without boundaries, to move freely between the holy trinity of women. No church would ever make me give up my body in all its lustful glory to a fleshless lord. For what purpose? To be tamed, to live in servitude, to be robbed of my mystery?

Why then should I remain silent just when the mortal world has decided to overthrow magic in favour of religion and rational thought? When our ways are about to be sacrificed to the Lord of Despair, he whose feet never touched this earth of mine?

I could have dreamed my way through such lunacy, deep under my trees, wrapped safe in darkling sleep and all that happened would never have happened. For the loss of one oak tree I put my curse on he who claimed my church, who had the arrogance to fell my cathedral. I might have forgiven him one of my glorious, bejewelled treasures, but Francis Thursby, Earl of Rodermere, would have none of it. Foolish jester. He had no idea at whom he jangled his bells.

Come then, follow me down, for I am but the crack between the words, a riddle to be solved. Come, follow me, into the shadow of a sorceress's spell and think no more of my presence. I am but the unseen, all-knowing storyteller.

No man should have dared to wake me. No man. No man.

II

There is little merit in sticking pins in time, in searching for a date to tie this story to. Suffice to say it is set in an England ruled by a faerie queen, a period of ruffles and lace, of wrought velvet and blanched satins, silk stockings costing a king's ransom. It is the age of imagination, when the philosopher's stone would make gold of your dreams. A time when the world became curved and the seas led to strange lands and brought back unknown treasures. It is the day when the play be everything, and all men's lives had their season there. And it would have meant nothing to the sorceress.

In her chamber deep underground she dressed in all her finery. Her petticoat was the colour of damask rose and in the embroidered stitchery lay her magic, ancient as snakes, the very weave of the cloth testament to her power. She wore her crown of briars on her amber hair, a ruff of raven's feathers, a farthingale embroidered with beetles black as jet. Her skirt borrowed from midnight's wardrobe showed the hem of her petticoat beneath. And in the witching hour she went to find him.

III

Invisible in her cloak the sorceress took the measure of the man before making her appearance. She had found Lord Rodermere at the refectory table where once the monks had dined in silence. He was a large, sprawling man whose doublet battled to contain his flesh. His small eyes that suited swine looked mean in a man; his nose dominated his features; his lips, hard, thin. It was not a handsome face and his fondness for the wine accounted for the redness of his complexion. The stags' heads on the wall were testament to his passion for hunting.

Lord Rodermere's father, Edmund Thursby, had been given the monastery and its lands by a king who, in need of a new wife, had the monks made destitute. The late Earl of Rodermere had lived there and done nothing to its chambers that were bitter cold even in the summer months. Neither had he touched the forest other than to care for it by good husbandry. He had applied the same principle to his land and his people. Unlike his son, he had had the wisdom to leave the great oak trees alone for he believed in the tales of the forest, of the sorceress and the wolf. Only those who did not live in those parts and were ignorant thought these stories to be no more than faerie tales.

When Edmund Thursby died, his son returned home from

fighting abroad determined to build a manor house from the forest, as if by the destruction of the oak trees he would be hacking at the roots of pagan beliefs. He had sworn to rid his land of superstitions, bring his peasants under the control of the church and there such nonsense would be banished, by force if necessary. He would prove that man is master of nature and if in the heart of the forest there were both sorceress and wolf, he would hunt them down with horse and hound and kill them.

Three mastiffs lie at Lord Rodermere's feet. His page serves him wine, hands shaking as he lifts the jug to refill his master's goblet. Irritated, Lord Rodermere pushes the boy away. For all his bravado he looks uncomfortable in the dining hall of shadows. His dogs stir, their hackles rise, they snarl. They sense an unknown presence.

'Quiet,' says Lord Rodermere. 'It is only the wind.' And, cursing, he demands more wine. The page, pale of face, refills his glass. 'What? Are you frightened of a breeze?'

'No, my lord.'

The muscles tighten in Lord Rodermere's neck, beads of sweat form on his forehead. His heart pounds faster than it should. He jumps when a log falls into the fire.

'More candles,' he demands.

More candles are lit and the unseen, uninvited guest takes pleasure in blowing them out one by one. The servants and the dogs back away from their master. It is only when he lifts his wine once more to those dry lips that the sorceress appears before him in a blaze of light. His lordship's hand loses its grip on the goblet which clutters to the floor.

Time stops. And her voice echoes in the rafters.

'Francis Thursby, Earl of Rodermere, I will grant you any wish you might desire if you will – as your father did and the monks before him – leave my forest be. I am prepared to be generous.'

'What godless creature are you? From whence did you come?'

He is wondering if this be the Devil in the form of a woman.

His deep voice quavers. 'By what trickery do you conjure yourself before me? Who are you to claim my oak trees and my land, to threaten me, your lord and master?'

'You mistake me,' says the sorceress. 'I do not threaten you. And you are not and never will be my lord and master. I have come to tell you plainly what you must do if you are not to feel the burden of my curse upon you.'

'What did you say, mistress?'

He is shocked that a mere woman would speak to him thus. He calls for his servants. He stands high and square and points to the sorceress and orders that this witch be thrown out. Not one of his men dares go near her. Lord Rodermere was not expecting such insubordination. His temper now well and truly lost to reason, he bellows for his steward.

Master Gilbert Goodwin, who was born in these parts and knows them well, comes quickly, his footsteps ring on the stone floor as he enters the hall and slow when he see the sorceress.

'Lock her up and call the sherriff,' commands his master.

Master Goodwin – wisely – stays where he is.

'Did you not hear me?' shouts Lord Rodermere.

'My lord,' says Master Goodwin. 'You would do well to hear her out.'

His lordship draws his sword.

'Do you disobey me too? Be careful, Master Goodwin . . .'

The sorceress raises her hand to silence the fool. She has had enough of his blabbering tongue. One look is all it takes and stock still he stands, mouth wide open, unable to move. The sword falls from his grip and, like the goblet, clatters to the floor.

'You should do as Master Goodwin suggests,' says the sorceress. 'You should listen to every word and mark it well. Fell another of my oak trees and I will put a curse on you that no man will have the power to undo. But leave my forest be and I will grant you one wish.'

She snaps her fingers and Lord Rodermere is returned to the trumpets and drums of his fury. He shouts at her as if the sound of his voice will have the power to undo her threat.

'Woman, your charms and other such trumpery be worthless. I damn you as a sorceress, a bullbegger.'

And before his eyes, she vanishes.

IV

The next day at dawn, to show his mettle and his belief in a higher heaven, Lord Rodermere felled the second stag oak – broader than three kings and taller than any church in those parts. The majestic tree had stood sentinel over the forest, half in shade, half in sun so that it knew both the woods and the fields. Autumn had not yet stripped the tree of its cargo of leaves, yet regardless it was crudely felled. Sap blood on the earl's hands, the sorceress's curse upon his soul. She wrote it on the bark of that noble fallen tree, words written in gold for all to see.

A faerie boy
will be born to you
whose beauty will
be your death.

Lord Rodermere laughed when he was shown it.

'What jade's trick is this?' he said to Master Goodwin. 'Does she think I would be soul-feared by such sorcery?'

His peasants trembled when they saw the words but not because of their master's threats. They knew from the ancient laws that it be a bad omen that the words be written in gold, that they be etched so deep into the bark.

A bad omen indeed.

For every oak that Francis felled, the sorceress's curse went deeper, slithering into the branches and the very roots of the Rodermere family tree.

As seasons passed and gathered years with them, one turret rose out of his grand house, then another, slightly taller, and finally the third turret rose higher, taller than the tallest oaks, a monstrous scar upon the forest. The sorceress's land was cleared to make way for a park, gardens, jousting grounds, orchards of stunted trees. The house itself had claimed four thousand and sixty of her oaks. Its banqueting hall, its chapel, its carved wooden panelling, its long gallery, its staircases – all from her oaks made. Those faithful trees told her the truth of that family, of the twisted knots of its unhappiness.

In their dying, dried-out whispers, they said, 'He has no son, he wants a son. Two daughters born, two daughters dead and still no son has he.'

They spoke of a house petrified, of Lord Rodermere's many cruelties, of his servants who shivered at his presence, of his wife who dreaded his voice at her chamber door.

It was the Widow Bott who told the sorceress what her oaks could not, she being the local midwife and cunning woman, and close with the servants at the House of the Three Turrets. The sorceress knew her well. There was not a babe born in these parts whose birth she had not attended except those of the daughters of Eleanor, Lady Rodermere. Her arrogant, bumble-brain, shit-prick of a husband never wanted the Widow Bott near his wife. The widow was a handsome woman, her own mistress and had not succumbed to his oafish charms. In a fury at being rejected, he had threatened to ruin her unless she lay with him, accused her of putting him under a spell, stated publicly that he distrusted her forest remedies and advised all godly men not to let her near their wives for he believed her to be a witch.

In that alone he was right and it was the powers of the sorceress that had made her so. He should have known no one lived in the heart of her forest unless she had invited them there. The monks who first claimed this land had been wise enough to fear the darkness of the woods where the sunlight had little power. They began to believe that at the heart of forest, in the darkest place, lived the Devil himself in the guise of a black wolf. These stories grew in the retelling until the black wolf took on monstrous proportions. It was dread of this beast that stopped many a brave heart from venturing deep into the forest but it did not stop Gilbert Goodwin.

When first the sorceress laid eyes on him he was but a lad, adrift in her realm. He showed no fear, only a curious interest in finding himself with night coming on and his path lost. And being alive to everything he watched the moon shine through the trees, bewitched by the darkness that lifted the curtain onto another forest more magical, more savage than that of his daytime wanderings. He climbed one of the sorceress's oaks and slept in its mossy hollow till morning. Then, refreshed, he found by her design the rich larder of the forest where he gathered mushrooms and there saw his way home.

He was apprenticed to the steward of the late earl, Edmund Thursby, and the earl wisely saw in him more than a glimmer of intelligence. Gilbert Goodwin had learned a great deal from the old earl. He had admired his care of the forest and respect for his peasants.

Master Goodwin understood his neighbours. They may well go to church on Sunday, sit through dull sermons, chill their knees on stone floors, yet he knew in their souls they prayed that the black wolf stayed in the heart of the forest and did not eat their livestock or their babes.

After the sorceress's oaks were felled the sightings of the black wolf became more numerous. Its very size and shape belonged to a deep magic that Gilbert Goodwin knew should be respected if you valued your life and your land.

All this the sorceress had learned for she oft walked invisible beside Master Goodwin, listening to his thoughts, though he was never aware of it. He had filled out the thinness of his youth, grown well-built with a kind, thoughtful face and grey eyes that saw more than many and a tongue wise enough to hold its peace until speech became necessary. Francis, Lord Rodermere, for reasons that he could not fathom, felt inadequate when speaking to his steward. Even in height, Master Goodwin was superior.

On a spring morn they stood together, side by side, in a graveyard of oaks whose stumps stood as raw wounds that broke from barren soil, their once ethereal canopies but a ghost's memory. Now in this new season there was no leafy protection from the rain that drizzled on leather and fur, that dripped from brims of hats. Gilbert Goodwin's thoughts that miserable morning were filled with sadness for the utter pointlessness of such destruction. He looked at the standing trees and wondered if they too were doomed.

'It is only a matter of time before the head of that black wolf is nailed to my wall,' said Lord Rodermere. 'If it were not for the quality of the hunting I would have these woods felled. That would put an end to the pagan beliefs of the peasantry.'

'The forest has stood for thousands of years, my lord,' said Master Goodwin. 'You are the first man to have had an axe taken to those great oaks.'

'Do not say that you, like my buffoon of a father, believe in all that elfin gibberish.'

'Your father was a wise man,' said Master Goodwin, 'and understood his people. I would call a buffoon a man who thinks he knows everything, is averse to all advice, who acts without knowledge and is driven by conceit, only to be surprised at the consequences.'

Lord Rodermere was unsure if he had just been insulted by his steward but not knowing how to respond if he had, he continued.

'You believe that some sorceress has the power to put a curse on me?'

'I believe,' said Master Goodwin, his grey eyes never leaving his master's face, 'that you would have fared better if you had let the forest be, and built your house of bricks and mortar. This forest has always been a place of great beauty and greater terror.'

Gilbert Goodwin's wit was too fast for the slow, wine-soaked brain of Lord Rodermere, who in order to enforce his authority said, 'You are not seen often in church on Sunday. Do you worship at a different altar?'

Master Goodwin did not answer.

'I thought you better than a mere peasant.'

Again the steward held his tongue.

'Never married?'

'No, my lord.'

'Why not? Is your prick so small it could bring no woman satisfaction?'

Gilbert Goodwin, well-versed in his master's rages and jibes, had expected as much. Lord Rodermere was thinking of his own baubles.

The hands of time tick on, the sorceress's remaining oaks, her elders, and her ashes – white trees of death – move imperceptibly closer to the House of the Three Turrets. For all his lordship's boast of glass windows very little light shines in and long shadows fall across his lordship's gardens and his lordship's orchards.

Lady Eleanor bears him a third daughter. The child lives, but smallpox makes her soft skin toad-blemished and only now does Lord Rodermere begin to wonder if he has indeed been cursed. He enquires of his steward where he might find the sorceress who visited him when he hacked the first oak. Master Goodwin tells him plainly that it is best he looks no more. This time Lord Rodermere does not laugh so loudly for the words of the curse are echoing in his empty head.

. . . whose beauty will
be your death.

V

One May morning, Lord Rodermere, out hunting with a party of friends, thought he saw in a thicket a vixen and set off after her until by twists and turns he became lost. He stopped and shouted out in the hope of one of his party hearing him. And all he saw and all he heard was the chanting melody of birds, quivering leaves, cooling winds, and shadows. The mocking echo of hounds and a distant horn confused his senses. A snake unseen slithered past and so startled his horse that it bolted, taking his lordship by surprise. It was all he could do to hold tight to the saddle and reins as his horse, wild-eyed, nostrils flaring, took flight. Low branches scratched his face and Lord Rodermere fought not to lose his ride.

He is conscious, perhaps for the first time, of how deep and far the forest stretches.

On and on they go, horse and rider, this way and that, he all torn and knocked about, unable to bring his horse under control for in the mind of the creature the snake follows faster than he can gallop. Into the darkness the horse takes his rider. He, too, wild with terror, for was that not the cry of a wolf? And all sight is lost and then it seems he has passed through some unseen curtain into blinding light. The ground beneath his horse is moss, soft moss, and from it rises an intoxicating perfume.

Lord Rodermere thinks to call out. He is rewarded not by the sound of the hunting horn but by a song that has such yearning at its heart that his horse becomes calm and he, enchanted, dismounts. Forgetting how he arrived here he follows the music which calls him on until he comes upon a clearing.

Through the trees, he spies a stream, and under a willow in the dappled light a maiden dressed in an apple blossom gown stands bare-footed in the shallow waters. He, all in wonder, lets his horse drink.

'Maiden, do you know this forest well?' he says. 'Methinks I am lost.'

She takes no notice of him or his fine horse. She ripples the waters with her toes. Her silence intrigues him.

'I am Rodermere,' he says.

She glances up at him, her eyes as golden as the sun, her skin rose pink, her hair as black as midnight, her face an enchantment. She says not a word. She takes his hand and leads him into the stream.

'No,' he says, 'my boots . . .'

And she lets go of him and walks out into the deep water where the stream whirls. Swimming away from him, her blossom gown floats free. The sight of her voluptuous nakedness, her loosened hair, flower filled, near undoes him. Disregarding his boots, his clothes, he wades out to her. But he is a cloven-footed lover whose grace lies in brutality. That, this sweet maiden does not allow and she casts him off.

Finding that his strength has no power over her, he follows her to the bank of the stream, desperate for his lust to be allayed, and there goes down on his knees and begs her to lie with him. She comes, puts her arms round his neck, kisses him softly on the lips.

If he had known anything of elfin ways he would have had the wisdom to climb fast upon his horse and ride free. For we are the stuff of dreams, void of time's cruel passing. We are creatures of freedom that only brush against the world of envious man whose desires are made dirty with guilt.

It is one of the sorceress's handmaids who now stands near-naked before him in all her ethereal perfection. Her strength will haunt him ere long he lives, the smell of her soft skin a perfume he will never forget or find again. She is what man wishes for in bed but freedom is her birthright: she will not be tied to hearth or home. She is mother, good, bad all in one and none is she. A friend, no friend of man be she.

The Earl of Rodermere is now tamed, unclothed, brought to his knees, and hers to do with as she will. No man has loved a faerie and lived whole to tell the tale. But such is the pleasure she gives him that long afternoon that there he stays in her arms, honey from her breast he drinks and all time lost.

The hunting party searched all that afternoon and into the evening until, exhausted, they returned home without Lord Rodermere. The next morning they went again to look for him. For a week the search continued but there was no sign of him. The parson prayed in the chapel for his master's swift return. The following Sunday, the earl's horse came home without its rider. Gradually, as the days become weeks and the weeks turned into months, the mystery of Lord Rodermere's vanishing deepened. Those who lived near the great forest knew well he was not the first to be elfin taken.

Only his wife, Eleanor, Lady Rodermere, and his little daughter, Lady Clare Thursby, kept their hopes to themselves and their prayers tight on their lips for both wife and daughter prayed – prayed as they had never done before – that Francis Thursby, Earl of Rodermere, might not be found.

Wife and daughter dared to believe that their prayers had been answered. It had been a harsh winter when even the birds had fallen from the sky, frozen by the cold. Surely, Lady Rodermere told herself, no one could survive in the forest in such unforgiving weather.

VI

Nine months have passed. It is midnight in the House of the Three Turrets. A servant sleepily attends to the fires before returning to his trundle bed. The cat, all whiskers and claws, sits watching the space behind the cupboard in hope of a mouse. The flea sucks on the sweet flesh of dreamers till he is ready to burst with blood. The distant church bells ring the hour. The dogs in the hall begin to bark.

Yes, this is the hour that will alter all the hours to come.

VII

The infant was brought to the sorceress at one of the clock, one minute after his birth, more beautiful than even she had imagined. There was no kiss upon his brow, no faerie wish to interfere with her curse, or so she supposed, for who would dare disobey her? So certain was she of her powers that she did not examine the babe – perhaps his beauty beguiled her but she took the word of his mother when she said she had not kissed the boy, that he was innocent of any wish.

What is done is done and one kiss would not have the power to interfere with the sorceress's magic. But she had no notion of what a mother's love in all its sticky gore was like. Only later did she discover that the faerie had lied and the sorceress was aggrieved that she had ever trusted her womb-ridden words.

Her task that morn was to make sure that Lady Rodermere took this infant as her own, to love and to cherish.

She placed the basket with the babe in it on the steps leading up to the great front door of the House of the Three Turrets. The dogs howled but the household did not stir; it was asleep, deep under her spell. She required only two people to be awake: Master Gilbert Goodwin, Lord Rodermere's trusted steward, and Lady Rodermere, Lord Rodermere's trusted wife.

Lady Eleanor was lying in her great bed, listening to the dogs. She watched the door and held her breath, every sinew in her body stretched to breaking. She stayed that way, suspended between sleep and wakefulness, taking short, sharp breaths until she could tentatively assure herself that there was no tightening of the air, no drowning of hope, no weighted foot upon the stair. Her husband had not returned. She lay back on the linen sheets, relished the chilly space around her, the warm island her body had made in the centre of that vast cold bed.

Lady Eleanor, unlike her lord, believes in the Queen of Elfame. She is certain that her husband has been faerie-taken and she prays that he might never be returned to the shores of her bed.

Through the large bottle-glass panes of the window a beam of moonlight falls accusingly on the carved wooden cradle. It has been in this chamber ever since Eleanor first wed Francis, Lord Rodermere. Three daughters born, one still lives. Over the years the cradle has come to represent her failure to produce a son, an heir for his vast estate. Tomorrow, she thinks, she will have it removed.

Her bravery wavers, for the dogs have not ceased their howling. She rises, puts on her fur-lined gown over her underdress, her feet bare on the chill oak floor, as cold as the fear in her heart.

Please do not send his lordship back, please do not.

Taking a candle, she opens her chamber door, listening for distant voices in that cavernous House of the Three Turrets. There are none. For a moment she wonders whether she should call for Agnes, her maid. Eleanor has always loathed the black whalebone beams of the long gallery, full as it is of oaken shadows. Hearing Agnes's peaceful snores from the adjoining chamber, she thinks better of it.

At the main staircase Eleanor stops and looks over the banisters. The dogs are now whining; why, she cannot fathom. Only her husband's steward is there. What could be the reason for the hounds to be so disturbed? She watches Master Goodwin. He is holding a basket, staring at its contents with a puzzled expression. Snow dusts his doublet and cakes his boots. The glow from the fire catches his face. A face to be relied on, she thinks, and in that moment she sees him for the first time, as if she had never noticed him before. Kind eyes, generous lips unlike her husband's mean, hard slit of a mouth. She wonders what those lips might feel like if they were to kiss hers. One thought stitches itself into another forbidden thought and she finds herself imagining Gilbert Goodwin being a gentle lover . . . and in that instant she knows what she wants, what she longs for: to be loved without leaden cruelty.

So the sorceress's magic begins to work, for tell me how does a cuckoo lay her egg in a magpie's nest if not with the help of nature's charms?

Lord Rodermere had never considered his wife to be a hand-some woman but that night Eleanor is not without beauty – a slight frame, delicate. Her hair is tumbled, sleep has given her a soft glow. As she walks slowly down the grand staircase, holding on to the balustrade, her gown falls open. The outline of her body, her breasts, show through the muslin underdress.

Gilbert Goodwin is suddenly aware of her and sees, not the wife of his lord and master, but someone vulnerable, lost; finds himself moved by the very image of her.

Eleanor and, she suspects, Gilbert Goodwin, knows there is another, invisible, presence watching them. This house of whispering oak seems always to be calling the forest closer, admitting its spirits.

'What is it?' she says.

Gilbert holds out the basket to her.

Her sad brown eyes take in the infant, fast asleep in the wicker basket, wrapped only in rabbit fur.

'Is it faerie born?' she asks.

'I do not know, my lady,' says Gilbert.

He does not think it an unwise question.

The babe lifts one small, perfect hand, nails as delicate as sea shells. She touches his finger and feels her heart being pulled towards the infant's, knotted round his.

'Have you ever seen such a beautiful child?' she says.

'No, my lady. There is a note.'

Pinned to the fur, written in the unmistakable hand of Francis, Earl of Rodermere, it reads, *This is my son*.

VIII

Later that St Valentine's Day, when the snow had settled thick and white, covering the truth of earth and the lies of lovers, Eleanor wondered who it was who had entered the house that bitter winter morn, who it was who had been intent upon mischief. In the quiet of that afternoon, as the sun once more began to fail and the snow fluttered at the window, she shuddered with the joy of remembering and felt not one ounce of guilt.

Gilbert, Eleanor at his side, had carried the basket up the stairs, through the long gallery to her chamber. Neither of them had said a word, nor had the infant announced its arrival. Gilbert closed the door and they waited, hoping that none of the servants had heard or seen them.

She whispered, 'My maid is asleep in there,' and Gilbert Goodwin silently closed the door to the antechamber.

Still the infant had not cried out.

At the end of the bed was a chest where Eleanor had kept the swaddling clothes and the sheepskin bedding that her babes had slept in when newly born. She took out what was needed and wrapped the babe in the long linen cloth before laying him in the cradle to sleep. His hand fought its way free to find his mouth.

'You will be needing a wet nurse, my lady,' said Gilbert.

'Not yet awhile,' she said and sat to rock the cradle, to think what she should do, how she would explain the child's sudden appearance. Could she claim the baby as her own? True, when she was with child, she had been slight, had never grown to the size of a galleon in full sail.

Back and forth, back and forth, the cradle rocks back and forth and with each gentle movement she feels a strange heat. It starts in her thighs and spreads up into her belly, into her very womb, up to her breasts. It is an overwhelming heat, the like of which she had never experienced before. She stands up abruptly and forgetting all about Gilbert, forgetting all about modesty, she throws off her fur-lined gown. Still her womb feels to be a cauldron of flame. She discards her underdress.

'I am on fire,' she says.

Gilbert sees her naked, her arms wide open and turns his face away.

'My lady, shall I call for Agnes?'

She looks at him and he turns to her, his full lips parted. She leans forward, her lips touch his. It is kindling for the blaze.

Frantically, she undoes his doublet. He pulls off his shirt, her hand slips into his breeches, she is pleased to feel his cock is hard. On the bed he parts her tender limbs, kisses her lips, her neck. He nuzzles her breasts and gently enters her, not with the violence she is used to, nor is the act over with the pain of a few uncaring thrusts.

Gilbert whispers, 'Slowly, my lady, slowly.'

He takes his time, waits for her. At each stile the lovers encounter he helps her over, and deeper into her he goes. Then, at the height of their ardour, when all appears lost, Eleanor gives a cry that wakes the baby, that makes the lovers pull away, she embarrassed by the completion of an act that she never knew could be so tender.

Gilbert climbs out of bed, picks up the infant and holds it to him. They wait for the knock on the door, for their sin to be discovered.

But there is not a sound, the house is still wrapped in an enchanting spell. The sorceress would not allow these two lovers to be disturbed. More needs to happen before the cuckoo is well and truly hatched.

IX

Eleanor looks at Gilbert, naked, holding the infant close to him and her breasts ache. They feel full, painfully full, just as when she'd had her own babes. Leaking milk, she takes the babe from Gilbert and begins to feed him. With each thirsting suck he assures his place in her affections. She looks up at her new lover.

'Tell me what has happened to us – do you know?'

Tears fill his eyes.

When the infant had finished feeding, Eleanor searched hungrily for a mark upon him for she had no doubt that her husband had been faerie-taken, no doubt that this was his child.

The infant fell asleep and Gilbert wrapped him warm and snug and laid him in the cradle. And as he did so, the steward felt that time had gathered itself in quick, aching heartbeats, each beat becoming a month, the months becoming nine. This faerie child was as much his and his mistress's – born in a flame of a desire – as ever it was his master's.

Gilbert awoke only when there was a tear of light in night's icy cloth. Eleanor had the babe at her breast once more.

She reached out towards her lover and whispered softly, 'I will not give up the child. He is ours. What will we say? What should we do?'

Gilbert kissed her.

'Leave that to me,' he said.

In a basket near the bed lay a heap of bloodied sheets. Blood spilt on the floor, jugs of water, pink in colour, clothes and all such stuff to dress a stage for a woman who had given birth.

When Agnes finally stirred she was confused first by how late the hour was, then mystified at the sight of her mistress propped up on pillows with a newborn babe.

'Oh, my lady,' said Agnes, 'why did you not wake me?'

'I tried,' said Lady Rodermere, 'but you were fast asleep and it came so quick upon me.'

'Was no one with you, my lady?'

Not a beat did Eleanor miss.

'Yes – Gilbert Goodwin.'

After all it was the steward's duty to make sure that any child born to Lord Rodermere's wife was no usurper.

'I am most truly sorry,' said Agnes. 'The thought of you being on your own, and you never knowing you were with child.'

Eleanor felt the smile deep within her and kept her face solemn as she said, 'If asked, perhaps it would be best that you were to say you were with me all night.'

'Willingly,' Agnes said.

And by doing so is caught in the nest of lies.

X

It was Gilbert Goodwin who after the infant's birth sent for the Widow Bott. The widow had delivered many a changeling child and watched them fade as bluebells in a wood when the season has passed. For the truth is, there are few children who have a mortal and a faerie for a parent and those that are born always have a longing to return to our world rather than stay in the human realm, and who can blame them. Changeling children, instead of being plump and round are sickly things that hang on to life as does a spider swing on a thread in a tempest. These changeling babes, left behind unwanted by the goblins, are placed in cradles where newborn babes lie and when no one is looking they take the child's form as their own. But not this half-elfin child. He was born to be the sorceress's instrument of death.

Lord Rodermere had often decried faeries as diminutive creatures made of air and imagination. But we are giants for we hold sway over the superstitions of humankind. I have hunted the skies, chased the clouds in my chariot, I have seen wisdom in the eye of a snake, strength beyond its size in an ant, and cruelty in the hand of man. Our sizes, our shapes, our very natures are beyond the comprehension of most. We are concerned with pleasure and the joy of love, we use our powers to shift our shapes, to build enchanted dwellings, to fashion magic objects and to take dire revenge on mortals who offend us. But for those we protect, such as the Widow Bott, we ensure their youth and health.

She has a far greater understanding in the knowledge of herbs and plants and their properties than many an apothecary, much more than the quack wizard, or so called alchemist, hoping to turn lead to gold, to cheat men from their money.

So it was important – nay, I would say it was a necessity – that Gilbert called for her, for she alone could sway all incredulity, she could assure any doubters that the sheets held the evidence of a human birth, not the blood of a slaughtered rabbit. In short, she would give weight to the child's arrival, confirm that he was indeed the son of Francis Thursby, Earl of Rodermere.

XI

The sorceress had no desire to remain at the House of the Three Turrets that morning. It pained her to see her trees used that way, their branches bent, carved into unforgiving shapes. Instead she went to the widow's cottage and waited by the fire.

It was dark by the time the Widow Bott returned. Wrapped against the cold, her cloak caked in frost, snow and she came in as one. Putting down her basket, she fumbled for a candle to light. The sorceress lit it for her, set the fire to blaze and the pot upon it.

'I should have known that you would be here,' said the Widow Bott. 'Well, I am not talking to the air. Show yourself, or be gone. I am tired and it shivers me when I cannot see you for who you are.'

For some reason she was out of sorts.

'You always know when I am near,' said the sorceress, to comfort her.

''Tis a pity that a few more folk are not as wise as me to your ways,' said the widow, dusting the snow from the hem of her dress and taking a chair by the fire. 'What mischief have you been up to?'

The sorceress laughed. 'So you saw the child?'

'Yes. He is more beautiful than any mortal babe should ever be. He has already won the heart of Lady Eleanor.'

The sorceress seated herself opposite the widow. 'You should be in better spirits,' she said.

'And what of Gilbert Goodwin?' asked the widow.

'What of him?'

'Never has a man been more lovestruck.'

'And Lady Eleanor?'

'The same. Do you intend to return Lord Rodermere? For he is not missed at all, especially not by his wife who trembles at his very name.' The widow stood, took a long clay pipe from a jug that sat on the mantelpiece and kicked a log with the heel of her boot, before sitting down again in her rocking chair. 'You have made a mistake if you think Lord Rodermere is of any importance.'

'He has dented my forest.'

'Will you put a curse on every man who fells a tree?' snapped the widow. 'Perhaps it would have been best if you had travelled further than the forest and seen what is abroad before you laid your curse, for there are many roads that lead now to the city and news travels both ways upon the Queen's highway.'

'Tell me,' the sorceress said, ignoring her jibe. 'Did you examine the infant?'

'Lady Eleanor would not let me hold of the babe. She seems as devoted to it as if it was hers and she has no need of a wet nurse. Though she did ask about the star that be on his thigh.'

The sorceress stood. 'What star? The child was blemish free. Did you see it?'

'No, for the infant was swaddled.'

'She is mistaken.'

'I think not,' said the Widow Bott.

'What did you tell her?'

'That such a mark . . .'

'Such a mark,' the sorceress interrupted, 'was not upon the child.'

The widow never once had been frightened of the sorceress. She shrugged her shoulders.

'I have no need to argue with you,' she said. 'If you say there is no star then what I say means little.'

'What did you say to Lady Eleanor?'

'That such a mark shows him to be of faerie blood and the star, a gift. She asked what kind of gift and I told her that only his mother could answer that question. She blushed when she realised that she had unwittingly confessed that the child be not hers, milk or no milk. She begged me never to say a word. She showed me the note left pinned to a fur and I assured her that her secret was safe.'

'Good, good. But there is no mark.'

'If you say so,' said the widow. 'But Lady Eleanor knows more of your ways than her husband did. She asked if the babe be a hollow child for she has heard of women who give birth to changelings and having no appetite for life, they mock a mother's love and fade away. I promised her this be no such child. Was I right?'

'Yes. Yes,' the sorceress said again and all the while the thought of the star worried her.

'You should not toy with us as if we be puppets,' said the widow.

'Come, that is unfair – I do not.'

'But you do. Look how many lives will be changed by your curse. You would be wise to leave it be, not have Lord Rodermere return to plague his wife, to accuse me again of being a witch. Let the good of his disappearance be your comfort.'

'No, what is done is done and cannot be undone.'

The sorceress watched the Widow Bott as she relit her pipe.

'So you know how all this will play out? How Lord Rodermere will meet his end?'

These questions annoyed the sorceress.

'My curse will come to pass. What befalls the players on the way has little to do with me.'

'I think you are mistaken. You are dealing with our lives.'

The Widow Bott pulled at the sorceress. But no one talks that way to her and she turned to leave.

'Wait,' said the widow. 'Wait. You know there is a reward for anyone with information about Lord Rodermere that would lead to his safe recovery?'

'They will never find him – of that I have no worry.'

'You may have no worry, but I do. They may never find him unless you will it but what you have done this day will bring to leaf a tree of questions that fools and mountebanks will try to answer, their brains baited by the riddle of the boy's unholy beauty. I will be marshalled and again accused of witchcraft. The monks feared nature's beauty, seeing it as a seducer, a tormenter of men. Even in the soft petals of the rose, they thought they saw the face of evil. Do you believe this child will go unnoticed, that his very looks will not be brought into question? How far do you suppose the news of his birth has already travelled?'

The sorceress said, 'Your word is enough, I am sure, to confirm that the child is the son of Francis Thursby, Earl of Rodermere. No one will question his parentage.'

'Again, you are mistaken.'

The sorceress had no interest in this. What concerned her was the star.

'Keep yourself to yourself, widow,' she said, 'and you will be safe.'

'Perhaps. But for how long?'

'Near seventeen years,' said the sorceress.

She was in no mood to contemplate consequences and as she lifted the latch on the door, she congratulated herself that her powers had not waned.

XII

The sorceress returns to her dwelling deep under her angel oak, whose veiny tendrils weave the domed roof of her chamber. Here stands her bed – raven black, the colour of dreams – with its canopy of stars. Fireflies light the room and gather, as do the moths, round one golden orb, a heavy pendant that swings slow across the chamber. She sleeps suspended between the streams of ages. Her spirit barely stirs to hear minutes passing. It is a parcel of time put to good use.

A moth's wing flutters and almost seventeen years are gone.

XIII

Something gnaws at the edges of sleep. Not the rhythm of the days but her passion for Herkain, the King of the Beasts. It is not wise, she knows, to let herself visit him even in dreams for it brings her to the well of her own emptiness. He who had the sorceress's very heart where all her love lay, who sunk his glorious teeth into its arteries, pulled it beating from her breast, left her heartless. He did not take her power, only her reason. She conjures the memory of Herkain's tongue licking the flesh from her to reveal her pelt in all its lush resplendence. Once, she longed to return to him, ached to feel his prick deep inside her, to feel his strength contain her, the howl of his whole being released into hers. When they lay together they were one, she his dark, he her light.

Memory can disturb even the deepest sleeper with its incessant chimes upon the mind. Does the sorceress deceive herself when she dreams again of Herkain? Or is it the infant's beauty that so enchants her that she cannot rest until she has the measure of the boy, knows what kind of fiend she has created?

Though he be half of faerie blood, all of him will be his father's child. His beauty will corrupt him and the years will make a monster of the man.

And she wakes. By the lantern light she sees that the hem of her petticoat is torn, a scrap of the precious fabric gone, her very inner sanctum violated.

A tear in her petticoat is an unbearable weakness. It wounds her as if it is her flesh that is peeled from her for that piece of fabric is a charm that would give the thief power over her.

Who would do such a thing? No mealy mouthed mortal could part the watery curtain that divides the world of man from faerie. No spirit would dare come near her. Was this Herkain's mischief? No, no, it was not he, of that she is certain. Then who?

Such was her fury, such was her malice, that she howled with the pain of it. And her faithful trees stayed silent and gave no clue as to who the thief might be. Her rage was uncontainable, she rocked the earth with it and heard winter shiver.

The sorceress dressed to hide the tear and against the season of snows she wore a gown made of summer gold, sewn with the silk of spiders' threads, embroidered with beads of morning dew. Its rubies ladybirds, its diamonds fireflies, hemmed with moonshine's watery beams; yet it was the tear in the hem of her petticoat that weighed her down for some mortal held its threads and by such stitchery, she was tied to them. She smelled blood, she smelled the shit and the fear of mortals.

She hardly noticed the cold or winter's white mantle. Rage kept her warm and fury brought on a blizzard. Only in the icy breeze did her balance return to her. All was frozen, held tight against nature's cruelties.

The Widow Bott, she will know. She will know who committed this crime.

She reached the clearing where the widow's cottage stood. A papery yellow light glinted through the slatted windows. The wind whirled the snow as she knocked on the door.

'Who is it?' said a voice.

'You know it is I.'

The widow unbolted the door that had never before been locked for she had no one to fear, not even the black wolf. She was wrapped as tight as her cottage, her clothes quilted against the cold. The fire flared in the draught of the open door and she closed it quickly, and moved to her chair.

'So, mistress, you come at last,' she said.

'I told you it would be near seventeen years,' said the sorceress, 'and true to my word I am here. What is wrong, old widow?'

The widow's hollow eyes as good as told her that something was amiss. She took the chair opposite her and the widow turned her face away. Where, thought the sorceress, was the widow's bright, piercing stare that dangled challenge in its light?

She thought to ask a simple question.

'The babe – what did Lady Rodermere call him?'

'He is called Lord Beaumont Thursby, but all that know him call him Beau.'

'He is now near grown, is he not? Ruined by the knowledge of his beauty and its power?'

'If that was your design then you will be disappointed. He has grown to be the sweetest of young men. If his beauty has any consequence it is to those who look upon him for, man or woman, it makes no difference, all are enchanted by him.'

'So, I am right,' the sorceress persisted. 'He uses his looks to make slaves of those who his beauty entraps.'

'Again you are wrong.'

'Impossible.'

The Widow Bott leaned forward and poked at the fire as if she had no desire to speak the truth.

'His sister,' continued the sorceress. 'That toad-blemished creature: surely she is bitter with jealousy?'

'Again, no. Powerful is the bond of affection between brother and sister. And tomorrow, their mother, Lady Rodermere, is to marry Gilbert Goodwin.'

'But she is still married to Lord Rodermere, is she not?'

'Not. The queen was petitioned to annul the marriage as Lord Rodermere has not been seen, alive or dead, for eighteen years come May. Please, mistress, I beg of you, let this be. Do not return Lord Rodermere to them.'

The sorceress looked at the widow more closely as she repacked her pipe and lit it, sucking in her sallow cheeks.

'What are you not telling me?'

'There is nothing to tell,' she said.

She was lying, trying to hide her thoughts, the sorceress knew it. One name escaped the store cupboard of her mind. Sir Percival Hayes.

'What are you frightened of?' the sorceress asked. 'Who is this man – this Sir Percival Hayes?'

The widow shivered. The sorceress caught her eye. 'I am waiting,' she said, 'and I am not in the mood to be lied to.'

'Sir Percival Hayes has an estate not far from here. Lady Eleanor is his cousin. When the earl vanished, Sir Percival went to the house and swore he would be found. He too had heard stories of people being elfin taken – it was a subject that much interested him. Cunning men and wizards made a path to the door of the House of the Three Turrets, promising that they had the charm, knew the spell that would release Lord Rodermere from the faerie realm. Two years of fools came and went, and for all their enquiries—'

'Yes, yes,' the sorceress interrupted. 'Nothing was discovered.'

'Mistress, let me tell this in my way.'

At last a spark of the woman she remembered.

'After two years had passed, Sir Percival sent from London his own alchemist, Master Thomas Finglas.'

The old widow was silent awhile and then said, 'He brought with him his apprentice, a lad whose skin was as dark as an acorn. They made a strange pair, the boy and the man. The alchemist, I was told, handed Gilbert Goodwin a letter from Sir Percival who wrote that Master Finglas was tasked to bring back Lord Rodermere from the faerie realm. You may well imagine that Master Goodwin was none too eager to welcome this guest. Near two years had passed, two years of managing his master's estate, of loving his master's wife, of sleeping in his master's bed. The last thing he wanted was his master's return.'

'The quest failed,' said the sorceress. 'The alchemist – you met him?'

The widow nodded.

'What sort of trickster was he? Soaked in books, steeped in knowledge, lacking in wisdom?'

The widow looked her straight in the eye. 'If you know all, why did you never come when I called for you?' She gazed into the embers of the fire and said, 'Master Finglas failed to find Lord Rodermere and his failure to do so turned Sir Percival Hayes against all such alchemy. He had me examined for witchcraft. He said there be reports of me dancing with the black wolf, he even accused me of casting an owl-hunting enchantment on Lord Rodermere. He said I worked with a familiar.'

'What led him to think this?'

'I know not. Sir Percival sent his steward here this Yuletide to collect proofs against me: cheese that would not curdle, butter that would not come, the ale that drew flat.'

The sorceress laughed. 'As if we would be bothered with such domesticity.'

'There is more,' she said. 'I be accused of bewitching Lady Rodermere's maid, Agnes Dawse, and by doing so cause her death. But I did nothing, nothing. I never even saw her when she was ill.'

Sleep had made the sorceress slow. She should have known from the moment the widow opened the door that the spell that kept her safe was broken and age had taken its revenge. She had cast herself from the sorceress by the folly of her tongue. The sorceress should have been more circumspect. The tear in her dress was a weakness that pulled her imperceptibly into the mortal world. Time is the giver and time the thief.

'You betrayed me, old widow. You spoke my name.'

Her fury rumbled the rafters of the cottage and she was in a mind to bring it down on the old widow and let it be her tomb.

'Do you not care what happens to me?' said the Widow Bott. 'Be it of no importance to you?'

'Some may think that a tear in their petticoat is of no importance.' The sorceress showed her where the cloth had been taken. 'If you can tell me where I might find the missing piece, I could be kind to you still.'

The widow peered at the hem and felt the fabric between her fingers. Snow thudded to the floor from a hole in the thatch.

'I think I saw it – but I cannot be certain.'

Then the sorceress caught it – a fleck of a secret in the widow's eye.

'Be warned, old widow,' said the sorceress, her anger a blood-red moon, 'for I speak willow words that, if I so desire, can snatch your soul away, turn your good fortune to bad and bad to evil. My magic is eternal. What is it you are keeping from me?'

The widow shivered.

'A scrap of your hem. He had it. The alchemist had it.'

Blinded by rage at what she had heard, such was her impatience to be gone that in all the Widow Bott had said the sorceress had missed the details. The truth, as tiny as spring flowers, lay unnoticeable beneath the snow.

XIV

That night, this night, midnight, the end of Christmastide. Father Thames has begun to freeze, so tight is winter's grip. Silent, soft, canny snow begins to fall; thick is each determined flake that gathers unrelenting in its purpose to make white this plague-ridden, shit-filled city.

On such a night in Southwark, the bastard side of the Thames, by the sign of the Unicorn where the houses bow towards one another, their spidery beams made solid with salacious gossip. There the torches that would have lent light to the street have long been defeated, but one paltry candle burns in the cellar window of the house of the alchemist, Thomas Finglas. A vixen trots up the narrow alleyway, her soft pads leaving paw prints that are soon to vanish in a layer of crisp snow. She sniffs the night air and sees at the bars of the cellar window a creature, not of human shape. For a moment their eyes meet. Then, with a nod, the fox sets off once more, her brush proud behind her, her breath licked with flames. At the back door, the sorceress hesitates and listens. From the cellar comes an unearthly cry.

Herkain's long-ago words return to her unheeded.

'Pride, my love, is the Mistress of Misrule.'

Pride? she thinks. No, it is not pride that brings me here, unless pride be the essence of my being. She is here to retrieve what is rightfully hers, a piece of her hem, perilous, too powerful to be taken by a mere mortal.

Unseen, a ghost, she steps into the house and as she enters the threads from the stolen hem needle into her, pull her towards this unknown thief. Quite suddenly she feels her powers wane, her magic weaken. Surely it is impossible that a man could possess wizardry equal to her own?

Not a sound do her feet make on the stairs and there, in a tattered, long-neglected chamber, the alchemist lies on his lumpy mattress. The sorceress can hear his thoughts as she can with most mortals. In the flicker of troublesome dreams he notes the bluish light, the bitter cold, and longs for a peaceful sleep to rob him of all conscious thought. He thinks the cause of so much waking is a dry brain and his continual fears, he believes, account for his lack of sleep.

But it is the memory of his late wife, deep buried, that is the cause. He had hoped with her death would go all the bell, book and candle curses that had tortured his days, made barren his nights. Half asleep he stares up at the canopy of the bed. His disquiet mind frets at the shabby drapes until in the fabric he sees the face of his dead wife, hears her voice crab-clawing at him.

'Nay, Husband. I would call you a murderer.'

And into the covers of his bed, he mumbles, 'It was your curiosity that killed you, woman, not me.'

Her cackle was as thick as his blood and just as black. 'Suspicion will always fall on you, husband. I made sure of it – a gift from my winding sheet. I might be dead and maggoty-eaten but the power of my mischievous tongue has outlived me, has it not, Husband?'

Thomas sits bolt upright in bed. He is a thin man, his eyes

hooded by anxiety. He has lost the optimism that had once given him an arrogance that marked him out, as if he alone knew the answer to all the world's conundrums. His mind is kept sharp with knowledge yet his wits are dulled by superstition and a terror of the power he has unleashed.

This dead wife of his is an indigestible piece of gristle. Her bitter words sit heavy on the right side of his stomach, a pain no remedy of his devising can ease. A cold wind moans into the chamber through the gaps in the glass. He hears the vengeful night conquering the current of the Thames, transforming water into ice. He hears with a heavy heart his late wife's waspish voice prattle on.

'I would call you an adulterer, a dealer in the Devil's magic.'

He sinks back and pulls the covers up over him.

'And you,' says Thomas Finglas, 'what brought you to our table apart from rumours and lies to make misery of my tomorrows? Never once an infant came from that barren womb of yours to comfort my days. Be damned, be gone.'

He thinks back to his mistress, his beloved Bess, her flesh so soft, her breasts so firm, her belly round. Her belly round that had given him his one and only infant, a secret to be protected from this cruel world and from his wife's vicious temper.

'You never knew the truth, woman,' he says into the hollow silence.

The sorceress is intrigued.

'Tell me, Thomas,' she says. 'Tell me the truth.'

'Bess . . . is that you? Bess . . .'

Sleep takes him, exhausted, in its kind embrace. And just as he dreams of Bess's round bottom, her soft cheek, just as he feels her lips upon his, downstairs something heavy falls.

'The cat,' says Thomas sleepily.

He cares little, for only Beelzebub now will make him rise

from this floating warmth of oblivion, from the tender-breasted Bess. All else can go to the Devil.

'The cat,' he says again, his eyes heavy, his mind at last clear of the past.

But it is no cat.

XV

There are two men in the house, heavy of build but nimble of foot, the stench of the river and the tavern on them, mercenaries in search of any paid work. Kidnapping, assault, murder, all arts they are well-versed in as long as they are paid and can own their own boots. Each step they take in hope of waylaying their prey.

Thomas's apprentice, John Butter, does not wake at the sound of the intruders. He is asleep in the kitchen. He, unlike his master, sleeps the deep sleep of youth. Walls may crash, trees may fall and still he would dream on.

Thomas wakes with a start. He tries to gather his dreaming wits and fails.

'Bess?' he calls into the darkness. 'In the name of God, show yourself.'

Swift are the two men. He has no chance to scream before he is muffled in a cloak, wrapped and strapped.

His two assailants are big-built, battle-dented men. Thomas is an easy customer. The knife held to his side tells him they mean business.

'Keep quiet and no harm will come to you. Make a sound and the knife will find its home in your heart.'

He is bundled from the chamber. The vixen slips out unseen before them.

The garden gate creaks back and forth in the wind. Thomas struggles to free his face from the cloak, shaking his head vigorously. From the low window of his cellar comes the high-pitched yowl and the vixen sees there again the feathered creature who stares out through the bars, eyes glinting; a halo of light outlines its shape, talons scrape at the glass. The image is disjointed by the round panes so there appears more than one and behind all a shadow of wings looms great. The sight seems to torture Thomas.

Under his breath he whispers, 'In the name of God be secret and in all your doings be still.'

Momentarily, the sound stops his assailants.

'What's that?' says one, lifting his lantern.

He points at the cellar window. The sound sends a shiver down their hardened spines. Not even in war, when the battle was over and men lay wounded and dying, had these two heard such a cry.

'Let us be gone from this cursed place,' says the other and pulls Thomas into the alleyway. And in that moment, not fully able to see his enemies, he tries to make a fight of it. His reward for his effort is a sharp blow to the head. He stumbles and loses consciousness.

The mercenaries take hold of an arm each and carry Thomas with all haste towards the river. If anyone had the gall to stop them they would say they were helping an old drunk home. But no one is about to see them and only their footsteps tell which way they are bound. By the water steps, not far from the Unicorn alehouse, they drag Thomas to where a barge is waiting. On board is a gentleman, dressed in black, his jerkin slashed through with red taffeta, a fur-lined cloak speaks of a wealthy master.

'What is this?' he says, seeing Thomas unconscious. 'Is he alive? I am not taking a dead man to the House of the Three Turrets.'

'He is not dead. He will recover soon enough. Now, where is the money?'

The knife glitters in the darkness. Neither party wants an argument. A purse of coins is handed over and Thomas is dragged into a curtained cabin.

The oarsmen push off and out into the slushy water towards the middle of the river where a ribbon of mercury is all that is left of the fast-flowing tide, for the Thames has by degrees begun to turn white. Behind the barge London Bridge looms monstrous high, and an army of buildings, a fortress to remind England's enemies that this country is ruled by a queen with a lion's heart.

When the river freezes it speaks; fragments of ice crackling with confessions of the murdered and the lost. On the ill-lit bridge the sorceress alone sees the frosted ghost of a young woman, a group of drunken men laughing, jostling her. She loses her footing and slips, tumbles unnoticed into the icy, churning waters. The voices of the dead bring an eerie sense of solitude to this usually frantic thoroughfare. Among them Thomas hears his Bess.

'Not long, my love, 'til we embrace again. Not long, my love.'

The river is near deserted. The oarsmen battle on, sweating even in the cold of this grievous night. Slowly the city disappears, past Westminster and out into the pitchy black darkness of the countryside.

XVI

But the sorceress cannot leave. Not now, not until she knows what it is that the alchemist has hidden in the cellar. Crude curiosity pulls at her and to the house she returns.

Still no one had stirred. Then she heard it, the frantic flapping of wings and scratching of talons, and she perceived a smell – pungent, musty, animal. Determined to see the creature she was at the cellar door when she heard a call.

'Master, master – is that you?'

A young man stared at her and through her to where the back door had swung open letting in the raw cold. Dark of skin and dark of eye, this, then, is the alchemist's apprentice. Unlike his master his thoughts were guarded and he kept them close to him. The sorceress found it hard to fathom what he was thinking other than the obvious. The footprints in the snow increased his fears. She followed him as he took the stairs, two at a time, to his master's chamber, cursing under his breath. One glance at the disarray of the bed clothes, enough to tell him what had happened.

In the apprentice's ebony eyes she saw the heat of the sun from an unknown world, the place from whence he was stolen. He knows better than his master the power of magic, knows it possesses a life force that not even death can defy. He survived the seas where the battle with the waves had been fought.

The wooden boat, weighed down with the thief's treasure, ill-equipped to deal with the fury of such a tempest, had been tossed as if it were a child's plaything and, limping into port, had brought him to these cold, anaemic shores.

Again the sound from the cellar. It is a noise that she sees he dreads and it is louder, more urgent than ever before. As he runs down the stairs, his thoughts, the ones she catches, have an energy to them, his whole being is more alive than the alchemist's. She listens hard. He hopes his master's secret is not to be discovered, he knows he must calm the creature in the cellar. She is in the passage when she hears a creak on the stairs and a young maidservant appears.

'Oh, lord,' she says, 'Master Butter, what has happened?'

Master Butter speaks with a stammer and he is careful not to trip over his words. He knows that his stammer is especially pronounced in the presence of a pretty girl. He does his best to sound commanding.

'Go into the kitchen, Mary,' he says. 'Stay there until . . .'

To his surprise she looks at him in a direct manner that has little fear in it.

'Do you want me to help you?' she asks, following him to the small cellar door at end of the passage.

For one moment he thinks he might laugh, the notion is so ridiculous.

'No,' he says.

The sorceress can see that Mary is new to the household and that she has never before met anyone like Master Butter. The colour of his skin, darker than the beams of the house. His eyes are darker still. He is tall. He turns to look at her as he takes his master's key. Her presence gives him courage.

'Be still,' he says into the darkness of the alchemist's cellar.

He opens the door, turns to make sure Mary will not follow and in that instant the sorceress slides in before him.

XVII

You are not from my realm, Thomas Finglas, and your magic confuses me. You confuse me, for I saw what it is that you keep locked in your cellar and she is not of this world. Did you steal her from Herkain's realm? No, it is impossible for any mortal to pass through that watery curtain into the kingdom of the beasts and return alive to tell the tale for the flesh of man is the sweetest of all meats. There is something more worth knowing. Perhaps she was sold to you, this winged beast. She would not be the first – the unicorn, the griffin made the journey and survived. But no and no again. And methinks that if a 'no' was a brick then a wall I would build with them. You go against the wool of me and muddle my thoughts. How is this possible, what potions, what magic charm did you use to create her? Was it by the hem of my petticoat or have you stolen more from me?

A knot of human making pulled becomes more impossible to untangle and yet the sorceress, knowing all this and more, cannot let it be.

Who are you, Thomas Finglas? You who possess power enough to rob me of myself, to flood my mind with your narrative. Who are you? There is trickery here. By what means did you find my chamber? Was it with a knife you cut my petticoat or did you pull the fabric from me? And why did I feel nothing? The cloth is as good as my skin. The pain alone would have woken me and yet I was numb to you. How can that be? These questions enrage me. Never before have I not listened to my instinct. It has ruled me. In the depth of my ancient being my wisdom echoes loud: return to your chamber, sleep and dream. Let time take care of the curse, not you. Not you.

Her excuse is the beast. And so she follows the barge which looks to her eye as a black slug does that leaves a slime trail in the thin surface of ice and snow. She has no choice but to stay close to this Thomas Finglas for he holds the answer to the many questions that sit, crumbs upon her lips.

The alchemist was conscious by the time he was helped up the steps at the watergate of the House of the Three Turrets, his mind making a mosaic of his broken thoughts that the sorceress furiously pieced together to find an answer. There was none. Overriding everything was his simple anxiety to be home. Now she listened far more attentively to all that the moth of his memory brought to the light.

He thinks his apprentice will not know the right words to calm his child. The thought of her escaping into the streets fills him with dread. She will be hunted like an animal, torn apart. She is still only a child, he thinks. Only a child.

And the sorceress thinks, she is no child of this world.

53

XVIII

It was a bitter dawn and snow illuminated the grounds. The light made beard shapes of trimmed hedges and in the distance, looming large through unnatural angles of bush and wall, the three turrets rose, each spire impaling the sky's tapestry. Surrounding all, the forest cast its shadows. The sorceress heard its familiar, deep, slow heartbeat. This was a place Thomas had never wanted to see again and he had a feeling – no, a surety – who it was who had sent for him and to know it made his bones cold as stone.

Two servants each took one of his arms to guide him lest he should slip. In defiance he pulled away. If death be waiting for him then he will meet it with dignity, not being handled as if he be a criminal.

One had to admire his courage and, in spite of herself, she did. The sorceress followed him up the steps to the great door where near seventeen years ago she had left a basket, certain of her powers. Where fifteen years ago Thomas came, certain of his powers. He is taken to an antechamber with no fire, no candle and there in the darkness he is left, the door closed, the key turned.

And then he says her name into the darkness of that worrisome chamber. How does he know her name? Fury rises up in her – and sinks back. It is never wise to trust a witch.

'You are here,' he whispers. 'I cannot see you but I feel your presence. I know it is not my Bess. I am right, am I not? It is you who have been watching me, listening to my very thoughts. Did you come for your hem? Return me safe to London and I will give it to you.'

'Where is it?'

Thomas jumps when she speaks. That at least she finds satisfying.

'Where are you?' He turns wildly this way and that and he cannot see her. 'Help me, mistress, I must return to . . .'

'To what? What is it – what is she – who you must return to?'

Here he stumbles.

'You saw her?'

'Yes, I saw her.'

'I beg of thee. She cannot – must not be discovered. She would be . . . John Butter will not know what to do to calm her. I must return home.'

'Tell me the truth of how you came by this winged beast and perhaps I will help you.'

He says as he might a prayer, 'She is my daughter.'

This cannot be, the sorceress thinks.

'Tell me how.'

And from the liquid dark of the chamber his wife is once more conjured, her voice set to nibble away at his paper-thin sanity.

'Yes, Thomas, tell her. Tell her of your whore and the beast.'

'I am listening,' says the sorceress. 'Tell me about the beast, Thomas.'

Again he floods her with his misery, his loss, the torn pieces of unstitched memory, a misleading patchwork of thoughts.

'I loved her,' he says.

'But she was not your wife,' says the ghost of Mistress Finglas whose tongue is blacker than Hell's back door. 'It was I who was your wife.'

'Quiet,' he shouts. 'Quiet, woman, stop plaguing me. What more do you want?'

No one comes to see what is wrong. The silence thus disturbed takes time to thicken upon them once more.

The sorceress hears then a crackle, a laugh.

'I want my house, my furnishings, my garden,' says Mistress Finglas. 'You went away to find an earl and came back with a whore, did you not, Husband?'

The alchemist's dead wife clings to him as ivy to a house.

With a sigh he lets go of all the fragments of his memory for the sorceress to knit together.

Some fifteen years before he and John Butter had returned from the House of the Three Turrets, bringing with them a maid to work in the house. Upon seeing that the maid Bess was quickening with child and no father to its name, Mistress Finglas, the good, Christian woman that she was, insisted that Bess be thrown out for her ungodly ways. Thomas forbade it. In revenge she had hagridden the girl with that venomous tongue of hers. The babe would be cursed by the hellwain, born boneless, horns on its head, fur in its mouth, a tail in its breeches.

Five months later, Bess began her labour. Not even the pain of the oncoming infant was allowed to interfere with the main meal of the day. Betwixt two courses the babe slipped slithering, bloody, between her mother's legs, and not a cry did either make. Bess held her close, and there they sat, tied together by the cord. She was baffled by the newborn's silence as liver-like, the placenta slopped onto the stone floor. She cut the cord with the carving knife, wrapped the creature and warmed her by the fire. Then served roast chicken and with the gravy quietly informed her master of their daughter's birth. Pushing back his chair hard he rose abruptly as it fell backwards. The noise of it startled his wife. She looked up from her plate, mouth wide open, stuffed with chicken meat, so that all the chewing and her few black teeth could be seen.

She said, 'What is it, Husband?'

And he, repulsed by the very sight of her, felt himself on the precipice of declaring a truth, the truth that was well known to all three of them.

Like the newborn babe he remained silent, even when his wife asked, 'Husband, where go you?' and gravy rolled down her double chins.

Downstairs in the kitchen Bess wept and showed him their newborn, eyes closed and silent, her tufted hair red like her mother's.

Mistress Finglas, puffing and hefting herself after her husband, demanded to know what all the fuss be about.

Then seeing the babe so still, wax white, said, 'I told you, I told you so I did, the pucklar would come and steal the bastard.'

Good, kind Bess, by then at her mind's end, screamed, 'If she be dead. So be me.'

Master Finglas gathered mother and child into his laboratory and closed and bolted the door against the fury of his wife. Mistress Finglas, knees bent, praying that wood might become parchment, stayed there cursing less the child should think to cry its way back to life.

'I hear a crow croak from the next roof, and you know what that means, Husband,' she shouted. 'A coffin in the ground, a coffin in the ground. Serves you both right.'

No answer came and on the second day, the door still barred to her, she took to boxing the ears of her husband's apprentice, demanding he open it.

'I . . . I . . . I cannot,' stammered the terrified boy.

Having beaten John Butter until the worst of her rage had

57

subsided, Mistress Finglas left him curled in upon himself outside his master's door, lifted her skirts high and crossed the stinking alleyway to the house of her neighbour. She huffed up the narrow stairs and there she stayed by the window and talked away the hours in unwise words. She knew, she said, what they be doing, her husband and the whore, they be eating the flesh of the unbaptised babe. Her jealous imaginings gave birth to rumour, its midwife being gossip that to this night still haunted the alchemist's good reputation.

On the third day, in desperation, Mistress Finglas cut up her husband's fur-lined cloak. The wanton waste of such a necessity gave her untold pleasure. She wondered what her scissors, razor-sharp, would feel like plunged into the heart of her cheating husband. On the fourth day she went to church, fired by the idea of Hell's vengeance and all the demonic winged beasts to be found there.

On the fifth day, the door to her husband's laboratory opened. Bess returned to the kitchen, her husband to his business, and neither had a word to say about the baby.

'Where is it?' demanded Mistress Finglas.

'Where is what?' asked her husband.

'The babe.'

'There is no babe.'

'You jest, Husband. I saw it with my own eyes.'

XIX

A key turns in the door, candlelight falls on the tormented face of the alchemist. A servant, carrying a gown, enters to find Master Finglas arguing with his dead wife, on the brink of losing his mind. The gown, which is far grander than any the alchemist has ever owned, pulls him back to the present. The sudden warmth that envelops him feels like the arms of his Bess, tears sting his eyes at the memory of her loving. He stands straight, rubs his hand over his bare head. He is escorted through the long gallery with its rows of paintings of the Rodermere family from the first to the present. He notices that one is missing, a shiny patch of wall marks out the square space where it used to hang. It was not a large portrait, yet he had considered it the finest there. It was of Francis Thursby, Earl of Rodermere, his hawk at his wrist.

The sorceress slips her hand into his. He stiffens, stops breathing for a moment, then squeezes her fingers gently. He is mystified by the softness of her skin. What did he expect? Scales? As much as she hates to admit it, by the hem of her petticoat their fates are tied to one another.

'Do not leave me,' he whispers as a door is opened.

The chamber they entered was hung with tapestries all depicting a hunting party. The riders looked out at Thomas; the hounds were running for the fox who, like the hunters, stared out at the viewer unconcerned, or so it appeared, by the nearness of danger. And in front of a roaring fire stood Sir Percival Hayes, Thomas's old master and benefactor. Whippet lean, his clothes extravagant; a ruff of Dutch lace that could be valued in acres of land was gathered round his neck. The effect of the ruff was to disjoint his head from his body as if the two were different domains serving different masters. His face was by far the more sinister. He had hooded eyes, a long nose, lips too full. He could be taken for a younger man yet look closer and the fine lines that wrinkled his skin gave away his age. He was known at court as the Badger for his dark hair had a white stripe through it. Once head and body were joined as one his whole appearance spoke of menace.

Fifteen years, thought Thomas, can so change a man. When he had been in Sir Percival's favour his master's face had been open to the world. Now it is closed, iron conclusions have crushed the dreams of the younger man, made him an unmovable force of convention.

In those distant days, Sir Percival wanted to know the mysteries of alchemy and more. He had sought out Thomas Finglas. Having sieved through all the cunning men and quacks in London who pretended knowledge of the chemical theatre, Thomas stood apart. He was learned, spoke Greek, Latin, French and German as well as he spoke English. His interest was not in what he considered the cheap trick of turning lead into gold, but in the faerie realm for he believed if its power could be harnessed then all the secrets of nature would be at man's command. Thomas had been with his master two years – in which he married, realised his mistake, and was able to do nothing but be bound to it for better or worse – when he had been sent here to return Lord Rodermere to the House of the Three Turrets.

XX

Sir Percival Hayes poured a goblet of wine, took a sip and helped himself to sweetmeats from a dish before him. He ate with a ladylike delicacy then slowly took out a fine linen handkerchief and wiped his fingers. At last he turned to Thomas.

'Do you remember, Master Finglas, when you came back to London from a summer of bedding a nursemaid and had the audacity to tell me that your work had been successful? And you produced this?' Sir Percival waved a scroll at Thomas. 'I dismissed you as a fraud, did I not? Threw you out of my house, along with that shrew you married. These days, I believe, your practice deals mainly with pimps and whores and cures for the pox.'

'Not entirely, Sir Percival,' Thomas muttered.

'Did I ask you to speak? No, I did not. I am talking, you are listening. After your departure I washed my mind clean of your nonsense, determined to meddle no more in the Devil's Cauldron. From that day forth, my role at the court of Her Majesty would be to root out superstition, hunt witches and those who profess to deal with the Devil's magic. In that, I have served Her Majesty faithfully. I cite you as an example of a cunning man, a mountebank, and from the reports my spies have gathered on you, I was right in my assertions.'

Thomas was trembling. The question he wanted to ask came out in a low whisper.

'Sir, why have you brought me here?'

Sir Percival poured his third glass of wine.

'Yesterday,' he said, 'my cousin Eleanor, Lady Rodermere, was wed to Master Gilbert Goodwin. The service took place in the chapel and afterwards there was to be a feast for the guests in the banqueting hall. I was there as a representative of Her Majesty. I had argued on Lady Rodermere's behalf that as Lord Rodermere had been missing for near eighteen years he should be considered dead and she free to marry again. So, tell me', Sir Percival drained the third glass of wine, 'did you pick a date at hazard? Or was it something you calculated on an astrological chart? Or was it decided on the throw of a dice?'

Thomas feels the pit of his stomach to be lead.

I watch you, Thomas. Beads of sweat pepper your forehead. You are caught in a quandary of your own making.

'Have you lost your tongue, man?' said Sir Percival. 'I asked you a question.'

Thomas mumbled and at last asked why is this important, why now is it so important that he should be dragged from his bed and bundled here?

She is pleased that he has roused himself and still has some fight in him.

Sir Percival stood and handed Thomas the scroll.

'Read it,' he commanded.

Thomas did not need to. He knew exactly what it said. After all, he was its author.

'Read it,' said Sir Percival again.

Thomas looked down on the grave of his own words. All that was written there was the date and the time of Lord Rodermere's return.

'Yesterday,' said Sir Percival, 'on the date, at the very time stated there, just as glasses were raised to toast the bride and groom, a dead man walked into the banqueting hall, a ghost at the feast. He looked not one day older than when he vanished. He was wearing the same garments; they were fresh, not a blemish to be seen. The intensity of the silence was so dense that you could hear the unsaid: "This is not possible." Because standing in the middle of the banqueting hall was Francis Thursby, Earl of Rodermere, returned, as he told us, after one day – one day – in the realm of the faeries.'

XXI

Mark me well – nothing good will come of my curse. I made sure of that when I cast it. If it had not been for the hem of my dress I would have no interest in this affair other than to hear of the death of Lord Rodermere at the hand of his beauteous son.

Alas, by her hem was she brought here to watch and watch she did as Thomas Finglas was dragged by Sir Percival as he might a reluctant schoolboy, through the long gallery and up the spiral staircase that led to the chamber at the top of the tallest of the turrets.

'If you want your freedom, Master Finglas,' said Sir Percival, 'then I advise you to conjure a rational explanation of what befell Lord Rodermere. Until you do, you will remain here as his physician.'

Those words gave the sorceress satisfaction and she left Thomas to his fate. In truth she cared little for humankind whose minds perpetually worry at their days and whose actions bring naught but destruction upon our world. Her spirit is not one given to melancholy. It is an emotion that belongs to man, along with endless regret.

The Widow Bott had given her a desire to see this young

Lord Beaumont. It would surprise her not if she too had fallen under his spell for such beauty was designed to have the power to awaken desire in all those about it. The sorceress wondered, though, why the old witch was not wise enough to know this and thought she must remember the dire consequences beauty has had on plainer mortals. Once, not that long ago, the widow had searched out the sorceress with a request from a gentlewoman of these parts who owned a fine house and fine horses but felt her looks to be her one tragedy. She asked if she might not be given a potion to make her beautiful. Being less bitter then than the sorceress is these days she could see the folly of such a wish and told the widow to advise against it. But the gentlewoman paid a higher sum to have the widow ask her again and the sorceress granted it. And then such was her beauty that it awoke evil in the hearts of all the good women of her acquaintance who turned against her and their jealousy was to be her death.

The sorceress judged that beauty in a young man would have the same potency as beauty in a woman. Impatient to find the boy, hither and thither she went and she heard the conversations and the thoughts of the household. Few of the servants remembered Lord Rodermere and those who did recalled him with no fond memory nor had a good word to say about him. All had heard stories of his debauchery and none doubted that he was a tyrant. There was not a young woman high born or low who had been safe from his lustful advances. The sorceress relished blowing on the dust of these old tales. She whirled them up on the winds of gossip so that by the afternoon there was not a settled mind to be found in the House of the Three Turrets. All wondered what was to become of their master, Gilbert Goodwin and his new wife, Mistress Eleanor Goodwin, of young Lord Beaumont Thursby and Lady Clare. The question weighed heavy in their hearts.

XXII

She finds him in the long gallery by a tall window, juggling three wooden rings. He has the art of it well but it is his face – no, his whole demeanour – that steals her breath and makes her delight in her powers. His hair raven black, thick his eyelashes of the same colour framing golden eyes. His lips sensuous, full, made for pleasure, he possesses a natural allure that shines in him, a charm, she would call it, that bewilders even her. He is both male and female, united in one body.

Up the three rings go as the sunlight that has failed to make an appearance all day breaks through the snow-filled clouds and casts him in a rose gold light. An artist would give his soul to paint him. He moves with a natural grace, the very air around him accommodates his being. Here is an ethereal creature who man or woman both would desire, would lose riches and reason for one night of passion. All then is as it should be. He is empty of emotion, of that she is certain. He is indeed almost perfect in every respect, his beauty but the mask of an unfeeling monster. Try as she might she cannot hear his thoughts; his is a shallow vessel, nothing inside his head but the mirror of his own perfection. The Widow Bott, blinded by his looks, had failed to see that nothing lay beneath the surface but her own imaginings.

The sorceress is not so easily duped. Oh, she thinks, but this is too joyous – he will be the light of all men's desire, he will be the heart that no woman can possess. Take pride in your work, enjoy what is about to befall those who enter his domain.

Beau catches the rings and puts two on a side table. He turns and seemingly stares directly at her. That disturbs her. He cannot see her, no man can unless she wills it and to prove the point she moves but the point is unproven: his eyes follow her. Under her breath she whispers to the icy draught words that protect her from the gaze of human eyes.

I am born from the womb of the earth, nursed with the milk of the moon. Flame gave me three bodies, one soul. In between lies my invisibility.

It does not ease her as it should.

'There you are,' he says.

He is speaking to her in her language. This cannot be. She holds her breath.

'Beau.'

The sound of his name comes from behind her. She moves further into the wooden shadows.

It was not her but his sister, Lady Clare, the boy addressed and the sorceress anticipates that she is about to see the nature of young Lord Beaumont. His sister's thoughts she can hear clearly and she will tell her her truth of him for the sorceress is beginning to think he has no soul. A pity about her face. If it was not so blemished the sorceress would say she was a striking young woman. She is of twenty-two winters with an enviable figure and holds herself well. The sorceress thinks she was a fool to worry that she might be visible – Lady Clare cannot see her.

What is this? Lady Clare laughs as he tosses a ring for her to catch and she is thinking that she would rather die than be without him, that the very notion of being parted from her brother is unbearable. And what does Lord Beaumont think?

Nothing. His mind is blank parchment that the sorceress can easily write upon and shape his character to her desires.

Beau smiles at his sister, takes her hand and kisses it. He looks in the sorceress's direction and seems to hold her gaze before he turns back to Lady Clare.

'We have not spoken in that language since we were children,' she says. 'This house seems full of spirits today. Beau, did we dream what happened to us in the forest?'

He puts his finger lightly on his sister's lips.

The sorceress waits to hear his reply expecting it to be cruel. And then she catches Clare's thoughts – glimpses of a memory dance in her head, children running into the forest – then they are gone.

Lady Clare sighs. 'We must put aside such childish nonsense. Alas, no one has the magic to alter what has happened.'

Speak, Beau. Let me hear your voice.

The sorceress goes to stand beside him lest she miss a word.

'Do you believe,' says Lady Clare, 'that it is possible for our father to return after so long without the years marking his disappearance?' Again Beau looks at the sorceress. 'What is it?' Lady Clare says, following his gaze. She drops her voice. 'Is someone listening?'

'These oak beams listen,' Beau says quietly. 'Have you seen our mother this morning?'

His is a voice a stream would envy, a voice that is neither low nor high but has a quiet command to it. Oh, Robin Goodfellow, look what she created in your honour.

'Not yet,' says Lady Clare. 'But, Beau, tell me you will leave with us.'

Delight of delights. The sorceress sees a tear in her eye. All this love for an empty shell of an androgyne, a man for all desire, shallow as a puddle.

'Sir Percival had the alchemist, Thomas Finglas, brought here from London last night,' she continues. 'He is locked in the turret with our father. It is hoped he may bring him to his senses.'

'Then there is even more reason that you must be gone before Lord Rodermere wakes further from his trance and his temper rekindles.'

He takes her hand and walks with her down the long gallery.

She says, 'He will not miss you, he does not know you. He does not believe you are his son.'

'That was last night,' says Beau, 'but he is by all accounts an irrational man.'

He gives her a look of such tenderness. The sorceress sees how well he acts the part. Oh, beauty, what a beast you make.

'What will I do without you?' Lady Clare says. 'Who will see me as you do?'

'It will be for a short time only, I promise.'

And he turns round and looks straight at the sorceress.

XXIII

It must not happen. Young Lord Beaumont must not leave this place. His destiny is to murder his father as I foretold when I wrote my curse on the bark of that felled oak. If the death of Francis Rodermere means the death of his son, what care I. He is a puppet and I the puppet master, his strings are at my command.

The sooner the deed is done the better for there is a wildness calling me, a yearning to relish once more my powers as an enchantress. I needs must be free to find a new lover, to be ravished by him. I have almost forgotten the alchemy of sex. This mortal world has twisted passion into such a bitter coil that it makes soil barren, fills rich earth with sand. I must replenish myself, lest all of me withers. Still by my curse I am tied. Still by my hem I am caught. Let it be done, let it be over.

My mood is black, thick. And sticky is the rage that runs through my knotted veins. The boy unsettles me, his look unsettles me. Did his mother lie when she said she never kissed the infant? And if she did what gift did she give him? I shake the thought away. No, he is empty of soul, of feeling, he is but a pretty knife to pierce a heart.

Thomas Finglas is locked in the tallest turret where Lord Rodermere prowls about as would a wolf. It is not a small chamber and is encircled by windows. Leaning against the wall is a large collection of mirrors. Some have lost their frames, others broken. All the shards reflect Lord Rodermere in a bright light of fury.

Thomas is seated, head in hands, the very picture of melancholy, as Lord Rodermere rails a vomit of angry words. Such a din is it that it has nearly defeated Thomas. Where are your powers now, alchemist? The painting that was missing from the long gallery is propped against the wall. Francis Rodermere looks no different than he did when he sat for the portrait some eighteen years before and this is what he wants Thomas to explain.

'If, as you say,' he roars, 'I have been lost for near eighteen years, why, tell me, have I not aged? I do not believe you. Neither do I believe that boy is my son.'

The sorceress has no wish to hear more of his meaningless curses. Sleep is the saviour of the insane, and she gives Lord Rodermere dreams of a May morn, of a stream, of a maiden. The first and last day of love. He flops onto the trundle bed and lies still.

Thomas looks up when the shouting ceases, startled by the abruptness of the silence. He stares anxiously round the chamber.

'You did not finish your story,' she says.

'Mistress,' he says, going down on his knees, 'please show yourself. Please take me away from here and I promise . . .'

'What then happened, Thomas?'

He rises, begins again.

'Slowly,' she says. 'We will not be disturbed.'

'She – my wife – caused the news to spread. An author, larding his lean words with thees and thous to make more of the story, printed a pamphlet claiming I had made a beast from a babe.'

'And had you, Thomas? Had you made a beast?'

'Bess begged me to revive the babe and I, confronted by so

much grief, knew not what to do but to experiment with my elixir of everlasting life, a potion no more proven than any others. I poured it into the crucible, stirred it over the heat, my heart warmed by my love's belief in me. I put in the feather of a bird, the wing of a bat, the hair of a cat, I anointed the infant's lifeless body with oil of acorn to ward off noisome things. It was Bess who placed her into the mercury. Together we watched her vanish in the silvery water and I was bewildered when she rose again – alive, unrecognisable, an abomination. Three years we kept her safe from prying eyes. But the rumours and gossip did not abate and neither did the nagging of my wife. She took out her rage on Bess. As the child grew, the sounds from the cellar became louder and my wife became more terrified. She plagued me with questions and hearing no satisfactory answer, threatened she would let the whole world know that I had the Devil living in our house. Soon after this threat, John Butter found her at the foot of the stairs. She was dying and the physician called to attend her could not – to my relief – explain the marks he found on her body, nor fathom what animal could have had the power to tear flesh from her bones. Blame fell on me and the strange sounds that came from the cellar. I was arrested on suspicion of murder and wizardry and that night . . .' He hung his head. 'That night Bess vanished, never to be seen again. I near lost my reason. All I had for company in the darkness of my cell was the cackle of my dead wife. I heard her all the time. "As long as I be alive, as long I be dead, I will haunt the whore." Why did I never hear my beloved Bess?'

He took a gulp of air.

'Go on, Thomas.'

'At the inquest my apprentice was asked where he had been the day his mistress died. He trembled on being questioned and appeared to be an idiot with little understanding. He stammered, tripped, fell and faltered over his words to such a degree that he was found to be incomprehensible and his testimony disregarded. But John is a wise soul. He knew I hoped to find peace at the Tyburn Tree. But it was not to be. The landlord of the Unicorn alehouse swore that I had been with him all morning until the time of the accident and no man, as far as he knew, could be in two places at one time. The charge of wizardry was unproven, the case against me dismissed. There was no relief. I have lived in torment ever since.' Thomas paused then said, 'Let me see you, mistress.'

She does. Abruptly, he sits, startled by the sight of her. She, the sorceress who time does not age, neither does her beauty fade. Her resources are various and plentiful and she will not be tied to any man, nor be his footstool or wishing bowl, to come hither, go thither. Now she will offer Thomas a way out of his troubles. If he accepts but fails to keep his end of the bargain she will bring such sorrow to him that his days will be unbearable. She smiles, feels light coming from her, her feet rooted once more to the ground. She will be glorious. Thomas is in awe of her. She takes pleasure in his surprise and watches his confusion turn to bare-faced desire.

'Promise to give me back my hem,' she says, 'and I will have you home.'

She bends and kisses his lips, tastes his hunger. He puts his arms round her, holds her buttocks and softly weeps.

'You do wish to return home, do you not?' she says.

'Yes,' he says. 'Yes . . .' And then as if remembering the reason he is locked up he turns to look at the sleeping lord. 'But how? Tell me how.'

'I will return Francis Rodermere's missing years. Then the question of where he has been will be his own to answer, not yours. Sir Percival will claim that he lost his memory and has only recently recalled where he lived or who he was, but, alas, has no idea where he's been.'

'You would do all that?'

She pulls back his gown, lifts his night shift, his cock already hard and of a goodly shape and her hand slips up and down the length of it, peeling back the skin.

He groans with pleasure. She stops. He opens his eyes, tries to take her hand.

'I promise,' he says. 'I promise that when we are in London . . . I promise on my child's life . . . I will return your hem.'

She lifts her silken gown above her belly and lowers her cunny onto his weapon, wet at the point.

XXIV

She enjoys such carnal acts and Thomas's desperation has a tenderness to it. He is not, as she would have supposed, a greedy lover. But she is in control, not he and her mind is elsewhere.

She is thinking it would be wise to trust the power of her curse and let it work its fatal magic. And yet she cannot for a maggot of a thought niggles at her: she fears the boy was faerie-blessed.

Lady Clare's deep love for her brother goes back to infancy. Her memories trouble the sorceress. She had willed Lady Clare to return to them but she did not, her mind flooded with thoughts of being so soon parted from her brother. Has the sorceress been too quick in her judgment? For it appears from the affection Lady Clare holds him in that he possesses a true beauty: he has kindness, love, intelligence. Not one ounce of his bastard of a father shows in him at all. When Beau smiles, it is a smile that would bring a queen to her knees. That is as it should but not the rest. Could it be that he as yet has no knowledge of his power? Lady Clare is not in one small part envious of his looks. The sorceress had imagined that she would loathe her brother, resent his beauty. Surely that is the pattern of human nature: to be shaped by jealousy, to be broken by envy. It shivers her to think she had been so unwise as to believe that her powers were incorruptible. She comforts herself with this thought: Lord Beaumont has many chambers of his soul yet to grow into. If he is not corrupted now there are years enough for him to become so.

No one interferes with her curses.

'Where are you going?' says Thomas Finglas. 'Stay, I beg you.'

Invisible once more, she is gone.

XXV

Mistress Eleanor Goodwin, still dressed in her bridal gown, was seated staring into the embers of the fire. Her husband Gilbert stood opposite her.

He was silent, immovable. It appeared that both had said all the words they had to say.

But Eleanor returned to the round. 'I will not leave, not without him.'

'My love, Lord Beaumont is right,' said Gilbert. 'If you stay, what will become of you? Of us? Remember what Lord Rodermere did to you? Think what he might do to Lady Clare.' Gilbert's voice softened. 'If Beau is seen to leave with us and Lord Rodermere decides he wants his son then our fates are sealed – he will come after us.'

'But to go abroad, to leave him here to that monster's mercy, how could you think of such a thing? You who love him as a son.'

'He will follow. You and Lady Clare must have time to escape and when you are safe, I will send a message and then he will be with us again.'

'Could we not stay in London and be closer to him?'

Eleanor looked up to see her son and daughter in the doorway.

'Is the the carriage ready?' Beau asked and his voice had a note of calm authority to it.

Gilbert nodded as if saying the words might reawaken the argument that had occupied their wedding night.

Beau knelt beside his mother.

'My lady, to stay here would be folly. You are married to Master Gilbert. Best by far you leave today and go abroad. Take my sister away from here. It is what you have long wanted. Sir Percival has advised you to do as much.'

'Only if you come too,' she said.

The sorceress has to admit surprise at this young man's elegance of language, his careful argument. She can see his speech holds weight. And she is wondering how she might make them stay here a while longer until the deed is done. But one look at Master Goodwin tells her it would be his knife, not Beau's, that would pierce the earl's heart and that would never do.

The wind whirled, the chamber door flew open and in the sudden breeze the fire flared.

Beau glanced up to where she stood as if to say, 'You are still here?'

Beau's words seemed to shake Mistress Goodwin into action. Her husband called for a servant.

'Bring the carriage and my horse to the front of the house,' he said, and he helped his wife to her feet.

This parting causes each of them great sorrow and it appears as genuine in Beau as it does in the others. Surely, thinks the sorceress, this is an actor playing his part, nothing more.

'How will I find you?' said Mistress Goodwin to her son. 'When will I see you?'

'I promise, soon,' said Beau. 'Now, my lady –' he kissed her hand '– the quicker you are away from here the nearer you will be to seeing me again.'

An hour later saw the carriage containing Mistress Eleanor and Lady Clare leave the house, accompanied on horseback by Gilbert Goodwin. The three cloud-capped turrets stared down on the walled forecourt to the gatehouse where the porter and other outdoor servants lived. It was they who ran out to open the gates, to wave farewell. The rooks cawed against the oncoming darkness as the carriage disappeared onto the main road. Beau stood bare-headed on the drive and only when it was lost from sight did he turn and walk back to the house.

I am torn. For this boy is everything he should not be and despite of it I am enchanted with him and his girlish looks. At the grand door where once I had come with a basket he stops, turns to look at me and holds the door open as if waiting for me to enter.

I am born from the womb of the earth, nursed by the milk of the moon. Flame gave me three bodies, one soul. In between lies my invisibility.

XXVI

Thomas was watching from a window in the turret as the carriage departed. He wondered why the young Lord Beaumont was not inside it, for there would be no point in the boy staying, no point at all. His heart missed a beat when he heard the door to the chamber being unlocked.

He turned and was about to say that he needed more time, when Sir Percival said, 'What have you done?'

Thomas, without looking at Lord Rodermere, replied, 'He sleeps.'

'Sleeps?' repeated Sir Percival. 'Yes, sleeps – and he has aged. Alchemist, I much underestimated your talent. This is indeed a remarkable transformation.'

Now Thomas looked at Francis. And indeed a miracle of sorts had taken place: the ravages of time had collided with him. Gone was the youthful man and in its place a withdrawn creature whose prick had aged more than the man himself so it would in future be an impotent thing that would cause him much frustration and not one ounce of pleasure. Lord Rodermere looked nothing like the portrait, the two images hardly reflected each other.

The sorceress's one regret is that she had not the chance to be there when young Lord Beaumont confronted his father. She would have chosen it to be different but Sir Percival was intent on having Thomas Finglas gone as soon as possible, regardless of the fact it was now night and the roads barely passable. A horse was brought that looked as reluctant to leave the stable as Thomas was to leave the warmth of the house.

'If, Master Finglas, you mention one word of what has happened this day and your part in it, I will not hesitate to have you charged with sorcery,' said Sir Percival.

He nodded at a servant who took from Thomas the gown he was given on his arrival. Thomas, in his nightshirt, sat astride the horse.

'But, sir, I will freeze to death.'

Sir Percival said nothing and the great door closed behind him. Snow was falling on horse and man as they made their way on to the impassable road.

Thomas will remember nothing of his journey and only come into himself again as he crosses London Bridge and its tongue-tied waters. There, numb with cold, he will urge on his horse until he finds himself haunting his own back door.

'Be I alive or be I dead?' he asked.

His conclusion, dull as it is, was that he was dead. There is something so pathetic in man's desire to know what state his flesh be in. How could he not feel the pulsing of his blood, the beating of his heart? And it strikes the sorceress that in all she has seen of him he possesses very little magic. He jumps when he hears her voice.

'I have kept my part of the bargain, now you must keep yours.'

Again he asks, 'Am I dead?'

Night had reached the hour when it wraps itself starless in its frozen cloth. The door was locked, the house in darkness. Thomas knocked with his fist. He knocked again. His teeth were chattering, his breath a white mist and these bodily signs comforted him and proved he was made of living parts. When still there was no reply he cursed his nick-ninny of an apprentice: was he deaf as well as stupid? Then his courage wavered as an altogether more terrifying thought came to him: what if his daughter had escaped and murdered again? Once more, Thomas raised his fist, ready to feel his knuckles hard upon wood, then stopped as the door all by itself opened into an abyss.

'John?' he called.

There is no answer but from within comes that high-pitched yowl.

XXVII

Thomas Finglas enters his house with shaking steps, fearful of stumbling over the remains of his apprentice and the serving girl whose name for the moment escapes him. He turns to where he supposes the sorceress is. Look at this learned man, this tormented Thomas Finglas. He does not possess one ounce of power. Now he searches for the sorceress as might a child, frightened of the dark and it occurs to her that the magic she feels in this house belongs to another. Thomas is shaking with cold or with fear, it is hard to tell the difference. In mortals both have a smell to them. In the passage he fumbles for a candle and then searches in vain for a tinderbox with which to light it. Not far from him is a scratching, talons on wood.

The sorceress lights the candle for him and he nearly drops it. His hands are shaking so violently that he is forced to use both. As he goes towards his cellar the back door slams behind them and the candle is extinguished.

'Did you do that?' he asks.

She did not.

Try as she might she cannot relight the candle. Now she is equally alarmed for the very air is filled with menace. Does the creature have the strength to play with her?

The laboratory door flaps, half off its hinges, and light spills from the hearth but there is no one to be seen. Thomas stares in at the chaos of this chamber, usually an ordered place that he keeps meticulously clean. It is in disarray; all his precious notebooks torn to shreds, the vials of chemicals smashed, his crucible overturned.

'Where are you?' he says wearily. 'Show yourself, Randa.'

In the silence the only answer is the breath of another – but where is she?

His thoughts are whirling about his head, all wrapped in guilt that he hopes the sorceress does not understand but she does and she fears that whoever is hidden in the shadows can hear them as well as she.

Anger at the meaningless destruction of all he holds dear causes him to spit out his curses.

'You, the bringer of my ruination, are you my punishment for the sin of adultery? This, my life's work, ripped asunder. Do you know what you have done? Where are you, you child of malice? Where is Master Butter?' he shouts. 'Where is Mary? Have you killed them as once you killed the mistress?'

Instantly he regrets what he said. He tries and fails to suck the words back into himself. He picks up papers, bunches them in his hand. He is whimpering. 'All my work, my books . . . they are irreplaceable. Monster! Yes, monster, a monster of my own making.' His thoughts, now unstoppable, reveal in their brutal honesty the truth of his feelings and fuel his tongue. 'I should have left you dead. I am disgusted that I had any part in the making of you. Half-human, half-animal – you have never shown any sign of intelligence, you cannot talk, nor do you comprehend what I say. My life has been ruined by you, ruined by the burden of a deformed imbecile who must be kept secret and restrained for as long as she lives – if only I can find chains strong enough to bind her. You have grown beyond my control.' And now he is shouting, shouting, 'What will become of me if you are discovered? What will become of you? Oh lord above . . .'

And all the pity for himself, for Bess, collides into a single thought: what will become of Randa when she is fully grown? The idea that this beast, this thing he calls child, might have physical desires he can hardly bear to contemplate.

'I should have left nature to take its course,' he says into the darkness. 'I should have let you die.'

In the shadows the sorceress sees a human eye, green as an emerald. She is listening, just as the sorceress is, to every mean, mundane word and thought that this pathetic man has. Near weeping with exhaustion, defeated by all he sees, he recites his charm to calm her. To calm himself.

'In the name of God be secret and in all your doings be still.'

She will not reply. She has never before answered him.

When she does speak her voice is deep and haunting and he is so stupefied by it that he loses his footing, stumbles backwards, feeling each word of hers as a blow.

'I am not still,' she says. 'I never will be. And whatever your God of retribution might say, I will no longer be secret.'

She screams a scream so piercing it shatters windows, sets dogs to howl. Now the sorceress sees the shape of the beast, she sees the glint of her talons. She hears the flapping of her immense wings. She hears Thomas Finglas cry out in agony. There is a rush of air and the beast is in the snowy garden and the sorceress is in time to see her silhouetted against the night sky, a magnificent winged creature who does not belong to the world of man. The sorceress watches enchanted as the creature tilts her head and inhales the thick, foul breath of the city. She opens her mouth and tastes the snow, stretches her wings to their full extent and swoops out over the river. And she is gone.

'Randa, come back . . . Randa . . . in all your doings be still . . .'

Thomas's words collapse in on him. The sorceress lights the candle. He is on his knees in the passage. Blood runs down the torn ribbons of his face, he looks like a martyr and she has little sympathy.

Revenge, she thinks, is the sweetest sweetmeat of all.

'My hem,' she says. 'Give me my hem.'

THE BEAST

'Tis my sole plague to be alone,
I am a beast, a monster grown . . .

THE ANATOMY OF MELANCHOLY
ROBERT BURTON

XXVIII

In my dreams I am not the beast. I am the child with childish thoughts. I run free on two stout legs, no spiked leather wings to weigh me down. I sing with unformed words that one day will turn into song, a language that will define me. I see my mother smiling, I see my father wake into a nightmare. Who am I, Mother, who am I?

She called me Randa.

She lied. I was no child. I was a malformed, half-wished-for babe. After only three summers I was a thing too strong for chains to bind.

And he, my father, thought me an abomination. I heard his thoughts, caught on the wishbone of his sorrows, tied to his mean regret. I was his greatest triumph and his greatest failure. No word dare he speak of this to her, his love, his beloved, his Bess, my mother.

Soft be she, kind be she, loving be she. She who knew what darkness filled my father's dreams.

I am old bones wrapped in young skin. I am the beginning and the end without end. I was plunged into mercury vapour and under those metallic waters, in that mirror, I caught a glimpse of time beyond understanding, of a past beyond regret. I knew things no infant should know, wisdom soaked into a deep, an ancient soul.

When my mother still lived she told me tales of fantastic beasts, of a land where I would be queen. Where I would not be alone.

'And will you come with me?' I asked her, her my mother.

She kissed me and told me of the House of the Three Turrets where she had met my father, of a boy born so beautiful that his mother forbade all mirrors, fearful that he might fall in love with his own reflection.

'Why am I not beautiful, Mother? Why?'

She whispered, 'Love will transform you.'

I heard the woman, she who called herself a good wife, wife a word of spikes to pin a husband to, the *f* of the word being the mightier weapon of all the letters for it has a cruel curve to its bow. Mistress Finglas, the good wife, she who whispered through the door that I be a hellwain, a curse upon all mankind. That they would come. Who would come? They would come. To take me to the slaughterhouse.

My father was right. He should have murdered me when he had a chance. Before I made my first kill.

I am three when I sink my talons into Mistress Finglas's lardy flesh and strip the fat from her. No one being home, she comes at me with a fiery poker. I am not frightened but I relish the fear in her eyes, the smell of terror a hard-won perfume. I pounce. Lard her flesh, steel my claws. I want to free the vileness, the slithering snake that lies buried in her entrails. But she does not move. I pull at her and all life is gone. I have consumed two of her fingers when John Butter finds me. I am surprised at how sweet such cruel flesh tastes. John, never fearful, not then when I still owned the enchantment of a cub, took the bones from my hand, said I must promise, Mistress Randa must promise, never to do it again.

No one else called me Mistress. Only Randa. One name sufficed for such a malignant thing as I.

John Butter cleaned me and sent for the apothecary. I watched the scrawny man as he entered the house. Hair the colour of pigeon shit, dirty ruff, smell of stale wine. He vomited on the stairs when he saw the good wife. A shame for there is nothing sweeter than the smell of fresh blood.

My mother asked me why? Why I had done such a thing?

I told her that Mistress Finglas had come for me, that there was a beast in her belly and I had tried to set it free but it must have been eaten up within her.

She held me in her arms, said she would take me to where I would be safe, that she would be back in a day and we would go by barge to the forest where stood the House of the Three Turrets.

'Where the beautiful boy lives?'

'Yes. And there in the forest lies your way.'

XXIX

I knew she was dead, my mother. The cord that bound us cut for ever. A vital spirit gone. My protector. She who understood her child and called her little one, my sweet Randa. Loss made the loneliness of my being all the greater, made the house smaller. All the words in me sank to the bottom of my soul. I saw no use in speech. Better a watcher be. So a watcher I became. My silence was confirmation to my father of my bestial nature, more animal than human. So he thought. Not so John Butter. I saw a tear in his eye when the iron collar was placed round my neck to rub away my feathers, rub raw my skin, let in the fury.

John Butter's thoughts are too fast. They gallop free of his mind. He sees what his master should be doing before his master knows it. John has chains like me. Unseen by the human eye, they run through his blood, jigger-jugger, tip-tripping his words on his tongue. It was John who smuggled me a book. Slowly I made the letters reveal their spell, not one word lost. There were pictures of beasts; a bear, a fox. No picture of me.

My father calls himself an alchemist. I know not what that means. He tells me he searches for a reason for my existence but I am here, Father. I am here, locked up. I exist, I live without a life. I hear him tell John that he knows not what to do with me, that if the truth of what he has done is ever discovered it would be better by far that he throws himself into the Thames otherwise be arrested, tortured and taken to the hanging tree.

I grew. All things do grow. Helped by love they grow, crippled by hatred, still they grow. My father became smaller. Fear shrank him. He would talk to the ghost of his breath, he would ask Bess what he should do. She never answered.

Yes, Father, tell me: what will you do? For I grow restless. Cramps hurt me, my bones ache. I cannot move, the space grows tighter. I dream of flight, wake in such pain within my limbs that I would tear myself apart to stop it. My screams bring my jailer, my father. Keys rattle, door opens with a squeal so that he curses and curses me more.

I, his daughter, worse treated than a bear. My only comfort the sky I see through the round circles of glass. It calls to me. Certain am I that there in its moving clouds I could stretch myself into my fullness, stop the pain that runs rattling through me.

I listen. Always I listen, watch the floorboards above me, the light that slips through the cracks. Where the voices fall is a place I am never allowed to enter.

Gold. All they want, those shoes and boots that walk back and forth, is gold. I hear my father say it is against the law.

But, Father, am I not against the laws of creation?

A gentleman and a lady came to the house, to his laboratory. What they said scared him. Their voices were not to be trusted. They were slippery, they spoke in one tone and meant something altogether different.

They came, again. They spoke loudly. They were not here to pry, the lady said. She was a great believer in alchemy, she said.

There be far more to the heavens than the mortal eye can see. She said.

The gentleman, his voice commanding, said they were here to take an intelligent interest in what my father had achieved.

My father denied everything.

'Master Cassell, Mistress Cassell, it is the stuff of tales,' he said.

When they had gone he came down to the cellar and, drinking from a flask, he sat with me.

'God lives in church,' he said, 'but you cannot see him. He is invisible. He can see you though. What will I do with you, tell me?'

I waited. I am good at waiting. Sleep, dream, listen. Note when the voice is strange, is dangerous.

A beast. I hear the word and stand to catch what is being said. You say one thing, Father, and do another.

'What if I was to tell you that I could sell you – a beast of such a fantastical appearance that you would be assured of an audience every night.'

Oh, Father, how you betray me.

Another day, another voice. For all the fullness of his sound I think this stranger is meaner than Thomas Finglas. My father is telling him that the beast – that I – am made in terrifying proportions. The stranger asks the price. The price of me.

'Nothing,' says my father, my keeper, 'as long as you never tell a soul where you bought her.'

I hear doubt in the stranger's voice.

Footsteps leave the laboratory. Door opens, door closes and all is silent except for the rustle of the wind. I close my eyes and dream.

XXX

I curl in upon myself and hope this bitter winter, muffled in white beauty, brings me my death. I will not survive this cruel night. It is a strange relief to know that I will be free of this body, these wings, the aches that torment me, the constant hunger. Best that it is over soon. A deformed thing, this self that no one wants unless to gawp at. My bones will become stones once more. My eyes are heavy, sleep is here to carry me away in its cold chariot.

I smelled the animal before I saw her. I pulled myself up to the small window and there a fox was looking at me, fire licking her breath. I heard my heart beat with excitement, heard the thud of blood. Then silence.

Someone is in the house. A stranger – no, two strangers. I am an expert in the weight of boots. Two men hiding their heaviness in soft, uncertain steps. They waver. I think this way they will come. Then the stairs creak, then all is quiet. I listen, straining to hear. Nothing. A nothing filled with everything. Air taut then it comes with a rush, something, someone pulled down, down to the back door. I am up at the window to see who it is, what it is. It is Father, bare-footed in his flapping nightshirt, fighting the air. Two men with him, a fluster of movement, a blow. I let out a scream, a rusty nail is my voice, a wild screech. And there is the fox, the brush of her tail disappearing. Silence once more but for the gate groaning in the icy wind. I wait. I wait. I wait. Then, in a moment of moonshine, the glint of the fox's eye meets mine.

I hear John call for his master. He runs up the stairs then down. Fast is John.

Footsteps at the cellar door.

'Be still,' he says. 'Mistress Randa, be still.'

It is the fox who pushes open the door, her snout before her. I feel the animal's warm breath and the iron collar falls with a clank from my neck, resounding on the stone floor. Then she is gone. As I wonder at this inexplicable freedom, John turns and runs back up to my father's laboratory. Boards creak, something is lifted, something bangs shut. A girl's voice, questioning.

'Stay here,' says John Butter. 'Stay back, Mary.'

But the girl is there, her hand to her mouth. I stand in the door so it cannot be closed again. I tower above John and know how much I have grown. He comes to me, holds out by its string a purse for Mistress Randa to take. For me to take. A purse.

He speaks in my mother's tongue.

'Keep this safe, mistress.'

Now I listen. He is not tip-tripping, his words stand upright like him.

'Hold the purse when you wish to pass unseen. Hold it by the strings and you will be visible to all. You understand?'

I do not take it.

He thrusts it at me. 'It is the hem of a sorceress's petticoat. It is powerful. You understand? The master never knew how powerful.'

I take it.

'Goodbye, Mistress Randa.'

Then they are gone too. The front door closes.

In my father's laboratory I warmed myself by the fire, too tired for flight. I found food and ate, then with the daylight sleep took me deep. I woke to find it dark again, and saw all the possessions that my father held dearer than me.

I tore, broke, ruined, spoiled them all. I took no pleasure in the destruction but said more to him in that one act than I would ever say in words.

I hear my father's wheedling voice. Tight I hold the purse and he sees me not. Behind him in the passage, a creature in the form of a woman with the smell of a fox. She sees me, I know she does. And I see the tear in her hem. I hear my father's thoughts and feel as little pity for him as he feels for me. He stands in my way.

I flayed his face. I spared his life.

In soft, beguiling flakes of snow I rise up, rise up into the clouds that have long been waiting to embrace me. The wind in my wings makes sense of myself, all of myself, and at last I feel myself whole.

THE BEAUTY

If I could write the beauty of your eyes
And in fresh numbers number all your graces,
The age to come would say, 'This poet lies;
Such heavenly touches ne'er touch'd earthly faces'.

SONNET XVII

WILLIAM SHAKESPEARE

XXXI

'You look like none of them,' said Lord Rodermere.

My father was in the long gallery where he stood studying the portraits of our ancestors. His face a shade of a claret, his velvet breeches, his overstuffed codpiece and his large mutton sleeves, all of the same hue, lent themselves well to my imagining him to be a bloodied joint of meat.

'Here, Lord Beaumont, with the nose of a buffoon, is your grandfather, a weak-willed man who believed in the magic of the forest. Fool. This here is your grandmother: if she had not been a countess she would have been burned for a witch. And on and on they go, the great and the ugly of the Rodermere family. Note, Lord Beaumont, not one of them possessed even a grain of beauty.'

He was drunk and rambled nonsense in his cups.

'My lord,' I said, 'I wish to relinquish my name, title and claim to the land I stand to inherit and to be free of any obligation to you.'

He turned from the paintings to me. He looked almost rational and for a moment I thought that he would agree and allow me to leave. I waited for him to say he did not believe me to be his son and that as far as he was concerned I could go to the Devil.

He paused before he said, 'You have her eyes. Golden.' Then fell silent.

Thinking he had nothing more to say to me I started to walk away.

'Od's my will,' he shouted after me. 'You will not leave. If you do I assure you of one thing: that my whore of a wife, my daughter, my bastard of a steward will all be dead. That is my curse upon them for their treachery. Do you hear me, my son, do you hear me? If you leave that will be their fate. You will stay here and learn to be a man, for there is little merit in looks that belong to neither sex. I ask you – are you a girl to be bedded or are you a man enough to do the bedding?'

'My lord, I do not know how I look for I have never seen myself in a glass.'

He refilled his goblet and his laughter echoed from the rafters.

'Never seen yourself in a glass? Was Lady Rodermere frightened of you falling in love with your own reflection?'

I saw no point in arguing with a drunk. I kept the rhythm of my footsteps and with each beat of my shoe I told myself I would be gone from here. It would not be long and I would be gone from him and this rustic place. I was restless to see the world beyond the forest. To see London. To see the play.

That night I lay in my bed and his words that I had given little value to began to worry at me. Whose eyes do I have if not my own? What did he mean when he talked of beauty? What beauty and why did he doubt my sex? I told myself this was a speech made by a mad man when the bottle had toppled what little reason he had in favour of folly. Yet still that flea of a thought kept me awake, itched at my mind.

When I was a child I had a feeling of not belonging to this world. I was unsure of everything except that I was loved by my mother, by my sister, and by Master Goodwin who I considered my father.

This feeling – of being a stranger in my own world – I put aside when at the age of ten, a tutor, Doctor Grace, arrived from Cambridge and under his tutelage I began to give less credence to childish doubts. I was a part of this modern age, the future belonged to us, the young. And in that I became more settled to the idea of the man I would become.

Learning taught me the guilt of words, the weight of knowledge; that there were many languages and all held their secrets. I had taken comfort in the stories of Ovid, the wisdom of Socrates, was reassured by the straight line of the written word, be it Greek or Latin. I believed without question that there was a rational order to be found in all things, even in the serpent and the circle.

As I grew I came to believe that my infantile memories had nothing to do with reality, but were to do with stories I had been told as a child from which my imagination had made a false truth. I had thought I remembered a chamber in the forest deep under a tree, a black bed therein with black drapes, a sleeping woman as young as dawn, as ancient as time.

Now I was confronted by the certainty that I had once seen such a chamber. I recalled the blueness of the woman's veins, that looked to me like the roots of trees when they emerge from the earth. Sleep could not hide her age, her skin, papery as autumn leaves. In that chamber I thought she would wake and tell me I was home. Yesterday I had caught a glimpse of her shadow in the long gallery. I was shocked to hear her thoughts as I had heard them when I was small: my beauty would corrupt me, make a monster of me. What had beauty to do with me?

True, I had never seen myself in a glass but many men had not. It did not follow that they had not a clear idea of who they were in the mirror of their mind. I was lean, my hair was dark. I had good feet so Lady Clare told me. But as to my face, in whether or not it be fair, I had little interest. I supposed it to be a face as ordinary as any other man's, flattered only by the light of youth. Yet it was that word beauty that danced wayward in my head and kept sleep from me.

The following morning Lord Rodermere called to him my tutor, Doctor Grace, and informed him that his services were no longer needed.

'Your son shows great promise, my lord,' said my tutor. 'He could be a scholar. I would even suggest he might attend one of the universities.'

'My son to be some learned coxcomb?' shouted my father. 'I would rather he hanged than study. It behoves the sons of the aristocracy to blow a horn call correctly, to hunt skilfully, to train a hawk well and carry it elegantly. Literature can be left to ninny-hammers.'

At least Doctor Grace did not suffer the fate of Master Finglas, put unclothed on a horse. A carriage was summoned to take him to London and I was much saddened at his leaving.

As he climbed into the coach, he said, 'From an unpromising beginning, Lord Beaumount, you have turned into a diligent student. Hunting, I believe, is useful for mastering the art of war. In learning lies peace.'

I returned to my chamber to find a glass had been hung on the wall and, for the first time, I was confronted with my own reflection.

No, it cannot be me. I appear unreal, my face a mask. What freak of nature stands before me? No man was given this unearthly appearance. What some might call beauty, I find monstrous. I am defeated by this, my own image. I had believed that the absence of mirrors was to protect my sister from the truth of her blemished face, that the reason the servants were not allowed to look directly upon us was to do with her sensitivity. It had

him that I have never seen on any other person. My own lack of appetite came from revulsion at watching such insatiable greed.

A thought came to me that alleviated the boredom of these meals. I began to imagine that I had poisoned each dish he was consuming. It shocked me to find that such a vision of his death throes delighted me.

We never talked while he concentrated on his plate. He sat at the head of the table and I chose the chair furthest from him. The dogs walked back and forth in hope of a bone or two. Conversation there was none, unless it was to rant and shout, and mostly he would growl at the servants demanding more, more, and more again. His temper terrified all those who waited on him for it was hard to judge from one moment to the next the high or low of his rage. Finally, the wine if not the food would soothe his befuddled mind until at last he would bellow himself into a stupor.

His hatred of my mother was vicious. 'That bawd was the dullest woman in bed,' he would shout. 'No womb for a son.'

I refused to rise to such provocation. But when he talked of my sister I was less tolerant.

'Three useless daughters your mother gave me. Two grave-stones and the ugliest bitch of all survived. Who would want to marry her?' he said. 'Looking into that face on your wedding night would be enough to wilt even the strongest cock.' This thought amused him greatly. 'I should have sent her to a convent where no man would be obliged to look on her.'

At this my blood would rise. In truth I was possessed by murderous thoughts and became afraid that my very being was not mine to command. I would fall asleep thinking of killing him; wake, and my first thought would be how to best do the deed in such manner that the finger of blame would not point at me.

If I could but banish all such notions from my mind, then I

might return to myself. How such a passion had come about in me I did not understand but I did not doubt that I would be his death if I stayed in his house.

I had all but given up listening to him, merely conscious of his beef-witted grunts, when one day he suddenly he stood and shouted at me down the long table.

'Did you not hear me? A sorceress put a curse on me.' He stopped abruptly and changed the subject. 'Beau. Bloody stupid name, Beau. A ninny-nothing name.' He swayed unsteadily back and forth. 'Tell me how it goes, the curse.'

I shrugged. This was the first I had heard tell of it.

'You are a dumb-witted knave, are you not?'

He took a chicken by a drumstick and threw it down the table at me. I did not move. Drink had spoiled his aim and the dogs obligingly cleaned up the mess.

He sat down heavily in his chair.

'I remember,' he said. 'Yes, I remember. The curse was written on the bark of one of the first oak trees I felled to build this house. Written in gold, those words were . . . a faerie boy will be born to me. You hear that? Born to me . . . whose beauty will be my death.'

He took another draught from his goblet. 'A faerie boy will be my death – and you could not kill a rabbit. I doubt you have the balls to do such a thing. So you see, old sorceress,' he shouted at the rafters, 'here is my son – Lord Beaumont, pretty Lord Beaumont, a faerie boy. I drink to my murderer.'

I did not lift my goblet. I felt for my dagger and through the fog of rage one grain of reason tipped the scales: it was the curse, this bloodlust on me, and I had been made a puppet.

'Why do you not drink?'

I knew it would not be long until he lost all use of limb and tongue. He slumped in his chair, his eyes heavy, his mind wandering in wine.

'I do not believe in the elfin queen,' he said. 'I do not believe in magic.'

I hoped he might say he did not believe I was his son.

'Witches,' he said, 'now that is another matter. As is the Devil. A woman with a will needs to be broken with a whip,' he said.

Dear lord, at that instant I would have killed him. He brought his fist down hard on the table so that the dishes jumped.

'Never marry a bitch with a forked tongue, for she will be off gadding and you will never know if your child is yours or some other sop's. Better by far lie under an old hedge, than with a young upstart of a bush.'

A voice in my head said, do it, do it. One blow and it is over. I stood up.

'What – will you come at me, pretty nothing?'

Sweat broke out on my forehead and I felt I was battling to stop myself falling on him and by doing so know myself to be his son.

'Who then was my mother,' I asked, 'if not your wife?'

'Beautiful . . .' he said. 'The most beautiful woman I have ever seen. The only woman to tame my prick. One day, one day was all I had with her, that was all.' His eyes began to close. 'One fucking day . . .'

His words slurred into sleep.

None of the servants dared move. I went to the end of the table, lifted his hand and let it fall. He did not wake. He would be like that until morning.

My father had taken up residence in the tallest turret and it took four servants to carry him up to his bedchamber every night. My chamber was at the far end of the house. I went to it through the long gallery for there was one portrait I wanted to look at again. A small painting, lovingly placed in an elaborately carved frame. Perhaps it was hoped the frame would detract from my sister's blemished face for against all advice she had refused to have her skin painted soft. The portrait had been returned by a suitor, much to the sadness of my mother and Master Goodwin.

'What use is a lie?' Lady Clare had said to our mother. 'The humiliation would have been even worse when he saw me as I am.'

The incident had been made more hurtful by there being no letter accompanying the returned painting.

I took the portrait to my chamber and there I turned the glass from the wall and compared our two faces. Surface deep, it showed me only the building that housed my soul, not the chambers therein. There was more honesty to the mirror when I broke it for then I was reflected in many sizes, many parts and many shapes, and not one could claim the whole truth of me. I knew then nothing could be trusted, that all things seen and unseen have many sides to them. Perhaps deep inside me I had always known. It mattered not if I had a cock – that did not make me who I was. The man, though, recognised the woman within.

XXXIII

I was fourteen summers when I felt the beast between my legs
wake with a hunger which only my hand knew how to satisfy.
My dreams of longing stirred into morning explosions. My cock
possessed a demonic need that defied all rational thought. My
head shrunk in favour of my small leg.

My limited knowledge went little way to explaining why
my thing demanded total dedication and stood to attention at the most inappropriate moments. How this sudden
transformation had come about bewildered and thrilled me
in equal measure.

As a boy, I would oft go to the Widow Bott's cottage and there
in the rafters of her thatched roof I would listen with fascina-
tion and cheeks full of giggles to requests for remedies to ease
the frustration of a soft cock, for potions to keep a man hard
until satisfaction on both sides had been achieved, or mixtures
to relieve the pains of pregnancy. Avoiding pregnancy seem to
be the condition most desired by those who visited the widow.
One man I remember came to the cottage clutching a religious
tract and said that he had tried with no good effect to scrub
all sinful arousal from him. Being then but a child I thought I

would never be so foolish as to be led by such a small appendage. How wrong I was.

By fifteen, the books that interested me most were not ones my tutor favoured. Instead of studying my grammar I studied a book on anatomy, eager to reach the chapter on reproductive anatomies where the author wrote of the spermatic vessels and explained how they carry blood to the testicles. I was fascinated by the account of the matrix of women and, having read each word thoroughly if not twice, I innocently believed that I understood the erotic conjugation of the present tense of the verb *To Be*.

I am your cock.
Thou art my prisoner.
She is your desire.
He is your master.
We are one.
You are a virgin.
They are all women waiting.

The notion that anyone was waiting was foolish. Master Goodwin and my mother were careful who they invited to the House of the Three Turrets and who they employed as servants. I neither saw myself nor knew the effect I had on those who saw me, yet for all my family's concern I could not always be protected.

The first mirror I ever looked into was in the eyes of Sir Percival Hayes's wife, Lady Judith. His marriage had been most unexpected as it was well known that he preferred the company of men – in particular that of young actors.

He arrived with his new wife for the midsummer celebrations. She, being twenty years younger than Sir Percival, was near my sister's age and soon became her confidante.

Her sky blue eyes appeared to me to be clouded by sadness. But Sir Percival had been with us less than a month when he was called away to court and the change in Lady Judith was remarkable. She noticed me and talked to me in a way that she had not before. I was flattered. She would press little poems into my hand, wait for me in the long gallery, compliment me on the way I looked. And once she stole a kiss. All this went much to creating on my behalf an emotion that I considered naïvely to be love. I, too, took to writing poems. They talked of a higher love that had to do with the meeting of two souls. Yet every night I thought more about the meeting of her body and mine.

These forbidden kisses, forbidden touches, forbidden longings began by degrees to drive me wild until all I could think of was Lady Judith. Her maid was a sour-looking woman who had obviously been given strict instructions to make sure that Lady Judith remained an honourable wife. I was cast down with the most profound melancholy, certain that under this watchful eye our love would be for ever thwarted. Then, quite unexpectedly, the maid became unwell, and from fear that she was carrying some unsavoury disease she was moved to a chamber far from her mistress.

One sultry night I had determined to risk my life to see Lady Judith and declare my love, nay, my passion for her, when the door of my chamber opened and there was she, naked beneath her gown. Even if God and all his saints had arrived at that moment nothing would have stopped me. Nothing.

I do not think we said one word to each other, our desire spoke for us. At last I saw a purpose in an unruly cock. Before the moon lost its kingdom, I told her I loved her. And believed that indeed I did for never had longing been so soothed in one glorious act.

Her maid, alas, recovered all too soon, and with that Lady Judith departed.

I am ashamed to say I had completely forgotten her when, some nine months later, I heard she had died in childbirth. It never occurred to me that I might have been in any way responsible for her condition.

What my affair with Lady Judith taught me was the perfect understanding of the meaning of the present tense of the verb *To Be*.

I am my own man.
Thou art my cock, not my ruler.
She is just the beginning.

XXXIV

Lord Rodermere, having rid himself of my tutor, must have felt that my head was no longer in peril of being infected with knowledge. My other lessons – in archery, in fencing – were allowed to continue, both being considered fair sport. As my skills improved I thought more than I should of fulfilling the curse: that my arrow would hit my father or my sword pierce his flesh. And in these thoughts I confirmed all that I dreaded becoming.

He gave me a rambling speech on the importance of mastering falconry, a subject that as far as I could tell had occupied the better part of all his learning. Here then was where I foolishly demonstrated my naivety – I should have had more wisdom, should have known what this hurly-burly of a man might do but, mindless of the consequences, I delighted to show off my haggard. Master Goodwin and I had caught her the last May and I had passed much time in her training, had sacrificed many hours of sleep so that she was not afraid of man or dog. Now being fully moulted, there was no better hawk and I was proud of her for my haggard could not be defeated or left behind by the speed of any other fowl. She sat easy on my fist, bare-headed and docile.

Lord Rodermere had spent a fair sum on a pair of soar hawks that had been brought from Essex. The morning did not start well. His two birds being new he was not fully acquainted with them and was much out of sorts to see how my haggard pitched high above his hawks and, soaring, claimed her quarry every time. I relished the sight of her rising into the sky, disappearing in the clouds, and felt as I always did when I saw her fly that I was with her. I thrilled to watch her drive down upon her unsuspecting prey, delighted in the partnership between man and bird, between food and reward – such a delicate balance. It would have served me better to concentrate on the relationship between father and son for in my excitement I did not see the jealous glint in my father's eyes.

The next day when I went to the eyrie the master falconer told me that he knew not how but my hawk was dead. I examined her and could smell the clouds in her feathers and saw the pin through her heart. I could have killed my father for that crime alone. It shook me that I could hate with such a passion. It was then I understood that this vengeful spirit that had become my ruler was not me and I acknowledged I had two enemies: my father and the sorceress's curse. I was determined that neither would defeat me.

Henceforth Lord Rodermere excluded me from his hunting parties for no man, not even his son, should be allowed to outshine him. I refused to be made a whipping post and such was my fury at the cruelty of what this tyrant had done to my haggard that he no longer objected to eating alone.

It was a winter's morning when I took a horse from the stable and rode into the forest to find the Widow Bott. I rode until I was where the trees made night of day and stood as castle walls against all travellers and there my mare became reluctant to go further and I dismounted and led her by the reins. Overhead the rooks cried and the only other sounds were the tread of my horse and the thud as fallen snow was dislodged from branches. I smiled as I remembered the widow's house in the clearing. I had a memory of telling my mother that I had found the eye of the witch in the middle of the woods. She had laughed, said that only a child could believe in such a foolish notion.

But Master Goodwin, when we were alone, had knelt down and, tilting my face to his said, 'Promise me, Lord Beaumont, you will not go that way again.'

'Why not, sir?' I asked.

He sighed and I could see he was troubled to know how best to answer.

In the end he said, 'Is it so hard to promise me that one thing?'

'No,' I said.

I did not keep that promise.

XXXV

My mare began to sniff the air, to paw the frozen ground. For all my coaxing she shied and reared when I tried to walk on, and would not be soothed. I could see fear in her eye. I felt it too in my heart but having come this far I had no intention of turning back. Finding no way to calm her I let her go and watched as she weaved her way through the trees towards a safer path.

I stood still, my knife in my hand. The sky darkened and I heard a roaring as if the wings of a great hawk were swooping down on me.

I am behind him. He has dark hair, thick, the colour of ravens' feathers.

He is before me. I had not imagined anyone as beautiful as this man. Golden eyes, eagles' eyes. He is graceful on the ground as I am in the air.

I am gone.

Whatever it was that had been so close by me vanished as suddenly as it came. I turned this way, that way – there was nothing. I caught my breath and moved on.

I found it as the sun disappeared behind the clouds. Isolated in a snow-filled clearing, that cottage, more tumbledown and haunted than I remembered.

I frighten you. I want to say, it is me, it is Randa. To ask how came you to be made in perfect symmetry to a design the gods would envy. To have beauty whose power makes jealous the sun. For when you came into the clearing the ball of flame turned its back to the heavens.

I had not seen the Widow Bott for many years. I was wondering if she would have forgotten the small boy who had often visited her when the door opened and there was a woman I did not at first recognise, her white hair tangled with ivy and feathers, her clothes dark and of many layers. Surely this could not be the Widow Bott? I remembered her with coal black hair, that she had been proud and tall. Had time really robbed her of all her colour?

I am lead. Father, could this man turn me to gold? If he loved me would I be transformed? What would he think if he saw me as I am? The whole of me. Would he think to slay me, consider my death less significant than that of any other being? Is my blood not as red as his? Are we not the same, alone in our different shapes?

The widow called out, softly. 'Bird, my little bird, where are you?'

I watched as she seemed to greet some invisible guest. She was about to close the door when, as if having been informed of my presence, she looked in my direction. To my surprise she called my name.

'Beau – Lord Beaumont – is that you? What brings you this way?'

'There are questions I must ask and I believe only you can answer,' I said.

She looked past me.

'You came on foot?'

I nodded.

'Alone?'

'Yes.'

'I no longer welcome visitors. They bring naught but trouble. You should leave.'

'Do you not remember how I used to come here, sit in your rafters and play?'

'I remember that you stopped coming. And after that they came.'

'Who came?' I said.

'Sir Percival Hayes's witch hunters came. Go home. I want no more trouble.

'Please, mistress – I beg of you.'

The widow sighed, shook her white hair.

'Did you not hear what I said? It was unwise of you to make this journey. I have nothing to tell you. Be gone.'

No, I must see him close. Let him in, let him in.

My quest was nonsense. I knew whose son I was and needed no confirmation.

I was walking away, purpose to my steps, when the widow said, 'Are you hungry?' and opened the door for me.

I hesitated. But this was why I had come and so I entered her abode. I had remembered the inside of her cottage being light, homely. Now it was an accumulation of shadows. From the rafters, garments hung, ghosts of her former self dancing in the candlelight. The place was thick with smoke which gave the illusion that there were no walls, just an infinity of dark space, that everything was afloat in perpetual night.

Now I see him close. Oh, what a cruel thing it was to let me live to feel this human emotion called desire. To long for what I can never have. I would give my life for one kind word from his gentle lips, to know he meant it. Would he call me Randa, Mistress Randa? No, he would not see me. He would see the beast.

I was certain I could hear the voice of another; disjointed

words not spoken by the widow. Who was there in the darkness? I sensed something, someone else. I felt I had walked into a trap and, making my excuses, again turned to go.

Do not go. Do not go. Old woman, make him stay awhile.

'Wait, Lord Beaumont,' said the widow. 'Sit, eat. Forgive my humour, I have lived too long on my own.'

I had eaten nothing that day and was sore tempted by the smell from the cooking pot.

She took a ladle, filled a wooden bowl and handed me bread and a spoon. The stew was of venison. It had been a cruel winter and by now most peasants had to rely on the remains of root vegetables and hope the spring would come soon. The widow looked too weak to be a hunter. She smoked her pipe and watched me eat.

I perched on the bench by the table, every sinew in me taut. And then I felt a breath on my neck. Whatever was in the forest was now inside.

I have green eyes like my mother. Lips like my mother. Breasts and a cunny like all other women. I have a need for love, a hunger for love, to know what love is and be terrified by it. As you are now by my unseen presence.

'Do you live alone?' I asked.

'Yes. As I said, I always have. Tell me then, my lord – what brings you here?'

'You used to call me Beau.'

'I used to have black hair.'

'Master Goodwin told me you were there the day I was born.'

'I was,' she said.

I was much relieved. It was madness to believe anything Lord Rodermere had to say. True, his disappearance was unexplainable, but that did not make me an elfin child.

'You delivered me into the world, did you not?'

'I did not,' she said. 'I was called to the house after you were born.'

And all hope crumbled.

'For what reason?' I asked.

'So all would know you were the son of Lord and Lady Rodermere.'

'And am I?'

She did not reply but said, 'Lady Eleanor asked me about a star on your thigh.'

'What of it?'

'So you have such a mark?'

'Yes, I do but . . .'

'She wanted to know its meaning and when I told her that only the infant's mother would know the answer to that question she begged me not to tell a soul that you had been found in a basket with a note written in Lord Rodermere's hand, claiming you as his son. But that did not stop her loving you as if you were her own.'

'Then who was my mother?'

'Do not ask these questions, Lord Beaumont. You are the son of Francis, Earl of Rodermere – let that be enough for you.'

'It is not enough. I have seen myself in the glass. I know this much: I do not belong in the Thursby family. I have a face that belongs to no man, no woman that I have ever seen and all of me is lost, blinded by an image that does not reflect me. There is too much that plays on my mind and makes me think I will lose my reason without rational answers.'

'I have none to give you.'

'The day after my mother's wedding to Master Goodwin I was in the long gallery and I became aware of the presence of another being. I saw an outline, the figure was translucent, and I could hear all the poison of the thoughts that ran through her mind.'

'What makes you think it was a woman?'

'My father speaks of a sorceress.' I did not want to say that

I was sure I had once seen her lying in her black bed, deep under the forest. Instead I said, 'She thought me a hollow man. She thought my beauty would corrupt all those I met. Is this sorceress my mother?'

'A sorceress?' said the Widow Bott. 'I know of no such person. This is dangerous talk, Lord Beaumont.'

I heard the sound of another, close by, and the widow looked round her.

'Who else is here?' I said. 'There is someone—'

'Go. Go now, Beau.' She rose to her feet. 'Leave the forest, leave the spirits herein and they will leave you alone.'

I said quickly, 'My father told me I was of elfin blood. I beg of you, mistress, tell me what that means. Who am I? Where do I belong?'

I, too, am not of this world, Beau. I, too, am lost.

'Did you hear that? You must have heard it. Please – tell me you did.'

'Enough,' said the widow. She opened the door and, to my surprise, pushed me out. 'Begone now and never come this way again. Never.'

I felt like strangling the truth from her and that made me wonder if I, like my father, was a monster. I stayed a while in the clearing, trying to calm myself and hoped against all reason she might change her mind. But the door to her cottage remained closed. A sharp wind had risen and I took shelter in a thatched lean-to where the widow kept wood for the fire, neatly stacked. Beside the logs hung the carcass of a young deer, brutally killed, its throat ripped out, its pelt in ribbons. It unnerved me for only an animal would have killed a deer in this way. I determined to leave the clearing before dark set in. Then I saw in the gloom a pelt stretched taut on a wooden frame. Tentatively, I touched the frozen fur and my body tingled, a sensation I remembered from childhood – excitement charged with terror. It was the pelt of a black wolf of monstrous size. I had grown up listening to folk tales of such a wolf as this. I could not think how the Widow Bott had come by the pelt, and it occurred to me that perhaps the gossips were right to accuse her of witchcraft. I ran fast from there in the dwindling light, feeling a ghost on my heels.

XXXVI

Randa is not a name I know. I have no reason to know it yet it is the name of the demon who speaks to me.

I thought at first the spirit of the wolf had followed me out of the forest but in all the tales I have heard of the great black wolf never once has it had a name. The wolf is always spoken of as 'he', and it is a female spirit that is here in my chamber, watching. I know not who she is or what she wants of me but I hear her as I heard her in the widow's cottage. I hear her often.

Randa who thinks me a thief. How do I know that?

I asked her.

'Why? Tell me why am I a thief?'

'Your beauty has stolen my reason.'

I heard her say it. What more evidence do I need to convince myself of my insanity?

There is no one here. I listen to silence, the shadows talk. Whatever this strange enchantment is, it tortures me. Brewed from a witch's hell broth, is it the Widow Bott's doing? I am certain of only one thing: it began at her cottage. Wolf or demon, it springs from there.

The forest I am as familiar with as the lines on the palm of my hand. I have never feared it. In all its seasons it has been a friend. Yet in the winter's light of that late afternoon I felt as if the black wolf was on my heels. Only when I reached the stone steps leading up to the front door of the House of the Three Turrets did I feel it retreat. My heart was beating fast and I bent over to stop the world from spinning, to find my breath in the chaos of my being. I glanced back to the forest and through the beech trees thought I caught a glimpse of something – someone – watching me.

A servant opened the door.

'We have have been worried, Lord Beaumont,' he said. 'Your horse is long returned.'

I had entered the hall, grateful to feel the warmth of the fire, when from high above there came the sound of shattering glass. I followed the servants as they ran up the stairs to see what had caused it and a glorious thought came to me that my father, sodden-witted, had fallen through a window in one of the turrets. It would have made sense to my mind if he had but what I discovered made little sense at all.

The large window of my chamber was broken. In the darkness it was hard to see how such damage had occurred. Little could be done until the morning and I spent that night in another part of the house, returning to my chamber the following day. I was mystified by the extent of the destruction. There was no doubt that something monstrous had flown into the window with great violence. There was no wounded creature, but among the glass shards, I spied a splattering of blood and in all the confusion lay one flame-red feather. The sight of it picked at the stitching of my sanity.

It was a week before I could return to my chamber and by then I had come to believe I was not alone.

Sometimes I hear her, other times I swear I smell her, smell a perfume only found on the paws of a dog, and just as mysterious.

Randa.

What if I have created you from my imagination, made a powerful spirit from air so that I might have a companion, a friend to keep me from recognising my profound loneliness, to argue me out of murdering my father. Or is this the tail of the same coin? But if you are of my doing then why have I conjured a woman and not a man? A man would surely serve the same purpose. But I hear your thoughts and they are of a sweet woman's soul. It is as if you are inside me, my little soul to keep me company. If that be the case then we are two parts of the same body and who is to say how much woman is mixed in with man? Or how much man is mixed in with woman when he first drinks from the cup of life?

'What do you want?' I asked. 'To drive me mad?'

'*Perhaps I am your sanity,*' came the answer.

'I doubt that. You are the dark side of the mirror, the face I cannot see. Sometimes I hear your thoughts. They fragment, dance me slowly insane and I am drunk again on another goblet of your sad song. Randa, whoever you are, my constant, invisible, unwanted companion, my only companion, who are you? What are you?'

How can I love what terrifies me? Begone, I beg of you, my madness, begone.

THE BEAST

XXXVII

If he could see my sad eyes and know me: a woman, not a woman, a beast, not a beast. A confusion of two made one. For what purpose, I know not.

But I am here, the woman in me strong. I long for the love that these breasts of mine ache for. I like the softness of them and imagine the rest of me a map still to be discovered, that his hands, Beau's hands, could find my skin beneath my fur and I would be free of my feathers. He would kiss the soft fruit between my legs and this kiss would wake me into human form, not this. Not this.

Am I here, or am I a thing of dreams? Half dreamed for by my mother, half longed for and all to be forgotten by my father – he who could make no peace with the god he prays to. A god who flooded the world, who made Noah, a man, build an ark that he might take the animals, and leave us, half-beasts to drown.

John told me stories of his land, his home. He said dreams had a power to them, that if you believed hard enough they could become the source of life. John was gentle, John who they called Butter. He thought butter be edible gold. Butter became his surname. Like my mother he spoke with a different tongue from my father.

My mother kept her other tongue in a glass jar, full of 'yes, mistress, no mistress'. It spoke kindly to a lord who had no ears to hear her, no eyes to see me with. When she spoke to me, only to me, did she use her own voice. She spoke of a boy who had been born cursed with beauty, who lived in a house with three turrets; of a wise woman whose cottage lay in the eye of a forest. I listened to her stories with a child's understanding and wondered how beauty could be a curse. A beast like me is a curse but never beauty, surely not beauty. She told me I was wrong for what if all who looked upon this boy fell in love with him? Then I thought he would be doubly blessed.

Alas, no. For the man behind the mask, she said, would never be seen for who he truly was.

The day I left my father's house I had nothing to hold me to the cloth of the sky apart from dreams. Up in the clouds, for the first time not weighted by fur and bone, my shape had purpose. My wings, filled with air, gave me grace, though I had little strength for flying. The cold had eaten into me and when I could go no further I found the cottage in the eye of the forest, just as my mother had said.

The wise widow came out of her cottage into the darkness. I showed myself as I was, not hidden in invisibility and I smelled no fear in her.

'My name is Randa,' I said.

'Randa? Be Bess your mother?'

She said to come in, she said she had food, she had rabbit.

'I am too big for your door,' I said.

She laughed and told me curl into myself, and there was space enough.

It was she who taught me to hunt. There is an art to it which took some learning.

Perhaps I should have stayed with her, content to sit by her fire. I took to liking the food in the pot. This would be the rest of my days, I thought, safe, and seen whole in the mirror of her gaze. I would put aside all thoughts of another life. But then I saw him.

I was hunting, looking for deer, not looking for him. But there he was upon his horse and all that was in me fell from the sky. The widow called him Beau. Lord Beaumont. I had not imagined a face like his, not his beauty beyond reason. I had not thought I could ache for a touch as I ached for his.

You were my dream, you are my future and I knew that I would never be parted from you. Not then, not now.

The wise widow said, 'Hush, little bird, he is not for you.' She said he had been born into a curse, that his journey lay in a different direction, that I should leave him be.

'Tell me,' said I, 'can the sun choose not to rise? Then I tell you, I can no more leave him be.'

He will never love you. Hard words, their point pierced me. I knew the truth of them and still I followed him to the House of the Three Turrets.

It will be enough to stay a little while out of the cold, to keep him company. I do not speak the truth. How can it be enough when I long for him to fill all the loneliness in me?

Under night's cover I watch you sleeping. High in the beams of your chamber is where I stay. I lick my wounds, pull out the splinters of glass, wait until I heal. I long to touch you. When I did, you woke with a shudder. A nightmare, you called me. Randa, a thing of night horses.

Your skin is as soft as velvet. Beneath its taut surface I hear your blood beat. Poets write sonnets to such beauty as yours. They talk of love. Such a small word is love yet its weight upon the soul is immeasurable. The L of longing, a fortress that crumples defeated into the O of a world of wooden hope, then the V, the void, the violence of desire, all held in place by the cheating E that promises an eternity of endings.

Will you ever love me as I love you?

THE BEAUTY

XXXVIII

Sleep is the only refuge from the mistress of my madness. Only in my dreams can I escape her.

In my dreams there is a house like no other I have seen. Not built from heavy timbers that hold the darkness, this mansion is made of brick and stone, its walls tangled over with ivy and roses, the windows of such magnificent breadth and height they would make a cathedral blush.

The chambers have double doors that reach to the ceiling and open onto vistas of rooms beyond. It appears uninhabited, for I see no furniture. Yet whenever I want to sit on a chair or think of a table there is the chair, there the table.

Every night I dreamed of the same place until by degrees I believed I knew it better than the House of the Three Turrets. Never did I see another soul nor believe it to be haunted. Outside, I knew – though how I knew I cannot tell – there were beasts.

That dream, that mansion became my solace, a reward for the daylight hours I spent under my father's tyrannical roof with a ghost my only companion.

I too wait for darkness but not to dream, to hunt. I climb to the highest turret. There are no windows, no glass to hurt me.

I let myself fall before instinct as strong as breathing unfolds my wings. They have grown more powerful with use. I hold tight to the purse of my invisibility. The deer runs, knowing I am above her. I can smell her fear, see the wildness of death in her eyes. The sharpness of my claws are swift in the killing and then the taste of blood-raw meat that still has a heartbeat to it.

I watch the square man with the cruel bones. You say he is Father, he with his feast of dead cooked animals. The sight of it is repulsive. There is an honesty in the chase, a humbling in the kill.

And you slip away from me into another place.

To sleep, to dream and to have no more to do with this waking world – that is all I desired. I refused to hear she who was my madness.

I cared little about my clothes. I left my doublet unbraced, my stockings round my ankles, failed to shave and was delighted to see the ruin of myself in any unsuspecting glass I happened to pass. I had little interest in daylight. It was the nights I longed for.

My father, being told of my melancholy, asked what ailed me.

'Daylight,' I replied, 'for its reign is longer by far than night's realm.'

He stared at me for a while and took in my shabby appearance.

'The mad are fools that no man should take seriously,' he said. 'I think I know the cause of your malady.'

He had his back towards me as he filled his goblet.

'Could it be, sir,' I said, 'that I am plagued and punished with insanity for your faults? Bad blood begets bad blood.'

I expected him to rise in anger but he was never interested in any answer that did not come from his own tongue, neither did he value any opinion that was not of his own making.

'I believe,' he said, 'that your need for sleep is due to the lack of carnal copulation. I would say it is the poisonous vapours of the seed too long kept in the testicles that affect the brain and heart. It is simple: your melancholy is the result of your virginity and an underused cock.'

I saw no point in contradicting him. It would have illustrated too much sanity on my part.

'There is a cure that will bring you to your senses,' he said. 'You simply need to indulge the bodily fluids with sexual delights.'

To that end whores were brought from London to the House of the Three Turrets, more, I suspected, for Lord Rodermere's entertainment than mine. Seeing that I had no interest in them, he partook liberally of the delights on offer. And though he did not say it, he decided I was beyond redemption.

My tutor Doctor Grace had often talked of the influence that the heavens and stars have upon the humour of our souls. If he was right I concluded that I must have been born under a most vexed and sorrowful star. Perhaps best to sleep and live in enchanting dreams that become nightly more precious to me than the solid earth beneath my feet.

Just when I was convinced that I had truly strayed from the road to sanity, at least in the daylight hours, something occurred that gave me hope that I had not lost all reason.

It was one of my father's servants who discovered, at the top of the tallest of the three turrets, above their master's bedchamber, the half-eaten carcass of a deer and the bones of numerous chickens and rabbits. The discovery sent fear running through the household and relief dancing in my soul. Servants who had held their peace began to talk of hearing scratching sounds at night, of being terrified to go into my chamber when I was not there, certain that within was something malign, something demonic. A bad omen, they said. It was a bad omen when the window of my chamber first broke for they knew no bird so great that could cause such damage.

What a hungry ghost you are, Randa. And for the first time in a long age I laughed.

THE BEAST

XXXIX

If the seas be wine Lord Rodermere would drink them dry. I watch him. He groans in his sleep and methinks he is a beast created by his own hand and knows it not; a little horned worm, jealous of his son, of his beauty. His youth.

He is filled with rotting meat that moulders in his gut, giving off ill humours and wretched dreams.

These nights, I, Randa, I go to his chamber out of fear of what Beau might do for I can see that he fights every day this murderous curse that urges him to kill this monster, this father.

Beau, sweet Beau, paces dagger in hand. He says this must be done if he is to find peace. What enchantment is it that has control of his gentle nature? He thinks I am his madness. I know I am his saviour.

Perhaps I should do the killing for him. It would take so little, I would be swift with this bloated creature of titles. Between the dream and the dying he would not know who had done it. I stand at his bed and watch him, a father, another father careless of his seed. He wakes and I do not hide myself but stretch my wings. His eyes wide with terror, he crawls up the bed, pulls the covers round his ears.

'Oh my lord, save me,' he whimpers and remembering another

lord he speaks long-forgotten prayers to his god, my father's god, as if that will protect him.

I delight in his terror, in my power.

Then the door to the chamber opens and Beau is here, dagger in hand. He sleeps and knows not what he does.

Invisible again, I swoop on him, drag him from the place. At the foot of the stairs to the turret he wakes.

'Have I killed him?' he asks, uncertain, and I whisper that it is a nightmare, just a nightmare.

He stops. 'Are you sure,' he says, 'mistress of my madness?'

The house rings with the screams of his father.

THE BEAUTY

XL

Once asleep my father rarely stirred until well past ten in the morning. The House of the Three Turrets could have fallen down around him and still he would be snoring. But one night he found himself woken from his stupor in a state of terror, sure that a huge, winged monster stood at the foot of his bed.

The following day, seeking spiritual guidance, he invited Parson Pegwell to dine and insisted I join them. We made an odd party. The parson was a fanatical pig of a cleric, who grubbed about in my father's trough for favours. Fearing there be none, he saw a way to secure his place by claiming that he could drive out the evil spirit.

'I have heard that a melancholic humour can encourage the Devil to enter the soul,' said my father.

'Precisely, my lord,' said the parson who due to the quantity of wine was failing to say anything precisely. 'The Devil is canny and only has to find a weakness to worm its way into you.'

Lord Rodermere thought about that. 'If my son has such a demon in him would it be possible for that demon to escape at night and haunt another?'

'It would need no encouragement,' said Parson Pegwell. 'I am certain, my lord, that what you saw last night came out of your son for I am afraid he is possessed.'

138

They spoke of me as if I was not present or had become invisible. Parson Pegwell talked more garbage than any lunatic, none of his thoughts being new but were full of superstition that belonged to a world fast fading. As I listened to them I wondered who here was the madman. I ventured not me.

'Can anything be done?'

'Yes, Lord Rodermere, most definitely, yes. We have the tools in the church, we have the power of prayer, the holy oils. These are enough to make even the Devil afraid.'

'Are they?' I said.

Both stopped, surprised, and stared at me as if they had forgotten that I was at the table.

'Yes, Lord Beaumont.'

'I fail to understand,' I said.

'What is it exactly that you do not understand, my lord?' Parson Pegwell pronounced each word slowly as if speaking to an imbecile.

'The New Testament records that the Devil was unafraid of even Christ himself. So why would he be afraid of your gibberish?'

Lord Rodermere laughed, despite himself, while the parson looked as if he had been nailed to the cross of misunderstanding.

'My lord,' he said, shocked that his ally should find what I said amusing. 'Laughter only encourages the Devil. This is a serious matter. I believe, if you would allow me, that I can help your son find his way back to the path of righteousness.'

I could see that my father had become bored with the conversation. Nothing much interested him for long unless it was to do with womanising, hunting and shooting. The church and its superstitions were to be negotiated and if none of it interfered with his pleasures he was happy to conform.

He finished his goblet of wine, stood up, stretched and farted.

'It is of no interest to me what you do or how you do it if you can assure me I will never see that hideous apparition again.'

With that he left the table.

Small men with mean eyes like Parson Pegwell remember every perceived insult against God. They are the hooks to be used in the future to ensure the fish does not escape the line.

As the parson watched my father walk away I suspected that it was not me he wished to catch but a larger fish by far, and one more useful to his ambition.

THE BEAST

XLI

This Parson Pegwell is alight with want when he talks to you, talks of saints martyred with arrows. He prays that his good book will save you but it is riddled with the words of a sacrificial son and of his father, a vengeful god who sent his ghost to violate a virgin. These stories of barbarism, the parson says, will rescue you from your madness. He brings you holy relics, vials of water and oils.

This ashen brimstone of a man, this mooncalf will never frighten Randa, never frighten me away, not with a book he does not understand. Only you can make me go, not him, nor his babbling lord. Parson Pegwell speaks words that lack belief and his hungry eyes never leave your face.

Randa understands.

I understand, and I wish I did not, that he too is blinded by your beauty. I have seen that look on all those who come into your presence and my heart is heavy to know that I am not alone in my love for you. This was my folly: to believe that you belonged to me. The curse is not only on you, but on we who look upon your face while you have no notion of the pain you cause.

I see the hopelessness of my affection. But Randa is different,

Randa knows you, unlike the others, Randa knows the man behind the mask. You are not vain, you are kind, honourable . . .

'Who are you, Randa?'

I hold my breath.

'Come, why such modesty? Show yourself, mistress of my madness. Parson Pegwell, if you believe him, has the power to chase you from my door with just a prayer. Have you nothing to say? At least then do me the honour of letting me see the cause of my insanity.'

'I meant no harm.'

My words are dragged from me and startle me as much as they do him.

'I know you have a voice, Randa, but do you possess a body to house the voice, a soul to keep it company?'

I do not answer. Neither do I dare show my self.

'What do you want of me?' he asks. 'Is it not enough that I am on the brink of losing my grasp on reason?'

I am too shy to tell him what I want.

'You have nothing to say? That is most unlike you. I often hear your thoughts. I hear my father is not to your liking and in that we share a common understanding. Come, Mistress Randa, if you will not talk to me then at least give me a glimpse of you. Are you a ghost?'

'I have a heart that beats.'

'Then I ask again, what shape are you who devours rabbits and hens and has the strength to carry a deer's carcass up to the tower? There must at least be a stomach to you. I imagine you have wings, or otherwise talons strong enough to climb stone.'

'I cannot say but that there be mystery to me.'

'Are you too terrifying to behold?'

'I have an ancient soul, housed in a different skin. I do not belong to the leaden world of man.'

'Did your father name you Randa?'

'My father wished I had not been born.'

'Who is your father?'

'A dealer in magic who understands it not.'

'Who is your mother?'

'My mother is an angel.'

'It was you who stopped me from killing my father, was it not?'

'Yes, it was me.'

'Why?'

'It is in my nature to kill, not in yours.'

'You do not know me. You see the mask, not the man.'

'I do see you.'

'No. You are like everyone else – they see what they wish to see when they look at me.'

'It is a curse,' I say.

'Never was a truth better spoken,' he says.

THE BEAUTY

XLII

In my dream I wander through my favourite chambers, alone as always. Then I see her.

I bow, beg her forgiveness and ask if she be the lady of the house. She looks in my direction and says nothing. She is a little younger than I, tall, with dark auburn hair that falls in heavy ringlets and frames her face. Her neck is elegant and bejewelled with heavy stones that gleam as do only true gems of value. Her features fascinate me. Dark eyebrows, emerald green eyes, her nose beaked, her lips full. She moves with such elegance, as if she is aware of all her limbs and the effect they make on the space around her.

'My lady,' I say.

She stares through me and goes to a glass that hangs on the wall in an elaborate and gilded frame. I do not remember it being there when I had entered that chamber before. It seems to me that the glass lights up with her reflection yet when I stand next to her so she might see me in it there is no image of me to be seen. All my presence does is cause her to shudder. I am invisible.

She walks away through the chambers, her fingertips touching the surface of the doors only to rest a moment before she moves on. Her gown, black as ebony, trails behind her. In the last chamber there is a chair and a fire burning in the hearth. I go closer, still she sees me not but her gown falls liquid velvet to the floor and she is naked. The sight of her makes my cock hard. She owns beautiful breasts, heavy but with a shape that a goddess would envy, berry red nipples so dainty a sweetmeat I could devour them. Being close to her gives me a sense of deep intimacy. She holds by the quill a long, fire-red feather and plays with it, running it through her fingers, brushing the feather down her neck, stopping there awhile. A smile on her lips, the feather begins its blissful flight, encircling her breasts, down her stomach then opening her legs so that I can see the black bush framing the theatre of her cunny. I long to suck the moisture from her. I feel my life will be over if I cannot possess her, if my mouth cannot be where the feather now rests. So engorged with desire am I that I shout, 'I am here. I am here.'

Then I awoke, never again to dream of the house or the lady.

XLIII

Parson Pegwell declared I was cured. If it was so I felt no different than I did before but having suffered such idiocy at his hands I knew that my madness had more sanity to it than I had supposed.

I was called to my father in his chamber and found him standing by the fire and Parson Pegwell seated, giving a sermon on what he believed had happened to Lord Rodermere.

'Witchcraft. You, like your son, have been put under a wicked spell.' My father was about to address me when the over-zealous Pegwell forestalled him. 'Lord Beaumont, I was telling your father that with the help of the good Lord I have rid you of your demon.'

I was still lost in the dream, dizzy with desire.

My father turned to me and said, grudgingly, that I did indeed have more colour and my eyes were not so wild.

'But,' added the irrepressible parson, 'we must remain vigilant and keep danger from door and hearth.'

'Quiet, man!' shouted Lord Rodermere. 'I have had enough of your prattle. I want no more of your preaching. If my son is cured then one thing I am certain of is that it has nothing to do with you. Get out.'

Parson Pegwell was not expecting such abuse. And there lay

the power of Francis Thursby, Earl of Rodermere. What made him a tyrant was that no one knew when the storm in him would break, and wherever the lightning struck it left its scars.

I decided that night to take one of my father's whores, hoping to conjure the dark lady of my dreams in the body of another.

My father's two favourite whores arrived as the evening's entertainment and with them was a young girl of about my age. Although her face and neck were painted white she did not fool Lord Rodermere. With his usual grace, he ordered that she be sent back from whence she came and he did not mean the whore house.

I found her in an antechamber, freezing cold. She told me her name was Gally.

'An unusual name,' I said.

'It comes from gallimaufrey, sir. It's what my mother called me. She said I was a hodge-podge, made from all the remains in the larder. I can see you were not made that way. Are you Lord Rodermere's son?'

'I have that honour.'

'The mad one?'

'The only one. And I am pleased to tell you, mistress, that I am now believed to be cured.'

She laughed and I knew I had found someone I could talk to, even fuck, and the thought excited me. I had been alone with Randa too long and I relished the idea of company, of conversation with someone who was not invisible.

I took Gally to my chamber. I hoped Randa might have gone hunting as was her way, but I felt her presence there. So be it.

We stood there awkwardly, Gally and me. I asked if she was hungry.

'Gutfoundered,' she said.

The manner in which she spoke amused me.

'My lord,' she said, 'have you never heard such words trip off the vulgar tongue?'

I ordered wine and food to be brought to us and while we ate she told me of London. I savoured every word. She had a liking for the play and the players, she said, though a more ragbag bunch would be hard to find.

'Some of them are little more than gallowglasses – mercenaries disguised as actors, nothing better.'

Suddenly, an unexpected feeling of merriment ran through my body. My cock had refused to lie quiet all day and was once more standing to attention, desperate for satisfaction.

'Would you like to kiss me?' she asked.

You do not love him, you do not know him. You do not know how long I have loved him. We are inseparable. Do not make me jealous, for in jealousy the demon lives.

Gally moved away from me.

'God's teeth! What was that?'

'Nothing,' I said.

'It was something,' she said, looking round.

I took her hand.

'It is nothing, I swear. Enough,' I said quietly to the past mistress of my madness. 'Begone,' I added.

'You sure you are not mad?' said Gally.

'Only with desire.'

She took my face in her hands.

'I would say there was some witchery in your looks. You could make a woman or a man believe the moon was the sun. What is your preference, sir?'

Her question took me aback and I was silent for a while before I answered.

'My preference is for an unattainable woman.'

She gazed at me and said, 'Married?' and before I could answer she began to kiss me until with a desperation I threw off my garments, giving my prick its freedom. I begged to see her without her clothes.

Gally undressed and what had appeared to be a young girl was in truth a boy not much older than myself. He had his cock and balls held tight between his legs so that he might be assumed to be of an indeterminate sex. The sight of him did not lessen the hardness of my cock.

'I see, sir, that I do not wither you,' he said.

'No,' I said. 'You intrigue me.'

Pushing me on to the bed, Gally bent down and was about to take the tip of my cock between his lips when he stopped and said, 'What is this?' He ran his finger over the star on my thigh. 'Is it a mark of the beast?'

'It is but a birthmark,' I said, impatient for him to continue.

'In the shape of a star?'

'Yes, yes, and it matters not, not at this moment.'

I cared little just then for my star or his sex. Girl-boy-boy-girl – all were one.

How cruel to make me watch you. How can I not see your skin, white on black. Two bodies ill fit, unfit and fit. The sky weighs down on me. My invisibility has hidden me from you and fooled me with the promise of the woman I can never be. I can give you nothing, nothing but moth dust.

You sleep wrapped in another's arms, your eyelashes brushing your cheeks. I am wild with a desire that never can be fulfilled. You have taught me to understand my isolation, that I belong not to this world. I belong nowhere.

My love, let me whisper soft into your dreams. I was not a figment. I was Randa, who loved you better than the life she was given. Goodnight, sweet lord. We will not meet again.

XLIV

Randa was not there. I woke suddenly, knowing the silence was different – deeper, darker – and I wondered if she had gone for good. I was giddy with relief. I was free, my mind once more my own.

To make sure, I said softly, 'Randa – are you there?'

'Who you talking to?' said Gally, waking.

'No one,' I said.

'Then come here.'

It was dawn by the time he-she rose from the bed and I watched fascinated as the vulnerable girl reappeared.

'Do you act?' I asked.

'I play the ladies' roles – have done since I was twelve. I hardly ever wear boys' clothes these days but sad to say the company at present is penniless, all as sick as could be with the Lombard Fever.'

'Are you ill?'

He-she laughed. 'It means sick with bone idleness due to the lack of employment. It can be the queen's whim or the plague that closes us down, but this time we have Shakeshaft, the old rogue of a theatre manager, to thank for our misfortunes, he having drunk the profits and pissed them out in the Marshalsea. Now all that is left to us is to peck for our pennies off the arse pickings of gentlemen. But for all that I am not at everyone's cunt and call. I have my pride. I came here as a favour to my friends.'

'Actors like yourself?' I asked.

'In a manner of talking and depending where you weigh the words. Anyone who sells themselves is a whore in part – even his lordship's parson, he who hides behind a screen playing for his own satisfaction while having a look at your father's attempts at rutting. You know what the other whores say about Lord Rodermere?' I did not. 'That his hammer be brittle. In short, he cannot keep it up long enough for anyone's satisfaction.'

That did not interest me but the notion that one could make a living by acting – albeit a precarious one – now there lay a road that I wanted much to travel.

Not knowing how to pay for such a night's entertainment I offered her-him a ring.

'No, you turnip,' Gally said. 'This one I did for the pleasure of it.'

'Is there nothing you would you like?'

'Sir, if I am honest, threads of the female kind would be greatly welcomed as they would help me find work.'

I gave her some garments my sister had left and accompanied her to the river where Master Sorrel, the bargeman, stood wrapped tight against the cold waiting for his passengers. I remembered that when I was young he would take me out on the river, talk of its tides and turns. He had been close to my stepfather and I felt ashamed that I had not seen him for a while.

Gally's friends came running up behind us, giggling with relief to see her. I handed them in turn to Master Sorrel. He took each by the hand and helped them into the barge.

'Lord Beaumont,' he said, 'this is yours.' He handed me a sealed letter. 'You must have dropped it, my lord.'

And without another word he rowed off, soon to disappear in the morning mist that clung to the top of the water. I saw the letter was addressed to me. It was in my mother's hand.

I went back to bed and read it. My mother, so uncertain as to the value or the safety of her words, had left blank spaces supposing that I might replace them with ones that better described her circumstances than she could. These blanks were puzzles and all I could conclude from the few words written there was that they were safe, living somewhere in London, that I was not to worry and that for some reason they had been to see the alchemist Thomas Finglas. It was a bittersweet pill, that letter. A bittersweet dawn that morning.

I could not believe that Randa would not come back. I told myself it was a relief to have my mind free of another's thoughts. But I said it with too much conviction and not enough heart for the silence felt louder and more lonely than it ever was before.

In my chamber that evening still there was no sign of Randa. How strange it was with no little soul to interrupt my thoughts, no one in my head to contradict me. No more poetry, no more sad songs. I became angry. I should brush it off, be eternally grateful to be sane again. And here is the rub – I could hardly bring myself to acknowledge it. I missed her. I had loved her, loved the voice of my little soul. I pulled myself up. Love? No, that is not the right word and yet I could find no better to replace it.

I sat staring at the fire. I did not join my father for he, on hearing how I had passed the night, was disgusted – not that I had spent it with a boy but with a blackamoor. It was almost too much for him to bear. It determined me of one thing: that I could not stay there much longer. Better by far to be my own master, make my own way in the world. I was well educated, I loved words; perhaps, I thought, a life as a thespian would suit my soul.

It came to me, a story that had long held sway over my imagination. It was of Hermaphroditos, a handsome youth who attracted the love of a Naiad nymph, Salmakis. She prayed that they might never be parted and the gods, more obliging than they are now, answered her prayers and merged their two forms into a winged youth. I imagined him with my haggard's feathers, female thighs and breasts. But when Hermaphroditos, like Gally, lifted her dress, there sat a penis and balls. The remembering sent a shiver of delight down me. I had learned about lust and the joy to be found in the sameness and difference of sex.

Gally never came again. That did not worry me. It was Randa who concerned me for she too was gone, never to return. As time passed I found it hard to confess, even to myself, that I was bereft without her. The only tangible thing I had left of her was a fire-red feather.

THE BEAST

XLV

Misery makes me careless. I have lived locked away, hidden in the shadows, invisibility my only friend. I belong nowhere, to no one, not even to myself. I am an abomination. I saw drawings in a book, in his, in Beau's book – of demons, winged and horned, spiked of tail. They prey on men. Is that me? Is it?

I climb the stairs of the tallest turret. I hope with all my being that my wings fail me, let me fall as a stone to ground. Alas, my will if not my soul has an irrepressible desire for the sky. It is my will that lifts me, lifts me above the forest. My eyes are wet, as John Butter's were when he chained me. There is a sob in me so very loud I dare not let it out. It would bring down the clouds, wake the dead trees.

I am lost in sadness. I am in the clearing by the widow's cottage. The Widow Bott called me little bird which I am not and never was. There is no ointment to soothe my agony, no potion to heal my broken soul. No knife could be as sharp, no sword as pointed as this pain of love, this love unreturned.

It is the fox, the vixen. She is here with her fiery breath. She came so sudden but I am invisible, she cannot see me. Smell me, yes. See me, no. Then why come to me in such a manner, with twists and turns? She is changing by degrees and I know her: red of hair, handsome of face, wise of eye, cruel of mouth. I know her. She who gave me my freedom. I know the sorceress.

'I want what is mine,' she says to me who is not there, who cannot be seen. Though she sees me. 'The hem of my dress,' says she.

I move fast away, hold the purse tight by its strings so she might glimpse me.

Wondrous. She says Randa has grown wondrous. She says this is not the place for me.

I fold my leathery wings about my naked breasts. There is no place for me.

She holds out her hand, her fingers long and gnarled, her eyes brighter than flame, alight with desire.

'My hem,' she hisses, 'my hem.'

Her gaze never falters. She points to the dark heart of the forest. She says, there, there is where Randa belongs. Still she holds out her hand.

I let fall the purse, my invisibility, my friend. And it is gone. And the sorceress is gone.

If the darkness be my death, I have no fear. I go where she pointed, into the forest to a place I think no different than where I was until mossy velvet brushes my feathers and my fur, and I enter the softness of spring to the song of a cuckoo.

THE BEAUTY

XLVI

Spring arrived. I had been kept prisoner under winter's bitter rule and my father's malice but now I knew my family were safe I determined to be gone from the House of the Three Turrets.

In late April, when the nightingales had begun their sweet song and sunny showers perfumed the air, I received another letter delivered by the bargeman, this written by my sister, Lady Clare. It was full of details from an orderly life unlike mine which was lived on the margins of chaos. I wanted to tell her about Randa but when I put pen to paper what I wrote belonged more to madness than anything that could claim reality, a fantasy of the irrational thought it most probably was. So I stuck to banalities and I did not tell her of the hawk, the house or the whores.

I hoped that I would receive many more letters, but if they were sent they all failed to arrive apart from one that started in the middle with no explanation of how the middle became so isolated from its usual companions, the beginning and the end.

It was concerned with the alchemist Thomas Finglas, not so much for what he had done but for what his apprentice John Butter had achieved in his place.

. . . for ever since Master Finglas's terrible accident . . .

What accident, Clare did not say. But it was John Butter who was responsible for the making of potions and she claimed that in the space of three weeks her skin had become less red and the worst of the blemishes showed signs of fading.

. . . I am beginning to feel more confident as to my appearance.

Most of what she had to say had more to do with Master John Butter than her complexion and ended abruptly with . . . *I will tell you all when next I write.*

That was to be her last letter. I heard no more from Clare or my mother and shortly afterwards it became quite clear that I could stay not a day more in my father's house without fulfilling the curse that I had inherited at birth.

XLVII

Parson Pegwell had become anxious that after my miraculous recovery he might no longer be needed. To guarantee his place in my father's affections he claimed from the pulpit that he alone knew who was responsible for Lord Rodermere's disappearance. This notion my father took to, for those lost years were a cause of constant concern to him. The parson, now certain of my father's attention, declared the perpetrator to be none other than the witch, Widow Bott.

Lord Rodermere remembered the handsome woman who had refused his advances. He wrote to Sir Percival Hayes asking what he knew about the widow. Sir Percival's steward wrote back to confirm that he had questioned her and had threatened to have her drowned if she did not name the demon with whom she worked. Now she was accused of a far greater crime: not only that of witchcraft but also for debauching my father, turning him from the path of the Lord.

The widow was dragged to the House of the Three Turrets and tied to a chair in the great hall. When Lord Rodermere saw her he could only imagine that he must indeed have been bewitched to have ever desired such a hag.

The parson thrust long pins into her body to see if they drew blood. Lord Rodermere had her clothes and cap torn from her and her head shaved. All this was done with unmeasured violence. From my chamber I had heard the widow's screams and, outraged, I attempted to stop the unfounded persecution and told my father he was no better than a barbarian. He had his henchmen drag me away and lock me in my chamber. It by then being evening and my father having other entertainments in prospect, he sent the widow naked back to her cottage, threatening that the following day she would be arrested and sent for trial.

The next day she was gone, much to the outrage of Francis, Lord Rodermere. Parson Pegwell was greatly aggrieved and that Sunday he accused his congregation of hiding her, warning that anyone found to have done such a thing would be hanged. Where she had gone no one knew, and no one claimed to know. Once again Parson Pegwell felt all the advances he had made with my father fall away. There being no Widow Bott to torture, my father returned to his main obsession: hunting.

He kept all manner of sport hounds that ran for the buck, fox, hare, otter and badger, though I secretly wondered if the chase was not an excuse to go looking for the watery curtain behind which all time was stolen from him.

I was never asked to join him. In truth I made sure that I stayed as far away from the man as possible for the desire to kill him never once abated. If anything, frustration and a lack of purpose in my life had increased it and I thought I would grow old under my father's bitter roof if I did not take action and by doing so free myself.

All at once everything changed and the cards life had thrown at me were tossed for a jester to catch and play with as he fancied.

My father had returned from hunting with some local land-owners. Usually, he hardly bothered to recognise my presence, yet for some inexplicable reason, I was called into the courtyard where he was sitting high on his horse. He bent and took from a huntsman a dead fox. The hounds were near driven wild by the smell of it and the noise was deafening until Lord Rodermere shouted for silence and the dogs became quiet.

I had known him long enough to tell by the tenor of his voice what mood he was in. There was a solemn note to it and in its quietness lay his true fury.

'This is Lord Beaumont Thursby,' he announced to his companions. 'My son.' There was a polite murmur that stopped when he said with distaste, 'My son – who is more beautiful than a girl.' He dismounted, took out his dagger, cut off the brush of the fox and threw its body to the dogs. 'You are not a man,' he said to me. 'You are nothing, a beautiful nothing.'

He gestured to his servant to take me to him. I shook myself free and went of my own accord. My father grabbed me by my hair and undid my codpiece.

'Look,' he said, 'he has a penis and balls yet they make a mockery of his face. Have you breasts, sir?'

Now I fought to free myself. I heard laughter as he smeared my face with the blood of the fox's brush.

'You disgust me,' he said. 'Are you not man enough to fight?'

He threw me into the dirt and the bloodied brush after me, then picked up his riding whip and brought it down on my back, again and again. I managed to stand and, head down, charged at him as would a bull. He fell backwards and the voice in my head screamed now, kill him, now, now. I found his dagger where he had dropped it and I was on him, the blade at his neck.

His servant was fast upon me and held me tight as, fighting for breath, Lord Rodermere struggled to his feet.

The hunting party was uneasy, unsure.

'Leave the boy be,' one gentleman was brave enough to say.

'We have enjoyed enough sport for one day. Come, my lord, let us drink some wine.'

Lord Rodermere was puffing, purple-faced. He turned to his companions, who, no longer laughing, did not know what to make of the play before them. He again had his dagger in his hand.

'Shall I cut the head off this half-formed changeling?' he asked. 'Have it stuffed and mounted on the wall in the great hall? Perhaps then,' he said as he went into the house, 'my true son will return.'

XLVIII

I felt my belly to be a furnace. My veins ran with molten fury that no rational thought could quench. It made a madman of me, a true madman, fooled into believing that I had a mind of steel and the will to murder my father. All that stopped me from such a reckless act was a fox cub.

I had gone into the house gasping for breath. I could see nothing, nothing but the colour of blood, smell nothing but the smell of blood, taste nothing but the taste of blood. I stood in the passage with my back against the cool stone wall, adjusted my shirt, my doublet, my breeches, and with blurred vision watched servants rush past holding platters piled high with food, jugs of wine vanishing into the white light of the sun. I cared little who saw me. Lunacy was my companion. The Devil urged me on to retrieve my rapier from the armourer. The knowledge that I would hang for my deed bothered me not a jot. I would kill my father and dance at his dying.

The kitchen echoed the sound of the fury within me – the clatter of pans, the shouting of servants driven by the irrational urgency of their master's insatiable hunger. I was about to cross the kitchen courtyard when I spied a covered basket, on top of which sat a large stone. I noticed it and did not. It was what I heard that made me stop. The sound of an animal. I went closer.

'There's nothing in there, Lord Beaumont, but dead vermin,' said a servant. 'The gamekeeper is coming for it when he has done.'

Again the soft whimpering. I lifted the lid and saw two dead fox cubs and from under their corpses a third sharp face stared at me, eyes filled with terror.

'Your lordship, I would not,' said the servant. 'They will be riddled with fleas.'

What did I care? I was riddled with rage – a flea would be a wholesome companion. I picked up the little fox and put it inside my doublet, I felt it curl up and fall almost instantly asleep. Taking a loaf, some meat, and an apple I walked away from the house into the waiting forest. Only there among the tall columns of the cathedral trees was I able to take in the sweet air. At last, soothed by the birdsong, by the hum of bees, by the shade of the green mosaic above, I found my balance. With each step I took deeper into the forest I told myself that I was one stride further from the man who I would never again acknowledge as my father. His seed may have given me life but that life, I reasoned, was my own. Not his.

That realisation began to cool the humours in me and I saw in the shadows the jiggering madman I could so easily have become.

By the time – what time? By this time I was deep in the forest in a moss-filled twilight where the trees huddled close together. I felt the wild thing inside my doublet move. I had long forgotten my companion, my reason for not going to the armoury, for not murdering my father. I sat on a log and put the fox cub down on the forest floor, thinking he would bolt as fast as his small legs would allow. Instead, he too sat, his head on one side, his blue eyes looking up at me. I had never seen a fox with eyes that colour, neither had I known a wild creature to be so tame. He took with delicacy the meat I gave him, not with the raw savagery I expected. When he had finished eating he wandered off and I was about to stand when he came back and jumped up on my lap. He pawed at my doublet, seemingly in hope of climbing back in. He must be wounded, I reasoned, but I had not seen any mark on his body. I examined the creature and, finding nothing, put him once more in my doublet. I had no wish to dawdle. Of all my ill-worked-out intentions, one was solid: I would not return to my father's house. The fox stuck his head out of my doublet, his eyes sparkled, his nose twitched but he showed no inclination to leave.

The only way to think of my journey was to imagine I was with my haggard, high above the forest, staring at the landscape below. I saw the vast expanse of wood hugging the river and beyond, in the far-off smoky shadows of the horizon, was the village I hoped to reach before dusk. The sunlight reappeared, shimmering, and I wondered if I might not find again the watery curtain that as a child I once ran through. But the more I walked, the more I realised that for too long my life had been steeped in forest stories and forest magic. Reality belonged to the world beyond these woods. If I was to go to London I must learn to walk with my feet firm upon the ground.

XLIX

I was in the middle of an imaginary duel with my father when I stopped for I heard chattering. And there, strung between two saplings, was a washing line where hung a collection of tatty shirts and thread-worn petticoats. In the gaps between the breeze of clothes I could make out what lay beyond – a large, canvas-covered wagon with lettering on the side that announced Master Ben Shakeshaft and his Medley of Players.

The name I knew, but how I could not recall. It hovered in my memory just out of my grasp. Not far from the caravan, in the centre of the clearing, was a long trestle table bearing the remains of a roasted chicken and round it sat a group of four squabbling men and a woman. The cause of their disagreement was to do with a lardy lad with a deep voice. Intrigued, I listened awhile.

'I never wanted to be a bloody actor,' he said. 'And it's not my fault my voice broke.'

'A nincompoop, Master Pennyworth, that's what you are,' said the large woman, who appeared to rise from the middle of the table and was made mostly of stomach and bust into which her face fell. Her features were that of a man, her chin hairy and whether her lumps and bumps were due to stuffing or flesh I could not tell. She had large hands with which she slapped the lardy lad.

'A worthless bottom of a boy – all cock and no tail that anyone might fancy.'

'Ow, that hurt, mistress.'

This drama much amused me and went part way to making me forget how angry I was.

A man stood on the steps of the caravan surveying the scene. He too was watching the argument with interest. A wiry fellow was he with a massive forehead and a long nose. Round his scrawny neck was tied a wide white cloth and in his hand he held a chicken drumstick.

'Now, now,' he said, addressing the woman. 'This is not helping, my sweet sorrow.'

One of the party at the table stood up and I wondered why I had not noticed him first.

He appeared the most educated of the group and in a voice that might roll over hills and be heard in the deepest valley said, 'Master Shakeshaft, my mind is worn thin due to imagining Master Pennyworth to be anything other than a fart-filled, ugly, pox-ridden, useless turd of an actor who could not fool a blind man into believing him to be a girl.'

'I said all my lines and in the right order, which is more than Master Merrymay did,' said the lad in his own defence.

Master Merrymay rose to object and was immediately dismissed with a wave of a hand.

'Pray tell me, Master Shakeshaft,' said the actor with a voice that would roll over hills, 'without a boy to play the female roles what do you suggest we do?'

'Master Cuthbert,' said Master Shakeshaft, 'it is but a little hurdle and it will be surmounted.'

Master Cuthbert took a deep breath and as if talking to a moon-headed calf said, 'In one week's time we are booked in

London to perform a new play at the Gate, and thus far we are in a storm of confusion, and no boy to play the female role since the last one left in a huff. This noodlehead would be more effective if he were to address sheep at a slaughterhouse for they would willingly lay down their lives to avoid listening to any more of his drivel.'

'We must consider how we will overcome the obstacle,' said Master Shakeshaft, tossing the half-eaten drumstick to the ground. 'I have a notion I see a chink of light.'

'Thank heaven and all its muses,' said Master Cuthbert. 'There was I imagining you had slammed the door on any sensible solution to our dilemma. Speak, Ben. I am trembling at the very thought that there might be a grub of an idea in that wine-soaked head of yours that once housed a brain.'

Master Shakeshaft seemed in no way offended by the actor's outburst. 'That is it, Crumb,' he said to Master Cuthbert. 'You have given me the idea and a pretty maggot of a thing it is. Why, it is simple. He –' he pointed to Master Pennyworth, '– he will play the part as dead.'

'Dead? Thunder my tongue! Oh, ye gods give me strength,' said Master Cuthbert. 'Dead – and I make love to bones? You mock our art, sir.'

'Better the bones be dead than they speak with a voice from the grave,' said Master Shakeshaft.

As I watched the scene, the little fox leaped free of my doublet and trotted into the clearing to retrieve the drumstick.

'A fox,' shouted the woman.

'Where, my sweet sorrow?' said Master Shakeshaft, reaching for his sword.

'It is but a cub,' said Master Cuthbert.

'It is vermin,' said the woman.

'Soon-to-be-dead vermin,' said Master Shakeshaft, advancing on the creature.

I would not let my fox be sacrificed to a drumstick and with the evening sun showing me in a golden light I made my entrance through the washing line.

The actors stared at me as I picked up the fox and, having their attention and naught to lose but my pride which anyway was long gone, I seized my chance.

Entirely forgetting that my face was covered in blood, I said, 'Perhaps, sirs and mistress, I might play the female role?'

L

I stood before them, clinging to a fox cub, my face a bloody mess, and not a word was said.

At last the silence was broken by Master Cuthbert.

'Do you always bring the sun with you to illuminate your face?' he said and added, without drawing a breath, 'Clean him up and he will do.'

'Rein in your desires, Master Cuthbert,' said Master Shakeshaft. 'Remember what we are trying to achieve: a play that will take London by the petticoat and jigger it until we hear the coins sing.'

'How could I forget?' said Master Cuthbert. 'If last night's disastrous performance is anything to judge our success by then I predict you will soon find yourself back in the Marshalsea.'

'Last night was not so bad,' said the theatre manager. He took a raw onion from his pocket and peeled it as he would an apple before taking a hearty bite. 'It was . . .'

'. . . a diabolical mess,' interrupted Master Cuthbert. 'A travesty. We could rightly be accused of being rogues rather an actors.'

'That is where you are wrong. We are Sir Percival Hayes's men.'

'"Were" is the word, Ben. Sir Percival is in the past tense because, if you remember, you pissed away the profits, and when Sir Percival found out he told you to stuff your onions up your arse.'

Master Shakeshaft shrugged and turned to me.

'We need a boy actor who can sing like a nightingale.'

It mattered not if I could or could not sing for having heard the name Sir Percival Hayes I had already decided to be gone from there and make my own way to the city.

'I cannot sing,' I said quickly. 'And I cannot act. I would be no better than a . . . a . . . a bare-arsed knave.'

Master Cuthbert laughed. 'That, sir, would give me joy to see.'

I bowed and walked away.

'Wait, sir, wait,' shouted Master Shakeshaft. 'Not so much haste, sir. You have taken the sunlight with you.'

Master Cuthbert stretched his long body. 'Come,' he said. 'Our bark is from Hell's kitchen, our bite is velvet to the touch. Sit, eat. Have some chicken. What is your hurry?'

Reluctantly, I sat at the table while Master Cuthbert introduced me to the other players whose names I instantly remembered and instantly forgot.

'And Crumb is what these shadows call me,' he added. 'Now,' he said, passing me a book. 'Read.'

'Do I stand or sit?'

'You read if you can read and it matters not a jot if you stand, crouch, sit or jump.'

It was by Ovid and I knew the work well. I read it using all the energy that my anger had released in me.

When I had finished the passage Crumb threw his arms in the air.

'There is a God,' he shouted. 'And your reason, Ben, for not taking a boy with a brain is?'

'Is that he has not been on stage before and . . . and . . .' He ran out of words. 'And you have a point, Crumb.'

Master Cuthbert laughed. 'If we have a play properly rehearsed and all you lily-livered lice learn your lines then with Gally's help, Sir Percival might reconsider his decision.'

'That point had not slipped the entrails of my mind,' said Master Shakeshaft.

Finally the queen's coin dropped. It was Gally who had spoken of the old rogue, the theatre manager. I inwardly smiled at the memory of her, of him.

'Clean the lad up and let us see if there is a woman beneath his fluff,' said Crumb.

Sweet sorrow brought a pail of water and handed me a cloth.

'Come,' she said, 'what is nature's damage?'

I turned my back to the table and washed my face but not well enough it seemed as with great impatience she took the cloth from me and cleaned me and shaved me.

I wondered if it would be possible to take refuge here and while this thought played in my head I became fascinated by the hairs that protruded from the chin of Mistress Sweet Sorrow.

'I was a bearded lady,' she said, 'one of the seven wonders of the world and never been further than Deptford.' She took hold of my jaw which made speaking impossible. 'God's blood, who are you?' she said, staring at me. 'Tell me, for you have the beard of a boy and the complexion of a girl.' I did not answer and she continued. 'You could stand on stage, say not a word and the audience would be satisfied and not feel cheated of their coin.'

She powdered my face and rouged my cheeks and my lips. My hair was long enough to be dressed. This all took place with nothing being lost in the quarrel between the actor and the playwright until I turned to face them.

'Well, I never,' said Master Shakeshaft. 'What enchanted forest did you come from, mistress?'

'I know not in which realm I belong,' I said, keeping my voice soft and remembering how my sister held herself.

Master Merrymay stood and raised his tankard to me. 'Beautiful,' he said breathlessly. 'A faerie queen.'

'What shall we call you?' asked Crumb.

'Beau . . .' I paused for a moment then said, '. . . Sorrel.'

'Master Beau Sorrel, we welcome you to the company,' said Master Shakeshaft. 'But not your fox.'

The fox had all along sat under the table by my feet. I picked it up and again walked away.

'Master Sorrel,' called Master Shakeshaft, 'you turn down my offer in favour of vermin?'

'He stays with me.'

Crumb laughed.

'Take them both, Ben. You never know, the fox might turn out to be the greater actor.'

LI

Time makes ghosts of us – the self is perhaps the dust of what we remember.

I remember that I had the remainder of that day, a night and one morning to learn my part. To my utter astonishment I found I had been given the lead role of Ann in *A Warning for Faire Women*.

'This is a mistake,' I said to Master Shakeshaft. 'It is far too important a part for a novice such as I am.'

'Come, young man, where is your mettle?' he laughed. 'You, at least, are something to look upon which is more than I can say for Master Pennyworth.'

For some foolish reason I thought honesty might save me.

'Sir,' I said, 'I have never before seen a play performed.'

'Never seen a play? In what hayloft have you been living?' said the theatre manager. I moved my mouth to answer. 'No, no,' he said, 'hold your tongue. The truth is always an actor's worst friend.' He took another onion from his pocket and peeled it. 'Crumb is an excellent teacher.' Taking a hearty bite, he continued, 'I agree it is a part that demands . . .'

'An actor?' I said. 'An understanding of the art?'

'Worry not,' said Master Shakeshaft. 'I would rather we find you to be a useless player here in the country than we bring you on only to discover you to be a useless player in London. If you prove to be a useless player – as I fear you might – then think no more of it, other than you saved a travelling group of actors the embarrassment of lacking a leading lady. Once we return to London there will be no shortage of talent hungry for a meal and the stage.'

Before I could think what to say he had shaken my hand and I had the impression that I had just been cheated but of what I could not say.

The play had to do with the true murder of George Sanders, a prosperous London merchant. He was killed by the jealous George Brown who was in love with Sanders's wife, Ann.

I was vexed enough to be given a role that at least demanded someone with knowledge of theatre, but then my troubles doubled.

'I cannot work out here in nature,' announced Master Cuthbert. 'We must take lodgings and the use of the upstairs room at the Wheatsheaf.'

I knew this to be a inn near to the House of the Three Turrets – too near for my liking.

'And how will we pay for it?' asked Mistress Sweet Sorrow.

Master Shakeshaft puffed himself up and taking hold of my doublet said, 'These clothes are too grand for an apprentice.'

And so it was that my clothes went to pay the bill at the inn where I arrived with the medley of players dressed in a lady's gown. Lodgings were not what Master Cuthbert most desired but the hire of the room so that I might be well rehearsed.

'It is your entrance that matters, Master Sorrel. Those few gestures tell the story to come, whether it be comedy or tragedy.'

'Or a great mess of a turd,' I said.

The lines were simple. It was the rest that proved a dance

hard to master and by the time the afternoon of the performance arrived, I felt as if I was to be taken to Tyburn Tree rather than appear in a play.

I was wound so tight with fear – fear of forgetting my lines, fear of being discovered for the fraud I knew I was, fear that I would be recognised – that I could hardly see or hear the audience. Paints and wigs do not an actor make, though I made liberal use of both in order that my disguise be assured.

The audience was full of sleepy drunks, and a hotchpotch of locals and landlords.

'Now, young Master Sorrel,' said Master Shakeshaft, 'remember all you have been taught and if you fluff your lines make the words up, and no one will be a penny the wiser. Whatever you do, do not stand there with your mouth open making vinegar of wine – these words are meant to be heard.'

The drums rolled, the play began and the actors ran onto the stage. What surprised me was that the audience carried on talking and chit-chattering. We were just a background diversion between the clinking of tankards.

I must have made a good entrance for to my surprise everyone fell silent. I gawped at the faces gawping at me. One man in the audience shouted, 'Do not be shy, lovely. Let us hear your voice.'

The words flowed from me, filled as they were with the passion of a woman intent on murder. Who better than I, I thought, to play this role?

What concerned me most that afternoon in the courtyard of the inn was that I would not be recognised and if that was the marker for success, then I achieved it. It did not occur to my father's henchman who watched the play with all the rest that he was applauding his master's son.

The crowning moment was when Crumb said, 'Well done, Master Sorrel, tomorrow we take the play – and you – to London.'

LII

It was the first time I had seen the great city and every sense in me was woken by the noise of bells. They rang for the day, the hour, they rang in a baby, they rang out a passing soul, they rang merrily in honour of a bride, they rang for work to begin and for work to end. All I could hear as we entered the city that fresh spring morning was the ringing of bells and the singing of larks. I was Caesar come to conquer, the rackety old cart a chariot. Sunlight danced on London Wall where flowers grew from the Romans' bricks. Then we were on our way along Cheapside where so many streets and lanes spoke of their wares: of leather, milk, and silk.

This was the time to put the past behind me. Never had I felt so alive as I did then and all that had gone before that moment seemed but dandelion seeds swept away by the breeze from the river. Here was my future. My purse at present was weak but I would in this city, out of its very clay, make my own fortune. This London was built for purpose, not for the idle and the shoe shufflers. Here, gold lay beneath the shit.

I overlooked one thing: I had brought with me a fox cub. A creature of the forest, of its magic, lay sleeping in my doublet undisturbed by all he heard. Only his nose twitched at every new smell.

As we crossed London Bridge I glimpsed a forest downriver; masts of galleons rising from the water while on the other side little boats and barges ferried people across with ant-like industry. All this I saw through the flap of the tent that covered the caravan.

'This is Southwark,' said Master Shakeshaft, 'home of the rogue and the rascal.'

We stopped at a house that looked over the river. It was neither tidy nor clean. And waiting for us in the doorway, hands on hips, was Gally.

As pleased as I was to see Gally, I feared she might say my name without a care to the consequences and all would be lost. She gave me a long, hard stare as I followed Master Shakeshaft and his wife into the house.

'What has the pied ninny cat dragged in today?' she asked Master Shakeshaft.

'Oh, that,' said my new employer, waving a dismissive hand in my direction. 'That is my apprentice, Beau Sorrel by name. A budding actor.'

'More a . . .' I began to say.

Gally leaned towards me. 'More an imposter,' she hissed. In a louder voice she said, 'A budding actor? If you say so, Master Shakeshaft.'

'I do say so. He will play women's parts and if he proves useless he can be the book holder or the prompter or do other such things that are necessary. But that face could sink a thousand ships. I wager that he, Beau Sorrel, is the money.'

I did not think that best described me, feeling more a feeble shadow than anything well-versed with substance.

He turned to his wife. 'Is there any wine, my sweet sorrow? For I have a mighty thirst, and a hunger on me that a rhinoceros would be proud of.'

'And with what do I buy this feast for such a vast and leathery animal?' said Mistress Shakeshaft.

Rummaging about in his pockets Master Shakeshaft took out a coin at which his long-suffering wife looked not at all impressed.

'The floor!' he said.

This command had everyone but me – for I had no idea what it meant – scrabbling about in hope of finding a sixpence and being much rewarded in their search.

I must have looked perplexed and, by way of explanation, Master Shakeshaft said, 'When I have largesse upon me I then take the monetary precautions fitting to my status and scatter what coinage I have about my person onto the floor. No better bank there be.'

'And you are no better than an ass to believe that,' said his sweet sorrow.

The theatre manager looked much wounded. 'Mistress, you might show me some respite.'

'Respect,' I corrected him.

'No, respite. The bitch always has a stick to beat me with.'

'Have I not good reason?' said his wife.

The chamber was low-ceilinged and the fire, when it was finally lit, gave off more smoke than warmth. The front door closed behind his wife and Master Shakeshaft stood on a chair and ran his hands along the top of the beams. He fetched down two bottles and winked at me.

'My sweet sorrow will only bother with the food,' he said, pulling a cork and pouring some wine into a dusty goblet.

The chair by the fire groaned as he sat down on it, still holding the bottle. He looked around at us.

'Do not feel you must keep company with me.'

Master Cuthbert said he would take his meal at the Mermaid

where he could pick up all the gossip and hear news of the latest plays.

'Lead the way, Crumb,' said Gally, 'for I have no desire to stay and listen to the babbling of a bumpkin who believes he can act, or a theatre manager who thinks a bumpkin can make him his fortune.'

'Hold that spiteful tongue of yours, Gally,' said Master Shakeshaft.

'Stuff an onion in it,' said Gally, taking Crumb's arm. She walked him purposefully to the door where she stopped and glanced back at me. 'There is much I have to tell you, Crum, and you will be surprised when you hear the truth of it. A scandal, no less.'

I felt that the game was up and tomorrow I would have to leave for I did not doubt that Gally meant to tell Crumb who I was. I jumped when Master Shakeshaft asked if I was staying.

'I hope so,' I said. 'I have not a penny to go elsewhere with.'

And in all honesty I was too tired to think what best to do. In the morning, I would have a plan.

'What is that fox going to eat?' asked Master Shakeshaft.

'The same as me,' I said.

Master Shakeshaft laughed. 'Apprentice, actor, fox, all is one and one is much of a muchness. It is hard to pull you apart.'

'Master Shakeshaft,' I said, 'I am not even a proper actor.'

'That is where our opinions differ,' said Ben Shakeshaft. 'I have all the conceit to believe you are; you have all the doubt to think you are not. I tell you this: a player is riddled with an equal amount of doubt and conceit yet once he struts upon the stage he becomes an empty vessel filled with the alchemy of the character he plays. No actor should truly know himself lest he becomes more important than the role.'

At that moment the front door flew open and in came his sweet sorrow carrying a basket laden with food.

That first night I slept on the table. At least the rats had trouble climbing the legs and in the main stayed on the floor where my fox had a feast. I stirred occasionally, hearing the scratches of tiny claws, the squeaks of doomed vermin.

In the morning I was woken with a kiss.

LIII

'What are you doing here, Lord Beaumont?'

I sat up with a start. Gally was leaning over me.

'Have you told Master Cuthbert who I am?' I said.

Hastily I rolled off the table, picked up my fox cub and fastened him into my doublet. 'Have you?' I asked again.

'No, I am full of admiration for your determination to leave your bastard of a father and that haunted house. But I am peeved, my lord, I admit.'

'Why?'

'Because according to Crum, this Beau Sorrel had the roughest men in the Wheatsheaf blubbering into their beer and I am not so happy about having a rival for the women's parts.'

'Then I will refuse to take them.'

'Oh, you will? Come on, madam, get off your pretty arse and let us find some breakfast.'

The house opened on to a narrow street darkened by over-hanging buildings that made night of day. It was crowded with noisy traders and, such was the clamour and confusion, the noise and smell that made up this stewpot of a city.

Gally was dressed as a man that morning but he wore a woman's painted face, his wig hung in long curls to his shoulders and he carried a feathered fan. He walked with such affected airs that we were much stared at.

'The bridge or a ferry?' he asked, linking his arm through mine.

'The bridge,' I said, having no knowledge of either.

We had nearly reached the end of Bridge Street when Gally stopped. He looked at my fox, then at me and said, 'What are you trying to do? Steal all my glory?'

'I am doing nothing,' I said.

'That is the problem.'

I did not know what he meant and said so. At that moment, a woman carrying a basket on her head turned to look at us and by some fluke tumbled over a street seller. Further along, two maids near succumbed to an accident and so it went on.

'Some might call it witchcraft,' said Gally.

'I would call it clumsiness. Or perhaps my fox caught their eyes.'

'If I was not so good at my trade I would be jealous. Have you not noticed that everyone else has blackened teeth while yours are ivory white, that the skin of most men and women is far from smooth and yours has not a blemish?' Gally started to laugh.

'What is it you find so funny?'

'You! We had better run before one of the women who are following us captures you and ties you to her bed.'

I turned to see that indeed there was a crowd. We started to run and did not stop until we reached the Mermaid.

When we were seated in the darkest part of the tavern, Gally said, 'Now, again I ask: what are you doing here, Lord Beaumont?'

'Trying to set myself straight on the course of life.'

'That,' said Gally, 'is a venture for fools.'

LIV

It amused me greatly to find I was working for a thief. Master Shakeshaft, I discovered, stole liberally other people's poetry, scenery and costumes. He was completely devoid of scruples, often poaching whole speeches without compunction. He had even been known to take other people's plays and put his name to them.

This was a world the like of which I had never thought I would encounter. I had been brought up to be an earl not an actor but perhaps one only knows oneself when the scenery of life is so abruptly changed. Before, I had been protected from the gaze of others; I was visible and invisible. Now in London's glass, I saw the dreams of others hung round my neck. With such a following of women I could have easily exchanged the table for a bed of feathers every night. That I did not was in part due to shyness but more out of fear that my own true self be apprehended.

I had hoped that my vengeful feelings towards my father might abate now I was free of him. But still I would find my thoughts gleaming with a murderous flame. The longer I lived in this city the less these bilious rages troubled me and it occurred to me that my madness might have been caused by the House of the Three Turrets itself. It was, after all, a place that from my childhood had been wraithed in spirits that had no more substance to them than an autumn mist. In London I was subject to such fogs. I knew the stage to be full of ghosts and shadows, I understood the paints and clothes, the tricks and trumpery that hide and alter reality.

Here then is a truth: man is a creature who feeds on stories as beasts feed on raw meat. We inflame our senses with such wild imaginings that our minds are but kindling for the tale.

What strange spell had I been under to make me believe that Randa was anything other than the desperate imaginings of a lonely, frustrated mind? Only with rational thought could I find some sanity in the curse I was told I had been born to. There was no proof – I would not take the Widow Bott's words for it. As for my beauty – why should that have any effect on my father's life? No, all this was but an evil given to me in the shape of a faerie tale.

'I will not be haunted by the sorceress's curse,' I said aloud.

My fox, asleep on the table, looked up with his head to one side then with a sigh curled upon himself again and slept.

I would not murder my father. It was not in my nature to enact such a violent deed. That is what I told myself then and yet I knew I lied.

I had made enquiries as to the whereabouts of my mother, sister and stepfather and discovered nothing.

'The question wears the crown,' said Gally 'The answer bows to another question, which is: if your family was so easy to find, would not Lord Rodermere have done so by now? And there is a whisper on the streets that his agents are searching for his son – who I know wanders round the city, his head in the blue sky of dreams, a butterfly waiting to be pinned.'

'What should I do?' I asked.

'What are you? A dunce? Act.' I started to protest but Gally interrupted me. 'No, you play at acting. You are wooden, stiff, and there is no movement in your mind or your limbs. Your words are mainly decoration, as is your face. Who are you? Go on, tell me – who are you?'

I said nothing,

'You like women?'

'Yes.'

'More than men?'

'Yes.'

'Then let me rid you, my lord, of all inhibition', Gally grasped my codpiece. 'Let us make your cock dance in the cunt. To win in love you must be bold, erect; learn how to woo the world and its horse.'

'You speak in riddles,' I said, laughing.

Paying no attention, she said, 'I want you to act. To be the lover, to be the hero, to be the heroine, to play the part, not just say the lines with a pretty face for a side dish.'

She flounced her skirts, went to her paintbox and told me to sit. She took a great deal of care in making my face to be that of a young maiden and completed the transformation with a wig.

'The challenge is this . . .' said Gally.

'What challenge?'

'The challenge,' she repeated, 'is to act the woman while speaking as a man.'

'Then should I not be dressed in woman's garb?'

'No. If you can make a bookseller treat you not as a madman, but as an innocent maid, if you can make him see only your face, not the garment you wear, then I will buy you dinner at the Mermaid Tavern.'

So said, we set off towards the great cathedral where, huddled together, was a collection of bookshops.

'Choose,' said Gally.

The shop was ill-lit and I can but assume that my face shone out for the bookseller eagerly asked how he could assist me.

'With a prayer book,' I said.

I kept my face down, my eyes up, my voice as soft as it could be – too soft for he leaned forward and I feared he would not be fooled.

'This one is a simply bound prayer book by Thomas Cranmer,' he said and handed it to me.

I took it and as I looked at its pages I began to believe that I might be an innocent maiden hoping for guidance. It came into my mind that I was about to be married and to a man I did not love. None of these thoughts did I dwell on, more that they formed into garlands. With every word I said, they began to feel less like lies and more like truth.

'I am to be married and I am a little uncertain . . . I know I would be grateful for . . . guidance . . .'

The bookseller took my hand and patted it. I quickly pulled it away lest he study it too long. And I blushed. Yes, I felt that I blushed.

Just then Gally entered the shop and made a near impossible situation worse. But the thought of a meal was all the encouragement I needed and I hid in the shadows while she picked up several prayer books then asked why they had no pictures in them of naked young men.

'Out,' shouted the bookseller. 'I will not have painted whores upset my lady customers.'

I was certain that the game was up but continued to study the book I was holding and to my great relief, it was only Gally who was shown the door.

'Out, you strumpet,' said the bookseller, 'and do not bring your vile tongue back in here.'

I believe I looked truly shocked and having no means to buy the book, said that I felt faint and needed air.

The bookseller was alarmed.

'Mistress – a chair,' he said.

'Nay,' I said – for some reason I thought I should have a country voice – 'Thank you, but I will come back another day.'

I had reached the door of the shop when he said, 'Wait, mistress. Here, take the prayer book. I see that you need its comfort.'

Gally, waiting round the corner, grabbed my sleeve as I left the shop.

'He gave me a prayer book,' I said. 'I cannot keep it.'

A learned-looking gentleman was coming towards us and Gally took the prayer book from me and said to him, 'The kindly bookseller gave me this but I cannot take it. Would you be so gracious as to give it back?'

We waited, I willing the gentleman not to steal it, and watched him enter the bookshop. Then we started to run, darting through the crowds, laughing. We stopped a few streets away.

'He could not believe me to be a woman,' I said when I had caught my breath.

'Of course he did,' said Gally and draped her arm on my shoulder. 'Lesson One – a success.'

'Lesson?'

'Yes, you half-baked faggot. That was an exercise in acting.' Gally stopped and threw her arms wide. 'Look about you – all these people rushing to and fro – what are they looking for?'

I shrugged.

'They are out buying dreams. They need to believe that you could be a beautiful, innocent maiden even though you are dressed as a man and speak as a man.' She stopped. 'You did speak as a man?'

'I know no other way.'
'Then to the Mermaid and to dine,' she said.

LV

'I have something I must tell you,' said Gally, once our food was served.

Well-versed in Gally's moods I could see her humour was much improved of late and suspected the cause to be a new bedfellow.

She leaned back in her chair and smiled.

'I heard a story about you.'

'Is this a riddle?'

'No, dear heart, this story was told to me by my new lover. He was once married – a grand mistake for his cock does not lean in that direction. His wife, Lady Judith . . .'

I felt the colour drain from me.

'Sir Percival Hayes is your lover?' I stood up. 'Do not say you told him where I am.'

'No, you noodle, be seated. Do you have so little faith in me?'

'Then why the story of Lady Judith?'

'The Badger was telling me, by way of sweet conversation after the noble act was well and truly rehearsed and played out in full, about the death in childbirth of his wife.'

'And what is this to me?' I heard my father's voice in mine and thought, oh Lord, who am I?

'The marriage,' said Gally, 'had not been consummated and Sir Percival's suspicions as to who the father might be fell on you – stop looking so alarmed, Beau. Badger told me that your looks made you impossible to resist.'

'I cannot believe that you and Sir Percival are lovers.'

'Why not? Come, no harm has been done. Your secret is safe.' Gally took my hand which I instantly withdrew.

'What petulance, Lord Beaumont. It is only due to me that Sir Percival maintains the Medley of Players. And he is eager to meet the new actor that has London by the balls.'

'No, absolutely, no. I might be able to fool a blind bookseller but Sir Percival – who has known me since I was born – never.'

'Do not concern yourself. I will make sure your paths do not cross.'

'Gally,' I said and pushed my plate aside, 'this farce will not have long to run before I am found out, either by a slip of your sweet tongue or a boast of another.'

'Never from me,' said Gally, 'never. You are my brother, my sister, a lover, a friend. Never. Throw yourself into the work and forget all else. Come, eat and be merry – for the time being at least all is well with the world.'

I had a lot to thank Gally for. I found my feet in London and began to enjoy this new profession. I could make the audience laugh and make it cry, and for once Sir Percival Hayes's men were given better places to perform in.

If I am honest, I do not think I could claim acting to be my natural calling but I played the parts of foolish maidens and equally gormless lovers and I found that if I believed wholeheartedly in my character, if I forgot who I was, that was a façade enough to hide behind.

Ben Shakeshaft put on a new play to outshine all others. *The Temperamental Ghost* had good returns. I played two roles, the Maiden and the Ghost. And in both, I was so far from myself that I could be true to the role I was playing.

Master Shakeshaft could not have been more pleased with the audience and the weight of his purse.

Naïvely, I thought that this was the way our fortunes would continue. But again, fate took me for a dance. One night while we were performing *The Temperamental Ghost* the theatre was shut down in fear of the plague. The audience went home disgruntled, the theatres in London went dark, nothing was to be performed.

'God's teeth,' said Gally, sitting down on an upturned barrel backstage. 'What are we going to do?'

A week had already passed and the ban was still in place and showed no signs of being lifted. There was no point in keeping the theatre on and Master Shakeshaft was again having the props and the costumes packed away and we, the company, were there to help. It was in the middle of this conversation that we heard Master Shakeshaft speaking slowly, loudly, and then ferociously.

'Do I have to make it plainer to you? Master Beau Sorrel is a man. Note that I emphasise that he is NOT a woman. If your mistress needs a companion the theatre is not the place to find her one.'

Gally's ears pricked up. She tiptoed nearer to the curtain that divided Master Shakeshaft from backstage.

'Not so hasty, Master Shakeshaft,' said Gally, pulling the curtain aside.

'It is no use,' said Master Shakeshaft. 'He speaks in the frog tongue and does not appear to understand a word of the queen's English.'

'I think you are much mistaken,' said Gally, slipping through the curtain. 'He understands exactly what it is his mistress wants.'

Master Shakeshaft started to repeat what he had said before but even louder, as if somehow the tone of his speech would be easier to understand.

I peeked through the curtain to take a better look at the Frenchman. He was immaculately dressed, wore a sharp Spanish beard and a pointed moustache. He looked as if he was well-versed in intrigue. Gally came back to me.

'Take care,' she whispered. 'This might be a trap of Lord Rodermere's devising.'

I could not see my father having sufficient imagination to hire such a man or to go to such extravagant lengths of deception.

The Frenchman was becoming exasperated. Thanks to Doctor Grace, I speak French fluently. Perhaps it was my curiosity that led me to offer to translate, albeit loosely, what the Frenchman had to say, for I wanted to know why, out of all our company, it was me he sought.

I stepped onto the stage and asked in French if I could be of assistance.

'This man,' he pointed at the theatre manager, 'has no grasp of your queen's English. But you speak French?'

'Yes, sir,' I replied, 'I do.'

And we continued the conversation in his language.

'Blood and thunder – is there no end to your numerous talents, Master Sorrel? What is the frog saying?' said Master Shakeshaft.

I looked at my master's expectant face and invented some rubbish that would not anger him.

'I am looking for an actor,' said the Frenchman. 'A Master Beau Sorrel.'

'I am Beau Sorrel,' I said.

'*Bien*,' said the Frenchman. 'Allow me to explain why I am

here. I have served my mistress since she was a child. It was her dowry that enabled her husband to become powerful. My lady is bored with the role expected of her as his wife and she has no interest in court. She fears that time creeps into her bedchamber at night to rob her of her beauty and she has taken decisive action to combat the ravages of age. Her stratagem is to stay awake at night and to this end, she desires a companion to entertain her and prevent her from sleeping.'

'What of her husband?'

He ignored my question. 'You will be well paid for your services,' he said, taking a purse from inside his doublet. 'And come the dawn you will be gone. She may want to see you again. She may not. It depends.'

'On what?' I asked.

'On how well you act.'

I was certain that the Frenchman was not in my father's employ. But that did not make him any less menacing.

At the sight of the purse, Ben Shakeshaft's attitude changed. He became full of apologies and ill-advised compliments of which the Frenchman took no notice.

'My mistress,' he said, 'requests that you wear these clothes.' He handed me a parcel. 'They are better suited for the role you are to play.'

One thing I had learned is that a ship is sooner rigged than a woman is dressed.

The skirt was quilted, the sleeves slashed and the embroidery very fine. It was without doubt the most expensive female garment I would ever wear. Still, I was not eager to be imprisoned in it. As a woman dressed in all this finery it would be near impossible to defend myself should the necessity arise.

Gally helped me and with much pinching, much girding, much clinging, I was pinned into the garment of a wealthy young lady.

'You could go to court in that,' said Master Shakeshaft when he saw the lavishness of the costume. 'You could be presented to the queen.'

Gally shooed him away and set to painting my face.

'Be very careful,' she whispered.

'Hurry,' called the Frenchman. 'The tide is on the turn.'

'Why do you say that?' I said to Gally. 'He is not my father's man.'

'No, perhaps not.'

'Definitely not.' And it sprung from nowhere – a longing to murder my father. I banished the thought and said, 'Lord Rodermere cannot abide foreigners.'

'Come,' called the Frenchman. 'There is no more time.'

'No wig,' said Gally. 'Your hair is thick enough without.'

She went again to her paintbox and took from it a light knife with the thinnest of blades.

'Here,' she said. 'Just be careful.'

The Frenchman was impressed with my transformation and his attitude towards me softened. We set off towards the river accompanied by a lamp boy and there on the inky waters of the Thames sat a river barge.

I had had time enough under Gally's tutelage to master the whims of women, their walk, their heaviness of hip, their uncertain step, and was helped into the barge with great care. I kept my head low and hid behind my dark locks and wavered as if in need of constant reassurance from the Frenchman before I could move. Such was my performance that I had every bargeman, including my escort, treat me as they might a wilted flower. All the while, the feel of the steel blade concealed in my garter was my only comfort in this most strange of circumstances.

The Frenchman sat next to me as the barge set off into the darkness of the middle of the river where the waters claimed neither bank. His voice had changed, as if brutality was not needed when speaking to a lady but his words were measured and the weight of them spoke of death.

'If one word of this adventure spills from your lips then you had better have made your peace with God for I will not hesitate to cut your throat and take out your tongue. You comprehend?'

I nodded and thought that I would be at peace only when I was on my way back to my lodgings and this night was done.

The house was unlit and it was too dark to make out exactly where it was but I could tell it was on the city side of the river. It had a watergate and the barge took us underneath where we disembarked unseen. The Frenchman escorted me up an elegant staircase and into a chamber. He left, the door closed, a key turned. What I saw made my heart sink for I was certain the chamber must belong to the lady's husband. The walls were lined with books and the room was dominated by a table on which there were piles of paper, used quills, and a decanter of wine. Two Venetian glass goblets stood waiting. But waiting for what? That was the question.

The lady entered from an antechamber. She wore a mask and was dressed in a loose-cut mantle of crimson velvet, richly embroidered and scattered with jewels. She sat at the table and studied me as if I were a specimen to be drawn, to be noted.

'You are more beautiful, more exquisite in person than you are on stage.' She poured the wine. 'Do you like women?' she asked, abruptly. 'I have heard that young actors who play the women's roles are much loved by men. Do you prefer men?'

'I prefer women, my lady.'

'Where did you learn to speak French?' she asked.

'Perhaps, my lady, it is best that you know as little about me as I do about you.'

She laughed. 'Very astute, Mistress Sorrel. Do you play chess?'

LVI

That night I played chess badly and lost to a woman whose face I could not see and whose mind burned as fierce as a flame. We ate, we drank and drank some more. I acted the companion, for that was who she had requested me to be.

'What is it like to be on the stage?' she said after I had lost my queen.

'There is fear and freedom in it in equal measures,' I said. 'If you do it well you can hide in the words of another.'

She made notes of what I said.

'Why is there so much time taken with entrances and not any given to exits? I have noticed that the actor, when he must leave the stage, seems in a muddle that near ruins the lines he has just said.'

I smiled for I too had wondered why that was so. It was Ben Shakeshaft's job as a plotter, I told her, to make sense of the exits and our places upon the stage.

'The entrance, Master Cuthbert told me, speaks of the play to come and is the key to the role the actor is about to perform.'

Again she took up her quill and made a note.

'Then Master Shakeshaft cannot plot,' she said.

I laughed, and curious to see her surrounded by so much paper and ink, asked, 'Is this your writing?'

'It is no one else's and it is of no consequence . . .' She stopped.

There was the sound of a door banging in some distant place in the house.

She waited awhile and hearing no other sound to accompany it she said, 'I have brought you here because I want to read you something that I have written. All I ask is that you tell me honestly what you think of it. If you feel it to be weak you must say so – I will not tolerate a lie.'

Her voice was beautiful and being read to by her was a delight, even in this bizarre situation. It was a play, a thing a thousand times better than Ben Shakeshaft's writing or any nonsense he had cobbled together.

'It speaks with a truth that few playwrights possess. Your words would only enhance an actor's skill, and I bow to your exceptional talent, my lady.'

'You are flattering me with false words.'

'No, my lady, far from it.'

For a while she was silent.

'My husband believes a woman can never own the cleverness or the wit of a man. Her mind is by its very nature inferior and subject to the ill-humour of her womb.'

Forgetting my role that evening, I said, 'Then he knows you not, my lady, and understands women even less.'

The mask kept her features still but her voice had a laugh in it. 'You know the art of dalliance,' she said. 'I ask you again: in all truth do you mean what you say?'

'Most sincerely, it is remarkable writing.'

She dipped a quill in ink and wrote on the manuscript.

'I wanted you here tonight to listen, to tell me the truth of my verse. If I had given it to your Master Shakeshaft, he would have claimed it as his own and would be fool enough to change the text. My husband would not consider my writings to be anything other than madness. I want you to put your name to my play.'

Before I could protest, we heard a voice that had in it an urgency, and for the second time that night I saw her motionless.

'Take it,' she said quickly. 'Do not let my husband see it.'

I slipped the manuscript under my petticoat as the door to the chamber was unlocked and in burst an explosion of rage.

'Why, my lady, do you lock your door?'

Her husband was twice her age and half her height, no taller than a child. By any stretch of the imagination, he was a ridiculous match for such a woman. And he was a seething cauldron.

'Checkmate,' said my lady of the night.

Finding us demurely playing chess, her husband was taken aback. 'My lady,' he said. 'Will you not introduce me to your companion?'

'This is Mistress . . . Sorrel,' said the lady. 'Mistress Sorrel – my husband.'

I stood and curtsied.

He glared at me and asked where I lived. I said Blackfriars and named a street that in my wanderings had struck me as presentable.

'With my mother, sir, she is a widow.'

I knew I was able to convince an audience that I was a woman and could only hope that in such close proximity I could convince this gentleman.

'How did you learn to play chess?'

'My father, sir,' I said. 'When I was but a child.'

He reached up and took my face in his cold, damp hand. His grip was powerful.

I pulled away, the innocent maiden from respectable Blackfriars, shocked to be treated in such a manner.

'Sir,' I said, 'I was employed to keep your lady company. If I have displeased you then I am most sorry.'

And more than aware of the manuscript, I lifted my skirts and made to leave.

'Wait,' he ordered. 'Did you keep age from midnight's door?'

'I hope so, sir. I was unaware of its entrance.'

'Good.' He called for the Frenchman. 'Escort Mistress . . . ah . . . Sorrel to her home,' he said.

I curtsied, regretting that my lady had told him my surname. Taking small steps, the manuscript gripped between my clenched knees, I left.

Gally was waiting for me when I was returned to my lodgings. My fox trotted in after me from what appeared to be a good night's hunting. Gally was so pleased to see me unharmed that she threw her arms about me.

'Leave me be,' I said, 'you smell of the Badger.'

'What did she want with you, this mysterious lady? Did you bed her?'

'Tomorrow, Gally. I will tell you all tomorrow. Would you unlace me?'

Before I fell asleep, I looked at the manuscript. Beneath the title, *My Lady's Revenge*, she had written the words, *A Tragedy by Master Beau Sorrel*.

LVII

Gally was the first person, after me, to read the play.

'*There lies a foul and grim thing,*' she quoted. '*And this is who I have wed. A man twice my age and who cannot satisfy me in bed.* Oh, I can see myself saying that line. *Unmask yourself, no longer such beauty should be shrouded.* God's teeth, but this is dramatic. It will have the audience on their toes looking at our play and not at the bottom of their tankards. Did you write it?'

'No,' I said.

Gally stood up and stretched. 'I do not want to know who the playwright is. But your name is on the manuscript and that will suffice.'

'What do you think Ben Shakeshaft will make of it?'

'It is not his usual dross so he will hate it.' Gally looked down the cast list. 'What part would you take?'

'Her twin brother,' I said. 'In a Spanish beard, I thought.'

'Oh, this is good – mistaken identities, blighted lovers, an ancient husband – all the ingredients for an outrageous success if acted well.'

She laughed. 'Her husband is the cuckold. Does it end badly?'

'Yes.'

'No!' said Master Shakeshaft. 'No, no, no, I will not put on another tragedy. We must make people laugh. Surely we can bring in some farce? You will have to rewrite it, Master Sorrel. As it stands, it is too much in the favour of the woman. Her husband appears a dribbling idiot.'

'Take it as it is, or do not take it at all,' I said.

'Give it to me, I will work on it.'

'No.'

'Remember, I am your master.'

'It will not be performed,' I said, 'unless every word of it is spoken as it is written.'

Master Cuthbert was reading the manuscript.

'This is fresh, original, Ben,' he said. 'I could bring something to the dribbling idiot of a husband.'

'It would be better – much better – if the husband were not such a fool.' Master Shakeshaft thought for a moment then said, 'All right. But if it is not liked, it will not be performed again. And, Master Sorrel, do not think I am going to pay you more for it.'

I had not seen my lady of the night again nor her Frenchman. His words of warning still rang in my ears. I thought often of that strange evening and through my lady's writing began to understand the frustration of wasted women defeated by foolish husbands.

After a while, I gave up any expectation of being invited to visit my lady. Rehearsals had started, and, to Master Shakeshaft's surprise, were going better than he had expected. My part being long, I spent my time learning my lines and found it easier while walking. I was on my way to the Mermaid Inn to listen to the gossip of the day and to discuss our play, for next week the ban was to be lifted and the voice of the actor would be heard again on the London stage. I had just crossed the bridge and was imagining the taste of the ale when I was accosted by the Frenchman.

'My mistress desires to see you, monsieur.'

To be honest, I was not sure it was wise for I had by then heard a rumour that I suspected had to do with my lady of the night. Her husband was a merchant who imported cloth and silks. He married a woman who, in her time, was considered the most beautiful and clever woman in London. He was a jealous man and became furious at the attention she received at court – especially from the young Earl of Seaton. To make sure no other man would be tempted by her beauty he killed her lover in a duel and disfigured his wife. She was never seen at court again, with or without her mask.

I wavered only for a moment and asked, 'Shall I change?'

'There is no need. The master is in Scotland. It takes a long time to reach Scotland and a longer time to return.'

I had not agreed to go with him, but I had not said no. I thought to myself that I was becoming a lot more familiar with tight corners than I wished to be.

This time the Frenchman did not speak a word as the barge made its way down the river, and I admitted to feeling a frisson of excitement at the thought of seeing her again. I was taken straight to her chamber. It was as it had been before except the connecting doors which had been closed were now open to reveal a large, four-poster bed. The room burned with so many candles reflected in bowls of water that they glimmered like stars on the ceiling. On the table, supper had been laid. Famished, I nibbled on a piece of chicken and waited.

I was examining the globe that she had on her table when I realised there was someone in the room. I turned and was discomposed by her appearance. She was naked apart from a pretty ruff round her neck and the wire cage of her skirt frame. Her skin was white, her breasts petite, her nipples dark. She was strikingly more lovely without those stiff garments that do nothing to enhance a woman's figure. On her feet she wore cork chopines which had the effect of making her look as if she was not quite connected to the floor, more that she hovered above it.

'My body holds the last remnants of my beauty,' she said, 'and I thought you should see it for my face ruins the picture. How go the rehearsals?'

'They go well, my lady. And they are amusing.'

'Amusing? It is a tragedy.'

I smiled. 'Precisely – and it has shocked Master Shakeshaft.'

'Then it will be a success?'

'Yes, my lady.'

'My husband permits Mistress Sorrel to be my nightly companion. It is an indulgence. He thinks it another sign of my lunacy. I do not care. I have wanted you since I first saw you on stage. Your beauty is unnatural – a charm, I would say.' She came nearer and touched my face. 'Smooth, without a mark. Is the rest of you made that way?'

'Apart from a star on my thigh.'

'I knew it. You are an elfin creature.'

'I am at a disadvantage, my lady.'

'How so?'

'You are naked in both thought and body and wear the gown of your birth with much elegance.'

'I thank you, Master Sorrel. I want you to make love to me. Does my forwardness offend you?'

'The reverse, my lady.'

I began to undress. She watched me until I stood before her, well risen for the occasion. Only then did she take off her mask. Her face was disfigured by a knife that had cut her from the corner of her mouth up her cheek and in a curve over her eye.

'My husband took not only my money but my beauty. Do you find me repulsive?'

'You are beautiful still,' I said.

She turned her face away. 'Then you, like all other young men, are careless with the truth and speak out of fear, not desire.'

I turned her face to mine.

'I have a beloved sister,' I said, 'who is disfigured by the pox. So much so that a suitor sent her portrait back without even the courtesy of a letter. But she, like you, has beauty. It comes from within her. Such radiance of mind and body can never be hidden; it is a light that will shine a lifetime and age will fail to dim it.'

I untied the ribbon that held the cage in place round her hips and removed her ruff. I picked her up in my arms and carried her to her bed.

In the day I rehearsed the play and at night I made love to the playwright.

Ben Shakeshaft, certain that the play would run for fewer than two performances, rented the Tabard Inn in Southwark where the performance area was small. He was a poor judge of plays and a poor judge of people. *My Lady's Revenge* ran for three weeks and each afternoon the inn was crowded. The audience in the galleries hung over the railings to hear every word and Gally's final speech before she sank the dagger into her breast was greeted with screams of horror followed by rapturous applause.

I had hoped that my lady and I might say a sweet farewell but it was not to be. On the night we opened I learned that her husband had returned. My last glimpse of her was when she came to watch the play accompanied, I learned, by Master and

Mistress Cassell, whose bored daughter had the face of a pug dog.

Ben Shakeshaft made a great fuss of the Cassells for, as he told me, they were friends of Sir Percival Hayes and had much enjoyed the play.

'And what of their companion, the lady in the mask – do you know if it found favour with her?'

'No,' said Master Shakeshaft, 'but she wants to meet you.'

I ran out into the courtyard in the hope that I might find her alone. But I saw only the Cassells, and Master Cassell was greeting my lady's husband.

Turning, I hid tight behind a pillar lest the merchant should make a sum of Sorrels and find in the answer there were two.

'You missed a good play, sir,' said Master Cassell.

Then I saw her, her motionless mask.

'There you are, my lady,' said her husband. He took off his glove, his fingers claws that sank into her wrist.

She flinched.

'I do not like the theatre, Master Cassell,' said the merchant. 'I have no stomach for the play.'

Much later I heard my lady and her husband had moved abroad to Paris. I knew she had loved me and I wished I had loved her, but I could not. Passion is blighted when it is not equally shared. And for all the skills of my trade, she knew the truth.

The last thing she had said to me was, 'Men long to mount women, women long for children, and all a child wants is a dog.'

THE SORCERESS

LVIII

'I will tell, kind heart, strange tales of man's cruel acts,' the oakman had whispered as the sorceress returned from but a day's absence. 'Come close, and let the wind rustle through my young green leaves the news from my roots, all knowledge known and yet unknown.'

She had rested her head against its great trunk, put her hands into the cracks of its bark. She knew before the wind whistled with words what it had to tell her.

'Your cubs are dead. Your lover slaughtered, killed by a crossbow's quarrel. Listen, can you hear the distant horn? The barking of the hounds?'

It cannot be, it cannot be. Her sweet cubs, her lover, his pelt so soft, who held her tight against the winter storm.

There is a truth to love that has no tie, no gods to deny the rhythm of the earth, the filling of the womb, no conscience to corrupt the seed. Only the season's call and the urgency of sex stripped of guilt. Both were free and played for more until life wriggled inside her vixen womb. Three born, blue eyes all, tongues so sweet that suckled her, their scent the perfume of the gods.

Who killed my cubs? Who killed my lover?

The great oakman shivered and with its many green-leafed tongues it spoke: Francis Thursby, Earl of Rodermere.

And such was her fury that the earth groaned. She ran to claim her lover's body and those of her cubs that she might bury them beneath the hawthorn tree. Their deaths would make the thorns sharper still.

I would pull down this House of the Three Turrets. I would shake it until its wooden teeth rattled, pile the oak beams high upon my back and carry them as if they weighed no more than feathers. I would build a bonfire and tie Lord Rodermere to a stake and light the pyre with a flame from the sun. When all had been consumed by fire, there would be a mark upon the earth that only generations of Rodermeres' salt tears would wash away. I would swallow this house, swallow it whole. I would suck in every nail, every bit of wattle and daub deep down into my stomach, digest it contentedly in sleep but for the curse. My curse. A boy will be born to you whose beauty will be your death. Young lord, where are you, you who were born to be my instrument? Where is my lover, where does his body rest?

'Thrown was he to the hounds, his brush lies trampled beneath the hooves of horses.'

Where are the bodies of my cubs, that I may take them to the hawthorn tree?

'One lost. Two thrown into a basket, their little necks broken.'

She heard the servants, listened carefully to all they said. They talked of nothing but Lord Beaumont's humiliation at his father's hand, of his beauty smeared with her lover's blood. Was this not cause enough? What more did Lord Beaumont need to exact his revenge, kill his father, free them both? Where then was he?

The servants said London; he would be well on his way. You can lose yourself in a city that size, they said. Or he has gone to find his sister, his mother and Master Goodwin before his lordship's assassins do. On one thing they all agreed: where the young lord was no one knew. She trembled with rage, not an ounce of compassion in it.

In the banqueting hall, before a feast of slaughtered animals, sat Lord Rodermere. Alive, far too alive. She will find his son and with all the means she possesses she will bring him back here to finish what she foretold in letters of gold.

In the green mantle of summer she lost her grief and relished the splendour of her perfect gown. She waited for the sun to begin the fall from its throne, waited for the wind to knock the apple heads together on the tree – the summer's adieu and the winter's forewarning. Only then to London does she go.

When the earth is covered in limestone and flint, when cart and boot make a midden of my soil, when nature is flattened by the weight of brick and timber from which no life springs, when all the comfort man has are lies and deceit and the only god he worships is to be found imprisoned in churches then man is truly lost in the hurly-burly insanity of the cities.

I remember a time when this river had no name, before they called it Temese, when it ran blue and crocodiles bathed on its banks. Here in its beds of fertile silt were planted not the seeds of a forest but the foundations of the city. In its walls once walked the griffin and the unicorn, now banished and turned to stone.

This is not my domain. This is land stolen from me. Here I am lost among the narrow lanes, its streets that stink of death and shit, of illness and of plague.

And where in all this whirling need and greed will I find him, my beauty, my Beau, my arrow of destruction?

LIX

At last goes she to the house of Thomas Finglas, a place she had no wish to revisit. She hardly recognises the building for it appears to have pulled itself up straight as if at last it remembered the reason for being there. A sign, newly painted, swings in the breeze. It reads, *Master John Butter, Alchemist*. In such a short passing of days all has changed. She studies the house well before she enters. She would have imagined that John Butter had married the serving girl, Mary. She remembered her as being presentable. She expects to hear the cry of an infant, the noise of a family, but the house is childless in its sounds.

One thing has not altered: the ever present ghost of Mistress Finglas, a poisonous odour hovering in the air, waiting to find another jealous soul for her green snake to take possession of. It has wrapped itself tight round Mary's heart.

The sorceress does not understand jealousy or perhaps she considers her jealousy to belong to a higher realm than that of this simple serving girl. She finds her in the bedchamber of Thomas Finglas. The place is wrapped in darkness and at first she sees her as a shadow. As for Thomas, he is but an outline. Mary sits next to him, feeding him soup from a bowl. He is not well but what ails him apart from the scarred face the sorceress cannot tell.

'Has Master Butter finished for the day?' Thomas asks.

'Nearly, master.'

'Good. Then he will be up soon.'

'There is one person on his list he has yet to see.'

'Who is that?'

Mary bites her lip. Yes, who, Mary?

'I do not know, master. It is a lady.'

The sorceress listens to her thoughts. Mary is not lying. She does not know the name of this lady. She prays it is not Lady Clare returned. For Mary had been in the cellar, the place where once they had kept the creature, and through the floorboards she had heard John Butter speak words of love, heard him kiss Lady Clare and more besides. When last she had come, he had bolted the laboratory door and Mary, with her eye to the crack, saw his arse rise and fall, rise and fall, and the lady's white limbs, all undone, twisted round his. And the little green snake bit Mary hard.

The sorceress sees Mary's secret. It worries at the serving maid, she fears that John Butter will learn of her treachery. Then what will she say? And how will she excuse what she has done?

She had paid for a letter to be written in words more elegant than ever she could summon in which she informed Master Gilbert Goodwin and his good wife exactly what kind of balm John Butter used to cure Lady Clare's condition and where on her body he used it. It had taken her time and coin to find the address and when she had, she paid again to make sure of the letter's safe delivery.

It is some months now since the letter was sent and it was said that the family had gone abroad. As Mary feeds her master, spoon by spoon, she is anxious that Lady Clare will return and then how would Mary explain the letter?

It was in his best interest, she says to herself. Yes, it was, and John Butter should be grateful.

The sorceress has heard enough. She is bored with Mary's common thoughts. Perhaps Thomas can shed more light on what has been happening here. She listens.

How long before the ferry man comes? How long before I see my Bess?

Nothing.

She is about to leave when she spies that the door to the laboratory is open a crack, enough for her to see John Butter seated in front of the fire, staring at the flames. She wonders at how master and servant have exchanged places.

She catches a thought of his. It comes back to him from the watery realm of daydreams when sleep has yet to catch him in its net of hours. His eyes are shut and she glimpses a silver fish of something near forgotten swimming through the sleepy seaweed of his mind. He is half dreaming about a midsummer's afternoon at the House of the Three Turrets when he was but a boy of twelve summers, and first he saw Lady Clare Thursby.

Tell me more, John, I am listening. Tell me, tell me more.

LX

John Butter is in a tree.

His master, Thomas Finglas, hoping for an afternoon of unbridled pleasure with the nursemaid Bess, has sent his new apprentice to find a four-leaf clover – a fool's errand, and John knows it to be so. He has taken delight in being free to play, to climb. From the tree he sees a little girl dressed in such a manner that she looks like a miniature lady. She must have been told by her nurse not to run for she is fighting an instinct that makes running essential.

'Beau,' she calls as she runs, 'Beau, Beau, come home. Please, Beau – where are you?'

She looks up and sees John Butter in the tree and, showing no fear of strangers, says, 'Please, would you help me find my brother? He is only two and he is missing. Our mother's heart will break if he does not come home.'

John jumps down, lands before her and kneeling looks directly at her. She stares back, her gaze defiant, waiting for him to turn away. Instead he touches her face.

'These are the honourable scars of a warrior,' he says. 'You have fought bravely, my lady, against an infallible enemy. It has left its mark but it has not touched your spirit.'

Many years later, when they have become lovers, Lady Clare confesses that she had thought him to be an elfin prince, for she had never seen anyone with skin so glorious and eyes so dark as his. Now John is thinking of Lady Clare full grown and the thought of her makes him ache.

No, John, no. I will not let sleep drown out all. I am a catcher of dreams. Come then, John Butter, let the past slide over the present, banish all notion of the future. Tell me what happened that day.

Little Lady Clare places her white hand in his. He remembers her utter faith in him.

'You will find him,' she says, 'I know you will.'

It does not occur to John as they walk deep into the woods that he has been cast in the role of a faerie prince.

'We must ask the forest to give back your brother,' he says.

'Will the trees listen?'

He does not answer because in a clearing between two oak trees stands the little lordling.

Lady Clare pulls her hand away from John's and starts to run towards her brother. John stops her for he understands exactly the danger the child is in. They must coax the boy back through the watery veil that separates the world of elfin from the world of man. If he does not come of his own accord he will be lost for ever. But the little boy vanishes in front of them and John Butter fears it is already too late.

'Where has he gone?' cries Lady Clare.

John tells her she must ask the trees to let him go then say his name again.

He remembers this, this moment, remembers Lady Clare pleading with the trees. He remembers the scent of the forest, the heat of the grass, the buzz of the insects. And the sun breaking through, a beam of golden light illuminating the place where Lord Beaumont had stood, indented with the tread of his shoe.

Lady Clare, near tears and terrified, stands straight, closes her eyes and softly calls her brother again.

'Beau – let us go home and play.'

Nothing but the song of a lark. They stand. They wait. How long John cannot say. Her little hand finds his again and the afternoon becomes early evening. Still they wait and all ties to the world are lost.

They hear his laughter before they see him. He comes running towards his sister, arms outstretched. She does not move but quietly calls him on. When he is near enough John catches hold of him. He wriggles to free himself and, realising he cannot, cries out, turns his head, pointing at the two oak trees as if he could see friends there.

A sudden wind roars in at them on a sea of leaves.

John, holding tight to Beau, takes Lady Clare's hand and they run until she can run no more. He carries them both, still feeling the wind to be chasing them. Only when they are out of the forest does John put Lady Clare down. Her brother is fast asleep on John's shoulder, his thumb in his mouth, and there in his fist is a piece of fabric the like of which John has never seen before.

It is the children's nurse Bess, frantic with worry and guilt, who runs to meet them; Bess who sees what Lord Beaumont holds in his small hand. Bess who gently takes it from him and gives it to her lover, the alchemist.

The sorceress has heard all she needs to hear.

Outside in the narrow lane she pauses and in the rush of people, she smells her own kin. There is a fox who walks beside his mistress. This sight stops her as it does many. His coat is lush, his eyes blue, and she is certain he is hers. The young fox smells her out, his hackles rise, his teeth bare. His mistress, her face hidden in the hood of a cloak stops and asks of the fox, what is it, who is there? And looks quickly about her. The door of Thomas Finglas's house opens and fox and mistress disappear inside, out of October's golden light.

She could laugh the leaves off the trees. This is why she has not found Beau Thursby. She has been looking for him in breeches when all along he has been hiding in petticoats.

LXI

Some say actors are the invention of the Devil, others that they are an offering to idolatry, responsible for the blossoming of vanity, the route of all iniquity. They say that the player is a master of vice, the teacher of wantonness – and in that the sorceress has much time for him. At least there appears some honesty in the glass he holds up for the reflection of his audience, a chance to see a truth so often lost in man's day-to-day manoeuvring. And among the minstrels and vagabonds is where she finds her actor, her beauty. A strolling player who takes the female role and so dressed in borrowed threads he has come here today to improvise his own drama.

She is intrigued. He looks the part but can he act it? She will take her seat in the same small cellar where Randa was held prisoner. The place has been cleaned and is empty apart from a bed and some bunches of herbs hanging from the beams. Here she will listen to the play unfold and in it she may yet discover a way of bringing Lord Beaumont to perform the part for which he was born. Alas, the applause he will not live to hear for it will be at his hanging.

She cares not whether he chooses to dress in women's robes or like a man go forth, dagger in hand, but in one act he will perform her curse and not even his quicksilver tongue can alter the role she has in mind for him. She listens and not a word is spilt that she does not hear, not an action taken that she does not know where on the stage it is performed. Yet still she cannot fathom Beau Thursby's thoughts; they are as before all blank. She blames this fault on her handmaiden who gave birth to him. The handmaiden, knowing of the sorceress's design, refused to have a puppet of her offspring made. But even had she bestowed on him the gift that the sorceress might not be privy to the machinations that whirl in his head, what of it? Unless by chance he can hear her and know what it is she thinks. That would be the cruellest of all blows.

So here then be two players: John Butter, heavy of heart, Beau Thursby in the disguise of a fair – nay, a beautiful mistress. The sorceress waits to hear their lines. Will his voice be low and deep and in it lie the truth of his sex? Beau speaks. Far from it. It is melodic and does in no way vex the ear.

'I am told, Master Butter,' says he, 'that you have healing hands. And the gift of talking to the faeries.'

Neither does his voice make one doubt the sex of the character he is playing.

'And that you alone in all of London know how to make gold from lead.'

'You flatter me greatly, mistress, but such trickery I leave to cozeners.'

John is wondering what this mysterious and pretty young woman has come for. A potion for the prevention of the plague? Possibly. The prevention of pregnancy? Very likely. A complaint of the flesh? It is hard to tell if her pallor be caused by nature or by an artful paintbox. This kind of work pays for the care of Thomas Finglas, and for Mary with her doleful eyes that follow him dog-like, wherever he goes. The income it provides he calls his steak and ale money.

John Butter asks how he can be of service and offers the lady a chair.

She declines to sit. The reason she is here, she says, is that she believes it is because of him, John Butter, that her mother and stepfather have taken her sister abroad and now she has no idea where they are.

John has misjudged the situation. This is another of Lord Rodermere's spies, come to seek out Master Goodwin and his family, to find where Lord Beaumount has vanished to. She is not the first – though perhaps the first woman.

'Wh-who is your sister?' John Butter asks. His voice has the echo of a distant stutter to it.

With the perfect timing that all actors need if they wish to command the stage, she replies: 'Lady Clare Thursby.'

The sorceress can feel John's relief. Lady Clare has no living sisters. These words are almost on his lips when he studies the young lady afresh and recalls where he has seen her before.

'You are an actor – I saw you at the Mitre last week performing *The Cuckold's Wife*.'

'Then if Lady Clare is my sister, who am I?'

John says the words as if he does not trust them to hold weight: Lord Beaumont Thursby.

'The disguise reveals the man,' says Lord Beaumont and hands something to John, demands he read it, asks what is missing from it. The beginning and the end, he says, only Master Butter knows.

In all dramas there comes a moment of revelation.

'Twice before I have called here. And twice I was told by a serving maid that if I was another of Lord Rodermere's men, then I should go to the Devil. I stayed away, now I can no longer. I ask you again – what happened between you and my sister?'

John starts to speak. His words fall over themselves, turn somersaults. Beau stops him and John becomes aware that the fox has his eyes fixed to the floorboards.

218

'Not here,' says Beau, his voice now his own. 'We are over-heard. The Three Feathers Inn at Bankside, in one hour.'

Does Beau know she is listening? Then she hears it, a creak on the stairs as Mary runs back to Thomas Finglas's chamber.

LXII

John Butter. Oh, John Butter.

Love seemed so easy, so pure when first you fell in love with Lady Clare and she with you. In its purity of lust a rose might blush for she was born with equal passion and felt she would never find a heart to house it. In you she discovered a palace where she might reign and her scars be celebrated as if they were a thousand stars upon her face. And though she told you she believed, as a child, that you were an elfin prince, she did not say – maidenly modesty forbade her saying – that in your sweet prick, honeyed with her juices, lies her kingdom.

All should have been well, a celebration of love in all its manifestations. Why is it not? This is an age when a vagabond can become a lord, an apprentice can become an alchemist. What frightened Gilbert Goodwin, the sorceress fancies, was the unwanted attention such a match would bring.

Can you hear me, Beau? I am beginning to suspect that you can. Then listen: your family is in danger and Gilbert Goodwin is right to worry. Your father has sworn to have them murdered.

If he has heard her, he shows no sign though she no longer believes that he is the empty vessel his looks suggest. In truth, she has stubbed a toe on her envy of his youth. His beauty is fresh, unpreserved, undeniable, whereas hers now craves the comfort of candlelight. These days she holds the shadows closer to her and the glass further away. Her sap rises slowly, her blood treacle black. He is her creation – why then should she be jealous? The cure for such distemper is simple: the sooner the deed is done and the grave marked out, the happier she will be.

She follows Beau and the fox down twisted lanes of bent, beamed houses to his lodging, a ramshackle place that smells of mice and is in such disarray even the fleas have fled.

How far you have tumbled, sweet lord. This life of squalor should not be yours. You should have stayed at the House of the Three Turrets rather than dwell in this midden. Where is your rage at the injustice of what your father has inflicted on your family? Where is your sword that should be itching to pierce his heart? Come fight, Beau – or be you a coward? You are either a very good actor, Beau, or you do not know I am here.

It takes him time to transform himself into the sex he was born with. So much is artificial in making women's shapes unnatural, as if they are divorced by design from their bodies. The white paint sticks glue-like to his face and without it he is more beautiful still. He does not love the mirror. If he was a woman, he would relish his image, fill his chambers with mirrors to reflect his perfection. Is it what others see that he cannot abide?

Leave this place behind. Fly away home, Beau. Do the deed for which you were born and free us both.

Nothing. She leaves Beau to change, content that he cannot hear her and is unaware of her presence.

She is glad that Randa left this place for if the creature had stayed she would have been seen as nothing more than a beast than the bear who is tied to a post in the amphitheatre while the dogs tear him to pieces. Entertainment fit for a queen or a king.

The sorceress thinks of Herkain, the King of the Beasts, and the memory makes her feel almost mortal and such feelings repulse her, sticky with longing, sour with bitter regret. Such an ancient story, she thinks, the bones of it well gnawed by many.

But that is all I have left – the cadaver of our love.

She was his queen in all but name. His wife, wounded by his infidelities, had long retired with her sickly offspring and it pleased the sorceress greatly that he had no affection for his heirs.

She told him when she found her gait had slowed with the weight of his fruits, and he would have nothing of her until the harvest came. But when it did, and she was once more herself, she found he had taken another mistress and it was for her that he held a banquet. The sorceress would not lightly suffer the humiliation of seeing him fawn over his new love. She went to the great hall and had the fruit of her womb served to Herkain on a golden platter, surrounded by apples, and there it lay howling at him. No Prince of the Beasts was it, but a mewling, puking creature in mortal form. There was an excited silence for the smell of such a dainty morsel drove the company to salivate. A rare feast indeed.

'Eat and enjoy,' she said. 'Months I spent preparing it, I laboured hard to bring it to you. This is all that is left of us. Its flesh.'

He picked up the thing and it ceased its crying. He lifted it to his mouth and she waited to hear his sharp fangs crunch on its soft bones. But he kissed its head.

'She will be called Aurelia,' he said.

She stared at him.

'That dish,' she said, 'is not worth a name.'

Heartless, he called her.

'Yes,' she said. 'You took it from me.'

Herkain banished the sorceress from his home, from his kingdom and sent her back to her realm.

Only cat and man torment their prey. At least in the Land of the Beast there is honesty in the kill, an understanding between the hunter and the hunted. Herkain was glorious, fast and clean, his talons as sharp as knives. Death was not negotiable as it is with sword and arrow. He left me with time without end to remember. My longing for him will not be darkened by the years.

The Three Feathers Inn is crowded with customers who have left the bear pit with a hearty thirst on them. Musicians play and the din of ill-advised chords scratch at the sorceress's ears. The losers are sinking their woes in ale while the winners with tankards of frothy beer drink to the health of the bear.

John Butter has secured a quiet corner. He is wondering what he will say to Lord Beaumont Thursby. He is wondering if he might have to fight a duel.

A scuffle breaks out, a sword is drawn.

'Outside with you,' shouts the landlord. He does not want blood on his straw.

Beau enters and the losers and the winners, even the old drunks, look up.

He is every part a gentleman. No one would take him for an actor. He knows how to walk across the room, knows he is the object of everyone's gaze and at the same time he ignores this attention completely.

John Butter is disturbed by the young gentleman standing before him for there appears not a trace of the lady he had seen but an hour ago. He asks after Lord Beaumont's fox.

'He goes his own way when I wear these clothes,' says Beau.

John notices the poverty, the threadbare doublet. These

mundane details do not seem to concern Beau. It is the letter he is interested in and the events that led to it.

Master John Butter is a private man, not given to revealing his emotions. But the sorceress can see he is fearful that Beau will accuse him, just as she suspects Gilbert Goodwin did, of taking advantage of a young girl's heart. But Beau puts him at his ease.

It was Lady Clare's mother, Mistress Goodwin, John tells him, who wrote to Thomas Finglas asking if he had a remedy for blemished skin. Thomas had replied that he was too ill to be of service but was sure that Master Butter would be able to concoct a remedy to treat Lady Clare's condition.

John talks around the point. The point is simple and the man is a fool to be ashamed. He and Lady Clare became lovers and someone wrote anonymously to inform Master Goodwin.

'After that I never saw her again. I made enquiries and learned the family had gone abroad – possibly to Amsterdam.'

The two men sit for a while and by degrees the conversation moves to other matters.

'I heard the play was cancelled,' says John.

Beau laughs. 'Master Shakeshaft is in prison again and we have no work until Christmastide when we are to perform for Sir Percival Hayes.'

John fears for Beau's safety. 'Is that wise?' he says.

And the sorceress thinks, very wise, for Beau will be near to his father's house.

'I am apprenticed, I have no say in the matter,' he says. 'I am caught between the Devil and . . . the Devil.'

John takes out a purse of coins. 'Here,' he says.

'No,' says Beau.

'Please, for Clare's sake.'

'You are a good man,' says Beau. 'Do you know who wrote the letter?'

John shakes his head.

It should be obvious to him who the culprit is and the sorcer-ess says the name to herself. She is pulled up short.

'Mary,' says Beau.

And before they say another word, the sorceress is gone.

THE BEAUTY

LXIII

So few of us are born to be ourselves; we are but the dreams of lovers, of mothers and fathers who long for us to step where their feet never dared. I was born to fulfil a curse, my fate decided, and my will is all that I have.

As a child I thought I belonged to you, sorceress, and took a keepsake from your petticoat, a piece of your hem. I knew you were there in the house of Thomas Finglas. I heard you nuzzling your way into Master Butter's private thoughts. I knew why you had searched me out. But my will is strong and I am prepared to do battle with you, you who have the infinity of time on your side, I who have but a human heart on mine.

That day in the Three Feathers Inn with John Butter I understood my impotence, that there was no remedy to be taken, no rational argument to be had with you. Your curse went deeper than the roots of the oak tree you wrote it on.

Ignorant steps had led me to being apprenticed to Ben Shakeshaft; naivety had convinced me that I could be an actor; stupidity had kept me waiting for my master's release from prison. In short, I was but a green rabbit who had been prettily snared and hung, ready to be stewed. I threw myself into what little acting work there was to be had, told myself I was my own man, my own master and believed not one word of it. And still I heard the echo of your words: *Do the deed for which you were born and free us both.*

That Christmas Eve found Master Shakeshaft, Master Cuthbert and I half frozen and fully lost on the queen's highway. Our wagon containing clothes, scenery and props was pulled by a horse that was more suited for glue than the road.

'Where are we?' said Master Cuthbert.

It was a good question with a bad answer.

We had been expected at Sir Percival Hayes's house that afternoon. By four o'clock darkness had already snuffed out all the light the day had to offer and forgotten to hang even a star or a moon for us to see by.

Sir Percival Hayes had commissioned Master Shakeshaft to write three new plays to be performed in his banqueting hall in front of his distinguished guests. He had told Ben Shakeshaft, after he had been released from debtors' prison for the second time, that if he let him down again he would disband the company and make a pig's purse from Master Shakeshaft's arse.

I earnestly wished it had been any other knight or lady than Sir Percival, a gentleman who knew me well and was bound, I thought, to recognise me. The only person in the company who knew my identity was Gally and she assured me that if I kept my head down and appeared only for the performance all would be well.

As the weeks of rehearsal passed I had convinced myself that she was right. With white paint, wig and the trappings that made up a woman, I had nothing to fear except a rumbling stomach. Never had I been so hungry as I was in those lean days leading to our departure. The notion of a warm bed and food a-plenty began to sway all other worries. Hunger does not a rational man make. If I was honest with myself, it was not Sir Percival I most feared but that I would be confronted by my father.

For once Master Shakeshaft had dug deep into his pockets. Money had been spent liberally on new costumes, on the building and painting of scenery, the making of masks and props. All were designed to fit into a caravan that they might be transported to and assembled in Sir Percival's banqueting hall.

But nothing Ben Shakeshaft did was with a generous heart. If a penny could be saved, if something could be bought cheap, got for less, found for nothing, then he would wheel and deal until he had a bargain. Having paid out handsomely on everything else he had scrimped on the horse and the caravan and before we had reached the city walls it was obvious that there was something wrong with the rear wheel of the wagon.

''Tis nothing,' said Master Shakeshaft. 'The road, that is all.'

By midday we were well behind the rest of the troupe who were in the carriage Sir Percival had sent for them. My fox became impatient and, smelling the wild woods, disappeared.

The only comfort was that I knew the way, though I was not foolish enough to say so. The House of the Three Turrets was not far from Sir Percival's house. And somewhere between knowing the route well and not wishing the knowledge to be known, sometime between daylight and darkness, we became lost. The horse refused to go further and we had ended in a solitary thicket. It occurred to me that the sorceress, the Mistress of Misrule, had followed us to make a mockery of our journey and I began to dread that we were in a trap of her making. I listened for her but only heard the dense silence.

'At least,' said Ben Shakeshaft, 'it is not snowing.'

As if on cue the first snowflake fell.

'Mistress Fortune has abandoned us,' said Crumb.

I lit the lantern, climbed down and examined the horse. It had lost a shoe. Inside again I found Crumb and Master Shakeshaft putting on costumes for warmth. Master Shakeshaft wore the ass's head complete with fur ears. I found a cloak and wrapped it about myself.

'There is a way out of this,' said Ben Shakeshaft, ever the optimist. 'By my reckoning we are not far from our destination. Let us leave the caravan here and go on foot to seek help before the snow becomes too deep.'

'Not wise,' Crumb said. 'We should stay here and make a fire.'

'With what?' said Master Shakeshaft. 'Our scenery and props? No, absolutely, no.'

'Mercy on me. We will die here then,' said Crumb. 'All because you, Ben, are a mustulent miser who values scenery over life.'

'Is it my fault we are lost? Who was it, Crumb, who said to take this path at the fork in the road?'

While they argued the snow fell thick around us. Then when everything seemed at its bleakest I heard my fox call. He came through a gap in the thicket beyond which I could dimly make out a shimmering veil. A shiver ran down me. When a child I thought that behind the watery curtain was where I belonged but now I feared that the sorceress intended to lure us there for her own ends.

'No – not that way, Master Shakeshaft,' I said.

But Ben Shakeshaft was not listening. He had climbed down from the caravan. 'Look, surely that is a house beyond that mist. By my troth, what did I tell you?'

'Wait, Ben,' said Crumb. 'It could be a trick of the light. And these forests are known for witches, for evil spirits . . .'

'You are pissing your breeches for nothing, Crumb.'

And before I could say that burning the scenery would be an altogether preferable plan, Master Shakeshaft had pushed into the thick, tangled mass of bushes and sharp, tearing thorns.

'Blood and bollocks,' he said, and continued to curse until he had passed through the veil. 'There is Sir Percival's house. We have arrived.'

Crumb followed. As reluctantly did I. Not far away was indeed a house, a house I knew, but it was not the house of Sir Percival Hayes. I stopped.

'Crumb, we should go no further,' I said.

'Ben,' said Crumb holding tight to my cloak. 'Let us go back.'

'Back?' said Master Shakeshaft. 'What are you? A pair of women? No, do not answer.'

Ben Shakeshaft strode off towards the gates and Crumb and I could only go after him.

There was a stillness about the place, as if time had stopped and I was convinced this was the sorceress's realm, this was her illusion, that she had tricked us to come this way.

Master Shakeshaft was near running towards the great front door when it opened. And it was then that I remembered where I had seen the house before. This was the house I had thought to be my solace, my escape from the voice of my little soul, from murderous thoughts of my father. This was the house in my dreams.

LXIV

Which of us looked the more fantastic that night I could not say; we three in our odd assorted costumes or the majordomo, but I would have wagered the majordomo by a whisker. He wore a mask of a human face, underneath his skin was given to moles with long protruding hairs, his eyes dark as a starless sky. He seemed to be having trouble standing upright, his gait was awkward, his arms long and ended in pristine white gloves that were at odds with his doublet and breeches. It appeared that I alone noticed these things for Master Shakeshaft and Master Cuthbert were so relieved to find shelter that neither were in much mind to question if it was the right place or not.

Our appearance was strange enough to at least warrant an enquiry from the majordomo as to who we were and what our business there might be. The fact that the front door had been opened unquestioningly as if we were expected was enough for Master Shakeshaft to have reached the reassuring conclusion that this was the house of Sir Percival Hayes.

'What did I tell you, Crumb?' said Master Shakeshaft as we were shown into a great hall.

Crumb said nothing.

'You know what you are? You are a panic of a man. Burn

the scenery, my arse, when we were so close to our destination. Ridiculous . . .'

His word faded to speechless awe when he saw the interior of the house. To me it was no revelation – it was exactly how I remembered it from my dreams: built for a different scale of being.

'Have the other members of my company arrived?' Master Shakeshaft's voice had less assurance to it.

The majordomo did not reply but waved away the words, as irritating to him as horse flies.

There was nothing to do other than follow him. He stopped as we approached two vast doors that reached the ceiling and without the inconvenience of touching them they opened onto what I knew would be a banqueting chamber. A long table was laid with the finest linen and three places had been set. A fire blazed and the burning candles – not tallow but beeswax – gave off a sweet perfume of summer heat, of meadow flowers.

Crumb looked at me. I shrugged. The majordomo made it clear that we were to be seated. Before us was set three large silver domes and from them came a smell so appetising that it made my mouth water.

'Worry heads, the both of you,' said Master Shakeshaft with a sigh of satisfaction. He gestured at the dishes. 'Look, we are expected.'

'But expected by whom? That is the question,' I said.

'By our host,' said Master Shakeshaft, lifting the dome off a platter. 'Never has a rounded breast of silver brought forth such deliciousness.'

It was a meal of many courses, all served by the majordomo, and it finished with the finest cheeses, figs, dried plums and fresh strawberries that tasted as if they had just been picked. So much food and wine on such empty stomachs made bloated fools of us all.

'This knife is gold,' said Master Shakeshaft, 'as, I suspect, is the plate.'

'And this glass,' said Crumb, lifting one of the lightest purple to his lips, 'I would say is Venetian – fit for a queen.'

'Sir Percival Hayes is a very wealthy man.' Master Shakeshaft drained his glass. It was immediately refilled and by the time we were shown to our separate bedchambers neither Crumb nor Master Shakeshaft were in a fit state to enquire of anything except sleep.

I lay in a carved wooden bed with clean sheets that smelled of lavender and dared not close my eyes. I listened and listened harder and wondered if I could hear the sorceress. All was quiet. And against my will I must have fallen into a heavy sleep.

I become aware that here is the same lady that I met before in this house of dreams. She is floating above me at the end of the bed, naked apart from a small ruff of intricate black lace. Her auburn hair is pinned up, tendrils fall tantalisingly to her nipples. I am aroused by the sight of her. She hovers and as I gaze up at her dark bush, she opens her legs and puts her fingers deep inside the softest part of her. From the folds of her cunny she takes a red rose. She holds it out to me. It is dripping blood.

Blood from the depths of my womb makes the rose red. I am not ashamed. I am the beast, the truth, the beauty within.

I enter the centre of the rose, each petal kissing and sucking me deeper into its vortex until I am lost in its fragrant sweetness. I come as if all of me has exploded and know not which parts belong where.

LXV

'I think,' said Master Shakeshaft, 'there has been a terrible mistake.'

We had eaten a feast of a breakfast and Ben Shakeshaft had enquired again after his players. Again there had been no answer but as the majordomo had not said a word in all the time we had been there we should not have been surprised. But this morning Master Shakeshaft was prepared to admit that we were at the wrong house.

The majordomo politely showed us to the front door. Outside in the fragile light of a winter's morn stood the horse and caravan. Both were in better state than they had been the night before – the horse shod and the caravan's wheel mended.

'Well, well,' said Ben Shakeshaft. 'A most gratifying and welcome sight.' It did not occur to him to express gratitude for the hospitality. 'How far is it to Sir Percival Hayes's house?'

The majordomo pointed to where the road beckoned beyond the iron gates which stood open awaiting our departure.

I whistled for my fox. He did not appear though I had no doubt that he would rejoin me once we had left the house of dreams and were back in the mortal realm.

Everything appeared set and for one glorious moment it seemed we would escape this house and no one would be the wiser as to the danger we had been in. Anxious to be gone I mounted the caravan and took the horse's reins, calling for Crumb. He heaved himself up and Master Shakeshaft was about to climb up beside us when he turned to take a last look at the house. And that was when I saw it. Amid the snow-bedecked foliage that covered the entrance to the house was one blood-red rose, so bright in colour that it looked to be a beating heart. The sight of it brought back my dream and with the dream a sense of unease.

'Come,' I said, 'let us be away from here.'

'Wait,' said Master Shakeshaft.

I heard myself say, 'Leave it.' I felt the words vibrate on my lips.

Too late. The deed was done. That idiot man had reached up and picked the rose. He stood smiling as would a clown with little awareness of the consequences of such a foolish act.

'I could not resist it,' he said.

The gates banged shut, the road lost. The horse and the caravan disappeared and both I and Crumb were thrown onto the snowy ground. The sun turned its back on the day and its light went out.

All that followed happened with great speed. From one majordomo three more were conjured. In a tangle of images each whirled past with such rapidity that it was hard to make sense of anything and all of it went against the grain of our understanding.

We were locked in a windowless chamber with one lantern that hung from the ceiling by a hook. Ben Shakeshaft, still holding the rose, was bone-white, his words coming out in stutters as if he had almost lost the power to speak.

It was Crumb who said, 'You knotty-pated fool, Ben, what

have you done? Why could you not leave it be? Why can you never leave anything be?'

'It is a rose. I did not think to offend anyone . . .'

'Do you ever think? A rose in winter? Did it not strike you as strange, that the rose might be valued?'

'No, no, never a rose . . .'

I knew that we would pay a high price for its theft, but I thought better than to say so.

'After all the generosity,' said Master Shakeshaft. 'Why would anyone miss a rose?'

His words ran out and time ticked and dripped and minutes leaked away.

'We will never reach Sir Percival's house,' said Master Shakeshaft.

It was not so much the woe of us but woe of himself that he lamented, his loss and all the wasted money he had spent. His days as a theatre manager were over.

Still more time passed and by degrees his anxiety turned to fury.

'I will tell it to the teeth of that servant when he comes back. He cannot hold us here against our will. It is kidnapping . . .'

'Curb your lip, Ben,' said Crumb, 'or I will curb it for you.'

I do not know how long we waited but at last the door opened and there was the same majordomo who had so unceremoniously thrown us in here.

For all Master Shakeshaft's brave words he became a shaking puddle as the majordomo took hold of him and dragged him bleating from the chamber.

There being no furniture, I sat on the floor and Crumb leaned against the wall, his eyes closed. All sense of possible freedom was lost when at last Master Shakeshaft was returned to us looking much altered, more ghost than human.

'Speak, Ben, or did they take your tongue? Speak,' said Crumb.

'It is not good … not good … at all.' He bit his lip.

'What is it? Come on, spit it out. Before it chokes you and kills us with the suspense.'

'This is the house of the beast, a creature too terrifying to speak of.'

'Did you see it?'

'My eyes blurred at the vision, my sight near failed me. I was aware of the smell of earth and iron, feathers and fur.'

'What is our punishment to be?' asked Crumb.

'We are to be meat for the beast's banquet.'

'You mean we are to be slaughtered?'

'Yes, yes,' shouted the theatre manager. 'Unless . . .'

'Unless what?' I asked.

'Unless.' Master Shakeshaft looked at me. 'Unless you, Master Sorrel, are prepared to stay. But it must be of your own free will, if not we will all be butchered – no better than cattle.' The old fool broke down and wept. 'Just for taking a rose – blood and bollocks – a red rose.'

'Then we are dead,' said Crumb. 'The compensation, I suppose, being that I will not have to pay my rent, or my tailor or the landlord of the Three Feathers. And I will no longer have to work for you.'

'But what will become of me?'

'In the physical sense? Or do you mean the spiritual?'

While they picked the skin off each other to no great effect, I thought of all I had overheard the sorceress say. If this was her house I doubted she would kill me. She had made it abundantly clear that my duty was to murder my father. Perhaps I could negotiate my freedom.

'What will happen if I agree to stay?' I asked.

Master Shakeshaft fell to his knees, clutching my breeches.

'Then we – that is, Crumb and I – will arrive at the house of Sir Percival Hayes, the play will be performed – without you, of course, but do not concern yourself, Gally will play your part – and it will be as if nothing untoward ever befell us. But I cannot bribe or corrupt you into staying.'

The door opened and a look of terror came over Ben Shakeshaft. The majordomo stood waiting.

THE BEAST

LXVI

He stayed. Beau stayed. I feel nothing, care nothing. He stayed. I will sacrifice his frozen body, let it be butchered for the feast. An offering to Herkain, the King of the Beasts, for his plate alone. The flesh of man be the sweetest meat of all.

Herkain, he who knew me as one of his own. I, a malformed creature, who belonged to no man, to no family, to no land, was brought before him. But he called me daughter. He, a king, unfolded my wings and showed me how to stand upright, how to be proud of my form. In his eyes, in the king's eyes, there was beauty in me. He held up for me a different glass and I saw my reflection, saw my strangeness, my magnificence.

This house is his gift to me.

Here I have lived and thought of Beau, of his beauty. And such sadness I feel, for he will never see me as does Herkain. Never see me as the king sees me.

The king comes often. He asks what is this sadness, what sadness is it that keeps me from his court? He looks into my eyes and he sees a splinter, a young man, a mortal. Who is he? he asks.

It can never be, I say, for he is the beauty and I the beast.

Herkain puts his hands to my face and takes away a tear. He drinks it in.

'I know the knot by which mortals tie themselves to time. Long ago I too was tied by its merciless strands.' He says that he knows the truth of love, that it is a stain upon the cloth that memory deepens with a blush.

I tell him the love I have for Beau no vessel can contain. I say the wine spills over. He is mine and not mine. I know him and he knows me not. I do not tell the king about the night Beau spent with the girl-boy, and Beau all hard to prove me weak.

When he is dead I will give his body to the King of the Beasts. I tell myself I care not. I turn away, give my orders and sleep.

THE BEAUTY

LXVII

The horse and caravan slowly made its way out of the gates onto the road beyond. The last I saw of Master Shakeshaft and Crumb was one gloved hand of each as they waved farewell to me, to be instantly forgotten by both and sit no heavier on their conscience than last night's ale.

I whistled again to my faithful fox but still there was no sign of him. A bad omen. The front door closed and freedom vanished. All that was left was the gravestone quiet of a deserted house and I was stilled with foreboding.

The wordless majordomo took me up the stairs and unlocked a door to a large chamber. There was little to recommend it apart from three tall, bare windows and an empty fireplace; not a stick of furniture to grace its size. But what held my eye hung from a meat hook in the centre of the chamber: a long, lush gown embroidered with crimson and gold threads and lined with black fur. It floated there without any reason for it was too high to reach without the help of a ladder.

I was resigned to being locked in but I was not resigned to what happened next. The majordomo pointed at my worn doublet and patched breeches, my hose and my boots. For all my protests he made it clear that they were to be removed.

He stood immovable, determined in his task and did not stop prodding me until I stood naked before him. Only then did he turn to leave, taking my clothes with him.

'Wait,' I demanded. 'I will freeze. A blanket, at least.'

My plea fell on deaf ears. The key turned in the lock and told me that my sentence was death. No man could survive naked in this icy place. If only I could reach the fur-lined mantle. But I could not, it was a tantalising fingertip too high. The exercise at least kept me warm but the sweat dried cold on me.

I said out loud, 'Is this what you want, sorceress? My death? Then it will not be long in coming.'

The gown falls to the floor. I put it on and the sudden warmth spreads across my flesh in such a sensual flood that I remember the dream and the rose. In the dim light I study the fabric: deep red velvet, embroidered with the richness of autumn colours. I do not think I have ever seen such a fabric as this except perhaps once when I was but a child. As I look at it I seem to enter the images, become a part of them. There is a fox, a huntsman, oaks, and a house with three turrets. I wrap the gown round me and curl into its black fur as if I was a dog.

Without the gown I would have died. Sleep was shallow. I walked back and forth trying to keep my feet and fingers warm. I think I see myself in the embroidered stitches on the gown. Exhaustion makes me believe that the small figures are moving and one says, *'Half-man, half-elfin – all of you forest born.'*

In the middle of that first night, the longest night I can remember, I heard a wild animal scream, saw a winged creature fly past the windows and knew not whether I was awake or asleep.

By the evening of the second day my bones were frozen. Defeated I sat in the corner and closed my eyes, expecting only death to hold the key to this chamber.

I woke with a start and saw a golden light. To my fuddled brain it made little sense. The chamber door was wide open. Pinpricks of candlelight showed me the way. I stood, stiff with cold, my feet painful, numb, and I walked – no, I hobbled from the chamber onto a gallery. At the foot of the stairs my fox sat looking up at me.

He did not come to greet me as was his usual way but waited for me to come closer to him. He set off, then turned to make sure I was following. With his snout he pushed open a door to reveal the banqueting hall. Not the chamber that Ben Shakeshaft, Crumb and I had dined in; this one opened onto the vista of chambers familiar to me from my dream. The table was set for two.

I went to the fire. The flames sent shadows across the walls and among them I thought I glimpsed the silhouette of a monstrous, birdlike creature with the spiked wings of a bat. It was the stuff of nightmares – those horses that gallop through the mind and drive it to lunacy. I held my breath, not moving.

Green eyes – human eyes – look straight at me through the red feathers that hide her face. Her nose is the beak of an owl. There is no doubting her sex – her breasts emerge from feathers and her cunny from the fur of a panther. Her mouth is the mouth of a woman but her talons are powerful enough to strip a man of his skin. What unnatural phenomen is this? From which strange shore did this spirit fly to frighten my life from me? The sight of her dispels the solidity of earth and I am falling through many worlds of disbelief before reason can make sense of my vision and my feet find ground firm enough to hold such alchemy as she.

I think I hear the creature speak.

'I am Randa,' she says.

The Beast

LXVIII

I punished him. I took away his clothes, saw his thin body, his shrivelled cock. I felt nothing.

I tell myself I feel nothing.

I lie.

I lie, all of me wild with confusion, the strings of my soul strung so tight that they screech with pain. I can no more let him die than kill myself.

Perhaps the cure for my infatuation will be the look of horror on his face when he sees me, sees Randa, sees this confusion of beast and woman.

In the banqueting hall I watch his face, whiter than snow, as he crumples onto the wooden floor.

Now, Randa: look and mark well the effect you have on him. He is fainting. He is terrified.

LXIX

My eyes deceive me – this cannot be Randa, she whose thoughts I used to hear, my constant companion who I called my little soul. I believed she, like me, was of the forest, elfin born – not this. No, I refuse to believe what I see. It is the result of my exhausted mind, of hunger, the vapours of an empty stomach – it dangles demons before me. I am asleep, lost in the death of a dark, dark dream . . . and if not? Think, think – this is not the first time I have seen such a winged creature. Rational thought tells me this malady has been brought about by delirium – my mind makes monstrous pictures, illusions conjured from the air. The creature is not here. I have a fever . . . yes, a fever accounts for this vision for there is no such beast, it is a fragment of a disordered mind, a reflection of myself. Before me stands the quandary of my whole being made into solid form. This is how I feel, this creature is the black side of my mirror. I am not beautiful . . . beauty be the monster.

I think I say that aloud. I close my eyes to stop the room spinning, to stop myself tumbling into Hell's inferno. May she be gone, may this apparition be gone. . .

Yet when I look again – when I look now – the creature is still here, spiked wings spread wide, leathery, veined.

'Forgive me, Randa . . .' – I am laughing – 'Forgive me, for I see you as a beast. Tell me that is impossible . . . tell me . . .'

Cold sweat breaks out on my forehead, vomit rises in my throat, a tidal wave rushes through my body, spilling out my insides . . . the chamber spins and I am falling into blood torn velvet.

LXX

In those half-remembered grains of dreams is the alchemy of truth. In this realm, behind the watery veil is where half of me belongs.

I wake, feel well again, with the clarity of vision that has long been lost to me or perhaps I never before understood. I float drowsy between thoughts and wakefulness. I note I am in a carved bed and through the window of this chamber twilight is giving way to a snow-laden night. A golden glow spreads from the fire burning in the grate to where I lie but apart from that the chamber is in darkness.

Now I realise I have lied to myself for too long. To what effect? That I might believe I belonged to the world of man, to deny I was faerie born.

She who gave birth to me loved me enough to protect me from my father. There has always been too much of the forest in my soul and now I think, what is there to prove that I am his child? A note left on a basket, scribbled in the disguised hand of the sorceress? The word of a fearful, cunning woman?

Perhaps my mother, she who bore me, knew better. She was of faerie folk who knew the magic to be found in nature. And so if I am not of Lord Rodermere's blood, then I have no part in the sorceress's curse, the curse which jarred my past and has blighted my future.

There is no more need to hide in women's clothes, to play a part upon the stage and pretend. Is that not what all actors do, pretend? And when the play is over, the audience gone, then does he not put away his costume and become himself once more? Not I. Not I. Determinedly I pretend I belong to the world of man, that I am my father's son and with that fantasy comes the chains that bind me.

In the shadows someone is watching me. A harsh, scratching sound betrays their presence.

'How long have I been here?'

'Three days,' the shadows answer.

'Randa?' I hold my breath. There is no reply. 'Forgive me if I insulted you. It was not you, Randa, not you, but the fever that made me see you as a monstrous being.'

'Then you saw Randa, saw me as I am. For what I am is the beast.'

I am back in my body, fully awake. Her voice comes from deep inside her, the voice I had learned to love. A voice I long to hear more of.

'Let me see you now, I beg.'

A silence thick with unsaid words. Finally her voice again.

'You hung an image of your own creation on my invisibility.'

'Please – show yourself to me.'

She takes so long to answer that I wonder if she has gone. I jump when she speaks again.

'You will dine with me, dine with Randa, tonight.'

There is nothing to see. A door opens, a door closes and the sounds echo throughout the house. She has gone. And I am left with thoughts that hover above me, detached from myself.

I let the weight of them fall into me. I who have been cursed with beauty, who have longed for the wildness of the mirror turned, longed for the beast, for the beast ... The harshness of a truth denied shocks even me: I will never find love in the symmetry of perfection.

This unknown companion, my little soul, she who I could not see, only hear, who now in spite of my terror I long to look upon – she is who I love.

Oh, night, do not be slow in your steps. I bid you come fast and light evening's candle.

The majordomo arrives without his mask and in the light of the lantern he carries, I see he has the face of a baboon, his ruff marking the divide between the simian head and the torso of a man. His arms are long and his hands without gloves are those of a monkey. It is his tail that holds the lantern.

By his manner of intimacy I can tell that he cared for me when I was ill. He takes my face in his hand and turns it to the light. His grip is strong and I have a memory of his touch, of fingers that ache to heal. There is a glint of pride in his eye and on seeing I am recovered he pats my face.

I am shaved and washed, all with silent efficiency. He disappears for a moment and comes back cradling the gown I had worn and feared I had ruined. Now I see it in a new light. He helps me into it and ties the cords at the front. It fits me as if it has been tailored for my body. He stands back and examines his work, then comes forward again and adjusts the gown so that it sits right on the shoulders.

'It looks well on you, my lord.'

'You speak?'

'Yes, as do you.' He hands me slippers and tells me to call him Papio. 'When you came here with the thief and his friend you spoke in a language I do not know, in words I do not recognise. But when you tossed in fever you spoke our language.'

'Tell me what she looks like,' I beg.

'My mistress is more glorious than ever you will be. To me your looks are ugly, an insult.'

'With that I would not disagree, but you have not answered my question.'

'She is the most magnificent of beasts. The like of her we have not seen for many an age. One day she will rule these lands.'

And I think, I will be beside her when the time comes.

I follow him downstairs to the banqueting hall. He lights the candles but they do not illuminate all of the chamber. I know she is here – perhaps in the room beyond. She has no intention of announcing herself.

I wait. And still I am patient. In the candlelight, again I study the fabric of my gown but now I see in its intricate stitches embroidered stories of magnificent beasts, kings and queens, far-off lands and castles that sit precariously high on rounded hills.

When I look up, she is there. I stand and hope my legs will not fail me. I bow and raise my eyes to hers. She is as I remembered, but I am ashamed of my reaction when first I saw her. What a petty man I am. I have only pale, white skin, the veneer of beauty. She is glorious in her unfathomable being. Who created such a magnificent creature, half of woman, half of beast, the whole more glorious than any puny man? Oh world, such unknown treasures do you possess if we have but eyes to see.

Her wings, two tall steeples, rise to a god that would say she is the Devil's own. And by her side is my fox. She lurches towards me and with her comes a perfume of iron, of earth. With difficulty she sits and the fox jumps up onto the chair beside her.

Three different dishes are set before us. My dish is a roast of mutton, served with the finest wine. For Randa, a bowl of dead mice; for the fox, a hen's carcass. His manners are not inclined to furniture and he takes the bird to the floor where he devours it. Randa peels the skin off the mice with her sharp talons as if their small bodies be no more than grapes, holds them up by their tails and crunches on soft bone with her sharp, pointed teeth. The wine swims in my head.

We eat, we do not speak. I have an advantage over Randa: I can hear her thoughts but her thoughts are a turmoil I can make no sense of. At last she breaks the silence.

'Tell me,' she says, Do I – I, Randa the beast – do I have a soul?'

LXXI

'You told me once your soul is ancient,' I say.

'My father was an educated man yet he believed in the Devil and in God. He taught me that a beast has no soul.'

'Was your father – the dealer in magic – was he like you?'

'My father, if he lives still, is an alchemist.'

He is thinking how is it Randa was born a beast? Shall I tell him my mother said it was nature's design for me? And that my father talked of the alchemy of transformation? And how he near sent himself mad with the grief of it all?

I am on the verge of giving myself away. Her thoughts interest me far more than what she has to say. Did her father create her? I must tread carefully.

'Were you cared for, treated well?'

'My father's apprentice was a kind man. My father's apprentice who called me Mistress Randa. His apprentice had more magic in his breath than did my father ever possess. He wept when the chain and iron collar were placed on me, the collar that burned my feathers away.'

'Who would do such a thing?'

'It was my father, the alchemist, who did it.'

'What of your mother, the angel?'

'Bess was her name.'

She loved me, loved me even when I killed.

To conceal my shock I pour myself more wine – which I know to be unwise.

'Pour me some,' she says.

Her eyes are bright, they never leave mine as her talons clutch the glass and lift it to her lips. Full, sensual lips.

'I killed her,' she says.

'Who?' I ask.

'She who spoke against my mother. Bitter tongue full of evil, her voice too loud, heard too far away. I was but a child, a beast too small to know my power. Her fingers tasted like butter. How could such vile flesh taste so sweet?'

You do not look away, but perhaps you play the part of hero. I admire you for that. But how long will manners that make fools of men keep you seated here? Ask me if Randa killed again ... ask me ... I dare you.

I will not for it would be as if I judged my fox for the killing of a hen when it is implicitly a part of his nature. Does she know I can hear her thoughts? Perhaps instinctively she does. She smiles, her lips blush red.

He sees me, sees the beast, and does not waver in his glance. I expected him to scrape his chair upon the floor and beg for his freedom.

Again I nearly give myself away, muddling what she says and what she thinks for her thoughts make me tender towards her. Speak to me.

'Speak to me, Mistress Randa.'

I had never thought we might talk like this, as if I, Randa, mattered to him, as if what I thought truly concerned him. But his beauty is an enchantment, it undoes me. I tremble to find desire ignite the embers in my heart, to flare again as if the flames had never been quenched. I cling once more to the possibility of love, a love in which I would be transformed. Banish the thought, Randa. Drink wine.

'Speak to you of what?'

'Of what you think, of what you dream.'

'I think,' she says, 'that nothing good will come of this. You once humiliated me and I wanted my revenge. Now I know it to be pointless.'

'Why did you not have the courage to show me yourself then when you stayed in my chamber and near convinced me of my insanity?'

'Do I not repulse you?'

'No. I am in awe. You are a mystery.'

She laughs. It is a high sound, wind rustling in summer leaves and I doubt not it is a sound that is rarely heard. I too laugh.

'Once,' she says, 'I believed that if you could love me for who I am, see me as I am and not flinch, that perhaps your loving would transform me, that there might be inside me another form more human, a woman waiting to be unwrapped.'

He says nothing. What can he say? Only that it would be impossible for him to make love to me, that the thought would wilt him. Oh, I am tired and this is all the sadness of uselessness. Tomorrow I will set him free. Tomorrow I will resign myself to this world and its beasts. And what of him, what of Beau? He will marry and be unhappy with his lot. If he remembers me at all it will be as no more than the stuff of dreams, tales to tell to his children while dancing them on his knee.

I want to shout at her: you are wrong, so wrong. Let me in, let me know you better. But I bite my tongue.

She stands, Papio comes to help her to her feet. I hear her talking to him and suspect it is about my leaving.

In the language I learned as a child, that Papio understands, I say, 'Randa, please, dear mistress, do not send me away.'

She turns to look at me.

'What point is there in your staying?'

'To know you better.' She says nothing and I say, 'Let me lie with you.'

'Why? To add a beast to your list of bedfellows? It is but the wine speaking. It has enchanted your eyes with rose petals and made me into an acceptable form. Go back to your wormy bed, Lord Beaumont, be gone. This is the Land of the Beasts. Here we feast on men like you.'

THE BEAST

LXXII

I want him gone for my soul is sick with the love of him, with longing for him, making a mockery of my senses. I disguise myself in dreams of what I might be if he, if Beau, was ever to truly love me. The eye of my mind makes possibilities where there are none. I labour hard to find joy in hope and I know the task to be hopeless. I fear I will study his face and when I do his golden eyes will tell me the truth of his loathing.

Does he think me half-witted? That I would let him lie with me? Is that the price he puts on his freedom? Perhaps I have misjudged him, given him more valour than he is worth.

When he is gone I will banish any thought of him. I will be a blown egg with only air to fill its oval space and let that be my heart.

I return to my chamber heavy of limb. I am no eagle that can fly into the sky, touch the sun and let it burn this pain from me. I know the truth of my being, I saw it mirrored in his eyes. I will have no man's pity and if that is the sum of his desire for me then, Beau, leave me to my dreams.

THE BEAUTY

LXXIII

I return to my chamber full of anger at the injustice of her words. She judged me too hastily, too harshly. What – does she suppose me a whore? And for all my rage at the perceived injustice, I realise she knows me better than I do myself. Her nature is the source of stars and shines just as bright; mine the world of words – words that have not wings enough to reach her.

Who have I loved? My mother, my sister, Master Goodwin. No one else. All else I might claim are moments of deluded passion.

What a clown you are. You who have so little liking for yourself, how would you ever have enough love for her? What conjuring cap do you need upon your head to make such magic happen?

It is not she that repulses me. It is myself, hidden in all this vile beauty, the truth of who I am concealed from human eye by the glamour of a charmed man. If I had one wish – one wish only – I would ask for it to be gone, to not be seen in the light that blinds and corrupts others.

I should have had the courage to speak with an honest tongue, to tell Randa that when she left me in the House of the Three Turrets, I felt abandoned. I missed her, missed hearing her thoughts. Yet tonight I said none of that truth. If I was a man, more a man than this, I would have said what I feel but I did not. I would have said that I know her.

While I rant my fox watches me.

'What am I to do?' I ask him.

Tomorrow I will be sent on to Sir Percival Hayes's house to be an apprentice to a thief once more, to be discovered and no doubt sold back to Lord Rodermere. What then? Held prisoner again in my father's house, the sword of the sorceress's curse hanging on a spider's thread above me. No. I am not a puppet to be pulled this way and that by the whims and fortunes of others. I am an educated man. Think. Tomorrow it will be too late.

This is the moment to act and perhaps by doing so I can change the course of my life.

I expected I would have to force the door and was surprised to find it was not locked. I picked up the candle and made my way into the cruel, black darkness. The house felt abandoned. I heard the creaking sound of neglect in its timbers. My candle flickered in the draught and threatened extinction. All around I heard the howl of wild beasts.

'Where is she? Where is Randa?' I asked the fox. He set off down the long passage, his brush straight out behind him.

I came at last to the largest of the large double doors. They opened on to a vast hall whose lofty timber beams threw menacing shadows across the floor. Nothing here apart from dying embers in a huge fireplace, and one tall, latticed window framed by blood-red velvet drapes.

It was cold and I was on the point of leaving when the window blew open, and the drapes, great sails of fabric, billowed into the empty space.

It would be wrong to leave this room to the elements. I battled to close the window and just then I smelled the earth and iron of her perfume. Still I saw nothing and went to leave. But my fox did not, he was staring up at one corner of the velvet drapes. I lifted my candle high and that is when I saw her there. I saw the winged beast, her talons sunk deep into the fabric. I stared and did not look away.

She descends, shredding velvet in her wake.

'I told you – it is not safe for you here.'

She stands before me, puts a talon under my chin and I feel it pierce my skin. She puts it to her mouth, licks my blood away.

I do not flinch.

'What is it you want?' she says. 'I have given you your freedom.'

I touch her talons, feel the power of them as if they were a prayer. I kiss them and Randa pulls them away.

'Do not play with me,' she says.

'I do not.'

Her green eyes never leave mine. At last she turns and in an instant she is hanging upside down from a beam, wrapped in her wings.

'Go away,' she says. 'Randa gave you – I gave you – you, Lord Beaumont – your freedom.'

'What if I do not want it?'

'Go back to your chamber. Leave there the gown you are wearing.'

I pick up the candle and furious to be so dismissed, slam it down again. 'You think me a thief? Here, have it.'

I tear the gown from my body, ripping the fur and the embroidered fabric, and toss it to the floor. It lies in a heap and I think my eyes perfidious for the fur lining moves of its own accord and takes on the shape of a black wolf. Stunned by such an unnatural vision my limbs that before were mine to control lose all such use. With a speed not known to man, this thing, this unmade thing of wolf fur, leaps on me and the minutes slow and it seems that the attack has lasted for all time. The thing grows, consumes me, swallows me whole. I hear Randa screech until I hear no more, smothered as I am, blinded in the suffocating darkness of fur. I cannot breathe. I cannot breathe . . .

Sharp teeth sink into my neck and I am thrown across the chamber, by what force I know not. Then it, the thing, is gone. I look up and there is Randa, terror in her eyes. I look down and cannot believe what I see.

THE BEAST

LXXIV

I did not know.

I knew. Randa knew well.

I had it tailored for him, a gown to match his beauty, not thinking that the precious fabric would ever be torn, that the tearing would set free – give life – to the skin that lined the garment. The vengeful spirit of a black wolf latched onto his host as a flea to a dog.

Randa, you lie.

Yes, I lie. It roared across my mind, excited my thoughts with its secret possibility that if he, if Beau, he who I love, should tear such a beautiful garment . . .

I knew the fabric would enchant him, knew he would stare in awe at the embroidered tales told in such small stitches. And if such a reckless act should release the magic, it would be just punishment for the scar he left upon my heart. A heart twice scarred; the loss of a mother mocking the loss of he who does not love me. Yet the scar he left I feel all the deeper.

Why did he search me out? I had made all clear to him, I had left open the door, not turned the key, given him, my lord, my love, his freedom.

What then made his shoes turn towards my chamber when the road waited so obligingly for him?

Desire made a beast of me. When he kissed my talons – my talons, not the slim, white hand of a lady – but my talons that kill – when he took them to his mouth, something stirred, unsettled all my human parts that scorn my dreams and leave me frustrated.

Beau stares in disbelief at his fur-covered limbs, at this unexpected transformation. His hair is longer, thicker, wiry and unruly. His body near unrecognisable. My heart races to think what would have happened if I had not sunk my teeth into the spirit's neck for the only part of Beau that I have seen before this moment is his beautiful face.

Slowly, unsure of himself, unsure of who this new self is, he stands. Taller than he was before, his bulk made greater by the fur on his back and shoulders. I move away, for the wolf may be deeper within him than his pelt. And I feel in me fear, both great and small, and know not what I have unleashed.

'I had hoped to be the alchemist of your transformation,' he says. It is his own voice, so dear to me. 'And now it appears I have unwittingly brought about my own.'

His eyes are sad and I hang my head, ashamed of my vengeful heart.

'You thought my words insincere. You believed I mocked you, that I played a part. You were wrong. It was only that I had forgotten the lines my soul should have spoken. I came to tell you that I missed you when you left the House of the Three Turrets. That is not a lie. For a time I thought myself glad to be free of you. But I was not. I was incomplete. Do you believe me, Mistress Randa?' He stretches out his arms, spreads wide his fingers tipped in fur. 'Now you meet me like this, can you believe I am speaking the truth? My truth, all I know of it?'

These words might set fire to me. I might burn in their flame for all eternity.

He pulls me back to him but I am lifted off the floor and fly hard against the wall. He has the strength of the wolf. And he is as surprised as I. For a moment my tongue loses all words and my head spins. He asks forgiveness if he has hurt me.

'I always thought myself a feeble man,' he says. 'Is this my punishment for being careless of your feelings?'

I shake my feathers, willing this all to go away. I have no words, only sounds. I think the spirit of the black wolf is a mighty one and I think it will protect him from the beasts in Herkain's realm.

'But will it protect you from me?' he says, and I am unnerved.

He comes to me, this man of wolf fur. I turn my head away. He turns it back to him, holding me tight about the waist.

He kisses me.

I knew not what passion such a tender kiss can kindle. He strokes my feathers.

'You are beautiful,' he says, 'far more beautiful than you know.'

It is on my tongue to say that these are but the words of the wolf spirit but he kisses me again.

I have two chambers. The empty one of wooden beams where, after I have hunted, often at night I hang; the other for the woman I wish I could be. It is lined with books that I can no longer hold, whose words I yearn to read, but my talons that when small were soft and malleable have grown to be instruments of slaughter. Here is where I sleep and in my quiet mind I envy mortals their hands that can turn the leaves of books and gather wisdom there.

We speak not and all the thoughts in my head are peaceful and here we lie and fit together in a different way than ever that I dreamed of. I wonder how such things have turned around to be this, and do not feel honourable in the part I played.

He says, 'You did nothing wrong. Had I known the consequences I would have done the same.'

I think, I am too slow. He has outwitted me. He is in my head and hears my thoughts.

'As I always have,' he says.

He kisses me again.

I taste a yearning in the sweetness of his tongue and recognise in it my own longing. Perhaps any other way than this I would have been too shy to let the rest unfold. He has such kisses in him and he strokes my feathers, caresses my fur, tenderly sucks upon my breast. And all the longing that I feel, the ache where my body holds the imprint of woman, the part that talons prove useless to satisfy, into that dark mystery of me he enters.

This act that in my mind made knots of love, I see in all its simplicity. He fills me and in that instant I am me, I am a woman, white-skinned and pale, my cunny clothed in its dark bush.

We sleep. I wrap him in my wings, hold his heartbeat close and trust myself to fall. In the morning I am I and he is half man, half wolf, all mine.

THE BEAUTY

LXXV

When we make love, in her wildness she sinks her talons into my back, the pain exquisite in its moment of bliss. She says that if she had hands she would stroke me as I do her.

'Your touch makes me feel a human, as if I am a woman who could be loved.'

From the scars on my back more fur grows.

I whisper into her feathers, 'How is it to have wings, to feel the air, to come home bearing the scent of clouds and snow?'

She hunts alone. I wait, feeling such hunger – for her return, and for her kill. The two emotions become one. It is with a sense of revulsion that I remember eating charred meat from the fire; the very thought is barbaric. I relish the soft, buttery taste of meat that still pulses with life, the warm blood of animals just killed. We eat together and nothing has ever tasted more vital than this. Sated, I take each of her talons in my mouth and suck the meat from them, lick the blood that runs down her feathers as she does my pelt.

This is all I want. This and for it to never cease. Here in our kingdom we rule.

The fox takes his time to sniff out and understand the change in me. He keep his distance.

Full from loving, from eating, we go into the chamber with the library and the furnishings from a life that is receding from me. I read to her, she hungry for words that I feel to be less important. I speak a different language without the past or future tense. This she notes. I reassure her: I am free, there are no strings of guilt, no ties of conscience, no chains of church to torment me.

When she asks me, what of the curse? I search my mind to remember what it is, why it is important, and tell her I cannot.

I beg her to take me hunting with her, to teach me to kill as she does.

'No,' she says. 'This is not you.' I howl and she holds me to her, saying, 'I fear the spirit of the vengeful wolf is becoming the master of you.'

It does not concern me. Why should it concern me? I am wolf.

THE BEAST

LXVI

It is the fox who shows me what I have refused to see. His hackles rise, his teeth bravely bared, he backs away from Beau. Beau, my lover, who has in devastating stitches changed into this other, this wolf, into a different kind of creature, one who I do not know, his beauty stripped from him.

Look, Randa, look at what he has become.

Where are his soft, golden eyes, his tender hands that stroked me, his gentle tongue that spoke to me of love, the love he had for me? This is not my lover, this animal is not he.

If passion is blind, then I possess no eyes. How could I love him yet not see these changes? His hands, his beautiful hands that once took me to a different sky . . . claws now, arrows in my heart.

Be I a jester to the truth? Have I killed him, my lover? Has Randa killed again?

Beau turns to me and I see him now for what he has become: a savage wolf with eyes of burning embers. With speed far faster than mine he tries to snatch the fox. The fox keeps Beau at bay. I fly at Beau, my talons the only weapons that have the power to hold him back. I seize the fox and take him up to the rafters with me. Beneath us, Beau, he that was Beau, circles, waiting for one of us, both of us to fall.

Have I left it too late? Have I? Papio is gone and there is no one here in this house of endless chambers. Only the wolf and me.

My world spins. I hold tight to the fox, rock him, powerless to calm the savage below. Beau has vanished into that vengeful pelt. He has grown in size, walks on all fours, from his fangs saliva drips. I hear his steel claws on the wooden floor, I hear his heavy breath, I hear him growl for meat, raw meat.

He throws his weight against the doors. Again, again, again. No words now, words all gone. Unable to escape, in his fury he turns upon the furnishings, tears the drapes to shreds, pulls down the books, snaps chairs and bed as if they be but kindling.

'Beau, my love, where are you?'

My cry drives him wilder and he leaps up as if he would kill me if he could only reach this high.

He stops as abruptly as he started and stands for a moment in a fallen forest of ruined objects. He stops, so I think and hope the man in him will return.

An explosion. Glass shards fly across the chamber, the lattice window shattered. He, the wolf, is no longer here.

I rush to the window, will myself to look down, fearing to see the wolf's body, Beau's body, crushed on the ground below. A scream is caught in my throat and I think I have let it out until I realise the sound does not come from me but from outside. It is the howl of the wolf and in the moonlight he shakes a shower of silver glass from his pelt and is gone.

A hunter am I. I follow him. Glad am I to feel the icy sky fill my wings. I glide, cushioned on pockets of air. Below me the great forest lies, brooding in all its dark secrecy, waiting for the dawn. Where is he? Where is my love? Snow falls. If I find him, persuade him to come home, perhaps make right what my jealousy has made wrong. All night I fly, I search, I pray. I think of my father and of his prayers, those endless prayers that his god never heard.

The day breaks, cracks the night sky. The bare branches of the great oak trees reach out to me. Fresh white snow covers the ground. Sharp be my eyes. The deer, the stag run criss-crossing through the trees but Beau I cannot see. Soon he will be returning from the hunt, aching to find a safe place to sleep until the moon calls him again.

I am close by the House of the Three Turrets. Below me a man mounts his horse and with his hounds rides out into the new day. I swoop down. There is no mistaking Lord Rodermere. He canters into the forest, followed by the wild barking of his dogs. The call of his hunting horn wakes the forest and rooks fly from their nests.

The sight of him brings a feeling of such foreboding: I know what Beau, my love, the wolf means to do and I am powerless to stop him.

Beau cannot be far away but the dogs have no scent of him. The rush of wind from my wings makes Lord Rodermere look up. He sees me and raises his crossbow, pulls back the bolt, takes aim at me and in that moment he does not see what I see. The wolf, my lover, springs at Lord Rodermere. The crossbow falls, the horse falls, the rider falls . . . the horse, wild with panic, scrambles to stand then gallops away, the terrified hounds following in its wake.

Lord Rodermere, stunned, is slow to find his feet. The wolf waits, watches. Only when the earl can see the glint in the wolf's eye, see his savagery, does the creature pounce and sink his steely teeth into the heart of Lord Rodermere. Into the heart of his father. A scream gurgles in his lordship's throat. He falls backwards, his arms and legs spread wide as the wolf tears his heart from his chest.

The rooks caw, the sun dances in the trees, the snow turns crimson in the morning light. The wolf has his prey by the throat, shakes him, shakes him, and I hear his neck snap. Only then does the wolf, does Beau, look up at me. He howls and drags his kill into the undergrowth.

Stillness returns to the forest. Bloodied snow is all that is left of the killing.

What have I done?

I have made a monster of a man.

THE BEAUTY OF
THE WOLF

LXXVII

I be wolf, no man my master.
All beast, all man, is one in me.
I, born in the beginning
before trees were named,
when the river ran blue,
I will be at the end of all ends.
A furnace my sinews of molten iron,
my claws are steel, vision blood red,
tongue black as my fur,
my mind ruled by the hammers of revenge.
I will find my killer.
This night is mine, his death my freedom.
To the house of the oakman's dead trees.
The moon, my light. I know the way.
I be the wolf, no man my master.
Morning snow untouched.
Comes the man, high on his horse,
hounds singing to the cry of a horn.
Hunger is all I know;
hunger is all I am.
In the morning forest I smell his blood,
Sluggish in sleepy veins.

He rides out,
the hounds do not follow,
wise to the scent of me.
This moment:
no man's past, no man's tomorrow,
the howl of eternity now.
I rise from the ground, cross space and time
to reach him.
To sink my teeth into his beating heart,
tear it from him.
Take him by his throat,
shake him until neck snaps.
A broken branch.
His eyes, wild, stare into flakes of falling snow.
By the arm I drag him,
let his blood replenish the soil,
feed the roots of barren trees.
My bones are from the earth,
Iron roots of the forest my skeleton.
I be wolf. No man my master.

THE BEAST
LXXVIII

I return to the house where the silence is loud, accusing. What has Randa done?

I scream my answer into the void. I, I, Randa, have caused my love to fulfil the sorceress's curse.

The silence is unforgiving.

I took a good man, a brave man and turned him into a murderer. How do I live knowing this?

I wish as I have never wished before that I could make time reverse itself. Have I lost him, my love?

All that he destroyed I leave where it fell; the broken chairs, my carved bed, the scattered books, spines split, autumn leaves their pages. I crouch to see the words, read one page then move to another book. Disjointed tales, the chattering of curious minds. Hope have I that I might come across a charm, a spell, to free him from the wolf spirit, to bring home to me my kind, gentle Beau.

I sleep. On the floor where I sleep objects from the chaos of his rage are illuminated in pools of of sunlight.

My faithful fox keeps me company, catches mice for me and lays them in rows. I have no desire to eat, to live. A name is all I own. I am The Beast.

I do not dream.

I wake at twilight to find Herkain standing over me. Behind him is Papio, returned.

The King of the Beasts says Randa will be queen here, but not with the spirit of a vengeful man-wolf at her side.

I realise the impossible weight of my grief and with bowed head I ask him, ask Herkain, how do I undo this enchantment? This cruel act, my terrible mistake. Is there a charm, I ask, that might take away Beau's wolf madness?

'You should have left the pelt be,' he says. 'But I am not here to talk of mundane matters. You must marry one of my sons. They are lazy beasts and not as handsome as you, yet they are of royal blood. You, Randa, must choose yourself a lord to be your master.'

What is he asking? No. Randa could not, I could not . . .

'Which one would you take?' he says.

Neither, I want to scream, neither, never. They are both idle creatures with stunted wings, one plump, one lean, and each near drowned in Narcissus's pool. Neither one have I a liking for.

The King of the Beasts says he would choose for me the elder of his sons.

'Of the two of them I would argue he has been less indulged by his mother. Though both, I agree, are of little consequence. But with such an alliance comes the surety of your place in this, my realm.'

I bite my lip until it bleeds.

'Please, majesty, reverse the charm.'

The gavel of his voice is a command. 'If I do this, you must let him go.'

'I will. After one night.'

'Let him go and marry one of my sons, whichever you wish.'

I nod.

LXXIX

Should I be so easily persuaded? What sentence do I condemn myself to? I tremble at the thought, for I have held tight to one belief, one hope, one wish, one prayer: that deep inside me, concealed by feathers and fur, is a woman waiting to be freed. I am of woman born. Every month I bleed as my mother did, the pain of the menstrual moons pulls my womb apart, cramps me over, curls me up. When the time comes I wrap my arms and wings about me, blood runs down my fur-covered thighs. And yet for all Beau's loving, I am still the beast.

I long to tell Herkain that perhaps I, too, have been cursed into a different shape, that in the shadows of my mind I see endless possibilities which amount to nothing. But I do not for I know with all my heart that I would lay my life down to have Beau returned as he was before.

Perhaps then he – man, not man-wolf – would make love to me and in the power of his seed transform Randa.

He told me when we lay together, before the wolf devoured him, that he, Beau, knew this house from his dreams. I asked did he see me in it. No. Not me. Not Randa. Only once did he see a young woman with hair so red, with skin so white, so pale. She wore her gown open, revealing her nakedness, and in her hand she held a red feather with which she played, '. . . here,' he said, and touched the secret part of me. I, laughing, told him I was jealous. What if I could be that woman and know in which realm I truly belong?

These thoughts dance through my mind.

Herkain draws with his staff two circles. I stand in one, he in the other.

I am ashamed of my hopes that betray his trust, of my ignorance that has brought about my downfall and near killed my love.

A blood moon rises, lazily pulling its heavy weight into the sky. Moonshine lights the chamber. All time, no time holds its breath.

Banish such thoughts I say, harsh to myself, for this is my kingdom, this my king. He who took me in, cared for me, opened my wings. He who said, and still says, that my form speaks the truth of who I am and the rest is an illusion of my desire.

And I want to say my mother was a woman, my father was a man. I remember the silvery mercury and rising from its waters, remember knowing all I could have been was stolen from me.

I jump when when he speaks.

'I forbid you to move from the circle for you will have no protection. If there is any interruption of this spell, Lord Beaumont will be for ever lost between the living and the dead.'

My father's prayer comes back to me. *In the name of God be secret and in all your doings be still.*

The moon has mounted its midnight throne. The King of the Beasts, staff in hand, calls into the darkness, a low rumble, a purr, that owns the pulse of the Earth itself.

'I command you, vengeful spirit – come back to me.'

All is quiet. So long is the quiet that it trembles with the fear of being broken.

Again Herkain speaks. 'Come back, great wolf, lay down your burden and be at peace.'

I hear something heavy downstairs; panting, steel claws upon the wood. He comes ever closer, with each step is a knock upon the stairs. My heart freezes. I know what it is he carries. Then he is before us in the darkness, amber eyes aflame. And with his jaws he drags the carcass.

'Lay down your burden,' says the King of the Beasts.

The black wolf comes close, lets fall the carcass half in, half out of Herkain's circle. I shiver when I see the dead meat of this man, a bloody sack that leaks his entrails. His eyes, wide open, stare at me, his face frozen in disbelief. Before me is the corpse of Francis Thursby, Earl of Rodermere.

I remember the words the forest whispered, the words that were written in gold on a felled oak.

A faerie boy
will be born to you
whose beauty will
be your death.

The black wolf circles, round and round. The doors close of their own accord and the wolf snarls, knowing he is trapped. Herkain calls to him again.

'Spirit, you have your revenge on he who slew you. The King of the Beasts sets you free.'

The wolf lunges at Herkain who does not flinch but raises his arm and sinks his powerful fist into the wolf's belly and begins to pull pelt from skin. It comes away reluctantly and as the fur is gathered in Beau returns. He stands upright, naked, bedewed with blood.

I fear this be his ghost and the man is gone. I fear that Beau be dead.

The pelt lies twitching on the floor. Herkain brings down his staff and the chamber fills with acrid smoke that turns to flames in which flicker the image of the hunter and the wolf.

Is it over? I do not know.

Beau, his eyes closed, is as white, as still as frost. Herkain has not moved from the circle. He twists his staff the other way and places it on the body of Lord Rodermere, calls for Papio, tells him to return the corpse to the mortal world.

'Tomorrow,' says Herkain to me, 'this young lord must be gone or his flesh will make a dish for our banquet.'

I nod.

'We understand each other well. I leave you, my lady, to undo what is left of the charm.'

'How can I? I do not own your staff – I do not have the power of life and death.'

'Do you not?' he asks and goes to the doors.

'But the charm, majesty . . .'

Not a word he says but with a bow he makes his exit and I am here with a shell of a man who looks like Beau and has no movement that life could own. I go to him, my wings trailing behind me, a vista of loneliness before me. If he should not wake? What then, my heart, what then?

I kiss Beau once to warm his lips. Twice, three times – and he opens his eyes. They are golden, they are his. Life pours back into my love.

He takes me in his arms and whispers, 'Tell me, will this for ever be so?'

THE BEAUTY

LXXX

It is the eve of my nuptials and I should be asleep and content in my dreams. I am awake. The bells of a distant church chime midnight, the unforgiving hour when yesterday tips what is best forgotten into the new day.

My betrothed is well educated and has all the attributes that any man might wish for. But I do not love her. She reminds me of a lapdog and is just as spoiled. Our marriage is to be an alliance of two families: the wealthy merchants, the Cassels, and the near-penniless family of Thursby, the Earls of Rodermere, possessors of the House of the Three Turrets and a forest. These stand in lieu of love.

I pour a goblet of of claret, stare into the dying fire and remember Randa. It is not wise to think of the last night I spent with her. All that is past is best forgotten. Wine is not the friend of wisdom, being better acquainted with maudlin thoughts and self-pity.

I wonder where you are, my little soul. After more than two years Randa still haunts me. The rose she gave me is dead but tonight it shines blood red in my memory. I tell myself that what happened in the darkness of her house was naught but a dream.

I had woken with relief into the light of her, her kisses. I had not done it. I had not killed. It was the destruction of her chamber that concerned me.

'Who did this?' I asked.

She kissed me again and said, 'None of this was your fault. I am to blame. Forgive me.'

I did not understand.

'I should not have given you the gown, the fur-lined gown.'

Slow was my mind. I could not make sense of what she was telling me and asked again if I had done the damage.

'No, no,' she said. 'Not you. It was not you.'

When did I start lying to myself?

All of my body was grazed. Papio brought up jugs of steaming water and I washed away the blood. I felt that I was born again into a new skin.

'You will heal,' she said. 'It was where the fur was pulled away.'

Fur? What fur? I remembered and I did not remember. The images came in steel-bright shafts of knowledge. Teeth and fangs sunk into another's flesh. Not yours. Not mine. Then whose?

I clung to her explanations as a drowning man does to a log.

In the broken mirror I saw the scars, criss-cross, razor deep on my back.

She bowed her magnificent head.

'Forgive me,' she said, whispered kisses in my ear.

I told her they were trophies of passion, that I was proud of every one of them. We both knew that was not what she was asking forgiveness for.

From tomorrow, I tell myself, as I have every day since we parted, I will think of her no more. But for tonight let me remember, remember all that happened that evening.

We dined on raw meat – I wanted nothing else. She told me that such longing would fade over time, as would the speed of my movements, the strength of my body. She was right. By degrees they have faded but not altogether gone. The one thing that does not fade – in my memory or in my heart – is Randa.

'This is where I belong,' I told her that last night.

We made love and I hoped, as much as she hoped, that I might be transformed into a beast or she into a woman, that we would meet in the same shape. So certain was I, I told her a hundred times before we fell asleep, that tomorrow we would wake the same.

We were just children, children wishing for the impossible.

I woke before dawn to find the bed empty. She was standing at the window as she always was.

'Come back to bed, my love,' I said.

She turned and said, 'I am, I always will be this abominable accident, this foul thing.'

'You are not, you are . . .'

She interrupted me. 'You cannot stay. You will be killed if you are not gone by the time the sun is up.'

'Killed? But why?'

She did not answer. Papio arrived. There was nothing generous in his step, in his gaze, and only menace in his eyes. He had brought my threadbare garments to put on me.

'A horse is ready,' he said. 'You must hurry.'

I went to Randa. Surely she would not allow me to be banished? We were each other's shadow.

She shook her feathers.

'Go quickly and think no more of staying.'

I have held onto this moment because I do not understand it and cannot let it go.

Randa walked with me down the great staircase and out into a morning of uncertain mists. There stood a horse.

We looked out of the gates to the road beyond; two strangers who had never discussed the depth of love or the weight of abandoned passion. My fox – her fox – trotted up the steps to Randa. I tried to speak, to plead for a life already gone. She turned her head away and pointed to a red rose below the first-floor window. Papio, sighing, climbed with great speed and brought it down to her.

'Take it,' she said. 'I give it to you as I gave you my heart – neither stolen.'

I mounted the horse, the gates opened and with such little effort I left a world of enchantment, one to which I have never returned and have no idea how to find.

Yes, Beau – tell me again: when was it you first lied? For all that has followed has been thorns on your tongue. Tomorrow I am marrying a woman I will never love. The wine jug knows what the heart dare not admit.

I love Randa.

I love.

LXXXI

Only the absence of time on my return made me realise its unbearable weight upon the soul.

I had been delivered with such speed to the House of the Three Turrets, from one world to another, that it had the effect of making me sick and giddy with the heaviness of travel and not knowing what hour I had arrived in, nor the day, nor the year. It was as if a part of me had been left behind. Now I know it was my heart.

The mortal world I find myself in once more is pulled by such a violent current; its endless seasons that toss and turn men's lives upon its tides of worry, of age, of sickness; of death the eternal fisherman that shares not his catch.

Such were my melancholy thoughts that morning when I dismounted and heard in the tolling of church bells a judgment on my ungodly thoughts, their doleful tone a reprimand even to this spring day that held such abundance of life.

I had no wish to be discovered or see my father again and with a weary step I took the forest road towards London. Quite what I would do when I arrived there or where I would stay I had not given much thought to. All the riches I had on me were one penny, and a blood-red rose whose value to me was priceless. I put my faith in the day being fair and the drum of my feet eventually bringing order to my scattered thoughts.

Wood pigeons cooed over the sound of the bells and I thought it must be Sunday and if it was, it went some way to explaining the persistence of their reproachful chimes.

I had not gone far when I came to the church among the trees – a gloomy building that once, before the Reformation, the monks had owned. It stood on the edge of the forest where the trees nibbled at its foundations. This was where Parson Pegwell gave his sermons, damning witches and all other such demons that he believed dwelled beyond its buttressed walls.

A funeral was taking place and two gravediggers were lining the grave with black velvet. I wondered who it was who had died for the fabric alone made me think itmust be someone of noble blood. A little further off by the churchyard gates, villagers had gathered. Those that could afford it wore black and all made me think of rooks. At the door of the church two banners stood. They bore our family's coat of arms.

Was he dead? Was my father dead? I was once more confused and it occurred to me that I had perhaps been gone for far longer than I had thought. What felt like a matter of days could well have been years. Had he died of old age?

I pulled my hat down and relied on my threadbare clothes, knowing that in them I would not be recognised. Both men were familiar to me for they had often worked for Master Goodwin. I asked who it was who was being buried.

'Bugger off,' said the first grave digger.

'Whose funeral is it?' I asked again.

'Look, lad,' said the second gravedigger who I knew to be called Master Tom, 'take this bread and if you are wise and not a ghost I advise you to leave with haste.'

'Is it some noble?' I asked

'Take this and leave, lad.'

I took off my hat and both men stared and stared again.

'Well,' said Master Tom. 'I will be buggered. By the Devil's own horse, we thought he had ridden off with you moons ago. We thought you were long dead.'

I put my hand out to the first gravedigger who took it.

'It is warm,' he said to Master Tom. They both bowed. 'Forgive us, Lord Beaumont, we did not recognise you. You have changed mightily.'

That thought had not occurred to me and I found it strangely reassuring to think I might have. If I had aged I felt no older.

'It is your father who is dead, my lord. It is his grave we dig.'

'When did Lord Rodermere die?'

'Three days ago, my lord.'

'Tell me how.'

The men looked awkwardly at each other, looked awkwardly at their shovels and then back to me.

I patted Tom on the back. It mattered not, for I knew what I was going to do and I cared little for the consequences. If my father is dead so is the curse.

The church was full of mourners and the voice of Parson Pegwell was as unforgiving as it always had been, dogmatic in its hypocrisy.

'I know that my Redeemer liveth, and that I shall rise out of the earth in the last day, and shall be covered again with my skin, and shall see God in my flesh.'

I pushed myself forward, person by person, until I stood in the middle of the nave. In the pews either side of the coffin sat my father's kinsmen and other landlords, all dressed in black gowns, sprigs of rosemary in their hats. The only face I recognised was that of Sir Percival Hayes. The rest – as was the audience to me when on stage – was a blur.

The parson was standing at the altar. At the sight of me he became a mute gargoyle and it was left to Sir Percival Hayes to take charge of this awkward situation. He rose from the pew.

The congregation fell into mutterings. I went to where my father's coffin rested, it too draped in black velvet.

'Open it,' I commanded. 'I wish to see my father.'

I could tell by the expression on Sir Percival's face that he knew not if he was dealing with a ghost or a mad man.

'My lord,' he said, raising his hand for silence. 'My lord, it is not . . .'

Before he could say another word, I interrupted him.

'As you well know, Sir Percival, I was born with a curse on my head. If the Earl of Rodermere is dead then I am free. Open it.'

Sir Percival lowered his voice.

'My lord, this is most unseemly. Is it not enough that you have my word on the matter?'

'No, Sir Percival. I must see for myself that there is a body to bury.'

I was not to be moved by argument nor by force. Sir Percival nodded to two attendants who took the velvet cloth from the coffin and the nails from the lid. By the time they had opened it the congregation was standing in hope of seeing the corpse.

Parson Pegwell went white at what was before him.

It was not so much a body more a butchered carcass that had been with great haste and little ceremony tipped into the coffin. The most recognisable part of my father was his face: frozen in terror, his eyes hanging from their sockets, his mouth open in a scream. I took my only penny and placed it there.

'He will be needing this when he meets St Peter at the pearly gates,' I said, 'for such a tyrant must surely buy his way in. One can only pray that God has a greater heart for forgiveness than man.'

The lid was hastily replaced and I walked out of the church and went to wait at the graveside.

By the time the woeful procession arrived to bury what was left of Lord Rodermere the sky had darkened. Parson Pegwell began, his voice quivering.

'Man that is born of woman hath but a short time to live . . .'
A roar of thunder broke across the sky. '. . . and is full of misery.'
Rain began to fall. 'He cometh up and is cut down like a flower.'

The signal was given and the two gravediggers slowly lowered the coffin into the earth. Whether it was the rain or a flash of lightning or Parson Pegwell's incoherent speech that distracted them, I could not say, but the loosely nailed coffin lid slipped and spilled a mangled hand. The sight was too much for the parson. The dusty, ashen tongue spoke no more and clutching at his heart he fell as a stone, face down into his lordship's grave.

LXXXII

My father was dead and with him the curse. The prophecy that had long haunted me had not come true. I was not his murderer – unless I could have inhabited two worlds at the same time. The thought worried me for I, the traveller, had returned from a place most mortals will never find. Inside me was a feeling, jagged and uneasy, a memory of a power in my limbs the like of which I had never known. And there it was: that echo of doubt. Had I, in another shape, in another place, killed him? Had I sunk not a knife in his flesh but deadly fangs? Banish the thought, I told myself, concentrate on this, my return, and open the door wide onto the future. I would bring my mother, sister and Master Goodwin home. We would live as we did before. Even as I said it to myself I knew it could never be. The past is only a memory of the present.

There was something foreboding about the House of the Three Turrets. In the golden light of that spring afternoon it had a garish appearance as if it was trying to hide the heaviness of its timbers. The building had undergone major works: new chimneys and fireplaces in every chamber; furnishings which had never been of great interest were now all resplendent. It was most out of keeping with the tyrant that once I called Father, a man of barbaric tastes who cared little for art or poetry and whose only interests were the hunt, whores and wine.

His old manservant arrived with a sombre suit of clothes for me to wear. I asked him what had induced my father to make such extravagant changes.

'A visit from Her Majesty, my lord.'

The statement seemed incongruous.

'The queen came here?'

'Yes, my lord.'

'Why?'

I waited for the answer. It was slow to be spoken.

'The forest, my lord.'

'The forest? Are you sure?'

'Yes, my lord. A great and terrible honour.'

I picked up a white ruff.

'No, my lord. Mourning requires black.'

It was only then that I noticed myself in the mirror. I was taken aback by my reflection in the amorous glass for I no longer possessed the enchantment of outrageous beauty. That blemish, that spell, that had so long defined me in others' eyes, had vanished. Randa, in the wildness of her lovemaking, in the ecstasy of pain, in the love lines of scars across my back – she had brought me into myself. She had changed me as I had failed to change her and sorry was I for that. My love, was I so devoid of magic?

Gone the glow from my features; gone the glamour that had the bewitched so many. The mask finally cracked. I have you to thank for that, my love. I am no longer afraid of the dark side of the glass.

LXXXIII

I went reluctantly to join Sir Percival and take my place upon the stage. I had no idea of my entrances or my exits, neither was I sure if this be Comedy, Tragedy or Farce. I would improvise and hope my performance would so convince him that it did not warrant too many questions.

Sir Percival bowed when I entered the antechamber to the banqueting hall where the feast was to be held for villagers and neighbours to honour the memory of my father. Sir Percival was almost unchanged, still an elegant man, only the flick of white hair more pronounced. I had never known if I liked him and I thought that feeling to be mutual. I knew him to be cruel but he had always been so very kind to my mother, and instrumental in bringing about her marriage to Gilbert Goodwin. And strange as it was to me, Gally seemed to love him. I was braced for the questions Sir Percival was bound to ask.

But he poured two goblets of wine, handed me one and said, 'What an unholy mess.'

I knew not if this remark related to my father, the demise of Parson Pegwell or was a general comment on the situation. He took a long drink then put down his goblet.

'Your father,' he said, 'was a fool and I admire you for having the courage to leave and take nothing with you.'

His anger interested me.

'You perhaps think, seeing all these changes,' – he stretched out his arms – 'that fortune smiled on Francis Rodermere. But it did not.' Sir Percival looked oddly uncomfortable. 'His pig-headed stupidity has brought this great family to the brink of bankruptcy.'

'But,' I said, 'the forest, his estate – his interests were, I believe, enormous.'

Sir Percival refilled his goblet.

'His lordship decided that he should marry again and have a legitimate son to inherit. He wanted to disown you.'

I smiled. 'That was my suggestion when he first returned here but he would not listen.'

'How I hate men like him. I loathe buffoons that believe money to be a shield against ignorance. Your father was a man of crossbows and gunpowder. Gunpowder that exploded without reason. But all might have been well had he not gone to court.'

'I cannot picture my father at court,' I said, entertained by the image.

'It is better that you cannot. Rodermere was a bore. He had always been a bore. No conversation, no charm, no wit. And certainly no talent for the Galliard.'

I bit my tongue to stifle the laughter that was growing in me. This was surely Farce in the best sense of the word.

'At court he was of interest only because of the story of his vanishing for eighteen years. It was a tale that had intrigued Her Majesty and one which your father's grape-soaked mind elaborated on.'

'But surely his lack of courtly accomplishments cannot account for his ruin.'

'No. And though grievous, it was not his worst offence.'

'Which was?' I said, mirth bubbling in my chest.

'Attempting to take by force one of Her Majesty's most favoured ladies-in-waiting.'

'In a public place?'

'In a passage at Hampton Court. He had relieved himself on the staircase, she saw him exposed there, he chased after her and . . .'

'He was an animal,' I said.

'Precisely. No better than a dog. He told me she had a look in her eye, and hips destined to bear sons. He was lucky he was not thrown into the Tower.'

'What was his punishment?' I asked, for I doubted that such a serious offence would go unreported to the queen.

'Your father was summoned by Her Majesty. She said she wished to see the enchanted forest that he boasted of. And more than that, she would dine with the King of the Faeries, the ruler of his land. Note: *his land*.'

'More,' I said, 'I note the word *king*.'

Whereupon Sir Percival, unable to stop himself, started to laugh.

'My apologies, Lord Rodermere, this is not amusing . . .' he said, wiping his eyes.

'How wrong you are,' I said. 'This is a true comedy of muddleheads. Pray continue.'

Sir Percival took a deep and measured breath and failed to compose himself.

'Your . . . your father . . . your father returned here with no wife and six months only to prepare this wind-filled house for the visit of Gloriana and three hundred courtiers, servants, cooks, et cetera, et cetera. Never subtle of mind, he took this honour to mean that Her Majesty had consented to him marrying the said lady-in-waiting, that her visit was as good as a blessing.'

I howled with laughter and Sir Percival, defeated, gave up all attempts to regain solemnity.

'The forest,' he continued, 'was to be abundant with walks to delight a faerie queen. Entertainment, music was to be provided and . . . and . . . and . . . ' Tears of laughter streamed down our faces. 'And – oh dear God – and the faerie king was to be the guest of honour at a banquet here.'

We fell back in our chairs and roared.

'It is good to laugh,' Sir Percival said when he could again speak.

'I take it my father did not comprehend the satire, nor the lethal nature of Her Majesty's wit. Did she dine with the faerie king?'

'Did she? No. As the gods would have it, it rained for the royal visit and all the forest entertainment was washed away. The queen pronounced herself deeply offended that the King of the Faeries had not been here to greet her.'

'This is Comedy.'

'My dear Lord Rodermere – it deteriorates further. Prepare yourself for Tragedy. Her Majesty found the house gloomy. The fires smoked and the garderobes began to smell. Fearing sickness, she and her courtiers departed after two days for more luxurious accommodation and before the royal carriage wheels were but a distant rumble your father was ruined.'

Sir Percival could not help it. I could not help it. We laughed. I laughed until my belly hurt. With tears in my eyes I asked what was left.

'Debts,' said Sir Percival.

'So the only souvenirs of Her Majesty's visit are debts and the smell of shit?'

'My lord, your understanding is impeccable. That is the sum total of your inheritance.'

LXXXIV

Shortly after the funeral I wrote to my mother and told her of Lord Rodermere's death. I did not tell her about the debts that now weighed down the estate.

I assured myself that Master Goodwin would know what should be done once they had returned. It was, I admit, one of the more cheerful thoughts that whirled round my mind. But such hope was dashed by the arrival of a letter from him.

A year ago, a cloth merchant I have come to know well had a ship arrive from Constantinople. Among the fabrics on board he found a cloth bag full of what he mistook to be onions. Having tried a few with a little butter and garlic he felt these Turkish vegetables were not to his liking, nor did they agree with his digestion.

I believed them to be bulbs of the lily type and told him so. He gave them to me. I planted them in the autumn and am now rewarded with the most intriguing flowers that have blossomed into cups of yellow and white. These bulbs are becoming highly sought after and will be extremely valuable. There is much that can be done with variation in colour if I knew but how, and I have, after much consideration, decided to invest all that I own into the growing of this rare plant, this tulip.

The letter made my heart sink. Surely this was folly. I had no idea what a tulip looked like and would never have imagined Master Goodwin to be so unwise in his business dealings. It seemed most out of character for a man so measured with money and who, in the years he had run it, had brought the estate into great profit. He ended his long letter assuring me that he, my mother and sister would be in England as soon as his business allowed.

I saw no point in writing to tell him of the financial woes I had inherited and instead did my best to salvage what I could from the jaws of the creditors. Land was sold, as were paintings, tapestries, silver and nearly every piece of furniture that was not physically joined to the structure of the house. The silver plate alone was of sufficient value to keep the bailiffs further from the gates than otherwise might have been the case. The forest I refused to part with.

It was the most unrewarding task. I could not have imagined that so many petty and trivial debts could add up to such a great sum that it amounted to near bankruptcy.

No, no, a thousand times, no – I had not forgotten Randa. The chaos delayed my trying to find her and when I did have time I realised I had no idea of the path that would lead me to her.

Once, when I was young, my sister told me, I had walked between the two worlds as if they were divided by no more than a curtain. Now my charm was gone and I possessed not the magic to find my way back to Randa. All I could do was hope. A thin thing is hope. It starts off rope thick and one pulls and worries at it until it comes down to no more than a spider's thread that eventually snaps.

I slept in my old chamber, kept the window open and hoped. Randa never came. I knew all my hoping had become but a thread when the rose turned the colour of dried blood. I had lost her and doubted I would see her again. I found it such an unbearable thought that I told myself it could not be – and knew it was.

Summer came, autumn was already waiting in the wings, blowing at the scenery, and Sir Percival introduced me to Master and Mistress Cassell.

Still my family did not return. Their letters were full of plans to do so but there was always something that prevented them from making the voyage.

By the time my engagement to Mistress Marian Cassell was announced I could congratulate myself on the estate being free of debts – in no small part assisted by a generous loan from Master Cassell. It had been given on the understanding that the house would be refurbished and made a suitable home for his daughter, my betrothed.

It was as if I was a sleepwalker watching myself, yet not attached to myself. I was doing this, I argued, for the greater interest, for my mother, my sister, for Master Gilbert Goodwin. Once the house was made ready they would come home. I refused to think that then I would be married.

The wedding was to be at the end of May and as the time approached I began to fear that the reason they had not returned was that Master Goodwin's affairs had not gone well and that he was too proud to tell me as much. I was in a mind to write to say that I was able to help him when I received a letter from Master John Butter. Even his name on the paper jolted me. It seemed to belong to another life. He asked if I, the Earl of Rodermere, would give my consent to his marrying my sister, Lady Clare Thursby. Master Goodwin had refused, fearing that it would jeopardise my own marriage.

I must be with her, he wrote. *I must be allowed to raise my son.*

THE BEAST

LXXXV

Beau is my last thought when I sleep; the first thought when I wake. I cannot breathe for the longing for him. I cannot live.

I look in the glass. Still I am more beast than woman. Why did love not change me?

Better death than this twilight life without him, trapped to live out my days in this unearthly shape, to know that he is a world away from me.

I cannot live.

Papio tells me I will recover, that I will forget, that it is in the nature of all beasts to do so.

I am not a beast.

I am a beast.

I tear at my fur, would pluck it from me if I thought it would reveal human flesh. But what of these legs that end in claws, what of these spiked wings?

Calm, calm, I tell myself. Calm. Close my eyes, think of Beau's hand so soft.

If I could but once more hold a book and by reading it find another story by which to escape this prison of my flesh. But it is impossible, my talons make it so.

The fox stays with me. No one comes to the house, I have

closed the doors, refused invitations to Herkain's court. I do not belong here in his realm. But if not here, then where? Where does Randa belong? I am a foreigner, in both lands an exile.

I know the hourglass runs not in my favour.

All the loathing I have for my shape twists the inside of me.

Did he love me? Or was it but a passing blindness for the truth of me would repulse most men. Did Beau close his eyes to such a vision and believe himself tricked by wicked witchery? Banish such a thought.

I would turn his passion into dust, yet knowing this, knowing how he would see me, still I must use all my willpower to stay, not to fly to him. Perhaps I would be cured to hear him say he could never love one as loathsome as me. Still I want the stars to guide me home to him.

Home. Oh, Randa, do you have a home? This house is where you live, home is Beau. I am sick of heart, of mind. Yes, the only cure is to see him. I would live in the rafters again, cling to the shadows that I might be near him.

Banish these thoughts, they are but fleas that suck the blood from me.

Has he forgotten me? Has he wiped Randa from his mind, found himself a beautiful woman to bed?

Banish these thoughts, Randa, banish them. All they do is turn the gravel of the mind, unrest the soul, allow the madness in.

No more do roses grow round the window.

Herkain has sent his emissary; the king demands I attend court. Papio called for the harpies to wash and adorn my fur with jewels.

I want to hide my breasts but was told that they were of such startling appearance that they should not be hidden. At least, I say, let me cover my nipples. Even that is forbidden. I take a pin and pierce them, the pain flooding me is a relief, a freedom from myself for it exists outside of me, unlike the pain of losing Beau. That is a wound that throbs without remorse.

The two harpies look at me in horror.

I smile. I long to scream, 'I am more human than you.' Though who am I to say so.

I take two jewels and wear them through the tender holes.

And, so adorned, to Herkain's palace.

What did I expect? Herkain's sons I had seen, a few of his attendants, never his courtiers.

The King of the Beasts sits on his throne in a vast hall; either side of him his stunted sons. I enter the great hall to silence. The court slowly bows to me and when they rise again I am surprised to see so many creatures as half-formed as myself, some with human heads and hands, all part-beast, all part-human. None as tall as I and none with wings.

I hold them out, my wings, and hear the whispered voices. Magnificent, they say. Randa is magnificent. Randa is a queen among the beasts.

Herkain comes to greet me. His eldest son lazily rises to his feet. He looks to be of small importance, his features those of a rat. He looks at me and turns petulantly to the queen, his mother, who sits behind the throne. Her small eyes, rat's eyes like her son's, glimmer in the darkness.

'Come,' says Herkain, and we walk out of the great hall into the bright sunlight. The courtiers herd behind their lord and master but he turns, raises his staff and they retreat. The doors close on them.

The king takes my arm. We walk, awkwardly on my part, down a gravel path into a formal garden. Herkain says nothing until we come to a lake and there on a stone seat we sit.

'Only once did I love,' he says. 'By that I mean truly love. Only once did I hear the song of passion playing deep inside me – until it struck the wrong chord and turned into a scream of despair, all harmony lost. Most of us play at love, profess love. Feel love, never. To truly love is to fall, and with age we grow brittle, become fearful of heights. Those of us who have loved, we silently carry the scars, smile kindly at those who tell us that their hearts might break and know they lie unto themselves. You, Randa, and I – we know what it is to feel beyond where wings can take us. Beyond words. We know we held the weight of it, we knew its tune. If it was all but a brief moment then that must be enough.'

'It will never be enough,' I say.

'I had a daughter who I loved beyond the weight of a crown. She was a human child, no mark of a beast on her.'

'How is that possible?'

'Her mother, my lover, was a creature of many parts that she could change at will. She wanted to bear me beasts of such nobility that my two sons would be of no consequence. They never were. I could not carry the weight of her love, it was a feather too heavy and I put it down. I knew it would be the undoing of me.'

'What happened to the child?'

'At five summers she could stay no longer and my heart broke with grief when she was sent to be adopted in the world of mortals. The family that took her knew not the truth of her.'

'Did you see her again?'

'Yes,' said Herkain. 'I did see her. I see her now, Randa. I see her echo in your eyes.'

THE BEAUTY

LXXXVI

I closed the chambers of my heart, I locked the door on my love and yet at night my thoughts of Randa escaped the prison.

What had I done in agreeing to marry Mistress Marian Cassell? I felt not one ounce of affection for her and I doubted if she had any for me. We were two ill-suited, wooden actors playing out our roles, directed in all our scenes by her wealthy father. It was his money that was going to support my estate by way of his daughter's generous dowry. In compensation the forest, the adjoining lands and the house would be saved and remain the property of the new Earl of Rodermere and his descendants. For what had I to offer? Very little. A title, a forest. A heart that would never love again.

I played my part. Was I not an actor? I did what was expected of me. I praised Mistress Marian with words of flattery, with words of love. I wooed her with poems meant for Randa that would make the sun blush and the stars jealous of the moon. She at least had the wit to know that they were not written for her. I gave hollow speeches at which she would yawn – for that I almost liked her.

Our courtship proceeded along familiar patterns with visits and the exchange of rings and gloves. This, then, was the stage dressed for a tragedy of two ill-fitted lovers.

The nuptial contract was witnessed by Sir Percival Hayes, Master and Mistress Cassell, the mayor and several aldermen of the city. I was congratulated on my choice of bride. Wine flowed and I needed no encouragement to take solace there.

I had intended to leave after the guests departed but Master Cassell had other designs. He took me into what he called his inner sanctum, a chamber given over to the study of alchemy. Everything was new and looked unused.

He had started, he said, in the hope of proving magic to be irrational and therefore impossible but later became converted due to making the acquaintance of an alchemist of impressive powers.

'It has, over the years, become an obsession of mine. Does the subject interest you, my lord?'

He poured me another goblet of wine. I should have left it and did not. I nodded sagely and wondered how long I would have to be there before I could make my excuses and be gone.

He asked about my father, the late earl. I had noticed that he often used the title as if making sure it was good enough and fit for his daughter.

'Your father, the late earl,' he repeated, 'disappeared for eighteen years.'

I wondered what was in the wine we were drinking for the chamber began to disappear under water. Master Cassell's eyes were on the side of his face, his mouth opened and shut, his words rolled towards me on a drunken tide.

'Extraordinary,' he added. 'Extraordinary.'

On that I wholeheartedly agreed with him.

'Sir Percival tells that an old witch cursed you when you were born and predicted that you would murder your father. But if I'm not mistaken, the late earl was brutally killed in a hunting accident by an enormous wolf.'

There in the shadows I see the wolf. For a moment I catch the glint in its eye then realise it is my reflection in the glass.

'The wolf grows larger every time in the telling,' I say.

I feel the power in my limbs, a spasm beneath my flesh.

'I did not kill my father,' I say out loud and regret it.

'Forgive me, my dear Lord Rodermere. I was merely taking a scholarly interest.'

I rise. I must leave. I have a longing for the cool night air, the lapping waters of the Thames as my barge takes me home.

Trying to keep my words from slurring, I bow, thank him profusely for his hospitality. But what is he doing? He stands before me. He says there is no need to leave.

'You are as good as wed to my daughter. Stay, my lord, make the contract binding.'

Master Cassell's voice is distorted. My words come not from me and they float into some middle distance. I am wading against the tide.

He opens the door onto a bedchamber that is lit with so many candles that I think it might be the inside of a church. The perfume in the place is overbearing. Mistress Cassell stands by the closed drapes of a four-poster bed. At a sign from her husband she pulls them back to reveal their daughter, fast asleep. Drugged, I imagine, like me.

I hear myself say, please, do not . . . but nevertheless she takes the bedclothes from her daughter and there she lies, naked. To my befuddled mind she appears drowned, her flesh white fish scales, her hair golden river weed.

Master Cassell's words float as jetsam on murky waters.

'We give our blessing, Lord Rodermere.'

I am wolf. I am wolf. I am drowning.

'No,' I say. 'Not until we are married . . . married in the sight of our lord.'

I push Master Cassell aside and moments later I am out of his house and staggering towards the river.

Mistress Marian and I saw each other seven times in all before the day of our wedding. I travelled to the Cassells' country estate on the river at Hampton to visit her and after my failure to comply with the merchant's wishes he was colder towards me and more inclined to talk business. Mistress Cassell grated much on my ear, her voice cat's claws on glass.

I bought my betrothed a small pug dog. It took against me which I found most amusing. She called it Bonbon. He yapped at everything and shitted and pissed on nearly every surface.

Both mother and daughter were obsessed with discovering secrets for the improvement of the complexion, the brightness of the eye, the glossiness of the hair, the smoothness of the arm, the throat. I did not care with what my future countess kept her skin smooth. Whether it be crumbs of bread, goats' milk and egg or the fat of a swan, all had the same effect which was to make her appear artificial. I found myself listening only when Mistress Cassell mentioned she had taken Marian to see an alchemist's wife who had a wonderful understanding of improvements to the skin.

More out of boredom than interest I asked the name of the alchemist's wife and was surprised by the answer.

'Mistress Finglas.'

'Is her husband the same Thomas Finglas who lives near the sign of the Unicorn in Southwark?'

Mistress Marian picked up her little dog.

'I suppose he must be the same to have a wife that bears his name.'

Why did I not possess the courage to declare my terrible mistake? Instead I did what buffoons do when they have dug their graves too deep and have not the wisdom to acknowledge it. I applied my mind to something else and so it was we stumbled – or rather I stumbled – ever nearer to the precipice of our nuptials.

LXXXVII

Our wedding was being arranged by Master Cassell and his wife. My suggestions for a modest affair had been richly ignored and it had become, by degrees and flights of fancy, grander as the days passed. Master Cassell was determined to ostentatiously display his wealth at every opportunity.

To my great amusement Sir Percival Hayes's players were to perform a masquerade at our wedding banquet. Such extravagance did much to brighten the eyes of my betrothed in who I perceived a resemblance to Bonbon when he was given a sweetmeat.

Spring came and embraced life, decorating the world at no expense in its mantle of greens. Nothing blossomed for Mistress Marian and me. It struck me that every feeling she might have possessed was locked away behind a whalebone façade, any doubt flattened by stomachers. The hollowness of our marriage would be illustrated in the width of her farthingale. She and her mother talked constantly of fashion. The descriptions of the costumes that were being made for the actors made me smile. I could imagine Gally's delight to learn she was to be attired in a skirt of silver cloth, a mantle of carnation taffeta. I smiled all the more to think of Ben Shakeshaft's reaction when he saw me, his once apprentice, whom he had abandoned to be eaten by a beast.

The plans for my sister's wedding, in contrast, were a relief in their simplicity. It was to take place in Blackfriars, soon after my mother and Lady Clare's arrival in London. Afterwards, a small supper would be given by the bridegroom at the newlyweds' home.

On an afternoon in early May I went to see John Butter to finalise the arrangements. I had agreed to meet him at his new house in Cheapside but was late arriving having been detained in Fleet Street in the many bookshops there. A troubled mind is best occupied. As always I found it near impossible to choose which volume to purchase from the multitudes of wondrously idle matter that seemed to be hatched every day from writers' quills. Nevertheless, I bought a fair collection; enough, I hoped, to distract me. In fewer than three weeks I, too, would be wed.

I walked past the house three times, so certain was I that I had made a mistake for the building was by far the most elegant in the street. When I did knock, the door was opened by a maid who curtsied and told me that her master was waiting for me in his study.

'Welcome, Lord Rodermere, welcome,' said Master Butter, rising to greet me. 'I am so pleased to see you.'

I was glad that the light was against my emotion being too well observed. In that instant I understood well why Clare loved him.

'What do you think?' he said.

'It is a fine house.'

'Come . . .'

He took me first into the garden before showing me every chamber. At the door to each he asked, 'Do you think Lady Clare will approve?'

'Everything,' he said, 'has been done with your sister's happiness in mind.'

In the last chamber was a small horse on wheels that he had obviously just bought. It made me sad that these two lovers had ever been parted.

'Fortune has smiled on you,' I said.

'Yes. It has taken hard work but I have many clients and have been blessed by being called to court on several occasions to attend Her Majesty, and to help her find a kinder paint for her skin. But enough. What of you, my lord?'

I could think of nothing so I spoke of my sister's dowry.

Master Butter said, quietly, 'We do not need or expect it. I have more than enough.'

I had received a package from Master Goodwin a few days earlier. In the enclosed letter he explained why he had not felt able to give his consent to my sister's betrothal and expressed his delight that all obstacles had been overcome. In the parcel were two sketches; one of the tulip, 'to show you where my money is invested,' the other a charming portrait of my sister and her little son. I gave it to John Butter. He took it nearer the light and looked at it with such love. I saw him wipe his eyes.

He turned to me and said, 'Tell me, my lord, that I am not dreaming, that she will be here soon and we will be married.'

I nodded.

He put the sketch safely away.

'Will you sup with us, my lord? There is someone who very much wants to see you.'

'Who?' I asked.

'You knew her as the Widow Bott.'

'I thought her dead.'

'She lives still.'

'But she vanished and no one ever heard more of her.'

'She came to London to Thomas Finglas's house. We hid her in the cellar and it was her remedies that saved my master. They married last year.'

I stared into the fire, ashamed I had not wondered more what had befallen the old widow. Then I remembered the maid, Mary, who had worked for Master Finglas and asked what had become of her.

'She left and I have no idea where she went, nor do I care. It was she who wrote to your stepfather – as you rightly supposed.'

I had forgotten all of that, of hearing the sorceress name her.

John Butter was about to say something more when Master Finglas and his wife arrived. In truth I hardly recognised either of them. Both in sombre clothes, and gone was all the wildness from the widow who now could easily be mistaken for a good, wholesome wife. Thomas's face was scarred, I noticed, but he held his head up and appeared to be much altered for the better since I saw him at the House of the Three Turrets attending my father.

Mistress Finglas came to me, took both my hands in hers and said, 'It is gone.'

'The curse?' I said.

'Not only that. The charm.' Mistress Finglas laughed. 'Forgive me, Lord Rodermere, it was such an unnatural thing, that beauty.'

We sat, ate and Mistress Finglas and I talked as people do when they have not seen each other for a while. We picked up stitches of the past, pulled through threads that had been lost, and all the time I was conscious of words unsaid.

It was Master Finglas who, looking around the chamber, asked John Butter to make sure no one was listening. He went to the door, closed it, and came back nodding.

Only then did Master Finglas lean towards me and in a whisper say, 'Tell me, my lord, do you know what has become of my daughter?'

'I did not know you had a daughter, Master Finglas,' I said.

'That is because I never had the courage to own her.'

I was bewildered and seeing all the solemn faces staring at me could only say that I was not acquainted with a young woman bearing the name Finglas.

'I am sorry, I cannot help you.'

'I believe you can, my lord,' persisted Master Finglas. 'Her name is Randa.'

Every sinew in me tenses. Can this man, this learned, paper-faced ghost be Randa's father? The unbearable cruelty of what he did to her near makes me forget my manners and it takes all my acting skills to keep my composure.

Any sympathy I had for him, for his scars, is gone. I am shocked again by the mental image of the iron collar that he placed round her neck when he should have embraced the uniqueness of his daughter. But I see in him, in this dull-minded man, a terror of his own creation.

As much as I am angered by his treatment of her no more can I claim righteousness. What does this secret self of mine fear that makes me deny the only love I have known?

In the shadowed candlelight, in this chamber too newly built to be infested with lies, I say, 'No, Master Finglas. I do not know your daughter. I do not know Mistress Randa.'

And glad I am that it is night for the day would scold me with its light.

THE SORCERESS

LXXXVIII

In my dreams I see her, deep under grey-green water. She opens her mouth, her words float towards me sealed in pearls of air. I try to catch them as they fall heavy into the silt of the river bed. Words I will never hear nor their wisdom ever know.

I wake, brush away troubled sleep and spring fills ancient bones with life. From a winter's bed I stir. In the mercurial dew I bathe and a new spirit inhabits this husk of mine. Above me sways the branches of my oaks, their pale, tender leaves translucent; the stained glass of my religion. I ask their roots for all the news these veiny gossips have to tell.

'Is Francis, Lord Rodermere, dead?'

Their answer as I expect: 'Dead and buried. The worms have had their fill.'

Rejoice, the curse is fulfilled. Time no more hangs on my mantle. 'Tell me, is his son buried beneath the hanging tree?'

'Before May is out he will lie with his new bride in his marriage bed.'

'But did he not murder his father?'

'No, not he, but the spirit of the great wolf long dead who found new strength in borrowed life.'

And all the softness of this morning's waking turns hard and
brittle in me. It is not over.
'Who dared interfere with my curse?'
Comes from their tendrils the spindly reply.
'Randa, Randa, Randa.'
My wits begin to turn.
What unnatural thing be she and from whence comes her
power? Randa, dare you make an enemy of me?

In due time, the sorceress dresses in May's sweet glory, holds
up nature's glass and there reflected back is her image. In fine
lines she sees upon her face a crack that has let age in. Is this
Randa's doing? Has she challenged the sorceress's authority?
If she finds it to be so, she will have her revenge on Randa, and
on Beaumont Thursby, Earl of Rodermere, and let all know that
she has willed it so.

LXXXIX

A wedding. The sorceress has no liking for such contracts, such binding prisons of hypocrisy. A blessing given, sworn in the eyes of a lord who knows not of this earth of hers and cares little what man does or says in his name. Better by far the couple had asked for her blessing for there would be a truth in her refusing it.

Much has been made of this marriage, that she can see. The drive leading to the House of the Three Turrets is strewn with flowers. Why should so many tender petals be slaughtered for this occasion?

No, she does not like weddings and even before she enters unseen she knows this marriage is wrong. Love has always been the one thing that can undo her but here there is none. She has nothing to fear. Money there is, money and rank a-plenty. And she is safe to wander through the chambers, to see the preparations for the celebration. The kitchens are a furnace, the tables full of slaughtered fowl – the swan, the peacock, the lark – waiting to be turned into dainty morsels. Servants work to prepare the banqueting hall. It is decked in more flowers of the fields as if bringing nature inside will encourage reluctant lovers to their bedchamber. Three days' festivities are planned. And then what?

She must find him, this boy, this beauty, her charm.

She goes from chamber to chamber in search of him and stops awhile in the great hall where a stage has been placed, draped in cloths of gold. Out of amusement does she dally. Among the curtains and the baskets of costumes stands a man in ass's head.

'What do you think, Crumb?' he says. A tall man steps forward. She takes him to be an actor for his costume too makes her smile. He has two horns upon his head. 'Well, Crumb, do I look like a beast?'

'No, Ben, you look like an ass.'

The first player takes off the mask.

'The trouble, Crumb,' he says, 'is that the beast's mask looks altogether too frightening for a wedding. Surely we are supposed to entertain the guests, not scare them.'

What Crumb says next interests the sorceress a great deal.

'Do you know,' he whispers, 'that this is the house of Beaumont Thursby, Earl of Rodermere?'

'You mock me. What, you think me a buttock? Of course I know whose house this is.'

Master Crumb sighs and is about to speak further when an enchanting creature emerges from behind a curtain. Her voice surprises the sorceress as it has much of a man about it.

'What Crumb is trying to tell you, Master Shakeshaft, you witless baboon, is that this is the house of your late apprentice, Beau Sorrel.'

'No, no, no, Gally. Very funny, very amusing. You jest with me. Beau Sorrel was no earl and Beau Sorrel is dead, eaten by a beast. And it would have been far worse had I not possessed the wit to save two of us out of the three. It was a tragedy but there was nothing I could do.

'Nothing you could do but write a play about a beauty and a beast,' says the enchanting girl with the voice of a man.

'And give it a happy ending as is expected at a wedding.'

Crumb throws his hands in the air. 'It is no use, Gally, he will not listen, will not believe that Beau Sorrel is not dead, not eaten by the beast. He lives, Master Shakeshaft, he lives as ever I do, and shits and pisses as ever I do. Now, how do I know this, Ben? Because I have seen him. Lord Rodermere is none other than Beau Sorrel.'

'Oh, rich, Crumb. Very full of wicked wit be you. It is a liar's pie that I will not sup on. I know what happened. It was I, not you, remember, who saw the terrifying creature – and it was hungry for human flesh.'

'Quiet,' hisses Crumb. 'Here comes Sir Percival.'

The actors stand to attention and bow as one.

This drama much delights the sorceress.

So here again is Sir Percival Hayes; he who does not believe in magic, he who tormented the alchemist, he whose henchman frightened the Widow Bott into revealing the sorceress's name. Dressed in a lordly manner, his face painted, he looks as artificial as his actors.

'What is that?' asks Sir Percival of Master Shakeshaft.

'It is an ass's head, Sir Percival.'

'It looks a much-used disguise, Master Shakeshaft. Where, pray, is the beast mask that was made to your design?'

'I have it, Sir Percival, but so lifelike is it that I fear it would alarm the bride.'

Master Crumb fetches the beast mask. It is a poor design but nevertheless, to the sorceress's eye, it holds a likeness of Randa. Oh, veiny roots of my great oaks, she thinks, what truths did you withhold from me?

'That feeble thing would not alarm an infant,' says Sir Percival and with a clicking of his heels and great authority he walks away.

The sorceress follows him out the hall and along the length of the house until he enters a chamber. At first she does not recognise who she sees: a handsome young gentleman, yes, who has strength in him and would make ladies blush with desire. But where is Beau?

'All is ready, Lord Rodermere,' says Sir Percival.

'I would have a moment to myself,' says the bridegroom, and in the dance of the morning light she sees the ghost of her charm still clings to him.

This was her beauty. Who took it from him? She listens to his thoughts that before she could not hear and now are hers for the taking.

Forgive me, Randa. Today I set my life on a different course and leave my dreams behind. I am only half a man and my lack of courage appalls me. I had such hopes for us. Look what they have become. I am the beast, Randa. I am the beast.

Picking up his gloves, he turns and for a moment seems to look at the sorceress. But she knows he cannot see her, can no longer hear her.

Sir Percival is waiting outside the chamber.

'It is a time for new beginnings, my lord,' he says.

No, she thinks. It is a time for old scores to be settled, once and for ever.

XC

Follow me down in the drizzle, follow me down on this grey May morn to the church where the wedding will take place.

Here is the grave of Lord Rodermere and with my finger all unseen, I write on the headstone as if it be butter and deep into the marble my words sink:

My curse.

Your death.

Let the joyful couple see it when they emerge from the church. I do not like these hollow buildings, these empty spaces of longed for answers. Let all believers float away up into the sky of my earth. Why have mortals not the wit to see that this ground, that this soil, is all there is to hold their heavy feet? They could not walk on clouds.

The congregation is made of the grand and the noble. Knights, gentlemen and their ladies all eager to seem younger than they are; false hair, painted faces, padded garments with much bombasting and quilting so they might appear better framed, better shouldered, better waisted, fuller of thigh. This sham fools no one. All here are in disguise, the truth of their puny flesh well-hidden in mountains of fabric.

Three faces she is pleased to see. Master John Butter is aglow, all worry stripped from him. He stands beside his new wife, Mistress Clare. Unlike the other women here, who take refuge behind their coyness and their painted façades, she makes no effort to hide her scars. This is the only honest couple among a congregation of hypocrites. They stand close to each other, finger tips touching. At Mistress Butter's side a small honeyed boy looks up at his mother. Next to the child is Mistress Eleanor Goodwin. Age has been kind to her. Her figure is fuller, she looks content and holds the hand of her little grandson. But where, the sorceress wonders, is her husband? Where is Master Gilbert Goodwin?

By the altar Beau waits for his bride and the congregation begins to sing. There are so many people that neighbours and villagers spill out of the church door and into the graveyard. She moves between the worshippers so she may have a better view of the proceedings.

The bride, snub-nosed, her long, borrowed locks falling about her shoulders, enters ready for the merry dance. Her dress, a garment Gloriana herself might envy, is sprinkled with jewels, the bodice cut so low that her breasts are on show for the delight of her soon-to-be husband.

Alas, Beau looks unimpressed. Perhaps someone should whisper to his bride that her groom loves an ill-formed creature; that snub noses and fakery are not to his liking.

At the church window she glimpses a feathered face with human eyes and she smiles. Look, Randa, he is marrying another.

One sneeze is all it takes for the sorceress to stop time, to make its greedy hands let go of the present and there they stand, lifeless puppets. Oh, how she relishes this moment before all things change. Beau stands beside his bride as if facing his grave. Never has such a handsome man looked more miserable. With this marriage he will be buried and it soothes the sorceress to think that, his charm now gone, there is no escape for him. He has been exiled from her world that was his by his birthright. He will live the remainder of his days with leaden feet.

She clicks her finger and time rushes in. The minister begins to speak and the bride holds out a ring to slip on Beau's finger.

And before she does, before all this is binding and irreversible, a fox walks into the church and up the aisle with assured steps as if searching for someone. At Beau's feet he stops.

The sorceress knows him, knows his blue eyes, knows this fox is hers. What better time to give the creature the gift of fire. After all, this is a wedding and gifts are expected.

There is a scream. The service stops.

Sir Percival approaches the fox with sword drawn. The fox does not move, fire licks its breath and Sir Percival backs away.

The bridegroom bends and holds the fox close. Only the sorceress hears Beau's whisper.

'Where is she? Where is Randa?'

And before Beau can act the sorceress is gone from there and swift she is upon Randa's trail. The creature's wings drag behind her and it does not take long to find her.

I have her. I have her and I will make her suffer for what she has done. He will never find her again.

Randa is surprised to see the sorceress.

'Come away, child,' says the sorceress with a sweet voice that hides the deadly nightshade of her feelings.

Pretending all the while to understand her heartache, she takes Randa into the heart of her forest, to the clearing, into the shell of the Widow Bott's cottage. She plays her role: the kind, caring sorceress.

'Why, my dear, are you here?' she asks.

Randa does not answer; grief strips all words from her. It pleases the sorceress greatly to relish her pain.

'Once I showed you where you belonged, in the Land of the

Beasts. It is dangerous for you to be here in this world for you will be hunted and killed.'

Randa looks at her with those human eyes.

'Leave me alone to die,' she says.

The sorceress's voice is harder now and she says, 'What made you think that a one such as Beau could ever love one such as you? You are a beast and always will be. These ornaments of human form you possess do not a mortal woman make you. How could he love you? Your very size and shape make such a match impossible. And he is in love with another – surely you could see that?'

'Did he marry her?'

'Yes.'

As the sorceress says it, Randa crumbles and says as if she cannot believe it, 'He is married? He married her?'

'Why, yes, child. Did you not see the ceremony take place?'

She nods.

Love is such a weakness and makes even a beast vulnerable. The sorceress blows a sleeping potion in her eyes, and seeing her lying there feels pleasure at her inevitable destruction. A body half of this world, half of another belongs to the earth. Let her remains feed the soil. There is, the sorceress admits, sadness in her form that predicts a future, that touches the past. Mortal and beast entwined.

The sorceress leaves Randa to dream. But a plan comes to her and she turns back. It pains her but she tears a corner from her hem and places it in Randa's talon. Vanish from human eye, Randa. Now Beau will not find her even if the fox leads him this way. The sorceress wants for her a spectacular death, watched by a queen, one the city of stones will not forget.

Follow me, oh follow me down, I sing as I return to the church.

XCI

The players of this wedding drama have lost their lines, the leading actor has left the stage and the audience, baffled, waits in silence at first. Then the whispering begins.

A fox, they say. Who would believe a fox would have the audacity to come into the church? It is witchcraft, certainly. And stories long forgotten, spider threads of embellished gossip, spin from one person to another.

When this comedy is over, I will sleep, leave mankind to his twisted dealings that do nothing but destroy my earth. I will sleep and treasure my acorns, gold beyond price. And when the wind comes and all mortals are blown away I will rise up, I will plant my seeds in the bones of the soil. But first to end what I began.

She looks around, notes that John Butter alone is missing from the congregation and supposes he has been sent to find the reluctant groom.

In the church, time becomes impolite. Minutes of hope tick slowly away and Lord Rodermere has not returned. She wonders if all these ladies and gentlemen can see that the folly of their rituals, by ever widening degrees, separates them from their roots in the earth.

The bride waits, stiffness fills her dress, her face, her whole being. And still her groom does not return. Alas, her thoughts are not of love lost, but the humiliation, all that comes with being so publicly abandoned in front of so many witnesses. She thinks, how will she find an earl to marry her now? A whale of self-pity swims through her. She catches the eye of Mistress Butter and, as often happens in church, her conscience trips on the mundane. She feels the pettiness of her words, the emptiness of her ill-conceived thoughts and regrets her hasty tongue. When first she was introduced to Lord Rodermere's sister, she had put her hand to her mouth and recoiled at the sight of her, and said, as if Mistress Butter did not have ears to hear, 'I will not be in her presence unless she is veiled.'

Alone now at the altar, she is embarrassed by foolish words that had at the time been so courteously dealt with.

Like everyone else, she turns to look when there is a stirring at the church door, a fluttering of excitement. A string of expectant faces, a wave of disappointment. It is not Beaumont, Lord Rodermere but Master Butter. Mistress Butter goes to her husband as does the sorceress for like everyone else she wants to hear what he has to say. What he says does not surprise his wife.

'Lord Rodermere,' he whispers, 'has taken his horse from the stable and left. I believe . . . I believe there may be . . . someone else.'

John Butter and Sir Percival Hayes speak together in lowered voices and are joined by Master Cassell. After a few minutes of hushed, agitated conversation, it is the bride's father who announces that the wedding will not take place. Not today.

No, not today. The sorceress laughs. Not ever.

The trees, her great trees, move nearer to the House of the

Three Turrets as if waiting to reclaim it. The chambers that once had light now are darkened by leafy greens. In the great banqueting hall, while musicians play, servants rush about making sure all is ready.

The guests trickle into the house, not knowing what to do but wishing to be out of the rain. The table is magnificent and they look at one another, embarrassed. But if they do not eat, it will all go to waste and so they sit, drink the wine and eat the food. The air is more suited to a funeral than a wedding. But then both occasions demand a feast.

Upstairs, in the long gallery, the stage is ready, chairs arranged, for after the banquet the play will begin. Master Shakeshaft has squirrelled away six flagons of good Bordeaux and one of port from which he takes the occasional swig. His thoughts are all about money and it is with a sense of relief he thinks of what he will be paid for today. But more than that, after the guests have seen the calibre of his work, he will be assured of many more such engagements. He has an imagination of tinder, fast to light, and it spirals into images of great wealth.

Only Gally seems to have the measure of the situation. She returns from the open window where below the bride and her parents walk, the bride weeping, her mother furious and Master Cassell was heard to say, 'He will pay. My God, how he will pay for this.'

'What is happening?' asks Master Shakeshaft.

Gally takes off her wig and scratches her head. 'It appears that young Lord Rodermere has not played his part. He left before plighting his troth.'

'Oh, very droll, Gally. Very funny.'

'I wish it were,' says she.

Oblivious, Crumb continues to rehearse his lines, perfecting the tone of his voice. Sir Percival enters the long gallery and all jump in surprise for Sir Percival's shoes have a particular sound to them, they click heavy on the wood. Everything about him is irritated, irritated that he has paid out so much money for nothing.

'The play is cancelled,' he snarls.

He is in no mood to be questioned.

'Sir Percival – wait one minute,' says Ben Shakeshaft. 'Would you be so kind, sir, as to tell us what has happened?'

'Leave. Take the costumes and go.' Sir Percival throws down a purse of coins, turns to Gally and says, 'Come.'

Ben Shakeshaft is about to speak again, but one look at Sir Percival is enough to make even this insensitive man realise it might be a mistake.

The other actors having departed by barge, the sorceress goes with Master Shakeshaft and Master Crumb as they set off at the mercy of the elements, the trunks of costumes rattling in the caravan. Ben Shakeshaft takes another drink from the flagon.

'What a miserable day, what a mismatched wedding. Blood and bollocks, what a waste of time.'

He is thinking it will take a miracle to get him out of the financial mire he is in and is wrapped up in the perceived injustice of it all. The drink has gone to his head, and he is not looking where the horse is going.

'Poor compensation, poor compensation indeed,' he says and hands the flagon to Master Cuthbert.

She watches them, knowing how easily they will bend to her will. Such merriment does this dance afford her. Master Shakeshaft could be sitting on a boat, he could be sitting on a bench for all the attention he gives the horse and the caravan. It is only with a little help from good fortune that he misses a collision with a much grander carriage that speeds towards them.

The carriage driver stops just in time, swears and shouts at Master Shakeshaft.

A head emerges from the window and the sorceress sees it belongs to Master Gilbert Goodwin. He looks to be a prosperous merchant indeed. She would much like to follow him but she must direct these two buffoons to do her bidding.

XCII

Why now do memories churn the silt of long-forgotten things?
Weddings, in their taut grimness of promises that no man or
woman can keep, have disturbed my mind. I have lived so long
and this is my one regret: that I did not see the infant for what
she was and love her for that alone. Did these hands give her
to Herkain? Did these feet walk away from her? Did these eyes
never wish to see her again, the only mortal child I have ever
borne? What madness was in me?

She leaves the players and their caravan and returns with haste
to the clearing where stands the Widow Bott's cottage. Pleased is
she to find Beau's horse tied up, the fox scratching at the cottage
door while Beau forces it open. Seeing nothing inside, he goes
out and calls for the fox. But the creature does not move.

Now she is uneasy for Beau looks set to go back in again and
she fears he might stumble across Randa's invisible body. She
calls the fox to her. It is a call no animal can resist and he runs
towards the sound, towards her.

Beau comes out of the cottage again and mounts his horse.
The fox, his mind fogged, trots back to his master.

She waits to make sure that neither returns then removes the hem of her gown from the beast's talon and binds her, folding her wings tight to her body. At the back of the tumbledown cottage is a rickety handcart, perfect for her purpose. She lifts Randa on to it. Randa wakes and in the moment before the sorceress blows the sleeping draught in them, again she sees something in the glint of Randa's green eyes and is shocked by her own sentimentality. The past clouds the present, she tells herself, and brings with it these maudlin thoughts. She shakes them from her head and sets off for the queen's highway. Before she reaches it she takes the shape of a simple old widow going to market.

Still it rains, the road is no more than a midden of mud. The cart with its heavy burden sticks firm into the earth. And there in the middle of the road, cart and she wait.

She hears them coming round the corner, Master Shakeshaft singing a drunken song. His companion seems to be no more sober.

'The thing is, Crumb,' says Master Shakeshaft, 'the thing is, drink keeps the rain from the soul. You might feel it on the skin but it does not sink in. Whereas if we were both sober we would know how truly wet we are.'

'Wise words,' says Master Crumb. 'And another little drop from that flagon would do me no harm. It is indeed a charm against the weather.'

'A miracle, that is what we need, my old friend. A miracle.'

Slowly they come into view. The horse, being sober, senses the way to London without the help of its masters. And it is the horse that comes to a halt at the sight of her.

'What is it, Daisy?' says Master Crumb.

'Daisy?' says Master Shakeshaft.

'Yes. It has been a mare since the day we bought it.'

'Well, I never knew that. A mare indeed . . . called Daisy . . .'

He starts to laugh and only then does it occur to him that they are not moving. Noticing her at last, he realises why.

'Out of the way, old woman, let us pass,' says Ben Shakeshaft. His words are slurred.

The sorceress has been waiting for them long enough and has rehearsed her part well. As if every bone in her body aches she limps to their caravan, looks up at the two of them and then at the sign painted on the side of the caravan.

'Be you actors?' she says.

'Yes,' they say together.

'Be you well-known actors?'

Master Shakeshaft puffs himself up, all turkey feathers.

'You might say we are very well known,' he says.

'Though not for the right reasons,' Master Crumb mutters.

'If you would not mind, mistress, kindly move your handcart out of our way,' says Master Shakeshaft.

'I cannot, sir. It is stuck in the mud. Be you going to London?'

'Yes,' says Master Shakeshaft, 'and we are in a great hurry.'

'I be going there to sell that,' she says and points to the hand-cart which is tilted in such a manner that the beast can be seen. The jagged edges of her folded wings protrude from the bindings.

'By the Devil, what is that?' says Master Crumb. 'Is it beast or man? Alive or dead?'

'Alive,' she says. 'It sleeps. It be a beast that my son caught in one of his traps. We cannot keep it for it is too big. We cannot eat it for it is too human. But I said to my son, who is gormless and a burden, that I will take the beast to London and sell it. I have been told I could get three pieces of silver for such a creature at the bear pit. And this be better than any bear, worth more than any bear.'

'It resembles a very large, flightless bird,' says Master Crumb.

'Take a look, sirs,' she says, 'if you wish.'

Cautiously and none too soberly both actors climb down and approach the handcart, Ben Shakeshaft drawing his sword. He quickly steps back.

'That . . . that . . . that,' he cannot finish what he is saying but takes another drink from the flagon and pulls Master Crumb away.

But Master Crumb brushes him aside and less frightened than his friend goes closer. He returns to his trembling companion and the sorceress hears their whispered words.

'That,' says Ben Shakeshaft, 'is the same monster I saw in the house, the same monster that ate Beau Sorrel. I swear to you, it is.'

'You are ridiculous, Ben,' says Master Crumb. 'Look at the thing – it is very peaceful. And anyway, Beau Sorrel was not eaten.' And being a little less drunk than Master Shakeshaft he says, 'Old woman, would you consider selling the beast to us?'

'It depends,' she says. 'It depends on you having three pieces of silver.'

Master Crumb takes from Master Shakeshaft's doublet the purse that Sir Percival gave him.

'What are you doing, Crumb?' says Ben Shakeshaft.

'Buying an attraction that will make us our fortune.'

'No, Crumb, no! Leave it be. Remember, it murdered Beau Sorrel.'

'How many times must I tell you,' says Master Crumb, 'Beau Sorrel lives.'

'No, no. It murdered and ate him. Once it wakes it is a terrifying thing.'

'You were frightened of that creature?'

'When it was awake. You never saw it when it was awake.'

'Think, Ben,' says Master Crumb. 'We could do the play – one performance only – with a real beast. Think of the audience we could attract. Think how much we could charge.'

'Three pieces of silver,' says the sorceress, 'and I will put in the sleeping draught and the draught you need to wake it by. But only use it once.'

'It is the Devil's own,' says Master Shakeshaft.

'And with the Devil's luck it could keep you out of the debtors' prison,' says Master Crumb.

The sorceress is much amused as they to-and-fro, coming down on one side of the argument and then the other. In order to hurry the conclusion she pulls the handcart wheels free from the mud and slowly starts to walk away.

'Wait, wait,' they both shout.

'Not so hasty, mistress,' says Master Crumb. 'You have a deal. Here – two pieces of silver.'

'No, sir,' she says. 'Three pieces of silver and I will give you the draughts you need to make it sleep and to wake it.'

Reluctantly they hand over the silver and she helps them carry Randa to the cart. The sorceress dusts her hands as they go on their way. Her part is done and she will not think of Randa again.

THE BEAUTY

XCIII

Three days I have been in the forest searching for Randa, growing more desperate with every hour that passes. All paths lead me back to the Widow Bott's cottage. I sit on the doorstep and from afar watch my fox sniffing the ground.

Whatever elfin charm I was born with is gone. I possess no more magic than any other man and perhaps less for I have made a shambles of my wedding and no doubt brought down the wrath of the Cassells on the head of my blameless mother. I refuse to think how furious Sir Percival Hayes is.

'Do you love Mistress Marian?' Clare had asked me the day before the wedding.

'Do you, who know me so well, need to ask me that?' I said.

We had been walking in the grounds of the House of the Three Turrets, wondering how such ancient oaks could have moved nearer to the house. We decided that in the night they must be pulled by their roots ever closer, waiting to reclaim the place that had robbed them of so many of their companions.

'Do you miss your beauty?'

I, trying to make light of the question said, 'What, mistress, are you suggesting that I am no longer handsome?'

Her face was serious. 'No, Brother,' she said. 'It was a strange enchantment and now you look yourself. Surely that is better?'

'I do not know,' I replied, which was the honest truth. 'Since first I looked in a glass I wanted it to be gone. And now that it is, I seem to have lost the magic that came with the curse, for without it I cannot . . . I cannot find her.'

'Who is it that you cannot find?'

'Randa.'

'John has spoken of her,' she said carefully. 'She is the daughter of Thomas Finglas. You denied all knowledge of her.' Clare was silent for some time, then said, 'She is half-beast, half-woman, is she not?'

'You think that is a bar to love?'

'Is it?'

'There is in her a woman trapped but I know not how to free her. You think me a misguided fool. Her father treated her abysmally, kept her chained in the cellar. He told her she had no soul.'

'Do you not think,' said Clare, 'that all men are frightened of what they cannot understand?'

'Yes,' I said. 'And fear turns to harm, to neglect, to murder.'

We walked on for a while in silence.

'My face,' my sister said, 'is the opposite of yours. It never held any magic, no mirror delighted in my image. Only you, our mother and Master Goodwin truly knew who I was and loved me. I once asked John if he could take away my blemishes and make my face as other women's are, would he do it. He shook his head and said that the marks are what made me and shaped me into the woman he fell in love with.'

'And he spoke the truth,' I said.

'I did not believe him, no more than I believed you when you told me the same. Then I gave birth to our son and something happened when he looked up at my face. He smiled and he smiles still. And I know now that love has transformed me.'

'I thought by loving Randa I could transform her.'

Clare took my hand. 'There is hope,' she said. 'It is an equation.'

I laughed. 'What equation, Mistress Butter?'

'It is to do with alchemy; the power of the opposites.'

'Tomorrow, I marry another.'

'You cannot sacrifice yourself for this house, to hold fast to the estate of a violent man. Look, the trees already have begun to reclaim what is theirs. Beau, do not do this.'

The rooks called out in a black chorus of agreement.

The fox returns and paws at the door. I push it open and with frantic energy he goes in and comes out, again and again. He has a scent. I remount my horse and follow the fox out of the clearing through the forest to the highway. Without stopping he turns towards London. Better, I say, that we go this way for the other leads to the House of the Three Turrets where a hangman's noose of debts and guilt awaits me. I am a madman in search of the unobtainable. What fools we men are to think that by one wish we can put right what fate has refused us. One stone lifted is not enough to make a mountain fall.

And so it is that I go to London and take rooms at the Unicorn, by the alchemist's house. I have enough money on me for the innkeeper to tolerate my companion. The fox is confounded by the futility of his search, the scent having disappeared among so many others on the road.

What kind of figure I cut I do not care as I go to Thomas Finglas's house. The river this morning is no nosegay; it stinks, a bitter, metallic smell mingled with shit. It is a smell I completely

334

forget when I am not in London and remember all too well when I return.

Heartache makes me careless of other people's clocks. I ring the bell of the alchemist's house and am surprised to find the door opened by Master Finglas himself. I say something to him – after all, you must say something when a door opens – and he takes me down the passage to a chamber I did not see before. It smells of beeswax and lavender and in the middle is a round table laid with their midday meal. Beyond, the door to the garden is open and the room is filled with sunshine. Mistress Finglas rises when she sees me.

I have so long thought about this meeting but I have forgotten the rigmarole that is necessary before I can say why I am here. I bow and apologise profusely for interrupting them at their meal. I say I will come back later if it is more convenient. I speak with such little enthusiasm that it must sound as if the very words exhaust me.

Mistress Finglas asks me to be seated. She looks so completely different from the wild woman who as a child I loved. She has gathered all the witchiness of herself and made it respectable. She pours me a goblet of wine and brings a plate.

'Lord Rodermere,' she says as she cuts slices of meat, 'I think you have not slept for five days.'

I nod and feed the meat to my fox.

I catch the look that husband and wife exchange. They must have learned about my wedding. I am so tired that it feels as if all of it happened to another person a long time ago.

'We heard, my lord,' says Master Finglas, 'that you were to be married.'

'Then you may also know that I walked from my wedding. Bad news has the ability to travel faster than good.' I drain the goblet of wine and say, 'Master Finglas, I lied when I told you I did not know your daughter.' He looks uncomfortable at the mention of her. 'I must ask you: do you know where she is now?' He says nothing and I am certain that he is weighing my words, unsure if I am genuine. To prove that I am, I say, 'I love Randa. And I have lost her.'

This statement is greeted by bewilderment on Master Finglas's part and recognition of its truth on the part of his wife. I can see that the alchemist thinks perhaps I have lost my mind and the declaration is a manifestation of my lunacy.

But Mistress Finglas says, 'Speak, Thomas. Tell Lord Rodermere the truth. Tell him.'

XCIV

I listen to Master Finglas's confession. He is full of remorse and feels the sludge of guilt for his treatment of Randa. He assures me he tried to contain the beast in her – but what could he do, he asks, especially after she had killed? She being only a child and not a child. If she had been discovered they both would have hanged. Even though he is nearer the grave than the cradle, his wife urges him on as if he was a child admitting to having pulled wings off butterflies.

I am no minister to give him absolution.

His memory has softened the image of his daughter, made her more human. He looks exhausted when he tells me that Master Cassell and his wife had once come to this house and asked to see her, the half-beast, half-child. He did not allow it. But what choice had he, what choice had he but to lock her away from prying eyes?

He touches his face.

'I was an arrogant fool as a young man. I believed myself to be London's greatest alchemist. It amuses me now for the truth is, as my dear wife says, that I lacked wisdom. And knowledge without wisdom is useless. I would have died if it was not for this kind woman. I did not believe I deserved saving. She mended me, she healed my face, my heart – but not my conscience.

'Bess. You will want to know about Randa's mother. Bess could neither read nor write yet it was she who predicted the date of your father's return. She knew the very hour – and the consequences. My Bess was born to magic, its deep secrets ran in her blood, she needed no books. She was my philosopher's stone and I, puffed up with conceit, refused to acknowledge it.'

Thomas Finglas looks embarrassed by his outpouring of feelings. His wife leans across to him and kisses him gently.

'All is well, Thomas,' she says. 'All is well.'

She takes him up to their chamber and I help myself to more wine, while I wait for her return.

When she comes down, Mistress Finglas takes a clay pipe from a pot near the chimney and sits at the table and lights it.

'He is a daft old bugger,' she says. 'It was fear made him cruel. But without his protection I would not be here today. No, I would not. When I left the forest this was the only address I knew in the whole of London. Thomas could have thrown me out to die on the streets, as many do. Instead he hid me in the cellar, where once he had kept Randa. But that be not why you come, Lord Rodermere. You be not here to hear the confessions of my husband.'

'No, mistress.' I got to my feet, impatient to continue my search. 'As I told you, I am looking for Randa.'

'Sit by me, my lord,' she says, 'and listen. I will tell you what your ears have not heard before. It was in the years after your father's disappearance, when I lived in the forest, that Bess came to me. She was with child.'

At this I sit.

'She was early in her pregnancy and I wondered if she had come, as many do, in need of one of my remedies to rid her of such an inconvenience. But she had not. She asked me a strange question. Be the child human or be it a beast? I pretended not to understand. Old widow, tell me the truth, she said. I thought the answer would determine whether or not she kept the infant and told her what my hands had seen, what my heart knew, what witchcraft had taught me. I told her that her babe possessed the power of both human and beast but I knew not the form the child would take, only that it would be a girl. She thanked me and there was such a smile upon her face. She begged me on no account to tell the sorceress. I knew who she spoke of, as do you, Lord Rodermere. But Bess said her name, such a powerful name, one best not spoken. Bess said it out loud. She said . . .' Mistress Finglas leans close and whispers a name unknown to me. 'And I felt that word as a tempest that had blown into my cottage, and I waited and held my breath, wondering if the sorceress would appear.'

'Did you hear of Bess again?' I ask.

'No. But when Randa came to my cottage, clutching the purse with the hem of the sorceress's petticoat safe inside it, I knew she was Bess's daughter.'

'And did you see Randa as she was?'

'Oh, yes, my lord. She be a marvel. Her wings, her feathers, her fur. And most men would claim she be a creation of the Devil.' Mistress Finglas's pipe has gone out and as she relights it, she says, 'You must sleep.'

'No, I will not sleep. I must first find out where Randa is.'

She shows me to the door and says, softly, 'Do you know of a theatrical gentleman, Master Shakeshaft by name? There are rumours, talk of a play he is to put on in the bear pit, for one evening only.'

'What is the play?'

'*The Duke and the Demon*, I hear.'

XCV

If you want to know the double dealings of London, the best place to hear the scurrilous news is by the river. I have never known a waterman not to be in full possession of all the gossip that this greedy city feeds off and there is rumour and scandal a-plenty to go round.

I take the public stairs down to where the watermen cry, 'Eastward Ho, Westward Ho,' and among their bustling company I search out the chattiest one and ask to be taken across the river.

The moment my coin is in his purse and his oars are in the water, I ask if he has heard a rumour about a fantastic beast.

'Now you come to mention it, a friend of mine, a close friend, related by blood, spoke to a friend of his, whose brother is a rum mercenary. He, having no regiment, was eager to take whatever work there be and has been employed to keep watch over a cage at the Paris Gardens. A quarrelsome man is this mercenary, not given to thinking or the making up of tales. He swore he has seen this monstrous beast, wings and all.'

Such is the sudden heaviness in my heart that I feel the weight of it could sink the boat. Why, I want to scream at the sky, why, my love, did you come back to this city that eats men and beasts alive?

My instinct, a voice I am only now paying attention to, tells me that before I do anything else I must find Master Shakeshaft. As I walk towards Cheapside and the Mermaid Tavern I begin by the power of too little sleep to almost convince myself that with rational conversation I could buy Randa's freedom.

I arrive at the Mermaid at the busiest hour of the day for the plays have just finished and it appears that every actor and their companies are here, thirsty for wine and ale. I ask one of the potmen if he has seen Ben Shakeshaft.

'Not here. The bear pit is where he be.'

I am on the point of leaving when I hear a shout above the noise of the crowd.

'Beau! Over here.'

It is Gally, standing on a bench. As I push my way through, she starts to sing.

'*Much ado at the church*
he refused to tie the knot . . .'

'Stop, Gally, please,' I say, pulling her down from the seat.

She throws her arms round me then turns to her companion.

'This,' she says, 'is the reluctant bridegroom.'

Her earnest companion glances up from his writing and studies me for a moment before he starts scribbling again.

'I must speak to you alone,' I whisper to Gally. 'And then I must find Ben Shakeshaft.'

'Then I must change,' says Gally. And before I can tell her that what she wears is not important on this occasion, she has disappeared into the throng.

'Sit,' says Gally's companion. And having no alternative I do.

'Much ado,' he says, 'and you refused to say the pretty oath of love?'

I nod and he seems happy to leave off any further attempt at conversation and turns to his writing.

I am asking myself one question: how will I free her? One

thing I do know is that I cannot sit any longer. Every bone in my body aches and the only cure is movement. I stand and the writer glances up at me.

'Leaving already?'

Again I nod and scour the room for Gally.

'Do you, by chance, have any good names?' he asks.

'Names for who?'

'For a witch – or sorceress.'

A name springs into my head, the name Mistress Finglas whispered to me.

'Sycorax.' I almost shout it.

'You do not mind if I use it?'

'No,' I said. 'Please do. What do they call you, sir?'

'Will,' he says. 'I am the spear, not the shaft.'

The tavern erupts in a bout of clapping. Gally has come through the door in a man's clothes, carrying a feather fan, an ostentatious cloak thrown over his shoulder. I think how much I have missed him. He and I make a dramatic exit.

Outside all the drama of him falls away.

'What brings you here?' he asks. 'I imagined you to be gone abroad. Are you ill? You look pale. You do not have a rash or . . .'

'Gally, listen. I heard a rumour that Ben Shakeshaft has a creature chained up in the Paris Gardens. I beg you – tell me that it is not the case.'

'I could. I mean, I can. And I would be lying.'

'Where did he find her?'

'He bought her . . . no, wait, how do you know that the beast is a she?'

'She has wings,' I say, 'but she has a woman's eyes, a woman's mouth, a woman's breasts and her name is Randa.'

'Oh dear lord – you know this beast? She has a name? But she is mute, she does not speak.'

'You have seen her?'

'Yes. I thought it – thought her – a freak dressed for the part, until she moved her wings'.

'Gally, where is Ben Shakeshaft? Where is he?'

'Wait,' says Gally. 'You go too fast. It takes time for my mind to whirl on such a thought as this.'

I think, this is hopeless, and start to walk quickly in the direction of London Bridge.

'Beau, do not walk away. Explain to me how it is that you are acquainted with this creature who is called Randa.'

I slow my steps. I know what I am about to say will make little sense to him and when I have finished I have left nothing out and I am waiting to hear him laugh.

But he takes me by my sleeve and pulls me into the Black Bear Tavern where he orders a jug of wine.

'Am I to believe,' he says slowly, 'that you love this beast – as you would your horse, or as you love your fox, but no more. Is that what you feel for Randa?'

'No, I am in love with Randa. I have loved no one else. She is why I could not marry. It is pointless, Gally, I cannot expect you to understand. It must confirm to you that I am indeed mad. But I care not what anyone thinks – I must save her and I will do it alone if need be.'

Gally's face is serious, all the laughter gone from it.

'Ben Shakeshaft, notorious debtor, crook and thief, has by his own admission had a stroke of good fortune. He bought your Randa on the queen's highway from an old crone. Never before in his life has he made such a shrewd bargain. There is not a seat to be had for the play and much speculation that our very own faerie queen will honour us. As will Sir Percival Hayes, the Cassells . . . the list of the grand and the noble goes on. If your plan is to free her from the cage before tomorrow then I am afraid it is impossible for the simple reason that she is guarded by mercenaries.'

'How many?' I ask.

'More than enough to kill you.'

'When last did you see her?'

'She was brought in for our rehearsal at the bear pit yesterday. Half the company was in much fear when they saw her though the other half said the beast was a fraud. She refused to play the part and lay curled on the floor until Ben Shakeshaft had one of his hired ruffians poke and prod her. She stood upright, spread her wings and everyone stood back aghast. If it was not for the chains I think she would have flown away. There was something so unworldly about her. And I thought, that is how I have felt all my days: half-woman, half-man, all beast.'

He takes a printed programme from his doublet and hands it to me. On the front is a very bad drawing of Randa. The play, *The Duke and the Demon*, is to be followed by a fight to the death between the demon and the bears.

'Do you have a part in the play?' I ask.

'I play the duke. And, yes, I will smuggle you in. But once you are in there, once you are in the bear pit, what will you do?'

'Keep the bears off her.'

'It is not enough.'

'I know it is not, but how I save her I have no means of rehearsing. I need a barge.'

'A barge?' repeats Gally. 'Beau, they will kill both of you.'

'Then I will die being true to myself, being true to Randa. I have no more time for lies.'

XCVI

I leave Gally and go again to the house of Thomas Finglas, frustrated that I have achieved nothing except to arrange to meet Gally at Sir Percival's house tonight. But first I must tell Thomas Finglas where his daughter is. I walk faster, then realise I am walking too fast and slow my pace – I do not want anyone to notice me, I want to remain anonymous. I knock on the alchemist's door.

'Back so soon, my lord?' says Mistress Finglas.

She leads me to Master Finglas's laboratory where food and a jug of wine are waiting on a table.

'Mistress Finglas, I have come here to see your husband.'

She says, as if it is a matter of fact, as if I have spoken the words myself, 'You have not eaten much today.'

She pulls back a chair for me. I feel at odds and do not know if I can sit. Only by moving can I stay awake.

'Please,' I say, 'I must speak to him. I can eat afterwards.'

'Eat,' she says. 'No battle was ever won on an empty stomach.'

I feel I am nine summers old again and reluctantly I obey her.

'Sir Percival Hayes sent word to him to attend Master Shakeshaft's beast, as he calls Randa, at the Paris Gardens.'

'Then I have wasted my time,' I say, feeling such anger at myself.

'My lord, you must listen to to what I have to say.'

I take a deep breath and try to keep my my rising panic under control.

'You speak your truth as I will mine. It will go no further than this room and when it is said it will be done with.'

'What truth?'

'Old fears do not die. I might be dressed as a respectable housewife, but my soul be that of a witch, a free spirit, a wise woman who knows the ancient ways. I ran for my life from the forest, from the place where all my roots are buried. I left everything behind and came naked to this city. And Thomas gave me shelter. Thomas told me, do not lose your truth. For that alone I love him. Other men have threatened me with burning, with torture and the rope. They told me I should not long for knowledge that is not woman's to own. That the things above us be not of woman's concern, the things below us, no woman should touch. And that those that do meddle in such things are Satan's whores. All the sorceress's knowledge is seen as superstition, though she knows of things above and below, she sees the past if she chooses, she sees the future if she wills it. When your father in his arrogance first chopped down one of her great oaks, she knew that the time was coming when this land will lose its trees, when the waters will lose its fish, when the seas will lose their weeds and die. She believed by stopping one mortal, she would stop many. You were born with a curse on your head, but they say the curse was broken. They say, my lord, it was not his son but a black wolf that killed Lord Rodermere.'

'What if I told you that they are wrong?'

'Tell me and I will tell you.'

'In Randa's house, in the Land of the Beasts, I wore a gown. The fur lining became a part of me, and I became a part of it. I possessed speed in my limbs that I had never owned before. My teeth were razor-sharp and I had a desire beyond desire for the blood of one man. As time has passed, these memories, these broken shards of glass shine back at me.'

'What do they show you?'

'I smell him. I smell his sweat as he sat upon his horse. My nose is alive with his scent. He comes through the trees, slices of him join then part and join again to become whole. I know he is armed. I smell the metal of the crossbow, sense the arch of the bolt and I am upon him. He is my prey and I am his death. His horse rears, throw us to the ground and gallops away. He lies dazed. Only when he saw me, when he knew me, did I sink my teeth deep into his flesh and feel such release, as if I had been trailing the world behind me on a harness and was at last free of its burden. When I saw what was left of my father in his coffin, I told myself it was the imaginings of my hatred for him that brought these visions. But I knew it was not and I did what men do when the truth is too sharp to hold: they sheath it in a lie.'

'It be as I thought,' says Mistress Finglas. She stoops before the fire and lights it. I am grateful for the heat. She takes out her pipe and lights that too. I watch the smoke rings and we sit in silence until her words float under my skin.

'Your father, Lord Rodermere, came many times to my cottage when my hair was black, my figure firm, my hips wide. I was, in those days, under the protection of the sorceress. He threatened that if I did not lie with him, he would have me sent to trial for witchcraft. Nine months after he disappeared, you were delivered to the House of the Three Turrets. I hoped that with your birth the sorceress might let things rest and not bring back your father. But her rage with man and with beast went deep.

'When Sir Percival Hayes sent his man to accuse me I spoke her name. Her punishment was harsh – as I knew it would be. But she made a mistake – an oversight – which led to another and then another, and I have kept the knowledge safe in my heart.

'Lord Rodermere came to see me after his return, to beg me to find your faerie mother. I told him I needed an offering, that I could not go without a gift. One day he came to my cottage dragging behind his horse the carcass of a great black wolf. I took the pelt, the offering to the elfin world, into the heart of the forest and there I left it. And walked away for I feared that the spirit of such a great wolf would rise again and search out the hunter who had robbed him of his life. When your father realised that your faerie mother would never return, he blamed me and set Parson Pegwell to bring down on me his righteous indignation.'

'The wolf's vengeful spirit would inhabit me now,' I said, 'if Herkain had not freed me. But my arms still have the strength, my legs can outrun most men. But what is the point in these confessions? At this late hour how can they save Randa?'

'I have need of your fox,' says Mistress Finglas.

'I have not seen him since last night; he often goes his own way. But you have not answered my question.'

'Your fox has been here,' she says. 'He screams impatient at the moon. He knows what I must do. Now, you go. Do you not have somewhere else you should be this evening?'

I rise, surprised to find I feel so light of heart, and I say so.

As I am leaving I ask, 'Mistress, why is it you need my fox?'

'That be your question,' she says. 'The answer be mine for the keeping.'

XCVII

We are interrupted by noise from the street.

'What is that?' I ask, for the sound reverberates through the wooden timbers of the house.

'It has started. I feared it would,' says Mistress Finglas. 'The ghost of my husband's first wife demands blood and revenge.'

I hear what it is they are shouting: that this is the house where the beast first struck.

'What do they – what do you mean?'

Putting on her cloak, she said, 'Come with me, my lord. I know a way where we will not be seen.'

I follow her out of the back door and along an alley.

We part at the river steps, I to take the ferry. I ask Mistress Finglas where she is bound. She would not say and just then my fox appears at her heels.

'Do not do anything foolish, my lord. There needs to be cunning if Randa is to be freed.'

I sit in the boat and listen to the waterman tell me about the beast. Oh, this city salivates with blood lust. For once Ben Shakeshaft has a play that everyone is braying to see.

*

In Blackfriars, I walk with measured steps past the shuttered shops whose windows are clamped shut. To my tired mind, the streets are but a playhouse waiting for this nocturnal tragedy to be acted out. Around me, a group of drunken men with torches and a drum cry, 'Death to the demon, death to the beast.'

I am grateful when I find Sir Percival's house, hidden behind a garden wall. The low gate looks of little importance and I pass it twice before I realise that this is the entrance. I ring the bell, and am ushered into an oak-panelled dining chamber. The table is so well polished that in the candlelight its surface shines as black as the river. The place smells of beeswax with none of the odours that make up the usual soup of family vapours.

It had been Gally's suggestion that we should meet here, assuring me that Sir Percival would help with a barge, with men if necessary, though in truth I doubted it. But with or without his or anyone else's help I am already determined that tomorrow I will use my sword and all my strength to save Randa. I know the futility of my plan, yet it brings some comfort as I wait in this chamber that is so unexpected. All is arranged to perfection with the eye of a connoisseur. In the centre of a wall hangs a portrait and at the bottom of the frame a little plaque says *Gallimaufry*. An androgynous creature brazenly stares out at the viewer. The portrait is of Gally. Her face, painted white, catches the viewer's eye and her gaze refuses to leave him. Her hair is worn high and covered in jewels, a ruff frames her face, the gown she wears is open and reveals her chest, one nipple pierced. But what makes it so striking a portrait is the expression of love upon Gally's face. It is directed towards one person: he who commissioned the painting.

Gally, who has always made light of her relationship with Sir Percival, has been caught by the artist's brush and revealed the truth of her feelings.

We have more in common than I had ever thought. Love does

not come as we expect. The earth is pulled towards a burning sphere, one star, one planet, that it cannot be parted from. Perhaps the same force rules our mortal hearts. Who is to judge the right or wrong of love, whether it is for a man, whether it is for a woman? Love trips us up, changes worlds, gives us eyes to see in a different light.

I become aware that Sir Percival is standing behind me.

'Do you like it, Lord Rodermere?'

'Yes,' I say, still staring at the painting. 'It captures everything that is Gally.' I turn to look at him. 'Everything that completes you.'

'Well observed, my lord,' says Sir Percival.

He takes me upstairs to his chamber, a chamber full of books, of curiosities, it is a place where magic is studied as if it can be rationally explained.

'You think me a hypocrite,' says Sir Percival, 'when I am so hard on witchcraft?'

I know not what to say, so I say nothing.

On his desk is a bright red feather. He hands it to me and I feel my heart leap with hope.

'Where did you find this?' I ask.

'I went today to see this beast that Ben Shakeshaft boasts of. It was in a cage at the Paris Gardens. When I bent to take a closer look, I saw it had human eyes, human lips. This one feather fell from the creature.'

'She is called Randa,' I say. He repeats the name. 'She is Thomas Finglas's daughter.'

He nods. 'I thought it was likely. Master Cassell told me some years ago that the alchemist was rumoured to be in possession of an unnatural creature. Do you study alchemy?' I say I do not. 'But you know it is the power of opposites?'

I say I do.

'Two Yuletides past, Ben Shakeshaft told me he lost one of his company – an apprentice was eaten by a savage beast.'

'She is not savage. And I am ashamed of myself. I should have tried to find her and instead I stayed to save the house and the estate. For what good purpose?'

'All is not lost. Master Goodwin has proved to be a clever businessman. He settled the marriage dowry with a tulip.'

'Master Cassell must have demanded a high price,' I said, wondering how I would every repay my stepfather.

'On the contrary – you had not sealed the bargain. Though I believe Master Cassell tried to make the contract binding. As I said, Master Goodwin is good with money – and with the pomposity of others. You still own your forest and your house.'

'They interest me little. All I care for is securing Randa's release.'

'I cannot tell you the pleasure it gives me to know you have not one ounce of your father in you,' says Sir Percival.

Just then a thunderous storm rages in.

'I am late but with good reason,' says Gally. 'I come from the Paris Gardens. You should know Thomas Finglas has been to see Randa.'

'I do know,' says Sir Percival. 'It was I who suggested to Master Shakeshaft that the alchemist visit the poor creature.'

'I must go. I must try to see her,' I say.

'Yes, go if you want to be killed,' says Sir Percival. 'But if you want to save her, then no.'

'Sir Percival is right,' says Gally, and hands Sir Percival a pamphlet. 'Ben high-and-mighty Shakeshaft has had them printed and paid rogues to plaster them everywhere in this fair city. The Paris Gardens is now awash with the crush of a vile-smelling crowd all wanting to see the beast. Master Shakeshaft has hung a cloth over the cage and people are queuing to pay a penny for a candlelit glimpse of her. Those who are well-off he charges three pennies and they do not have to queue.'

Sir Percival read the pamphlet aloud. '*The wonder of London!*

The beast! The female demon! Will the bears have strength enough to fight this force of evil and save the duke? Presented by the Shakeshaft Players.'

'Yes, that bastard told me,' says Gally 'as if he had just succeeded to the throne of England that he was now his own master and no longer needed the patronage of Sir Percival Hayes. And, I being your spy and "tail end" as he called it, was sacked. Here.' He threw down three silver coins. 'This is your loan repaid, courtesy of a shit-faced theatre manager. God's teeth, what are we going to do now? If we try to save her, London will have us stoned to death.'

'Was Crumb there this evening?' I ask.

'Now you come to mention it, he was not. I cannot imagine he wants much to do with this catastrophe. He is a proper actor, not some cheap showman.' I pick up my hat. 'Beau, stop. Where are you going?'

'To find Master Cuthbert.'

THE BEAST

XCVIII

The guards call me Beast. They say I be Hell-born, a demon.
They do not know my name. I keep my voice hidden in the cave
of my body; only to myself do I say, 'Randa.'

I sleep to wake to sleep again and I cannot tell one from
the other. Perhaps all be the same: lives wrapped in sheets and
shrouds.

I think men's feet rarely feel the ground. When it is dark, these
men that smell of sour cruelty light a fire and drink. Drink and
sit and talk of monstrous women. They say they know that she,
the she is me, they say they know that the monster, the monster
is me, has a cunt with teeth. Teeth to eat our cocks with. Drink
makes them brave with stupidity. They bet on who will have
the courage to enter my cage. Touch my breasts. I let out a long,
high scream.

No one comes.

I hang suspended in time with no idea which way it slips from
me. People come to stare, to gawp, their mouths wide open, foul
breath and rotten teeth. They taunt me through my bars. With
sticks they prod and bruise me. I see their ugly, greedy faces.
They whisper sweet obscenities. Or politely say that Noah would
never have taken that on the ark. She be a devil on earth. The

monster has no soul. I have soul enough to love, soul enough to know that without passion this life is but a hollow cage with or without bars.

The thief who stole my rose, my jailor, who I remember on his knees, trembling, frozen hands in prayer, white-faced, begging, weeping for his life. Then realised that a bargain could be struck. He did not hesitate, he gave up Beau's life as if it were but a fleck of dust upon his doublet. He came here, and with him a man dressed in the armour of wealth. His hands were gloved. I was too tired to lift my head, my vision blurred.

'And you found it on the road to London?' said the man of wealth.

'That I did, Sir Percival, and a fortunate thing it was too.'

'Pray tell me why, Master Shakeshaft.'

'Because I have sold every ticket the bear pit has to offer, and it is rumoured that Her Majesty may attend the performance.'

The man of wealth crouched. I saw his sharp face; his dark hair streaked with white. His eyes met mine and softened. I felt a feather fall and he picked it up.

His face was gone, his shoes still there. So was his voice.

'By the look of the creature, it has not long to live. And if it is dead the audience will want their money back and most probably set the dogs on you for a fraud. I believe it is my three silver coins that bought you this creature.'

'That is debatable, Sir Percival . . . '

'You are known, Master Shakeshaft, as Sir Percival Hayes's Men. I will not have you make a mockery of my name with this dying creature. I am interested in the play, the theatre. This sport, if you can call it sport, may be the pastime of kings and queens but it is not for me.'

They have both gone. All is lost in the nightmare of sleep and I hope I do not wake again. My head and all my feathers hurt.

My fur rubbed wrong, and all my limbs ache. My lips are chapped, my wings, their leathery perfection, torn. And all, all of me is pain.

If death comes, I will welcome it, cling fast with my talons to its bony frame. Death has the power to set me free, to cast off this shape that has done naught but torment me.

I think I hear my fox, Beau's fox, crying to the moon. His eerie call sends the caged dogs wild, makes the bears, my neighbours, roar, a desperate call for freedom, a longing for the wildness of solitude.

In my shell I hide, my body armour worn for battle.

They took me chained from my cage, dragged me to a roofless circle rising three tiers high. And in the sawdust they attached me to a post while they rehearsed their play.

One actor – I heard his name, they call him Gally – he alone was kind. He argued in my defence that this was barbaric. Look at her, he said, she is not all beast.

I did not play my part. I wrapped my wings round me and in my sleepy head I saw the sky above. I longed to catch the clouds, to fly until I could fly no more and fall, a dead stone, to my grave.

In dreams, there is no post to chain reality to. I do not know if my father is here or not for my days are so blinkered by the shutters of sleep. I think he kneels beside me. I think I hear him say my name, call me Randa, call me child, say he has come to help me. Say that Beau loves me.

Beau. I say his name.

'Yes,' says my father, this dream figure, this kind father, he who never was kind before. 'Beau loves you, my child.'

'Beau is married,' I say. 'I do not want his pity. I do not want your pity.'

'No, my child, he is not married. He saw the fox breathe fire and walked from the church.'

356

'But I saw, saw, saw my heart in half.'

This new father, this father I have never had, strokes my head. He helps me drink a potion and it tastes of honey. He asks what I have eaten. I tell him I have not, I will not. I will not eat horseflesh.

He asks the guards for water. And I feel the coolness of it wash over my feathers and clean my fur. There is fresh straw and I sleep.

Did I dream him? Did I dream he said his name? Did I dream that Beau did not marry? But the sorceress told me he did, told me that he loved his bride.

My life is but a fleeting moment of waking and all the rest is sleep.

THE BEAUTY

XCIX

In this winking evening of blind panic I make my way to the Mermaid Tavern where the cats go a-gossiping and there among the muddle of people I find Master Cuthbert. He is sitting by himself, nursing a costly sack posset, surrounded by screwed-up paper. He looks as if half of him has gone abroad while the other half cannot remember where he left his pride. He is so past the point of sobriety that he hardly notices me when I sit opposite him.

'Well,' he says to no one in particular, 'I told Ben Shakeshaft it was not acceptable, not honourable, not what an actor of my calibre should be doing. I said, "That beast is as good as dead." That is what I said.' He flops onto the table and I shake him awake.

'Dead? The beast?'

'No. Not yet. Soon will be.'

I try to keep my wits calm, refuse to be rattled by a drunk's vision of the truth.

'I need to know, Master Cuthbert,' I say, 'if you are happy to have lost your patron, Sir Percival Hayes.'

'Me? Me? No – I want nothing more to do with it. I am an actor, not a damnable dragon tamer. I regret, yes . . .' he bangs his forefinger hard into the table as if it might yield under attack. ' . . . I did not know it was sick.'

'You mean Randa.'

'The beast. Look, Beau – Lord Rodermere, whatever part you are playing today – look, you cheery fellow, if you had got married, done what you were meant to do, we would have performed our play, gone home. I would have been sober and none of this would have happened.'

'None of what?'

'Do you know what he said to me?' Crumb continues.

'Who?'

'Master Ben Shakeshaft, of course. He said I should keep my tongue for the play. He said that if I wanted my share of profit I should keep my complaints to myself.'

I put my arm about him and finding him surprisingly light lifted him to his feet.

'What you doing?'

'Taking you home.'

'Do you know, Lord Beau, I have drunk so many coins . . . magic is what it is . . . I have changed coins into drink. And not one of those drinks has done anything but made me feel more maudlin.' He starts to wave his arm around. 'You were not a bad actor, Beau. Showed promise. Wrote well. This is the age of the play . . . the play be everything.'

We have set off towards his lodgings when he stops again.

'There, see that?' He points out the posters stuck to a wall and bellows to the moon. 'Ladies and gentlemen, Master Ben Shakeshaft presents. Note my name is not written there. Does Sir Percival know what the buffoon has done?'

'He does.'

'Then woe is me. All is lost. I will be cast into the streets, a pauper. Best you leave me here, Beau my lord, let me get used to my new home for the streets are where I am bound.'

The bells of London chime midnight and still I hold on to him.

Crumb lives in a sorrowful set of rooms in an attic. In the summer it will be too hot and in the winter, I imagine, too cold. The window stares mournfully over the rooftops of London. I put him down on the bed.

'Sweet boy, beautiful boy. That is what you are. That is what you are . . . not dead, not eaten . . . a beauty.'

I sleep little on a broken-down chair listening to the raucous snores of an inebriated thespian.

In the morning Crumb is a sorrowful sight.

'I need my chamber pot,' he says.

And I think it best to leave him, saying I will meet him downstairs. The noise of farting and shitting and groans coming from the attic are not pleasant to hear.

I wait in the street, in the only puddle of sunlight the narrow lane has to offer. Shutters are pulled back, a cock crows and the orchestra of London begins to tune its instruments to the discord sound that is the music of this city. Above the increasing din I hear a cry: 'Today a beast will be seen in the bear pit.'

I am about to go back to find him when a very fragile, white-faced Crumb appears.

'I thank you for bringing me home,' he says, holding up his hand to shade his eyes from the light. 'But I must be at the bear pit. I am supposed to have written new lines to make up for the loss of Gally. So if you will excuse me, Lord Rodermere, I will say good morrow.'

I have not waited this long to let him slip away and once again I take his arm.

'Breakfast,' I say.

Reluctantly he walks with me towards the river and we stop at the first tavern we come to.

I order bread and butter and an omelette for both of us. And two pints of ale.

'You will feel better after you have eaten,' I say, pushing his plate to him.

'I cannot.'

'But I insist. Do you want me to write the speech for you?'

'I would be most grateful, Beau – my lord – if you feel up to it.' Slowly, he begins to eat. 'Why are you doing all this?'

'You need another actor – a replacement for Gally.' I take a deep breath. 'That actor will be me and I intend to rescue the beast from this lunacy.'

'Oh, no. No, no, I cannot help you.' He looks around, his voice becomes a whisper. 'It is impossible, cannot be done. The crowd will eat you alive if the bears do not.'

'What if I told you that Sir Percival Hayes is planning to reform his players and ask you to be his new manager?'

Crumb thinks about it.

It takes me less than an hour to write the necessary speech and I mercilessly steal lines from *Tamburlaine* for London loves a revenge play, loves the violent drumbeat of language.

Crumb has finished his ale and is much revived.

I hand him what I have written.

'I am an actor from Stratford,' I say quickly. 'Green about the ears, good with animals. Painfully shy, alas, yet when on stage gives a passable performance.'

'What is your name?' asks Crumb.

I can see he is slowly warming to the idea.

'Master Sydney Dale.'

He thinks about this then says, 'You look too smart as you are.'

He hands me his battered hat and I give him mine. We exchange cloaks.

He studies me again and says, 'It will not work. Ben is bound to recognise you.'

I put myself into the part of the duke and say the lines I have just written.

'Good, very good,' says Master Cuthbert. 'But can you play both parts – the duke and the shy country lad – all day?'

I nod.

'If you can do it,' he says, 'it will be the performance of your life. But still I am not sure how you will save the beast.'

To be honest neither am I but I am wise enough not to say so.

'The thing that goes in our favour,' says Crumb, sounding more his old self, 'is that Ben believes Beau Sorrel was eaten by a beast. Let us hope and pray that he still believes that when he sees you.'

C

I have never seen so many people in one place as there are this day in Southwark, and all of them with one mind as to their destination: the bear pit, to see the slaughter of a beast.

'Tears are what set us apart from the animals,' says Crumb. 'Only we savages cry.'

We make slow progress.

'It does not give one much faith in the quality of mercy,' says Master Cuthbert. 'More it confirms that man is a blood-thirsty monster.'

Around the entrance to the bear pit the crowd proves to be a near insurmountable obstacle until one of Master Shakeshaft's men recognises Crumb and lets us both in. Before me is a roof-less, round building, not at all unlike a theatre.

I keep my hat pulled down, my walk awkward, and, too shy to look anyone in the face, I follow Crumb. The place stinks of cruelty, of animals confined in small spaces, of dirt and sweat. I stand in the middle of the circular pit where the only stage prop is the post to which the poor bears will be chained and I look up at the three tiers of empty seats that in a matter of hours will be packed with a braying mob.

Ben Shakeshaft is so delighted to see Crumb that he enters the amphitheatre as if he owns it. I am fortunate in that he hardly seems to notice me.

'Come to your senses?' he says to Crumb. 'I knew you would. Now, my old friend, did you see the crowd?'

'I am not a blind bear,' says Crumb. 'Of course I saw the crowd. And I smelled it.'

'Then you saw coins on legs, for that is what they be. Walking silver, all destined for our pockets. Who . . .' he turns to me, 'is this lubberwort?'

'A replacement for Gally – to play the duke. Master Sydney Dale, an actor from the country, new to London. He says he is good with animals.' Crumb repeats the words. 'Good with animals.'

'Is he now?' says Master Shakeshaft. 'And where, my lad have you acted before?'

He does not look too closely at me.

I mention the Curtain.

'Only a small role,' I say.

'Is this the best you could find? he says to Crumb. 'He is all elbows and toes, an awkward saddle goose . . . no, Crumb, no.'

'Does it matter?' asks Crumb. 'No one is here to watch the play, only to see the beast being killed.'

'But I have a reputation as a great writer of plays and magnificent events and – that reminds me – where is the speech I asked for?'

Crumb hands it to him. 'This is good, Crumb. Almost of the same calibre as my writing.' He looks at me again and I think he has recognised me but then I see that another kind of maggot is worming its way into his brain. A thought has come to him as I hoped it might.

'Good with animals . . .' he mutters, and taking Crumb's arm, moves him out of my hearing.

I wait, holding my breath, my hand upon my dagger.

I hear Crumb say, 'It is no use you mumbling, Ben, I cannot hear a word you are saying. Speak louder – there is too much noise and I am going deaf.'

'I cannot persuade anyone to go into the beast's cage to administer the potion.'

'Well, I am certainly not going in there,' says Crumb.

'No, but that lad looks idiot enough,' says Master Shakeshaft in a stage whisper loud enough for me to hear, 'just tell him it is a harmless beast, that he has no need to worry. All he has to do is put this potion on its lips and it will wake the beast up.'

He turns to look at me and smiles. I act the shy imbecile, eager to please.

He comes towards me, clearing his throat.

'You are not frightened of animals, are you, lad?'

'No, master,' I say and do my best to look as innocent as a newborn lamb who has yet to hear he is bound for the slaughterhouse.

Master Shakeshaft takes me by my sleeve and we set off, followed, three paces behind, by Crumb. We walk past lines of cages where the mastiffs are kept and into the Paris Gardens. Here are the cages that house the bears. Their pitiful faces stare out; their dark, terrified eyes glimmer. Still I play my part. One wrong step and all will be lost.

Randa is in the only cage with a sail cloth thrown over it. The place is seething with fine gentlemen and ladies eager to hand over their coins and have a peek at this living demon. In charge of the mercenaries is a brick wall of a man.

'I think it be dead,' he says to Master Shakeshaft. 'I cannot be sure, but it does not move.'

'Get these people out of here,' hisses Master Shakeshaft. 'They will have a chance to see the beast in the bear pit like everyone else.'

When the crowd has left he bends down and lifts the corner

of the cloth. 'Where is it?' he says. I can hardly stand still and, taking my movements as a sign that I am frightened, he grabs me and looks around him. 'If there is anything amiss in there, you come and tell me. Do not go blurting it aloud – do you hear me?'

I nod and he gives me the potion.

The brick wall of a guard, his sword drawn, opens the cage. I hesitate, though all of me is with her before he has even turned the key.

'Go on, lad,' says Master Shakeshaft.

He pushes me in and the guard locks the cage.

The sail cloth makes the cage dark and it takes time for my eyes to adjust. When they do I see Randa is lying on her side, her wings wrapped about her. I go to her and she does not move and I feel I am standing at an abyss of loneliness for I am certain she is dead.

Kneeling beside her, I whisper her name. She does not answer. Her eyes are closed and I say it again.

'Oh, Randa, forgive me for being such a fool. Would that I could turn the hands back on every clock – I would never have left you. I should have stayed, my love.'

Still she does not move.

'All right in there?' calls Ben Shakeshaft and I think, if she is dead I will kill him. I will kill him, I care not for the consequences.

'Just getting used to the light, master,' I say.

'Beau . . .' she says my name so softly that I am not sure I hear her. 'Is it you? I am dreaming. I dream, dream of my father, I dream that he has become a kindly man . . .'

'You are not dreaming,' I say and stroke her feathers and kiss her. She unfolds her wings and I lift her into my arms. She is so weak. 'I have a potion to wake you.'

I kiss her again.

'This is potion enough,' she says.

'Are you sure everything is all right in there, Master Dale?' shouts Ben Shakeshaft.

'Yes,' I say. 'The creature is moving.'

'Good lad. Now give her the potion.'

'I just have to get close enough.'

I help her to sit. She looks at me and smiles.

'Tell me I am awake,' she says.

I stroke her feathers and I know she is dying.

THE SORCERESS

CI

I dream I see my daughter. She stands on the riverbed, silver sunlight dances on the pewter surface of the water. The ferries criss-crossing the Thames pass as clouds above her. Here, with the pike and the eel, with the trout and the salmon, lies her realm, these watery weeds her fields.

She speaks, her words float towards me in hundreds of tiny bubbles. They rise towards the light and are gone. Only one word do I hear.

Randa.

The sorceress wakes and she knows that her mortal heart beats too fast. Her ancient soul knows that if it fails her she will be leaving her shadow behind.

Quiet, my troubled mind, it was but a dream, be still. It is but the stirring of dead leaves rustled by the spring breeze, come to remind me of things long gone. Let the wind blow, blow it all away.

And she is surprised that she cannot milk as much comfort from that thought as she should. All of her is heavy, as if for the first time she knows the age of her bones. And everything and all and nothing weighs her down.

There by the long passage that leads out to the sunlight, she sees him, the confirmation of all that she dreads, the harbinger of bad news. The fox, her fox, her kin, stands watching her, his blue eyes shining, a curl of flame on his breath. He is here to fetch her and she follows him.

Under the canopy of her emerald-bejewelled oak, in its soft, dappled shade, she sees a woman dressed for church, cloaked in pious thoughts. She holds a basket. The sight of her worries the sorceress for she knows well the way men and women act when they find themselves lost in this, her forest. They are rightly terrified. But not this woman. Not she.

'Who are you?' asks the sorceress. 'What do you want with me?'

'Do you not recognise me, Sycorax?'

She says her name. How dare she say her name.

'Of course,' says the sorceress. 'I know who you are. You are the Widow Bott. Do you think that your wifely clothes will protect you, that the cross you have round your neck will save you? Go away before I kill you.'

The Widow Bott does not move.

'You do not know me,' she says, 'and I begin to wonder if you ever knew me. I may wear these clothes, but my spirit is still wild. I come alone, I hide behind no Lord, no cross. I be here to tell you a secret that I have kept from you. Now I should give it back. You can have the leadenness of it and then you can decide what you will do.'

'Go away, old widow, you are rambling. You have nothing to tell me that I do not already know. Not of the past, not of the present, not of the future.'

'Of trees and earth, of rivers and sky, your knowledge be deep but of mortals and their hearts your knowledge be shallow.'

'Be careful, old widow, for you tread too near me.'

'Then I be not close enough.'

'Beware,' the sorceress says. 'I warn you.'

'My name be Mistress Finglas now. I be married to the alche-mist Thomas Finglas.'

'What is that to me?'

'Your daughter was Thomas Finglas's lover.'

The sorceress laughs. 'What story are you telling me? What lies are you weaving on your loom? Go away.'

'Long ago, a little girl of five summers was brought to my cottage by a creature, half-monkey, half-human. The little girl, though, was beautiful. The creature told me his name, it was Papio, and he was from the Land of the Beasts where the child's father was king. He said it be too dangerous to keep her there and that she must not be discovered. I asked who should she be hidden from and he said from her mother, who wanted nothing for her daughter but her death. He handed me a purse of gold coins and with sadness he left. I called her Bess. Her name – as you know well – was Aurelia. I could not keep the girl and I took her to live with an elderly couple who had longed for children. They loved her dearly. She had, they said, a way with stories and talked of the Land of the Beasts. They asked me if what she said be true and I told them no. When Bess was sixteen she went to work at the House of the Three Turrets.'

'You lie,' says the sorceress. 'This is some story patched together to hurt me, your revenge for what I did to you. I do not believe a word you say. Go, leave me.'

But still she stands there and still she speaks.

'After some few years, Bess was made nurse to the children. Then Master Finglas was sent here to find Francis Rodermere. Thomas and Bess became lovers and when she knew she was with child Bess came to me. She asked me if her babe be mortal or beast and I told her she be either or both or one and the same.

And that was the last time I heard anything of her – until the day Randa found me.'

No, no, no. I hear my blood beating in my ears, I feel my arms lose their strength, the sea pulling away from my soul, the wave of regret near drowning me. And still she does not move.

'It was she, your granddaughter, Randa, who freed Beau from your curse of beauty. It was not Randa, but he, taken by the spirit of a black wolf, who killed his father. And Herkain who freed him from the wolf's spirit. Today the lovers will die in the bear pit in Southwark before a crowd longing to see blood spilt. Today perhaps your jealous heart will find peace.'

CII

One truth told, and the threads of her life are pulled apart, unravelled, revealed. Too late, too late. How could she have let her malice stitch such a thorny gown? Did love murder all other desires, rot the good in her? Only now she sees that it was her unbridled jealousy that made her destroy what she should have cherished.

She has wind and invisibility on her side; fury is her engine. And she is there.

I am in London. Look at them – so many people in the rat alleys of this city. I would tear walls apart, pull houses and churches down, let the river break its banks to find her. But where is she? I go downstream, letting the dragonfly ferries show me the way. I see a round building, flags flying. But it is empty, its doors closed, and the crowd snakes past towards a second, larger building. Here she must be for the noise rises from its circle, rises above the chimneys. The smoke of words is thick: kill the beast, the demon, the Devil. In the cages the mastiffs, red-eyed, wildly barking; the place stinks of humans, of the shit and fear of animals.

And then she sees him, the man they call Crumb, the man

she sold her granddaughter to, and she is ashamed. Three silver coins to bring her here, to this Hell-mouth.

His thoughts are laid out for her to hear. He thinks he should be gone now, now before it is too late, before Ben discovers the truth. What truth she cannot see.

'It was given the potion, was it not?' says his companion who she knows to be Master Shakeshaft.

She waits and listens, searching their thoughts to find where Randa is, in which cage she is imprisoned.

'Perhaps it takes time for the potion to work, Ben,' says Crumb.

She sees that it hurts his head to talk, that his brains are swimming in stale alcohol.

'Blood and bollocks . . .' Crumb winces as Master Shakeshaft stamps his foot as would a spoiled child. '. . . what is Master Dale doing?'

'He is with the beast, still trying to wake it,' says Crumb.

'I blame you, Crumb, for bringing that stupid lad, that half-cooked toad of a blithering idiot. I should never have let him in the cage.'

As much as it pains her to acknowledge it, she thinks this small, frantic man is not unlike her. He blames everyone, never himself. Never herself.

Crumb reminds him that only Master Sidney Dale was prepared to go into the cage. There it lies, a fish bone of guilt – he fears that Ben will discover Master Dale's true identity. The smell of this place makes him feel so green, he wishes he did not feel so rough. Now she sees who it is he is hiding. It is Beau, her beauty. The horror of her revenge comes back to her.

'I will go and see it for myself. And you will come with me,' says Master Shakeshaft. 'After all it was your idea that the lump fish should give the beast its potion.'

'Then you wake it,' says Crumb, 'and quickly. We will be castrated if the beast does not soon appear roaring wildly and hungry to attack.'

'Roaring wildly? We – you – you, Crumb – bought a useless, sleepy animal.'

She leaves them in the stew of their disagreement.

Where are you, Randa? Cage after cage she passes, full of bears. Only one of these small prisons has a cloth thrown over it. And outside stand two mercenaries more drunk than sober.

'What's that?' said one.

'What's what?' said the other.

And by then she has the keys. She dips under the sail cloth and unlocks the cage. In the gloom, Beau is cradling Randa in his arms. Around her lie fallen feathers. She is neither beast nor yet woman, but a transformation has begun.

But did not she, the sorceress, who knows better than anyone the true shape of passion, did she not tell Randa that she would always be a beast?

The sorceress sees what she has failed to see before: Randa newborn, perfect, lifeless. Aurelia, not Thomas Finglas, never he, drops the feather of a bird, the wing of a bat, the hair of a cat into the crucible. The babe rises from the mercurial waters, half-beast, half-human, but alive.

If she had not been blinded by conceit, by pride, what wonders the sorceress could have taught her granddaughter. And now she understands. In the Land of the Beasts Randa had the power to break the spell of beauty. Only in the mortal world does Beau have the power to give her back her human form through the alchemy of love. But not here, not in this barbaric place.

Beau whispers to Randa; he kisses her. She opens her eyes, emerald green as the leaves of her trees.

'Have you come to gloat?' she says to the sorceress.

'Who is there, my love?' asks Beau. His face is wet with tears.

'Can you not see her?' she says.

'Sycorax,' says Beau. He neither flinches nor is surprised. 'Is this what you wished for,' he whispers, 'when you sold her for three pieces of silver?'

Behind them stands Death, waiting to take her. The sorceress gave life once to her mother; she cannot give the gift of life again.

She knows what she will do. She tears the hem from her petticoat, places it in Randa's talon and watches her become invisible.

Master Shakeshaft and Master Crumb are outside, still at odds with one another.

'As I said, it is best that you go in first, Crumb, as Master Dale knows you.'

'But you, Ben, have the natural authority that I lack,' says Crumb.

'Oh, very well. But you are coming too.' They enter the cage together, holding each other by the arms. 'Good beast,' calls Master Shakeshaft, 'oh, kindly beast, where are you, gentle creature? Now is not the time for shyness.'

These blinded mice of men, their feeble eyes not yet adjusted to the gloom, cannot see Beau who with great care manoeuvres the invisible Randa onto his back.

When he is able to see him, Master Shakeshaft is confronted not by a beast, but by a ghost.

'B-B-Beau Sorrel? Be you a phantom come to haunt me? It was not my fault you were eaten, not my fault . . . Crumb!' he shouts. 'Look, it is a ghost, it is Beau Sorrel!'

Beau moves to the open door of the cage.

'Out of my way,' he says. 'If I am dead why bother with me?'

'Crumb,' says Master Shakeshaft, 'did you see? Did you see the ghost?'

'No, I saw Master Sidney Dale. I saw an actor, crushed.'

'Are you sure? But what of the beast . . .'

'I think,' says Crumb, edging towards the cage door, 'that the potion is working . . .'

I relish this moment. I have begun to reveal myself: fox of face, wing of bat, feather of peacock. Fire on my breath. This is the truth of me, this is how Herkain, the King of the Beasts knew me, loved me. And in this form I served our daughter to him on a platter, for how could one as glorious as I have given birth to a sprawling, puking infant?

The terror in the players' faces delights her.

You foolish men, you are but lice in my feathers. You want the beast; you have the beast.

Beyond the cage Beau is making his way to the river. An odd sight; a man weighed down with the invisible burden of his love upon his back. She catches a glimpse – a shadow – nothing more – of Randa's wings trailing in the mud.

In the bear pit my fury knows no bounds. How dare men mistreat the bears, mistreat the dogs.

My howl would honour the wildest tempest. I free the animals, bring the building tumbling down, I spread my wings and take to the sky.

To the river I go and on the foreshore I stand and look up at the bridge. In my mind's eye, I see again her ghost, my daughter, my Aurelia. Her slight frame crossing on that dark night, on a journey home to her father Herkain to tell him of his granddaughter. The drunken men, laughing, unaware, and she in the river, an accident.

The crowd has followed me, screaming. What care I now? Now that my clock has long gone with age and near run out of hours.

I say my words, they ripple on the changing tide, they are heard in the cities, in the forests, on the ears of the dead and the living. I say them loud as the river takes me into its dark embrace.

No man should have dared to wake me. No man. No man.

THE BEAST

CIII

Beau is with me.

Until I felt his heart beat I knew not in which of two spheres he belonged: the unstitched seams of consciousness or the loose threads of dreams.

'Why do you love me?'

I think I spoke aloud and I felt then his tears on my fur, his arms round me, his lips on mine.

Was that his answer? Such a sweet answer that I asked the question again.

'My little soul,' he said, 'what a question. You are the mirror in which I see the truth of myself.'

'The dark side of the glass.'

'No,' he said with such passion as if words alone can save me. 'You are the light.'

Was it the power of his kiss, in which lay the truth of his love, that began it? A strange sensation in my head, my feathers falling from me, my beak gone. A face revealed. What kind of face? I could not tell in the reflection in his eye. I wanted to ask – in all my filth, I wanted to ask – does it please you? And still feathers fell. Alas, my pelt does not lose its hold on me, nor do my wings, my talons.

I am too weak and sleep plays heavy with the curtains of my mind.

I fear time cannot hold me, that there are no more hours I can clutch before I sink into infinity.

In moments of wakefulness I heard the bears growling, the distant rumble of a drum, a trumpet blowing. I heard voices howling for the demon. I know who it is they howl for.

Beau rocked me, rocked me.

'Go home, my love,' I said. 'You cannot save me.'

'You are my home,' he said. 'I left you once. I will not leave you again.'

I looked up into his face. Did I speak when I told him I loved him?

If Death should creep silently upon me now, if he should try to reel me in, a feather-furred fish, then Beau's words would catch him.

'You will not die. I will not let him take you.'

The sorceress. Why has she has come?

She speaks and to me her words are but dead leaves. Her season has passed. She puts something, a scrap, in my talon and I am lifted onto Beau's back and I wonder if I am dead after all for I cannot see myself. And I remember her purse, the sorceress's purse. And such a sleep-filled head as mine cannot make reason stand straight. Yet still I see Beau, feel his spine beneath my breasts, feel his strength carry me.

I concentrate, try to wake, to pin my eyes wide so that they might see all. A thousand faces pass us.

'Hold on, my little soul,' says Beau and moves me so gently higher on his back.

Someone is standing on my wing and we cannot move, never will move again.

But something has happened. I feel it in the fear – the terror – of those around us, its perfume is of iron and of beating blood. It is behind us. Beau looks, I dare not.

'Do you see her?'

'Yes,' he says.

'It is not me?' I ask. 'You are sure?'

'No, it is not you, it is Sycorax.'

A yowl of rage, a wail of venom, a wrawl of fury that shakes the ground and sends people scattering. But we are moving away from the madness, down little alleyways, along tight lanes. I can feel his exhaustion, the strength ebbing from him. Then a voice shouting, coming towards us.

'Beau!' A voice well-versed in drama. A voice I recognise. Gally is his name. 'Where is she?'

'I am carrying her.'

'Beau, there is no one . . .' He puts out a hand and touches my fur, my wings. 'God's teeth!'

He helps Beau carry his invisible burden to the water. I smell the river.

A gentleman. I know him too, it is the man of wealth. He too asks where I am. His is the voice of authority. Gally takes his hand, his gloved hand. How strange the details are so alive. It is a gloved hand of disbelief, a gloved hand of a rational man. He touches me and quickly pulls his glove away.

'My God,' he says and crosses himself.

Other voices, all men. They say be quick, they say to leave, they say something terrible is happening at the bear pit.

We are on the barge and I feel the river beneath me, the rhythm of the oars in the water rocking me gently. I hear my mother singing.

In the distance a pall of dust and smoke rises into the afternoon sky.

'Has the bear pit fallen down?' says Gally.

'It is the sorceress,' says Beau, quietly. 'She has taken her revenge.'

CIV

'My little bird, you have the look of your mother about you.'

I am no longer on the river. Where am I?

The Widow Bott, her sleeves rolled up, is washing the dirt from me. Gently she cleans my face. Where once was a mane of red feathers is now a mass of curly hair.

'Where am I?'

I am sitting on a stool, my tattered, torn wings spread out on the floor behind me.

'The House of the Three Turrets,' she says.

'Beau – where is he?'

My voice sounds strange even to me.

'Hush, little bird,' says the Widow Bott. 'He be here. You were asleep when he brought you to this chamber. He too must wash.'

Footsteps running down the passage towards us and the door flies open. Here he is, his arms around me, lifting me. His hair is wet, his body naked beneath his gown, he smells of lavender and musk and my tattered wings – crumpled, discarded gowns – fall from me.

I move my shoulders and my neck, feel my hair tumble down my back.

'It be a birth of a different kind,' says the widow. 'But no less difficult for that.'

What am I being born into? I long to be fully awake, to know who I am.

When I am dry and smell of rose water, when my eyes are too heavy to stay open, I see my mother, my mother of the river, here in the chamber. In her arms she holds my broken wings that once knew the weight of clouds.

'Sleep, my child,' she says. 'Sleep, to rest, to heal.'

When I wake again I am in bed, wrapped in crisp white linen; I wonder if I am dead, if this be my shroud.

'Is this where they take you when your life is spent?'

'No, my love.' Beau is beside me, he whispers into my hair, tells me Master Butter is here. I see John Butter's face. He speaks of the silvery water that once I rose from.

The Widow Bott is gone. My mother is gone. My wings are gone.

It is dark now. The servant lights the candles, closes the door, tiptoes away. The house echoes with the sound of contented conversation. Beau holds a cup of wine to my lips, it tastes of nectar. He lies beside me.

'I remember your father's laugh,' I say. 'Raucous and mad.' I look up at Beau. 'Break this enchantment as I broke yours. Wake me. Wake me into myself, wake me into you.' I kiss him. 'Oh, if I had hands, what I would do.'

He pulls back the linen sheets, strokes my stomach and where he touches me, my body begins to melt. I have such need of him, and my need is met with equal passion. He is deep inside me and slowly we become one. Fur, skin all the same. He takes my talon, puts a claw in his mouth, sucks it and I am lost in his touch, alive in him. Forgetting the damage my claws can do I hold his back and am shocked to feel as never before the softness of his skin. In the candlelight I can make no sense of the reflection in the window, two lovers intertwined. Where is the beast? Where am I? Who is he making love to?

He kisses my thighs, he kisses all of me and velvet is my skin. I shudder with delight, with a pleasure so intense and I am rising from mercurial water, born into a new skin.

I wake at the first light of day and see I have hands, long fingers, seashell nails. I see all my fur and feathers gone. I own the body of woman.

'Is this me?'

'It is you, my love. Extraordinary beyond words.'

Beau helps me from the bed and I feel the wooden boards beneath my feet. The weight of my bottom makes me smile; my new skin is to be danced in. He turns me to the mirror and in its elaborate and gilded frame I see Randa, no shadow of the beast, just myself as I am. Flame-red hair, white skin, green eyes.

I see Beau.

I see the wolf.

I see us.

AUTHOR'S NOTE

Of all the fairytales, *Beauty and the Beast* is without a doubt my favourite. It's a fascinating tale which has been told in many ways. When I was a young woman, it struck me that the genders were the wrong way round. Surely it's women who are most susceptible to casting themselves in the role of the beast? Fearing our bodies to be out of control, we diet, we shape ourselves, we self-harm. We worry about our selfies, re-examine our images for imperfections and, though we don't admit it, we often see the beast reflected back at us.

Young men can be heartbreakingly beautiful, a beauty which in later life is lost to something completely different, and it was this that I wanted to examine when I started to write *The Beauty of the Wolf*, a novel where sexuality is not pinned down. The hero and heroine are only too aware of their images and the effect they have on other people. As it was in the age of Elizabeth I, so it is today — sexuality is more fluid, less defined, and it is for that reason I placed the story in the rich setting of Shakespeare's England.

I want to thank my editors at HQ, Sally Williamson and Clio Cornish. Many thanks go to Adam Mars-Jones who very kindly read an early draft and made some perceptively important suggestions; and to Jacky Bateman whose work on this book has been immense. She has a wicked eye for detail and continuity, and a great ability to keep me on track; 'thank you' seems slightly inadequate. And not forgetting Lisa Milton whose enthusiasm I am most grateful for, especially as this book sits slightly at odds on her list. Last but not least, my thanks to my agent, Catherine Clark. I'm very blessed to have one of the best agents around.

Writing is a solitary business and I'm not as good at selling my books as I should be. So, finally, I must give a great big thank you to the publicity and sales team, the unsung heroes of publishing. Without all their hard work, where would I be?

ONE PLACE. MANY STORIES

Bold, innovative and
empowering publishing.

FOLLOW US ON:

@HQStories